Acclaim for the *Shelter* series

'A gripping read… I read it one sitting…
a definite contender for my book of the year.'

Crime Fiction Lover

'A deeply layered web of hidden identities and secret alliances…
a thrilling, bloodthirsty, novel.'

Buzz

'A powerful and dynamic piece of writing. Uncomfortable, taut,
brutal, it will shock you out of complacency and hold you gripped
right to the end. A wonderful piece of writing.'

Cambria

'Fast action, convincing dialogue and intricate, long-range
plotting… every twist ratchets up the sense of danger and
disorientation… it should also come with an X rating and a
warning that it is not for those of a nervous disposition!'

Welsh Books Council

'A gritty read full of wonderfully drawn, complex
characters… a tremendous roller-coaster of a ride that
barely gave time for a pause for breath before there was another,
often unexpected, turn of events'

Newbooks

'It's not just about solving crimes, it's about the emotional impact... an unusual and interesting tale that keeps you guessing.'

John Gordon Sinclair, actor and author

'A cast I'd very much like to see more of, even though I did have to read the book from behind the sofa, peering through my fingers and hoping that someone would keep me safe from the bogeymen. But its descent into a particularly horrific abyss is tempered at all times by the quality of Gittins's writing.'

Crime Review

Secret Shelter

For Tomi

Secret Shelter

ROB GITTINS

y Lolfa

The characters in this book are entirely
fictional and are not intended to bear any
resemblance to anyone living or dead.

First impression: 2015

© Rob Gittins & Y Lolfa Cyf., 2015

The publishers wish to acknowledge the support of
Cyngor Llyfrau Cymru

Cover design: Matthew Tyson

Paperback ISBN: 978 1 78461 073 9
Hardback ISBN: 978 1 78461 188 0

Published and printed in Wales
on paper from well maintained forests by
Y Lolfa Cyf., Talybont, Ceredigion SY24 5HE
e-mail ylolfa@ylolfa.com
website www.ylolfa.com
tel 01970 832 304
fax 832 782

CONFIDENTIAL REPORT FOR THE COURT
Case No: 4587
IN THE FAMILY COURT

SECTION 7 CHILDREN ACT 1989 REPORT

CHILD CONCERNED: Child 4587
                                    (Name withheld)
                                    (Female: DOB withheld)
PARENTS/OTHER CHILDREN: Withheld

NOTES: Appropriate referrals by AOT have been made to all relevant
          departments – cf. 14/89657/4587. Recommendation of
          CBT inside a PICU facility as an absolute minimum, BUT:
          cf. note below;

SUPPLEMENTARY NOTE:
FOR THE EYES OF CLINICAL DIRECTOR ONLY.

*Jon, over the last twenty years we've liaised on hundreds of different
cases. My approach, as you know, has always been founded on the
belief that no-one is beyond help, that nurture will, with the right
intervention, always triumph over nature but this case, I confess,
has finally made me wonder.*

*Make up your own mind, my old friend. Spend thirty minutes in
the company of this little monster, and see what you think.*

PROLOGUE

S HE'D NEVER BEEN spooked by death.

Life and the living definitely gave her the occasional nightmare though.

The nurse looked down at the prone figure on the bed. Now and again, in the early days, there'd been something; the odd ripple of an eyelid, a small but definite blink as she reacted to some sudden noise somewhere. But for weeks now there'd been nothing.

The nurse checked the usual vital signs, recorded the latest findings in the log she re-filed at the bottom of the bed, then turned to go. In the early days too, she'd talk to her, hoping that something, anything, might get through. These days she couldn't get out of there quick enough.

On a whim the nurse held the door open just for a moment as she made to exit, then slammed it, hard against the jamb, looking at the young woman all the while.

Nothing.

Not even a flicker.

It was like caring for a living corpse.

On the bed, Mo stared at the ceiling as the nurse exited, closing the door rather more gently behind her this time. Not that she exactly had much choice, the ceiling was all she could stare at right now. But it wasn't the ceiling she was looking at with its cats-cradle splinters in the paint around the central light socket, or the small spider she could now see creeping along an almost invisible web to consume its latest catch.

All she was seeing was him.

The man.

The man whose name, or real name at least, she still didn't know and now never would.

She'd felt flattered by him, the mystery man, at the start; pathetically, tragically, she knew. But now she only felt one emotion when she thought of him and that was simple terror.

Not that she showed herself to be flattered at the start of course. Not that she even admitted it to herself. And if you'd told her beforehand that would be even remotely how she'd have felt, she'd have cocked her head to one side and looked at you in that way that used to so amuse her friends and family. Mo had always had the disconcerting ability to look patronisingly scornful and indulgently sympathetic at the same time, to make anyone feel more than a touch stupid and shamefaced with just that simple, sideways, glance.

When she was younger her parents had wondered if she should harness that ability in some way. A couple of teachers at parents' evenings, minds clearly working along similar lines, had floated the possibility of stage training for the slightly-precocious young girl and she'd taken part in a couple of amateur productions, but for some reason she just didn't take to it.

But since then Mo – she'd always hated her full name, Maureen – had drifted. One relatively low-level office job after another had come and gone. Relatively low-level boyfriends had come and gone also. Then he walked in.

He – the man – the man whose real name she still didn't know – had called to check on some housing stock that had been earmarked for sale. The local council department where she used to work was handling it. The housing stock in question was the usual sort of thing, a local authority block fallen into the kind of disrepair that made it uneconomic to maintain any longer. A couple of lawsuits from tenants who'd been injured by falling masonry and loose floor tiles had hastened their hand and an early and probably cut-price sale was now on the cards.

They'd had a couple of approaches from interested parties, both of whom Mo knew reasonably well; small-scale local developers, shifty types with an eye for a quick profit and she'd handed over the relevant tender documents without comment, glad to see them on their way.

Then the door opened behind them and everything changed.

There was an advert she used to watch on television where female workers in some office somewhere would time their midday break to coincide with the arrival of an impossibly-hunky window cleaner. She used to shake her head at the innate naffness of it all, not to mention the considerable unreality. Most girls she knew simply did not stand and stare at even ultra-hot guys in that way. In fact the hotter the guy, the less likely they were to do so.

Then that all changed too.

Maybe it was the accent. She couldn't place it but it was definitely foreign in some way, European-sounding and exotic.

And OK, the upmarket car glimpsed outside in the visitors' car park definitely helped. She didn't know the exact make or model at the time, but that didn't matter. All she did know was they didn't see too many of those parked among the regulation hatchbacks and family saloons, and the new arrival's obviously-expensive suit also complemented the more than pleasing picture.

But it was the eyes that really swung it for her. They were ice-blue, yet still warm somehow. All of which led to Mo, albeit with the traditional and token show of reluctance, agreeing to meet the somewhat exotic visitor in her lunch hour for a coffee to discuss the housing situation in her home city a little further. He really would appreciate, as he'd told her, some advice regarding the local scene.

Mo wasn't listening of course. She barely took in a word he was saying in fact. She was bathing instead in the warm hue of his eyes. They simply glittered, there was no other word for it. One of the other girls in the office had also noticed them – in truth, there wasn't a girl in that office who hadn't noticed them or him – and wondered if he was wearing some sort of fancy contact lenses or something.

Mo had no idea if he was wearing contact lenses, if the car he was driving was leased, if the physique that bulged beneath his well-cut suit was due to the flattering lines of his expensive clothes or whether he had a body, as well as eyes and a car, to die for, but she already suspected she was going to have one hell of a lot of fun finding out.

He – the man – the man whose real name she still didn't know – was simply unusual. He wasn't the sort of individual who normally made an appearance in the drab surroundings of a local Housing Department. And maybe that's why Mo had done it, she would later reflect – too late of course. Maybe that's why she felt the need to make herself and her job sound more interesting than she or that job actually were. Maybe she wanted to keep up in some way.

Or maybe he'd steered the conversation in that direction himself. Later still, much later, she'd desperately try and think back but the plain truth was she just couldn't remember and she had a lot of time now to do just that.

Look back.

Remember.

Suddenly, Mo felt a hot burning behind her eyes and had the nurse still been in the room she might have felt more encouraged. Or she might have just checked her airways, cleared her sinuses, believing it to be no more than a simple motor reflex, damage to the nerves supplying the tear ducts perhaps, causing her eyes to water. Mo knew that the nurse, so caring and solicitous in the early days, was now like the consultant, her family and her dwindling supply of friends. They were all slowly but surely giving up on her and Mo couldn't blame them. In their position and confronted by a patient like her, she'd do the same.

But it wasn't a simple motor reflex or damage to the nerves supplying her tear ducts. It was emotion, raw emotion, boiling inside her even if her face remained expressionless. And the hot burning she felt were tears that never fell. Tears for all that had happened to her, for the life she was now living, for the person she'd now become.

She'd imagined living a thousand different lives in the past, but never this one.

Please God, not this.

But God, quite obviously, hadn't been listening because now this was all there was.

After that first coffee in the nearby café, the enigmatic stranger with the ice-blue eyes had next taken her to a strange restaurant that had just opened down in the Bay, with a distant view of the Senedd across the water.

When they first walked in, she thought it was must be short staffed or something. Apart from a sole figure on the door waiting to escort them to their table, there didn't seem to be any waiters. In fact, and aside from that sole figure on reception, there didn't seem to be any staff at all.

But the place was packed and every other diner on every other table was tucking into their appetising-looking food. There just wasn't anyone handing those diners their plates of food or filling up their drinks. An increasingly bewildered Mo took her seat which was when she realised there didn't even seem to be a menu on the table. A quick glance round the bustling room confirmed there were no choices chalked up on blackboards on the walls either; which was when she saw the mini iPads in the very centre of the immaculately-arranged place settings.

And, as Mo looked round the restaurant again, she could now see that each table was furnished with similar iPads, one for each diner. And several of those other diners were already studying the screens, while others were using the special marker pens provided to tap in their choices.

It was cabaret, of course. You made your selection via the screen and then everything arrived at the table via some sort of concealed delivery system, a buzzer announcing the arrival of the food, leaving the diners themselves completely uninterrupted for the whole of the evening ahead.

Which was unusual and quirky and it instantly put Mo at ease in a way that sitting in the company of a relative stranger listening to a snooty head waiter intone a litany of that night's specials would never have done.

The light changed shape across the ceiling as the door opened once again and another nurse now came in to make another of the regular checks. But then the nurse paused, picked up a local listings magazine from a nearby chair and began leafing through it, planning her own upcoming weekend in all probability, debating the choice of that very same restaurant perhaps.

Mo remembered that he – the man – the man whose real name she still didn't know – had started the evening by telling her about a trip he was going to make that summer. He was taking time out from his busy work schedule to complete a long-cherished trek to a place she'd never heard of, somewhere in South America. His mother, recently-deceased, had family connections there and it was a trip she'd always talked of making herself, a promise she'd never got round to fulfilling and, now, never would. So he was going to do it for her, fulfil her promise by proxy.

Was it then that she'd started to try and match him like for like? Was that when she started trying to sound interesting too? And was it all totally unprompted? Or had she been played, as she now suspected, by a master at the very top of his game?

The truth was she didn't know. All she remembered was that she started to talk about this one house in particular her department looked after. It was just about her only link to anything even remotely unusual and special. And even though she'd signed all sorts of official forms and understood the absolute necessity of that house and its purpose remaining secret, in the warmth of the moment, in that wacko restaurant with food appearing as if by magic and a man with the bluest of eyes sitting opposite, she'd started talking about it.

And yes, she had more than slightly elevated her involvement with the house and its inhabitants, past, present and future. If she was being absolutely honest with herself – and there wasn't a lot of point in being anything else right now – she'd been looking out for signs of boredom from almost the moment they took their seats. She'd seen it once or twice before with other men she found particularly attractive. She'd seen the way their eyes would begin to glaze over ever so slightly as the evening wore on, the way they began to shift in their seats as they quite clearly began to wonder whether there was anything more to their young companion than an admittedly pretty face and a fairly impressive rack.

But her new companion didn't seem even remotely bored. And his eyes did not glaze over. And he didn't move a muscle as he remained seated across the table from her. Gratifyingly, his eyes actually started to widen as she told him some more details about that one house in particular.

Mo had made it crystal clear she wasn't going back to his place. Very definitely not on a first date. Call her old-fashioned, which had to be preferable to anyone thinking of her as a slag, but she'd laid down that particular ground rule as subtly but as obviously as she could just as soon as they'd left that strange and somehow wonderful restaurant. But she was still a little miffed that he'd accepted it so easily and, momentarily, she felt that familiar insecurity again.

Was it her?

Was that why he'd just accepted her veiled instruction with such good grace?

Had the evening not gone as well as she'd imagined, was he more relieved than disappointed that she wasn't going back with him to what she imagined was an impossibly beautiful house to match the expensive suit and the luxury car and, in truth, was she just a little disappointed too?

But then she was in that lovely car, sitting on that soft leather and seeing the lights on the dash illuminate as he started the engine, a low rumble sounding, close but distant at the same time.

She next remembered thinking the lights outside were bright, really bright; in fact they were actually hurting her eyes a little, which was when she started to close them and she remembered music playing softly too and then suddenly she felt tired.

There was just a moment when she also remembered feeling amused. She was out on a date, a first date for God's sake, she couldn't fall asleep! And then, suddenly, she was flopping all over the front seat of his car.

And then she felt a stabbing sense of panic because this wasn't right, it really wasn't and then that was it. That was the moment she entered what she now called the nightmare zone which was where she'd been ever since.

Mo remembered them driving on for a few more miles as she lay in the passenger seat beside the now-silent driver, unable to move, unable even to raise her voice above a whisper.

Then Mo remembered them pulling up in a lay-by. She remembered the lights of what must have been other cars and lorries flashing by, the sudden rush of noise as engines approached, blaring momentarily outside, then fading, lights playing on the roof.

And she remembered his voice pressing her, asking her questions he really shouldn't be asking, test questions she realised now as he tried to assess just how malleable she'd become under the influence of whatever he must have slipped into her drink at some advanced point in that evening, presumably debating whether he needed to administer any more.

When did she lose her virginity?

What was her favourite sexual position?

Did she still masturbate?

Private, strictly private, matters she'd barely admit to herself let alone to a stranger.

But she answered. And she did admit to all sorts of things. And then he moved on to what she now realised once again was the real matter of the moment.

He told her he wanted to know all about the safe house she'd told him about back in that restaurant. He wanted to know all the details. Who lived there? Who used to live there and, if she didn't know, how could he find out? Who looked after the place? When did they visit? Was there always an officer in attendance or were there times its occupants were left alone?

And, once again, she told him. She told him everything she knew, she even told him half-forgotten details she dredged from her memory, details that she'd probably never have remembered at all without the drug he'd administered.

Then he told her to smile while he injected her with what she now knew was a new drug because she'd heard the doctors grouped around her bed discussing it, the drug that was not only going to rob her of all movement but also the power of speech from that moment on as well.

And she did, she remembered that only too clearly. She actually did what she was told to do by the man whose real name she still didn't know, she actually smiled.

Mo moved, ever so fractionally, or at least felt as if she'd moved, even though the nurse, still by her side and still absorbed in her magazine, didn't register any movement at all.

Mo knew she should tell someone about the questions he'd asked. Mo knew that the place she'd told him about housed people at the highest level of risk and she knew that she'd probably severely compromised them by everything she'd said. And if she could have told someone then she would, if only to pay back the monster who'd done this to her.

It didn't help her growing frustration that in the last few days she'd actually remembered something new. That was also courtesy of one of the ever-present magazines littered around her room as another of the nurses, one of the male ones this time, had held up a picture of what he described to a colleague as his dream car which was a black Range Rover Vogue. And as she, briefly, saw the picture she realised that was the make and colour of the car her attacker had driven that night.

Mo looked back at the present-day nurse, her head still bent over her own magazine, now marking up a couple of possible options for the weekend ahead with a pen.

But Mo couldn't say any of that of course. She couldn't tell anyone about the man with the ice-blue eyes or his questions or his car or her betrayal of the safe house.

He'd made sure of it.

PART ONE

THE LONG GAME

I .

KIM CAME OUT of the flat struggling, as ever, to manoeuvre the buggy over the small step that led down to the pavement. And as she did so, and not for the first time, she silently cursed whoever had first decided that a modern-day child's buggy should be constructed from the same components and weigh roughly the same as a Sherman tank.

Inside, Aron stirred slightly as the wheels pressed back down onto the pavement. Kim paused for a moment, fearful, as ever, but then her precious bundle settled back to sleep.

Kim exhaled a silent sigh, a young mother's muttered thanks to the Gods of Good Slumber, then moved on only to pause once more as she suddenly wondered if she'd deadlocked the door to their flat behind her?

Instinctively she glanced back, but then shook her head. She had. She remembered the lock sliding into place behind her as she pushed the buggy out onto the landing; why had that thought even popped into her head like that?

Kim looked back at her sleeping child, gave herself a slight, remonstrating, shake. She had absolutely no wish to retrace her steps back up that steep flight of stairs to check on a door she could definitely remember locking behind her a moment or so before and, equally definitely, waking Aron along the way.

Kim walked on, becoming swallowed up as she did so in the moving crush that surged, day-in, day-out, beneath their first-floor window, sometimes keeping the baby awake, sometimes – because times were tough and money was tight right now – providing Kim and her partner, Jamie, with their evening's entertainment as they took in the sights and sounds of the free floor show below.

Kim pressed on some more, now passing students heading for the nearby college, girls in summer dresses, boys in slogan-emblazoned T-shirts and cropped shorts, fellow-members of a community in transit in a neighbourhood constantly in a state of flux. It was one of the reasons they'd chosen the area in the first place – that and the relatively low rents.

This part of Kim's home city was anonymous. That's how Jamie had always described it anyway. A melting pot of different nationalities, ages and creeds, meaning no-one stood out as exotic and different. And being anonymous, not standing out, very definitely suited Kim and Jamie right now.

Kim paused at a traffic light, waited for the red light to change to green and the beeping that would signal it was safe to cross while all around students took their chances as gaps momentarily opened up in the passing traffic; and Kim let her mind run on her partner, the father of her child.

Of course, what Jamie really meant was that the people living inside those parts of those cities could become anonymous, could live their lives in ways that would escape detection or observation, but she hadn't pointed that out because that's what love was all about, wasn't it? Not making your partner feel small.

Jamie had never done that to her. Not like her bastard of a first husband. He'd made something a profession out of it over the few unlamented years they'd been together, but Jamie was different.

Kim heard the beeping sound waft over the crossing, paused for a moment to make sure it wasn't one of the students imitating the electronic signal for a joke – she'd seen others caught out like that before – then pushed the buggy along the thin avenue of tarmac to the safety of the pavement on the other side. A short distance along was a supermarket, but she paused by a small greengrocer instead. The produce wasn't quite as fresh and the choice very definitely not as plentiful, but the prices were roughly the same and she always preferred, if possible, to favour the smaller independent shopkeeper with her trade.

Kim listened, smiling, as a small group of nearby students pondered what to do with a zucchini and whether that was the same as a courgette. Then she collected her own few groceries, adding on impulse a zucchini which might or might not be the same as a courgette, before pushing the buggy back along the street towards the small flat that was now more of a home to her than the four-bedroomed detached house a few miles and a lifetime away had ever been.

Even with its gravel drive that wrapped itself around the seemingly-ubiquitous ornamental fountain.

And the small but expensive car she'd been bought for a birthday.

Not to mention the John Lewis store card.

Now she walked everywhere and carried her cut-price produce home in plastic bags she recycled until they fell apart, but who cared? Not Kim, for one.

At the same traffic lights she paused again, this time in the company of a Big Issue seller, a middle-aged Asian woman. Kim had seen her standing in various locations in and around the area lately. The woman looked, quickly, at Kim but then looked away again, some sixth sense at work, dismissing her as not the type, maybe sensing richer pickings, somewhat paradoxically, amongst the groups of students now flooding into the nearby campus.

Kim reached into the buggy, took out her purse and bought that week's magazine. She was rewarded with a smile that seemed to bathe the world in light for a moment before the beeping was heard once more and Kim moved on.

Kim tucked the magazine into a bag under the buggy. She'd read it later after she'd given Aron his mid-morning feed. Sometimes there were jobs advertised in the back which she'd cut out and show to Jamie.

Kim knew how much he hated the work he was doing at the moment although he'd never admit it and she knew why. If he did, she might imagine he was feeling pressured, coerced into a life he didn't want by circumstances neither of them had really expected, but that simply wasn't true. The truth, as he'd pointed out on more than one occasion in the past and would probably also point out on many similar occasions in the future, was that it was a small price to pay for the life they now shared.

Because that's what love was all about too, wasn't it? Being considerate of a loved one's feelings. Taking those feelings, however misguided or mistaken, into account.

Coming back to the flat, Kim took out her key, and made to fit it in the lock of the communal front door, but it was already slightly open. She paused for a moment, eyes creasing in irritation.

It drove her wild, the people in the ground-floor flat did it all the time, just walked out without making sure the door was closed. Time and again she'd hear them from upstairs, letting the door swing carelessly behind them, unaware it hadn't properly locked into place.

Kim moved inside, pushed the door shut with as sharp a retort as she dared, hoping to send some none-too-subtle message to any careless neighbour still inside. She might have wanted to make some sort of protest, but she really didn't want to disturb Aron.

Then she hauled the buggy up the single flight of stairs, the smell of fresh fruit and vegetables from the groceries resting on the pannier shelf just about winning the battle against the slightly musty smell that always wafted up from the old and stained carpet lining the walkway and landing no matter how often she cleaned it.

Aron was just over seven months old and was their first child. And he wasn't going to be the last, not if Kim's new partner had anything to do with it. Jamie had already told her he wanted six, which might be pushing it a bit, but she might be persuaded to go for three.

Or maybe four.

A now-smiling Kim pulled her key out of her purse, opened the lock of their own door. Maybe they could make a start when he came home the week after next. He always was as randy as a stoat after a stint away on the rigs. Not that she'd seen too many stoats, randy or otherwise, but she'd read it in some magazine or book somewhere and the phrase had stuck.

Kim pushed the buggy inside the flat. And she was feeling stronger by the day now too, more able to cope with the thought of putting her body through that sort of ordeal again. She'd had a rough time of it with her first childbirth, a thirty-six-hour labour no less thanks to an epidural that had gone wrong, although as she'd kept reminding herself, that was absolutely nothing compared to the agony of her recent break-up and divorce. She'd have swopped a thirty-six-week labour for that.

Kim checked again on Aron, still sleeping inside his buggy and decided to leave him there for now. If she left the kitchen door open he'd be in sight all the time. Then she took out the bags from the buggy and turned towards the small galley at the end of the hall.

Which was when she felt it rather than saw it. A shadow, suddenly appearing in front of her. A sudden and totally unexpected presence blocking out the sun that always streamed down the small hall of their flat at this time of day, but not today.

Today, the sun was obscured by something.

Or someone.

Then the whole world seemed to explode in front of her. And Kim again felt rather than saw or heard a white-hot light with what sounded like an ear-shattering clap of thunder right in the centre.

Then there was nothing.

A few moments later, Aron stirred fitfully. The infant, some instinct at work, felt for his favourite toy that Kim and Jamie had christened Kitty, even though they weren't sure if it was a cat or a dog.

It wasn't the first toy they'd bought him but it was the one he'd loved from the start. From the day they'd first placed it in his cot, he'd reach out for it, kneading it with his tiny fingers, holding it close, refusing – sometimes even in his sleep – to let it go.

Only Aron couldn't find Kitty. If it was in the buggy it was out of reach. So he looked for his mother instead.

He spotted her quickly enough. She was a metre or so away. But she didn't approach as she usually did. And she didn't stand over him as she'd always done in the past either, didn't lean down, her face close to his, smiling down into his eyes, brushing her lips across the soft down on his head. She was just lying on the floor. Her face was turned towards him and her eyes were open and those eyes were looking straight at him, he could see them, the pupils wide, but she wasn't moving.

She was just lying there.

Staring at him.

And now Aron didn't only want his favourite toy, now Aron was hungry too and he began to squirm against the straps that were still securing him. Then he squirmed some more, getting increasingly agitated by the moment.

Then he began to whimper and then he started to cry.

Which was when Aron paused, momentarily disorientated. Because as the first of his cries had sounded, music started up, soft, but with a pounding beat, from somewhere close by.

Aron started to cry again and the music suddenly increased in volume in turn. Then Aron began to yell and the music sounded louder still as if there was some sort of competition going on.

Who could make the most noise?

Who could drown out the other?

Aron cried for another hour or so as the music continued, but then he began to falter and then he stopped, perhaps because he was growing tired or perhaps because he was already beginning to realise this kind of extended effort was going to prove pointless.

All the time the body on the floor by his side didn't move. The face that always broke into the broadest of smiles the moment he woke didn't change expression either. And there was no smile.

His mother's eyes moved; Aron could see them flicking from side to side, increasingly panicked as he cried louder and louder, demanding the attention he'd always taken for granted up to then.

But that was all. That's all he could see. Just a pair of eyes, helpless, flicking from side to side as she stared back at him.

Nothing else.

2 .

THE SLIM, TWENTY-SOMETHING, woman pulled up outside the security checkpoint, held her identity card flush to the electronic reader and waited while the sole guard on duty checked her registration number.

By her side, her companion and colleague, some two years younger and already beginning to exhibit signs of a paunch, was still absorbed in the file that had similarly absorbed her the previous evening and which had robbed her of most of her previous night's sleep as well.

Ros looked at him while they waited. From the look on Conor's face, it wasn't going to do too much for his next night's sleep either. Then she looked up at the building in front of them.

Ros, full name Ros Gilet, had been the youngest of all witness protection officers in the country at one time. Now time was moving on and that mantle had passed to others. Nothing ever stayed the same, a lesson Ros had learnt, perhaps only too acutely, at very definitely too early an age.

Ros looked across the nearby water towards an all-white hotel with a roof shaped like a swooping wave and, beyond, at a distant city that was also changing by the day, or so it seemed to her. But maybe that was her brain trying to blot out the horrors swimming around her unconscious right now, horrors that were so clearly absorbing her still-silent companion.

The horrors and their aftermath they would have to deal with in just a few moments' time.

Ros looked towards the checkpoint again, beginning to grow impatient. Once, that is, the sole guard on duty had actually found her registration number and swung open the flimsy barrier that separated this particular outpost of the city's thin blue line from the rest of the world.

Ros and Conor had visited Murder Squad many times before, but all previous visits had been made to their old offices in a large Victorian house sited in a leafy suburb some three or so miles away, a house which sported, incredibly so it always seemed to Ros, two palm trees outside.

Whichever seemingly-hopeless romantic had first planted them and why was now lost in the mists of time, but Ros only hoped he'd lived long enough to see the fruits of what must have seemed a lunatic labour. The palm trees in question were now well over six metres tall.

The suburb in question was growing now too, attracting an eclectic mix of students, university lecturers, young professionals and media workers, all of whom had moved into the area over the previous few years prompting a similarly eclectic array of cafés, restaurants and coffee shops to spring up in turn.

Many of Ros's previous meetings with a department that had always regarded hers with deep suspicion, if not outright hostility, had been in one of those often-crowded coffee shops, with Ros usually sandwiched between a wall and a coffee machine that operated at such a volume it drowned out ninety per cent of all conversation.

Ros always suspected the choice was deliberate, designed to put herself and her department at a disadvantage from the start of any exchange, a charge that Masters, the Head of Murder Squad, always treated with the contempt he clearly felt it deserved. They just served good coffee, he'd always pointed out.

By Ros's side, Conor's attention was still focused on the file, his features settled now into something resembling fascinated revulsion. Ros, still waiting for the security guard, looked round some more.

But now Murder Squad had moved to this purpose-built unit on the site of the old Cardiff docks. The days when the locale rang out to the sound of ships unloading wares from all around the world were long gone, and the land had remained largely derelict until the general regeneration of the neighbouring area had started to spread, ripple effect, ever further outwards. It all prompted a number cruncher in some resource department somewhere to do some calculations and come to the conclusion that it made a lot more sense to concentrate several local police departments in one location. And if they could take advantage of the reduced rates and rent offered by the local council in respect of all that abandoned land, they wouldn't only make efficiency savings but actual cost savings too.

All of which meant that the local council were happy to gain another high-profile tenant, the number crunchers in the resource department were happy at the apparent savings clawed back from an evermore beleaguered budget, and the local office supply companies were more than happy at all those orders for new desks and chairs.

The only people not happy were the various police departments who now had to leave their vibrant suburb with its eclectic population and equally eclectic array of cafés, restaurants and coffee shops. They were even less happy at decamping miles out of the city centre to a wasteland populated by one over-extended warehouse, a single canteen, an array of open-plan rooms with no actual desks, just hot-desks – whatever they might be, the largely bemused new tenants were still trying to work that out – and a daily trek of fifteen minutes' walk each way to the nearest eatery for lunch.

The drive would have taken only five minutes, but as there was never anywhere to park that wasn't really an option.

The security guard on the gate nodded, satisfied at last, his finger finally tracing Ros's registration number as he scrolled down his log. Then he handed her a large, laminated, card with the word 'Visitor' emblazoned on one side, the other side blank, and told her to park in bay number five, leaving the card visible on the dash. Then he opened the gates.

Ros drove on, swinging her car into bay number five, the rear end slewing over bay number six at the same time. Ros left it there, looking up at the windows now looking down on her.

Ros had never experienced too much in the way of a warm welcome from this department before and, courtesy of the somewhat-incendiary file she was now carrying and Conor was still reading, she didn't expect that to change now.

But Ros was to be proved wrong.

Masters, mid-forties, no-one seemed to know his exact age, carried another copy of that same file towards a meeting room. The support staff that oversaw the building had offered him something called a Pod for his upcoming meeting which, so far as Masters could see, consisted of a moveable Portakabin-style space with glass partitions where one might reasonably have expected walls.

Masters had no wish to spend the next few hours entombed inside such a contemporary horror and proceeded to inform the sweating support staff that in characteristically forthright terms. Now the meeting was to take place in a room complete with a ceiling, walls and a door – accoutrements Masters had always taken for granted before his department's enforced exile from what he was increasingly coming to regard as civilisation.

Masters glanced down at his mobile as an electronic alert told him his visitors had arrived. Masters looked out of the window onto the too-distant skyline and for once didn't feel that habitual weight of wary anticipation settle over him as it had on so many similar occasions in the past. This time Masters was actually glad to have Ros on board, to appropriate the corporate-speak of the support staff he'd so comprehensively terrorised just a few moments before.

Then the door opened and the female officer herself, complete with usual sidekick, came in.

Ros was much as he'd have expected, the usual closed book, emotions firmly in check, no hint of how she was feeling on her face.

But Conor was somewhat easier to read. Partly that was because this used to be his old department and, even though Masters had made some sort of connection with Ros in the last couple of years, he still knew Conor better. Partly it was because Conor's whey-faced expression made his current feelings all too clear. But mainly it was because Masters shared those feelings too.

Criminals he could handle. Witnesses, the vast majority of witnesses anyway, he could deal with too. At heart, Masters and Conor were like most coppers, at home with traditional villainy, souls with whom they could feel some sort of connection, fellow human beings motivated by the usual imperatives of greed, jealousy, avarice or just plain and simple lust.

But this case was different. Anything involving a traumatised child was always going to be, but once they factored in all this particular traumatised child had seen, then Masters had to confess to feeling more than a little out of his depth.

And that was just for starters.

Five minutes later, coffee had been distributed along with a small selection of biscuits. Bottled water, still and sparkling, had been placed on the table along with an array of plastic glasses. It was, again, a far cry from the kitchen in Murder Squad's old offices with its random collection of chipped mugs emblazoned with the names and mascots of assorted football teams, local and otherwise, although rumour had it they were still to be found in some unpacked carton in the new building somewhere.

Ros looked again at the file on the table in front of her as Masters's newest recruit and latest addition to his team, a late twenty-something male called Hendrix, kicked off the briefing by handing out some more loose-leaf pages to be added to those Conor and herself had brought with them.

'A couple of Black Rats took her in last night. At first they thought they'd got a runaway on their hands.'

Ros checked the age of the young girl in the report.

Six. Which seemed more than a little young to be having the sort of mother and daughter clashes that would provoke a night-time walk-out and, almost as if he could read her mind, the new recruit continued.

'Or they thought maybe they'd got an abandoned child on their hands. Mum out somewhere, kid left to fend for herself.'

There'd been a spate of them lately, children left home alone to use a phrase culled from an old movie Ros had seen once and then promptly forgotten. The local paper had whipped itself up into a frenzy of self-righteous indignation about it all recently too, particularly after one of those local mothers had appeared on a daytime TV chat show in an attempt to defend herself. She'd been, predictably, crucified for her pains. But she'd been treated to a night in a local hotel near to the TV studio the evening before her appearance by the production company behind the whole farrago so it hadn't been a totally aimless exercise in her eyes at least.

'When they first found her, they thought she might be suffering from hypothermia too, it's been cold the last few nights and she only had a thin coat on.'

Masters stepped in, not for the last time during the briefing.

'Then they called the duty quack who realised pretty quickly that whatever was wrong wasn't exactly going to be sorted out by heating up a hot water bottle.'

And then some, Ros silently reflected.

Partly to distract herself, temporarily at least, from the reports open in front of them all, Ros eyed the new recruit now taking up the briefing again.

At first glance Hendrix seemed to be hewn from the same stone as the rest in that troubled, and more than occasionally-troublesome, department. Reasonably fit, looking as if he worked out adequately if not obsessively; no wedding ring, although that didn't signify too much – most of the men in that department removed them while on duty anyway.

Partly that was a typically macho response to jewellery. Mainly it was not to give any of the hard-core psychopaths they habitually encountered any sort of leverage. A married man had a stake in something, meaning he then had something to lose.

But it was the eyes that always marked out those in Murder Squad in Ros's admittedly-jaundiced experience. Eyes that looked as if they'd lived a thousand lifetimes, as most of them had. This one didn't look quite so prematurely embittered as some, and certainly not as scarred as Masters, but then he'd only just joined.

Give him time.

'The girl – Kezia – didn't say too much at the start but once they got her back to the local nick it all came spilling out. One of the interviewing officers has a young girl of his own and he managed to strike up some sort of rapport. Not that too much of what she said made a lot of sense to begin with but at least they managed to get an address out of her, a nice little number on the outskirts of old St Mellons.'

Hendrix stopped as Masters once again took over.

'So with Kezia still not making too much in the way of sense the Black Rats decide to go and take a look for themselves. Five minutes after getting there they decide to force their way in after not getting an answer even though all the house lights were on and they could hear music.'

Was it empathy? Or just an over-active imagination? Sitting across from Masters, the file still open in front of her, Ros couldn't decide. All she knew was that it always happened.

The more acute the horror, the more visceral the crime scene detailed in any report, the more vividly Ros's imagination seemed to take over, turning a second-hand account into something so closely resembling a first-hand experience it was as if she herself had actually been there.

As if Ros herself had witnessed it all too.

The smell came first. It always did. It had been the first sensation that assailed her years before when she walked in on her first ever scene of bloodied butchery involving a never-to-be-forgotten family called the Kincaids.

Acrid, bitter, high-pitched, if a smell could be said to possess a pitch. Something outside all normal parameters, the type of smell that would cause animals to cower and which spelt one thing and one thing only; extreme and imminent danger.

But, initially at least, everything appeared normal as the two officers moved inside the hallway. No sign of a struggle, no evidence of any sort of forced entry. A quick check on a well-appointed kitchen just off the hallway revealed nothing untoward there either, and the rest of the downstairs rooms also revealed no lurking horrors.

Meaning whatever had so seriously spooked the young girl now in their care was upstairs.

Where the music was playing.

Where the smell seemed to be strongest.

Not even seeing the file in front of her now, Ros, the empathetic, invisible ghost journeyed with the two uniformed officers as they made their way up to the first-floor landing and to a bedroom door half-open in front of them. The music was coming from the other side of that half-open door, the same song repeating itself over and over on a loop, a song that sounded out of time somehow, modern and yet not, a song neither officer could immediately place.

Then again, identifying a tune wasn't exactly high on their list of priorities.

Ros, the officers' now-constant companion, stepped into the room with them, hovered in the doorway while one stumbled back outside to be sick, the other just about managing to reach inside his tunic for his radio to summon assistance before he too vomited on the expensively-carpeted floor; although what assistance could practically be rendered in this instance was already in some serious doubt.

The body – a male – looked like a carcass in an abattoir. He was lying on the bed, arms and legs secured by some sort of twine. Blood was everywhere, skin flayed into ribbons by what looked like a million different stab wounds. This wasn't a human being any more. This was butchered offal.

By now the first officer's colleague had joined him from the landing and it was he who saw the second victim. Up to that point, and perhaps understandably, the figure on the bed had claimed all their attention but now they could see that there was another body slumped on the floor.

This second figure, another male again, clutched a large, boning, knife in one hand. He actually appeared to be uninjured save for a large slash across his throat, extending from ear to ear, almost providing him with an extended second mouth which seemed now to be frozen into a permanent smile.

Another knife was lying by the victim on the bed. A reconstruction would later match its serrated edge to the throat wound suffered by the man on the floor. Presumably, at some stage in the ongoing torture, the victim on the bed had somehow managed to pick up one of the knives discarded by his assailant. Perhaps the attacker had become careless or perhaps he believed his victim was already beyond making any sort of protest regarding the horrors that were currently being inflicted on him.

But he was wrong. Because that victim, probably acting on some kind of auto-pilot by then, must have lashed out with the knife and slashed, in a single arc, the throat of his attacker.

That injury wouldn't have been immediately fatal, the second victim would have had to wait for unconsciousness courtesy of his failing blood level before death finally followed, although it would probably have taken place in a matter of minutes.

The victim on the bed may not have been so lucky.

Years before, at the scene of the torture and subsequent killing of the Kincaids, Ros had knelt down next to the body of the youngest victim, a ten-year-old boy called Cai, his upper body intact and undamaged but his legs virtually severed at both knees by the force of a shotgun blast. That young boy had been similarly destined to bleed to death, watching his life literally drain out of him although he'd probably been rather more transfixed by the sight of his helpless mother being anally raped by the handle of that self-same shotgun.

To blot out the unwanted, unwelcome memories, Ros turned her attention to the last few pages of the loose-leaf report before her and to the final entry on the part of the officer tasked with the unenviable duty of reporting all they'd seen that night.

Then, suddenly, from downstairs, they'd heard a noise. The front door had just opened. A second or so later and with the officers literally frozen, ambushed by all they'd just seen and uncertain as to who or what they would see next, they'd heard footsteps on the stairs.

The officers had looked at each other. So who was this, another assailant come to check on the handiwork of a fallen companion?

Which was when the bedroom door had pushed fully open and a young girl had walked into the room. For a moment the officers had just stared at the small, slight, figure in front of them but she didn't even seem to see them.

She just looked, flawless eyes wide in wonder, at the blood covering every inch of the walls and floor, at the stricken corpse slumped by the side of the bed before her eyes finally settled on the twisted creation splayed out on the bed itself.

By Ros's side, Conor frowned, puzzled.

Like everyone else in that briefing room he'd read the summaries in the various reports contained in the file they'd all been handed the night before, but there was something else in the additional reports that had just been given to them by Hendrix, something different.

Conor imagined those additional pages were some sort of corroborating testimony of some kind, but in fact there were clear discrepancies.

The macabre tableau was as he'd read previously, the position of the two corpses was also the same as was the occasionally over-graphic description of the damage wreaked upon the splayed body on the bed.

But in the report he'd been handed the previous evening, the girl had been found wandering the streets, a discovery that had led the investigating officers to that scene of medieval barbarity in the first place.

In the subsequent report, the one they'd just been handed, the girl had walked in on it all.

Conor frowned. What the hell had happened, had she been allowed to head home from the police station all by herself? Or was this a different girl altogether? And now, as he read more closely, there were other inconsistencies too. The age of the girl seemed to be different on different pages of the report and the internal geography of the property seemed different at times as well.

'Ma'am?'

Conor looked across at Ros, catching at the same time an identical look of puzzlement on Hendrix's face as he too scanned those same reports.

But Ros didn't look puzzled. And neither did Masters. Their expressions betrayed a very different emotion, one Conor had difficulty identifying at first perhaps because, in the case of Masters at least, it was something he'd never seen on his face before.

Because if Conor had to describe it in a single word, the only word he could have used was, fear.

'The girl.'

Conor hesitated. Minor discrepancies in a scenes of crime report weren't uncommon. Eyewitnesses to any cataclysmic event often reported differing, even occasionally-contradictory, impressions of the same experience. But these weren't minor discrepancies.

Ros nodded, ahead of him already it seemed.

'That's not the girl.'

'What?'

Across the table, Masters closed his file, the expression on his face saying it all. If only all that was contained therein and all it opened up thereby could be dispatched so easily.

'The second file, the one attached to the report you were given last night, was from a different killing. Years ago.'

For a moment Ros looked again at Masters who looked back

at her, a shared experience clearly being unwillingly revisited, infesting the space between them.

'The victim back then was a woman while this victim was a man, but the injuries inflicted on her were virtually the same as those inflicted on our present-day victim. His name is – or was – Roman Edwards by the way. He was known to us.'

Masters didn't elaborate as to exactly how or why for now. He just pressed on.

'There is another difference in that the original attacker discovered at the scene was known to us too. At this moment we have no idea who the present-day attacker might be, for reasons that will become clear once you read to the end of the report because I, for one, have no wish to provide a summary.'

Conor and Hendrix weren't looking any the less confused but Masters was rolling on anyway. Plenty of time for further explanations later.

'But that aside, everything else is virtually identical.'

Masters continued, the two reports still face down on the table in front of him.

'Meaning we haven't got a simple murder on our hands.'

Masters looked at Ros and there it was again, that same reluctantly-shared experience.

Ros nodded back, taking it up herself now, spelling out the same conclusion she'd also reached, equally unwillingly, the previous evening.

'We've got a copycat killing as well.'

3.

H E'D BEEN ENCASED inside the body bag for over three hours. And now he was beginning to wonder if it had all been something of a waste of effort.

Jamie had arrived at the heliport in the company of a group of men he'd always termed the usual suspects. Men, like himself, who were going to spend the next two weeks away from whatever home they were either working to support or from which they were seeking to escape.

Because it was always one or the other in Jamie's experience. No-one did this kind of work unless they had to. If there was anyone amongst that usually-taciturn group who opted for this life out of pure and simple choice, he'd never met them.

On their arrival at the heliport it had been the usual routine. They'd each been handed their heavy-duty, rubber-sealed, immersion suits – the so-called body bags – flotation devices designed to keep them more or less alive in case the helicopter, which was currently cranking up its labouring engines out on the launch pad, crashed into the freezing waters of the North Sea.

Then they'd watched the usual safety video about boarding life rafts as well as instructions on how to remove the helicopter windows in the event of becoming trapped inside.

It was a safety video Jamie had watched many times before, but never understood why it needed to be so brutal in tone. All the ones he'd previously watched on commercial aircraft before taking off for some holiday somewhere had always been so much softer in tone, almost apologetic for even broaching the possibility of a potential disaster. In this, much harsher world, the on-screen commentator seemed to relish it. Jamie put in his earplugs, blotted it out.

Then they'd walked out onto the tarmac towards the wheezing chariot that was going to take them out over all that spume-exploding water. Like every other helicopter they'd travelled in lately, it looked patched-up and old and for a good reason – because it was.

Jamie crowded into the narrow passenger cabin and for the next two hours it was much as it had been on every previous trip. No-one spoke, there was little point anyway, no-one could hear you if you did. And most of his companions kept their eyes tightly closed for the whole of the buffeting ride and not because they were tired but for another all-too obvious reason – because they were scared.

Jamie looked down at the water now just metres below. Once, he felt a violent drumming as one particularly furious wave actually smashed against the underside of the fuselage.

And then it happened. Two hours into the three-hour flight the intercom crackled into life and the pilot, visible in the open cockpit ahead, advised them that the weather at the rig was fifty-fifty.

It was the music that had done it.

Up to that moment, the moment Kim first heard the click of the on-off button, first heard the music begin to percolate through the small flat, she thought maybe she'd had some sort of stroke, which was almost unthinkable at her age, but what else could it be? What else could explain this sudden, devastating and total paralysis?

Then Aron started whimpering and her heart lurched as she realised she couldn't reach out to him, couldn't offer the comfort he was demanding, the comfort that was his right. Every instinct inside her battled her suddenly-useless body as spirit frantically attempted to impose itself over flesh.

When Kim realised she could do nothing, that whatever silent signals she was attempting to send from brain to body didn't even seem to be heeded, let alone acted on, she thought it was the worst moment of her life.

But it wasn't.

Because as Aron now started to really belt out his cries, as yells began to replace his formerly soft whimpers, she heard someone turn on the cheap CD player they'd bought for the kitchen – a tinny song beginning on what she'd soon realise was the repeat programme, a pre-programmed cycle which meant one song would start the moment another came to an end.

Someone?

Kim stared, unseeing, into a middle distance populated by no-one she could see, but who was quite clearly there nonetheless.

How the hell could there be someone in their kitchen, turning on their CD, playing their music?

Kim tried to move again, but once more she couldn't. At the same time she saw Aron find Kitty. As his fingers moved, restless, up and down the prison that was now his buggy, he suddenly felt the soft fur of his comforter and closed his fingers over it, bringing it up towards his mouth.

But the young baby's fingers were clumsy and he fumbled the manoeuvre and the small toy slipped from his grasp and fell onto the floor.

Kim watched him kick and cry and then kick some more and it might have been her imagination but Aron seemed to cry more for his lost toy than he'd cried in the whole of the last hour for a feed that had always been produced on demand.

And Kim knew why. Because no-one did what they always

did when he'd cried like that before, no-one reached down and put his toy back in his outstretched hands, and no-one did that because she still couldn't move a single, fucking, muscle.

Kim kept looking at Aron as he kept looking down at Kitty.

And felt her heart start to break.

A few hundred miles to the north, Jamie looked through the window at the water below, his mind running through options, computing possibilities.

Fifty-fifty was a clearly understood code. It meant there was now a clear doubt they could land. If the weather outside deteriorated any further they wouldn't even be able to get near the docking platform. If that happened they'd have to turn back which meant they'd miss the start of their shift.

In those circumstances what happened next was simple. The rig workers currently waiting on that platform for their own helicopter ride back to shore would remain there for another week while their replacements cooled their heels on dry land.

And Jamie could now almost see the mental calculations taking place in the minds of the men around him. They were all there, like Jamie, because they needed the money and every one of them was now trying to recalculate their finances in the event of a week's lost wages.

But Jamie was doing a very different kind of calculation as well. Because, yes, he needed the money and, yes, Kim and Aron needed it too. But what price do you place on watching your child in the first few months of his life, on being there when he wakes, watching him as he falls asleep, experiencing at first hand all those simple, precious moments which, once missed, can never be recaptured no matter how many times you pore over them later on some smartphone or camera?

So Jamie's mind was running, not on money, but on train schedules instead.

If they did have to return back to the helipad, Jamie was heading home and that was as in straightaway. He could get the lunchtime service, change trains in Edinburgh and be back in Cardiff mid-evening. He could then be back in their flat, a few miles from the city centre train station, less than half an hour later.

And now Jamie began luxuriating in the sudden possibility that had opened up before him. He might not even call Kim beforehand, might just let himself in and see the expression of stunned wonder in her eyes, drink in her always-welcoming, sunshine, smile.

Suddenly, Kim saw her. The someone who was in their kitchen, the someone who'd put on their CD player and who was now playing their music.

Or at least Kim saw an arm come into view as that someone bent down and calmly and coolly placed a small camera on the floor.

The arm wasn't rough or muscled; it was quite clearly the arm of a woman, possibly a young woman from the honed skin on view. But whoever it was didn't reveal herself any more and she certainly didn't take any notice of the crying baby a metre or so away either. All the woman's attention was on the camera instead.

Kim watched as her visitor's fingers flicked a couple of buttons. Kim couldn't see which ones, just kept watching as those same fingers checked the lens a couple of times making sure, so Kim was slowly realising, that she had herself and her small baby in view.

Then another switch on the side was flicked and a red light suddenly appeared, presumably meaning that the record facility had just been activated.

And, slowly again, Kim began to understand one thing even

if she understood nothing else. She knew now that she hadn't suffered any kind of stroke. Some sudden and terrible affliction hadn't robbed her of her ability to move and communicate, or at least no natural affliction.

She realised now that she must have been shot with something. Thinking back, that must have been what that explosion of light and noise was all about.

So what was this? A robbery that had gone wrong? Had she disturbed a panicky intruder who'd then lashed out with some weapon or something?

The only problem with that immediately-unconvincing little theory was that the intruder in question was quite clearly still there, was still in their flat and she didn't seem to be looking for anything to steal and her actions didn't look even remotely panicky right now either.

More of the woman was now visible, although her face was still just outside Kim's peripheral vision and all the time Kim's eyes framed a silent question to which, she was already beginning to suspect, she wouldn't receive an answer.

What are you doing?

What – the fuck – are you doing?

Another hour later and with the full horror of the answer only slowly dawning, Kim began to realise exactly what she was doing.

Jamie knew he shouldn't even be thinking like this. Only the previous evening both Kim and himself had reconciled themselves to the fact he'd be away for the next two weeks but Jamie couldn't help it, his spirits quite simply soared at the prospect of being away for less than a single day instead.

Jamie looked round at the faces on all sides of that narrow passenger cabin and he could see the same emotion on all those faces too. Even though every single man in that cabin was in the same sort of pressing need as himself, their spirits were quite clearly soaring in exactly the same way.

And Jamie knew that for a fact. Because when the pilot came back on the intercom a few minutes later to tell them that the weather had eased and that they would be able to land after all, an audible soft groan echoed around the whole cabin. Men who'd hardly looked at each other up to that point exchanged rueful smiles.

And Jamie smiled ruefully too as the helicopter now began to descend. A few moments before he'd been planning every second of the unexpected holiday he was to share with Kim and Aron. Now he wouldn't be seeing them for another fortnight at least.

Jamie looked out of the window at the waves which were beginning to calm as, below, the low cloud parted and the tiny helipad on the rig could be seen.

But as Jamie stepped from the helicopter twenty or so minutes later there was some consolation at least.

The rig manager approached, an email in hand. It hadn't been delivered to Jamie's personal laptop as the broadband connection to the rig was down – for the workforce at least, and not for the first or last time either. So, with only the main feed into the control computer working, Kim had sent her message there instead.

Jamie read the email, a warm glow spreading inside him as he did so. Kim had often sent him similar emails in the past, some small reminder of home to keep him company and cheer him up at the start of a shift, but this was different. Because Kim ended the simple message by telling him all about something that herself and Aron had been working on, some kind of show apparently.

Jamie wracked his brains, tried to imagine what she was

talking about. It was far too early for their baby to start walking, but maybe he'd started to say something at least halfway intelligible; maybe Kim had taught him to mimic his name or something.

Jamie looked at the email again as, all around, colleagues began preparing for the first of their twelve-hour shifts as the previous crew boarded the waiting helicopter for their own ride home.

Then Jamie looked up at the sky as the helicopter's blades started to turn once more, praying for a spell of decent weather that would restore the connection to his laptop.

Then he'd be able to view for himself whatever show his partner and their baby were currently devising for Daddy.

4.

LEON CHECKED HIS messages on his iPad. They were the usual collection. Dry-mouthed enquiries as to the treats he might be able to offer from equally dry-mouthed punters he'd probably never see. Time-wasters in other words who he immediately discounted. So far as that breed was concerned this city, now his adopted home city, had more than its fair share.

But one message seemed more promising. No name as yet, which wasn't unusual at this early stage, but the woman in question had contacted him three times over the previous twenty-four hours. She seemed to have done her research too. She'd already identified a couple of girls she was interested in and, if he could confirm the availability of at least one of them, then they might be able to do some business later that day.

Leon let himself out of his canal-side apartment on Rokin and walked up to Amsterdam's famous Dam Square before moving on to De Wallen. He hadn't managed to get to bed till four that morning and it was now barely noon, but some of the less attractive offerings were already inhabiting a few of the nearby windows.

Leon barely glanced at them as he passed, something the women in question seemed almost to expect. The pecking order had always been clear. The younger and more attractive women bagged the prime spots in the evening, the further down that sliding scale you descended in terms of looks and appeal the earlier your working day began.

As he turned a corner at the end of the narrow street Leon caught sight of himself as he passed one of the now-vacant windows. A decade or so before, had he been a different sex, he'd probably have been one of the area's late-night habituées. These days he'd be lucky to scrape into the early afternoon shift. For not the first time in his life Leon proffered grateful thanks to the gods that he'd been born a man.

He'd come to 1012 a few years previously. 1012 had always been the postcode for his adopted city's famous/infamous red-light district but it had also come to possess a different signifier in the last few years as well. Project 1012 was now the official code for the big clean-up that had recently been taking place. Over half the window-front brothels had now been closed along with roughly the same percentage of the equally famous/infamous cannabis coffee houses.

The campaign to close the former had attracted heated opposition from most of the area's working girls who were adamant that sweeping away the legal brothels would simply drive them out onto the streets. In the windows, so the argument went, everything was safe, out in the open. The girls could see their clients. Everyone, and not just their clients, could see them. And, apart from the usually brief periods when the curtains were drawn, everyone could see everything else too.

Leon entered one of the coffee houses that had so far escaped the cull, ordered a double espresso and headed across to a far table to await his appointment. On the way he passed two ageing, if not positively ancient, prostitutes chatting to a film crew who were making a documentary on the oldest members of the city's oldest profession.

Leon knew them, although not professionally. He'd never employed either. Both were in the early seventies and were quitting due to galloping arthritis which was making the demands of their working day too painful. As he moved on, Leon caught a brief flash of their conversation. One of the locally-famous duo, a mother of four, was estimating the number of men they must have serviced over the previous fifty years. Between them, the two sisters solemnly agreed, the total must be pushing at least four hundred thousand.

Leon settled himself at a far table, facing the door. He used to run a few working girls himself but now he operated a much more lucrative trade. Courtesy of a previous profession, he'd always had a keen interest in what might be called the more voyeuristic side of his chosen calling. There were always going to be those infinitely more interested in spectating than participating. Most of the girls regarded that type of punter with world-weary irritation, but not Leon. He'd realised from early on that the real money actually lay there these days.

Leon ran a couple of websites, but websites with what might be called a twist. Filming may have been strictly forbidden in and around the streets of De Wallen, but behind the closed doors of the three hundred or so tiny one-roomed cabins that still offered sexual services, it was a different matter.

Leon had started by filming a couple of clients who wanted a record of their often-dubious sexual endeavour to take home as an equally-dubious souvenir. But then one particularly brave or foolhardy soul had uploaded his own DVD clip onto the internet. The clip went viral, crashed Leon's server and a new idea was born.

Now Leon offered a virtual experience as well as the more usual physical encounter. Of course a punter could just watch if he or she so chose. But that same lucky punter, after viewing the action and checking out the wares, could then press a button and pre-book exactly the same experience for themselves.

And the really neat part of it all was that Leon really didn't need to put a lot of effort into the various offerings he provided. Supermodels were very much not the attraction these days, in fact the more ordinary and everyday the body on view the more his new punters seemed to like it.

It was the key difference between his old and new business. Back then it had all been airbrushed models and boob jobs. Now it was the girl next door who seemed to be the main attraction. And as ordinary and everyday a girl as possible.

The client who'd contacted him the previous day had specified no filming was to take place during her encounter, which was absolutely fine. She'd also made it clear she wanted a face-to-face meeting with not only himself but the merchandise in question, which was a sensible precaution too. Quite a few of his more choosy clients wanted to check out the goods on offer with their own eyes before making a final selection. The tricks that could be performed these days courtesy of Photoshop had littered the world with many a disappointed and disillusioned punter, which was never good for trade.

Leon checked his watch, a Patek Philippe, one of the few indulgences he'd managed to bring with him from his old life, even if almost everything else had fallen by the wayside. Then he looked up from his table as the door in front of him opened bang on the allotted minute. Something had told him this one would be neither a moment early or late. There was just something about her messages that hinted at a more than usually-punctual soul.

Leon pasted on a welcoming smile as a young, twenty-something, woman approached. She seemed to have a companion with her which he hadn't expected, but which didn't particularly bother him.

What did concern him more was something in the way she moved, something almost familiar.

But the sun was shining in from the street behind them and her features were momentarily in shadow, so a still-smiling Leon just half-rose, extending a hand as he did so.

Then he saw just who was now standing opposite him and

a moment later he saw just who her companion was too, which was when Leon's welcoming smile vanished.

Four hours previously, Ros, Masters, Conor and Hendrix had been in the 51 Executive Lounge at Cardiff Airport.

Ros had first flown from there on a family holiday as a small child. Any sort of lounge back then had just been a distant dream for most of the small airport's business travellers. Now it was a necessity, at least for one of their party.

Left to her own devices, Ros might have killed the waiting time in the airport's small selection of shops. The presence of Masters meant those shops being swiftly bypassed as the DCI led his small party past the waiting gaggle of hard-pressed parents looking after fractious offspring, and into the relative sanctity of what was little more than a boarded-up cupboard offering a pitifully-small selection of convenience snacks.

But it was, at least, a relatively private cupboard, making it rather more fit for purpose so far as Masters was concerned than the public areas outside. If he'd had to spend any time on the surrounding concourse then blood, quite clearly, might have been spilt, so Ros duly followed him in. She'd no wish to send those fractious children off on their annual holiday with an atrocity imprinted on their impressionable eyes. Ros and her fellow officers had witnessed more than their fill of those lately.

Ros eyed Masters as he settled himself into a large armchair, eschewing the coffee on offer from a nearby machine, contenting himself with bottled water instead, frustrated and, in his eyes at least, with good cause.

The previous evening, Masters had stared at a computer screen in mounting impatience. Thirty minutes previously he'd typed in a name, an age and a last-known address and had been waiting ever since for a response.

If Masters was in luck then a match would come back from HOLMES, the police's national computer, or the Home Office Large and Major Enquiry System to give it its full title.

If he was out of luck, then an alert would be flagged and some operative somewhere would intercept his request. Masters had no idea who they might be or where they might be based and also knew he wouldn't even be able to begin to find out.

If Masters's request was intercepted then the operative in question would crosscheck the name that had been flagged with a file, the contents of which would be accessible only by two passwords which had to be submitted in sequence and within a strictly defined timescale and which would then immediately be reset by another and quite different operative with the original passwords discarded.

Then a simple message would appear on Masters's monitor.

No matches.

A few seconds later a message comprising just those two words duly flashed before him.

So a tense and increasingly irritated Masters tried a more direct approach, making a call which was answered by a woman giving only a number in place of a name.

Masters repeated the same request he'd just sought electronically and his call was transferred to another voice, male this time. Once again, the voice was identified only by a number.

Masters once more gave the last-known name, age and address of the man he was seeking as well as spelling out, now with some considerable force, the very pressing reasons why he was so anxious to trace this particular individual.

Masters's respondent didn't speak during the whole of the tirade, only requesting Masters's own details including his rank and number at the end of what was fast becoming a litany of barely-suppressed bile.

Then the owner of the male voice, identified only by a number and not a name, had cut the call. He'd next made an internal check on his caller and had then requested a confidential check on that DCI's current quarry.

The search took some time as the information was contained in a series of interlinked files all of which were, once again, accessed separately by a set of now-different passwords, but finally the owner of the male voice had an actual name on the screen before him. Or, more accurately, he had two names on the screen before him. A name from what was very much the past, and a name that belonged to the present, along with details of that new individual's place and date of birth, his national insurance number, his passport and driving licence, his medical history and even his school exam results.

That life history was all fiction of course, but would now be as real to the person in question as to anyone else walking the streets outside those anonymous offices staffed by persons identified by numbers instead of names.

The owner of the male voice stared at the fictional creation on screen for a moment. Then he picked up the phone.

Back in his office, a frustrated Masters stared at his own phone, destined, as he was fast coming to suspect, to remain unenlightened and he was right.

Because the owner of the male voice identified only by a number and not a name now dialled a quite different number instead.

Ros really shouldn't have been surprised that Masters had attempted to subvert a system designed to protect a man he himself was seeking to protect in turn.

Jukes or, to give him his full title, DCI Jukes, her immediate senior officer, hadn't even made a pretence at taking any sort of offence when he'd briefed her on the attempted transgression an hour or so after taking that call from the owner of the voice identified only by a number.

There was little point and both Ros and Jukes knew it. Had they tasked Masters on his attempt to breach department protocol he'd probably have countered with some fine-sounding thesis about testing that department's security systems or some similar exercise in obfuscation.

Had they pressed him further, Masters might have pleaded a communality of purpose which would have been yet another exercise in evasion.

Or, more probably, he might just have ignored them.

Either way, it didn't much matter. The days when either Jukes or Ros found the activities of Murder Squad in general, and Masters in particular, a matter of surprise or even note were long gone. Murder Squad and Witness Protection were, always had been, and always would be, two very different sides of what was supposed to be the same judicial coin and the reason was simple.

Witness Protection was charged with keeping a witness safe until such time as that witness could be delivered to trial.

Murder Squad also wanted to keep that witness safe up to and including that trial, but there all common purpose, if any existed in the first place, evaporated.

Witnesses were a means to an end for Masters. So far as he was concerned, they were individuals to be mined for whatever information, insights or leads could be profitably extracted from them and then dismissed.

The problem being that once that information, those insights or those leads had been profitably extracted and thrown at some heavyweight villain in some Crown Court somewhere, many of those witnesses were then severely compromised. While Murder Squad celebrated yet another conviction in some nearby bar, Ros's department had a living, breathing, human being to deal with, an asset extinguished so far as Murder Squad were concerned, a charge, often a lifelong charge, for Ros and her cohorts.

A living, breathing, charge, such as Leon.

They found a different coffee shop within moments. The shop used by Leon was a regular haunt, so Ros had quickly established, and therefore susceptible to compromise. Such an eventuality was perhaps unlikely, but on that matter Ros and Masters were in complete agreement. Given the events of the last twenty-four hours it made absolutely no sense to take any unnecessary risks.

Ros and Masters seated themselves in front of a giant wall-mounted mural featuring, somewhat improbably and amongst others, the faces of Queen Beatrix, Hu Jintao, Dmitry Medvedev, Barack Obama and Silvio Berlusconi. It seemed an unholy combination but perhaps, as Ros reflected, that made this new setting oddly fitting. Because what had brought the three of them together was a far from holy matter too.

'Roman Edwards has been found dead.'

Masters plunged straight in, no preamble, no small talk.

Leon stared back at him. If he was surprised by Masters's bombshell announcement, he didn't show it. If he cared, he didn't show it either.

Masters reached into his pocket and slid a scenes-of-crime photograph across the coffee table. Leon looked down at it and now there was rather more in the way of a reaction. To the clear disgust of a couple of visiting tourists, Leon turned to his side and had to exert considerable self-control to stop himself being violently sick on the floor.

Ros sympathised. If she'd been shown that photo without even the ghost of an attempt to prepare her for what she was about to see, she'd have probably struggled not to deposit the contents of her airline snack over that same floor as well.

A calm Masters continued, ignoring the stifled retches coming from the figure in front of them.

'As you can see, he met his end in something of a brutal manner. As has probably also not escaped your attention, the manner of his demise was, shall we say, rather eerily familiar too.'

'For fuck's sake.'

That was a gasping Leon's only contribution to the exchange so far but he seemed to get his message across, gesturing at the offending image at the same time, a clear instruction to get rid of it.

Masters barely seemed to notice.

'There was a child's comic I used to buy, years ago.'

Ros and Leon looked at him, the scenes-of-crime photograph still on the table in front of them.

'There was this puzzle that used to come out each week, two pictures side by side, they looked the same but actually contained several subtle differences. The game was to identify as many of those differences as you could.'

Masters smiled, seemingly lost for a moment in his memory. Across the table, the staring Leon was recovering, but none too quickly.

'I've been through these two sets of pictures time and again.'

Masters tapped the file.

'And if there are any differences in the staging of these two crime scenes then I've missed them and believe me I really don't miss that much.'

Leon didn't reply. He still couldn't. But Ros could see he wasn't about to disagree.

Masters picked up the photo and studied it some more.

'This new crime scene could almost be a reconstruction, in

fact, let's go further, it is a reconstruction and virtually in its every detail too. This time, it's involved Roman Edwards. In the original crime scene it was, of course, your brother, Joey.'

Then Masters paused.

'The problem we have is that the details of that original crime were restricted to a highly select circle.'

Masters nodded at Leon.

'Yourself, obviously.'

Masters gestured in his own direction.

'Myself.'

Then Masters inclined a head towards the still-silent Ros seated to his left.

'Your handler and her senior officer, but no-one else, no-one at all which leaves us with a second problem.'

Masters leant close to Leon.

'Of the people inside that highly restricted circle, I know for a fact that I didn't commit this new murder.'

Masters nodded again at Ros.

'I assume my colleague didn't either and even though I've never liked the anal-obsessive who masquerades as her immediate senior officer, not even I suspect DCI Jukes of moonlighting as a defiler of bodies on this somewhat extreme scale.'

Masters nodded back at him.

'Which just leaves you, Leon.'

Masters nodded at him again.

'Did you do this?'

Leon only gave the slightest shake of his head by way of a response but it couldn't have been more eloquent an answer if he'd shouted it from one of the nearby, steeply pitched, rooftops.

The look on his face said it all too. The photo that Masters had now just placed back in the file in front of him may not have been before his eyes any longer, but its every detail was still quite clearly branded on them.

As was the original crime scene of course.

The one that had banished him from that world to this, believing he'd left that old world behind forever, now only too well aware that didn't seem to be the case.

Masters nodded once again. It was the answer he'd expected, as had Ros. Both officers would have been astonished indeed had Leon responded in any other way.

'Which leaves us with a third problem, I suppose.'

Conor left his hotel feeling more and more like the useless appendage he was turning out to be on this trip.

The official line was that Hendrix and himself were there as back-up, but for what hadn't been explained to either of them. They were both aware of some threat to a former witness, but the level of threat was being communicated on a need-to-know basis and it had been made crystal clear to Conor and Hendrix that they did not.

Conor imagined that might provoke some sort of fellow-feeling from his new colleague in Murder Squad. In fact it provoked nothing. As in absolutely no response at all.

But Conor had persisted, suggesting that the two of them might spend what was quite clearly going to be a night off in some local club or other. There were a few tucked in and around the nearby Leidseplein, the best of which were easily identified by the long queues already snaking outside, but in any event Conor had done a little research himself on the way over.

Studio 80 probably had the best sound system in the city although OT301 was reputedly well worth a look. There were also some decent rock bands touting their wares in the neighbouring Melkweg and Paradiso if Hendrix felt like working off the day's frustrations in the form of some heavy-duty head-bashing.

And if that didn't float any boats, Conor had also suggested an evening sampling the delights on offer in Wynand Fockink or De Twee Zwaantjes, or possibly even Prik if Hendrix favoured company of the more male persuasion.

Conor didn't know exactly what Hendrix might be into when it came to that sort of thing. How could he, he hardly knew the man? Which was rather the point of the evening Conor had in mind.

It had been like talking to a visitor from another planet. Hendrix had just told Conor he already had plans before melting away into the night, almost before Conor had a chance to realise he'd just been well and truly blanked.

Conor assumed Hendrix had booked himself in for a spot of sex tourism instead, which would have been reasonable enough. Conor wouldn't have indulged himself, not in these more or less happily-married days. But he might have tagged along to some sex club or other to watch a floor show. Why be so coy about it, that's what Conor didn't understand? Then again there was more than one thing about Masters's new sidekick that Conor didn't understand.

Maybe that's why he always felt so unsettled in his company.

Or maybe that was down to something else.

Back in the coffee shop, Leon was becoming more and more agitated.

'This could all be one giant set-up you do realise that, don't you?'

A belligerent Leon stared at his two companions.

'A smoking, fucking, gun and you two have just fired it.'

Ros shifted in her seat, uncomfortable. It was exactly the

point she herself had made to Masters and Jukes just a few hours previously.

'Whoever did for Roman had worked out the very first thing you'd do, that you'd break cover, come and find me, so if this is some sort of trap you've not only fallen into it, you've dived in, head fucking first.'

By Ros's side, Masters nodded, sagely. Like his silent companion, he was also aware that Leon had a point. It was a point that had not only been raised in that initial briefing back in the UK, but a point he himself had pondered, and at some considerable length too.

Before it had been ignored.

'It's a risk.'

Leon stared back in disbelief, not just at the statement but at the clear note of unconcern that underpinned it. Little matters like any clear and present threat to Leon's well-being didn't seem to score too highly on Masters's list of priorities right now.

Ros stepped in, quickly, as she'd stepped in many times in the past, attempting to liaise between a panicky witness and the man from Murder Squad. Masters would often delight in playing games, pushing a witness, taunting them indeed, ever-desirous of assessing the calibre of the man or woman who would one day stand up in a witness box and say all they'd promised to say when they first entered the protection programme.

Sometimes there was good reason for that. Sometimes a whole case rested on the shoulders of that witness and Masters needed to know, right from the start, whether he and his department were throwing in their professional lot with the shakiest of flakes.

But sometimes there was no reason for Masters's game-playing, no witness on whom they were relying, no evidence, real or imagined, to test. All of which held out the possibility that in those cases, and perhaps in this case too, Masters truly could not give a shit.

Ros took up the reins.

'Balanced against that was the risk involved in leaving you here, unaware of what may be a new threat, ignoring the possibility that this isn't some elaborate smoking gun as you put it, but something else.'

Leon stared back at her, now more lost than at any time since this unwelcome exchange began.

'Something else? What, for fuck's sake?'

But Ros sidestepped that one and pressed on, mainly because she didn't know. None of them did. That, partly at least, was the point of this trip.

'So, first, you need to be reinvented. We can't guarantee your new identity hasn't been compromised and second, we need to move you close to home. If this copycat killing is the first shot in some kind of twisted game, then we need you back under the kind of protection we simply can't offer if you stay here.'

'But this doesn't make any sense. There's no-one around from the old days. Roman, yes, OK.'

Leon tailed off, beginning to look hunted now.

'But he was the only one who knew anything about all that.'

Masters shrugged.

'Maybe Roman told someone.'

'Who? And why, for fuck's sake?'

Leon nodded back towards the scenes-of-crime photo, the tip of which was still visible, peeking out from the top of Masters's file.

'And even if he did, who'd do something like that? There was only one sicko who'd ever pull off that kind of stunt and he's dead.'

Leon tailed off again, struggling against the ever-present memories flashing again through his head.

Ros just looked back at him, remained silent.

An hour or so later, Ros walked along the same city streets Leon had patrolled just a few hours before.

All around her stag and hen parties headed for the six-and-a-half thousand square metres of usually-suspect and occasionally-genuine pleasure afforded by the area circumscribed by Niezel in the north, Nieuwmarkt to the east, Sint Jansstraat in the south and Warmoesstraat to the west.

Ros had spent some time in the city herself in her late teens, although never as a part of any hen or stag party. Ros's excursions then, as all her excursions before and since, had always been of the strictly solo variety.

In any event, Ros was making for a very different sort of destination, somewhere she'd come across on one of those previous excursions and a place to which she always returned whenever she came back to a city she'd once briefly adopted. A city that, unlike many of the locations she'd visited as a sole traveller back then, always felt as if it had adopted her in some way too.

And, as she walked on, Ros's mind drifted back to one of the elements of the modern-day murder she actually found the most disturbing.

Roman Edwards had been butchered in exactly the same manner as the original victim. That original victim had been a young woman called Toya James.

Leon's brother, Joey, had been her attacker before Toya had lashed out with that knife and killed him in turn.

But, unlike Toya, Roman hadn't actually felled any attacker. The figure slumped by the side of the bed had certainly fooled the investigating officers when they'd first walked in on that new crime scene, but perhaps they could be forgiven for not inspecting it all that closely.

Because that figure wasn't human at all. It was a mannequin, dressed to resemble the previous attacker, complete with trademark slash across the throat.

A copycat murder had been committed, Roman was ample evidence of that. But the mannequin was something else. The mannequin completed the tableau, removing all doubt that this was indeed a message of some kind. The problem being that no-one had any idea as yet exactly what that message might be.

Then Ros slowed. And she slowed because ahead of her she'd just seen someone.

In probably the last place she'd have expected to see him.

The plane took off at ten the next morning.

Ros, Masters, Conor and Hendrix settled back in their seats for the short flight home. A few rows ahead was Leon, separated from his companions, to all intents and purposes just a lone male making a business trip back from the Continent; in reality watched over all the time by every one of them.

But it wasn't Leon who was the subject of Ros's albeit-discreet attention right now. As the plane banked to begin the journey across the North Sea, Ros looked across at Hendrix.

Ros could see a small book open on his knee. The book seemed at first glance to be a guidebook but it was also a history text too. Its subject was the Begijnhof, an enclosed courtyard in one of the quieter parts of the city they'd just left, a small settlement dating from the early fourteenth century.

Originally constructed as a sanctuary for the Beguines – a Catholic sisterhood who lived like nuns although they took no monastic vows – the tall houses were still to be found grouped around a small square overlooking a well-maintained garden. No traffic noise intruded, augmenting the almost-sanctified atmosphere. Amsterdam's oldest house, the Het Houten Huis, also claimed sanctuary there.

Ros had come across it by accident years before but always made a return journey whenever she could, a pilgrimage in a sense. It was the closest place to heaven as far as Ros was concerned and she'd never heard any other soul so much as refer to it before, which made it all the more surprising that she'd seen Hendrix in that same square the previous evening.

Hendrix had been doing pretty much what Ros always did whenever she made one of her visits. He'd simply been sitting there, drinking in the atmosphere, immersing himself in it all.

Ros stole another sideways glance across at her oblivious companion. If she'd had to pick a location of choice for an off-duty cop in Amsterdam, she'd have made a list beginning and ending with locations illuminated with lights, mainly, if not exclusively, of the red variety. To find one on the site of a fourteenth-century convent impressed and disconcerted Ros in roughly equal measure for reasons she couldn't quite understand.

Then the plane banked again and Ros looked down once again at the file on her knee.

Then Ros returned to the matter of the moment, Hendrix, dismissed as so many others had been similarly dismissed over the years.

For his part, Masters had taken no notice of Hendrix or indeed anyone else on that plane ride back to the Welsh capital. Masters looked out of the window at the coastline below but didn't register that either. Unlike Ros, he didn't even glance down at the same open file on his lap. All Masters could see right now was a house.

The house was much like any other, a small links-terrace, unremarkable from the outside. It was uninhabited for most of the week or so it would seem to any inquisitive neighbour, but as most of those neighbours didn't usually inhabit any of those surrounding houses for much more than a few weeks themselves, not many were that inquisitive anyway.

These occasional inhabitants though were unlike any that a neighbour, inquisitive or otherwise, could possibly have expected to see grouped together in one cramped front room.

In one corner was a wildlife campaigner sporting a Greenpeace T-shirt and frayed blue jeans. On the sofa was a tattooed skinhead, boots crudely painted in the colours of the Union Jack. A bearded university lecturer, out in the small kitchen, could be heard debating a fine point in a Marxist text he was holding with an animal rights activist who was demonstrating some counter point in a leaflet he was waving in front of his companion's face.

It looked like some bizarre social experiment. Some doomed attempt to bring together all manner and types of opinion and argument in one single space, an exercise that in any other place and at any other time would probably have resulted in some quite serious injury.

But not in this room. Not with these myriad examples of the human race in all its multi-coloured and multi-opinionated guises. Discipline in here would be maintained at all times. These individuals never let down their guard.

Masters looked across the room and let his eyes settle on the only woman present that evening, a curio in itself. This had always been very much a man's world, at least until protests such as the one outside the American cruise missile base at Greenham Common in Berkshire a few decades before. Then, female police officers had been selected and dispatched to join the women protesters and report back. But even after that female recruits remained rare and Masters still wasn't sure why. Maybe it was simply down to the right type of woman not coming along all that often.

Masters shifted position slightly as the plane began its descent for landing, declining at the same time the offer of a last drink by a steward patrolling the small club class compartment of the plane. And Masters, once again, let his mind drift back to that strange gathering of even stranger souls.

Masters cleared his throat, a signal that he wanted silence, a signal instantly respected by all, be they bearded lecturers, tattooed skinheads, animal rights activists or wildlife campaigners. All eyes, including Anya's, the new female recruit, now swung his way.

Masters reached into his bag and took out a small wooden shield, the point of that gathering that night. It was rare for an officer in this sort of unit to receive an accolade of this type but the activities of the officer in question, Jack Ryan, the tattooed skinhead with the Union Jack boots, had very definitely merited such an honour.

Masters read out a prepared homily as Ryan kept his eyes modestly averted, looking down towards the floor.

But Masters wasn't looking at him. Masters was looking at the new female recruit again and all he could see was the naked desire, almost bordering on greed, in her eyes.

It was only too obvious what she was thinking and feeling. All Anya wanted, all she craved indeed, was to hear those same words paid in tribute to herself.

Masters looked again at the eager young woman and started to smile.

This was the one.

This was very definitely the one.

Back in the small commuter plane Masters looked at Leon those few rows ahead, just staring out of the window at nothing.

Then Masters looked back out of the window himself, his mind once again on that house and that young woman.

THERE'D BEEN TWO days of silence since that first email to the main office on the rig.

Since then none of Jamie's phone calls to the flat had been answered, although that wasn't all that unusual. Kim would sometimes walk the local streets and parks for hours, desperate to get out of a flat that was roughly the size of the smallest spare room back in her old house, the house in which they'd first met.

Not that Kim would ever draw comparisons of course, as Jamie knew. It might have sounded like criticism, as if she resented her current circumstances and lifestyle and was comparing it unfavourably with all she had before.

Jamie knew she didn't feel that way but it still couldn't be easy for her. His new partner had gone from a life of plenty, in material terms anyway, to a life that was anything but.

But that's what this job on the rig was all about. Give it another year and they'd have enough saved for a deposit on a proper home of their own and then they could leave that rented flat. Give it another year again and they should have some savings behind them too. Then Jamie would come ashore permanently, as they'd agreed, and they'd become the full-time family they all wanted to be, just the three of them from that point on.

Along with whoever else might come along of course, as a now-smiling Jamie reflected.

He knew there'd be those who would blame them for their current, straitened, circumstances. Kim was a married woman after all, complete with stepdaughter, when he'd first called into the house that day to do some work in the garden and found her in the small summerhouse, pretending she hadn't been crying at the same time as trying to hide the angry bruise that was already spreading across her cheek.

It wasn't any of his business, Jamie had told himself at first. It was a husband and wife thing. He didn't know too much about the man who was paying his wages. He certainly suspected some of those wages had been acquired by less than legal means, Kim's former husband having a local reputation as a middling-league chancer. But that, as Jamie kept telling himself, was also none of his business.

Jamie had just buckled down to the landscaping he'd been contracted to carry out and attempted to put everything else out of his mind.

Then he'd heard the voices.

First, there was his voice, hostile, accusatory and very possibly drunk as well. Then there was her voice, Kim's voice, pacifying him or at least trying to pacify him until a hard crack sounded around the garden as their latest exchange ended like so many others had ended in even the short time he'd been working there.

And then there'd be more tears which once again Kim would try to hide, yet another bruise she'd spend hours attempting to conceal.

Jamie had also heard the voice of Kim's no-nonsense mother as she made her increasingly frequent visits back then, insisting that Kim had made her bed and now she had to lie in it, that this was just a rough patch, that every couple had them, she just had to hang on in there.

And anyway what was the alternative? Walk out with nothing – because that's what she'd come into this marriage with, and that's what she'd be leaving with too if she did anything really stupid.

In one respect, Kim's mother was right. She'd certainly

walked into her marriage with nothing. But Kim had walked out with everything she'd ever wanted, as she'd always made clear to Jamie. Because she'd walked out with the man of her dreams.

The man who'd been there to pick her up when she'd fallen so low she thought she'd never get out from under what had become a vicious cycle of abuse.

The man who'd extended a simple hand of friendship to a woman in need, only for them both to realise there was so much more than simple friendship developing out of it all.

Not that Kim's mother or the rest of her extended family saw it that way. In their eyes she was a stupid cow who'd bagged a wealthy husband and had then run off with the hired help, and their attitude was now much the same as the husband's too.

Good riddance to bad rubbish.

And that mother and the rest of her extended family also warned her in no uncertain terms not to come knocking on any of their doors when her new world turned cold, as inevitably it would.

Only their new world hadn't turned cold. And that hadn't only just been down to the fact they'd fallen in love, it was all down to the simple pleasures, as Kim called them. Little treats she devised that may not have cost any money – every spare penny was well and truly destined for that much-cherished house fund – but small moments which still meant the world to them anyway.

Jamie smiled. Just like the one she was lining up for him that evening. At six o'clock. The Aron show as she'd called it in her first and only email so far, the mysterious spectacle she'd promised him.

Jamie had quickly secured the grudging agreement of the rig manager to access and use the office computer. So even if the broadband service to the rest of the rig was still playing up, he wasn't going to miss it.

And in fact he wasn't the only one because he'd never been able to resist boasting about his beautiful baby boy to his workmates and quite a few had now decided they wanted to put a face to a much-lauded name and attend as well.

This evening.

Six o'clock.

Jamie simply couldn't wait.

Kim couldn't believe it. For a moment or two, maybe a few minutes, maybe less, she'd actually fallen asleep. And as that realisation overwhelmed her, she almost felt her mind give way.

She could do nothing right now, nothing at all apart from stay awake. She couldn't speak, couldn't move, she certainly couldn't reach out to her baby whose former shrill sobs had now begun to mutate into occasional howls of weak bewilderment.

Previously, lying awake at night, she'd pray for him to settle as he stirred and grumbled in the small crib next to hers and Jamie's bed, but for the last few hours, aside from those brief, unforgivable, moments when she'd lapsed into temporary unconsciousness, she'd willed him to keep on crying, to let her know he was still there, was still all right.

But for the last few minutes, maybe longer, she still had no way of knowing, she'd allowed sleep to claim her and that realisation lacerated. The only thing she could do in her whole useless world right now was to try and remain focused and she hadn't even been able to do that.

Kim whimpered a succession of silent apologies but then, with a sudden jolt, she again felt rather than saw the door open behind her. For a moment she wondered if it was her mind playing tricks, inventing small sounds to punctuate the emptiness, but then light played on the opposite wall.

Then she heard a soft footfall meaning someone had definitely come in behind.

And, presumably, it was that same someone too.

Kim still couldn't move her head and all she could see was just the same female arm. Yet again, she felt rather than saw her new companion's eyes on her and Kim filled her own eyes with a hundred questions, the same questions that had been torturing her for what seemed like days now, trying desperately to establish some sort of exchange, willing her visitor to read the silent appeal in those eyes, to stop this and stop it now, whatever this was, it didn't matter, she simply didn't care any more.

Could the woman even begin to read her silent imprecations? Of course not and Kim knew it but she babbled them, silently, all the same.

Kim wouldn't do anything about this, she promised, she wouldn't even tell Jamie about it if she didn't want her to, this could just be between the two of them, they could write it off as some strange game or something, none of that mattered.

The only thing that mattered right now was reaching out to Aron, the only thing she remotely cared about was picking him up, blessing his lips with the sustenance his small body was clearly craving evermore desperately.

Then, all of a sudden, Aron himself came more into view as the woman reached down, adjusted Kim's position on the floor slightly.

And with it, Kim's stomach suddenly lurched and a thin dribble of vomit trickled from her mouth.

Kim's visitor made the last of her final checks on the recording equipment at the same time as she made sure the camera caught her monitoring the respective temperatures of her two captives.

For the mother the symptoms were complicated by the drugs she'd been using to keep her sedated, but it wasn't ever going to be the mother who was the main focus here. That was the downward regression of the infant.

Mild dehydration, so her researches had assured her, would commence almost immediately, leading in turn to the anticipated results. Tiredness, irritability, as well as a decreased urine volume. Conscientious soul that she was, she'd removed his nappy at one point to check, an action she'd also made sure had been captured on camera.

The baby would also become confused if not actually disorientated, even though at that early stage there'd only been a water loss of around one to two per cent.

Moderate dehydration would start a day or so later. Then there'd be no urine output at all. And then the irritability and confusion would be replaced with lethargy and even the occasional seizure, with the baby's eyes becoming evermore sunken.

Now the estimated water loss would be in the range of five to six per cent.

That morning her researches had predicted severe dehydration with the infant's heart and respiration rates beginning to increase to compensate for the decreased plasma volume and blood pressure. His temperature would now begin to rise as well.

Water loss would now be in the range of ten to fifteen per cent.

Kim's visitor noted with satisfaction the thin, grey, trickle of liquid from the mouth of the mother, ample evidence if any more were needed that her researches had been forensic in their accuracy.

So, and turning to the final moments now, there was one camera shot of which she was particularly proud. It hadn't been easy to achieve and when she'd first thought about it she didn't know if it would even be technically possible but now she thought she'd actually managed it. And if she had, then it would make the final image, she perhaps immodestly reflected, something of a masterpiece.

The small baby was going to be reflected in the eyeball of the mother. So – and if she could capture the moment properly – it would be as if the viewer were the mother herself watching their own child slip away, powerless to do anything to prevent it. It was the sort of shot that would guarantee near-mythic status, especially if she could hold it as long as possible when the time finally came.

The moment an infant died and you could see the realisation in his mother's eyes that he was gone.

Kim's visitor checked her watch, re-checked all her calculations. Then she nodded. All her estimates had pointed to the same end point and she saw no reason to change that now.

This evening.

Six o'clock.

And she simply couldn't wait.

6

Ros COLLECTED HER car from a small pound at the rear of the airport. Over the years it had become an unofficial car park for officers from all the emergency services. It was a perk of the job, saving a trek across acres of former fields to a distant parking place and a car crammed in amongst a thousand others, a location usually forgotten within moments of entering the distant departure lounge.

Ros waited half an hour for an airport tow truck to remove three cars barring her way and wondered whether she really should have just taken the shuttle bus instead.

Driving out of the airport she hesitated. The quickest route back to the city centre was a short six-mile hop via the site of an old farmhouse that had been named after a dovecot according to some sources, but was now a clogged and chaotic intersection above a by-pass that was usually clogged and chaotic as well.

According to a local guide Ros had once found, there'd been a crossroads there for centuries, originally marking the intersection of an old turnpike as well as the start of the old road to the ancient settlement of St Fagans. Ros had spent one entire taxi ride from the airport back to her docks apartment absorbed in such trivia and she knew why. It was an attempt to silence the inner voice that always deafened her on those kinds of journeys, the same voice that was sounding inside right now, calling her – siren-like – to make a small detour.

Ros hesitated a few moments longer. Then, just before she reached the intersection in question, Ros swung off the road.

Suddenly, she was in a different world completely, or at least that's what the small village connected by a loop to the main road always seemed like to her and maybe it was. Less than a mile away, shoppers poured into oversized metal sheds, each indistinguishable from its faceless neighbour. Here, it was like stepping back centuries, but Ros wasn't there for the sightseeing. As with her visit to quite a different location in a different country the previous evening, there was an element of pilgrimage involved now too.

Ros parked on the main street outside a large church. She turned off the engine which probably constituted some kind of mercy killing. She really was going to have her car serviced one day. Then she stared straight ahead over a low wall towards a well-tended graveyard.

Two of Ros's relatives were buried there. Not that anyone aside from Ros, one other family member and a strictly limited number of high-ranking police officers would ever have been able to identify them as members of Ros's family. Their names, dates of birth, and even the dates of their respective deaths had been changed long ago. To all intents and purposes the two bodies lying in those two coffins weren't even mother and daughter and they certainly weren't Ros's mother and elder sister.

Ros didn't even know the names they'd been allocated. She'd only discovered their final resting places courtesy of some late-night investigation amongst files she wasn't ever supposed to view. But at no point since had she actually completed the final leg of the journey, travelled through the small gate and on into the graveyard itself and paid her respects at any closer quarter.

For now it was enough to do as she was doing right now, to simply sit for a while a few metres away.

Then, from down the high street a small flotilla of vehicles made an approach as a funeral cortege hove into view, a hearse at the head of the small procession. Looking further down the road, Ros realised there were cars parked all along its length, mourners exiting now from every one. Ros started her engine again, turned round in the road and left the village courtesy of the same loop that had brought her there in the first place.

Along the way, Ros reflected on another graveyard somewhere, a grave she hadn't identified as yet and probably never would where another sibling lay, a sister called Braith whose brutal murder had plunged Ros's former life into madness. Somewhere, in that other graveyard, lay that other total innocent, but this one had been destined, unlike the ones Ros had just left, never to witness the chaos visited on her family.

Over the years Ros had come to see that as a blessing.

Ten minutes later, Ros pulled in through the gates of a new residential development overlooking an old and restored waterway. The bored concierge tipped her a slight nod of the head by way of a greeting, but Ros didn't see him. Because all of a sudden she found herself staring at another relic from the past.

Ros took a deep breath, pointed the short bonnet of her car at a parking space sandwiched between two flowerbeds. Most of the parking spaces on the complex were of the traditional variety, one sited beside the other. After suffering months of disruption courtesy of Ros's habitually inaccurate parallel parking, the long-suffering residents had lobbied the management company for a single parking space for her sited far away from the rest and Ros was duly granted a somewhat dubious exclusivity.

For the second time in twenty minutes, Ros put her engine out of its misery. Then she looked up at her father now standing by the driver's window. For a moment neither spoke and Ros felt an all-too-familiar dislocation settle inside.

Ros had once read about the differing experiences of survivors, how some bonded in a way none outside their joint experience could possibly understand, making them, from that moment onwards, almost brothers or sisters-in-arms.

But some had the opposite experience. When looking at fellow-survivors, some saw only the original horror, not the support mechanism that had carried them across to the other side. All that a voice or a face from the past did for them was to bring that past back into the present, corroding it in turn.

Ros wouldn't go that far when it came to her father, a man once known as Macklyn and a man Ros still thought of by that name. Even now, after all this time, she'd never quite been able to get used to his new one and neither, she strongly suspected, had he.

Father and daughter had managed some halfway decent times together in the years since their lives had been hijacked by events completely outside their control. They'd taken day trips, had celebrated, in some muted way, some milestone, a job, a birthday, a usually-quiet Christmas lunch.

But the knowledge of all that happened all those years before still hung heavy between them, all the more so as they rarely referred to it to the other and could never, of course, refer to it to anyone else.

When she was growing up Ros had felt that the world simply wasn't big enough for the kind of secret she was expected to keep inside, that she had to tell someone about it or it would eclipse everything. She'd like to say she'd worked through that, as other survivors sometimes managed to put behind them all they'd experienced and move on. At other times Ros just wondered who she thought she was fooling.

'I found this.'

Macklyn began, as he often did, with no enquiries as to his daughter's health or well-being. Macklyn resembled Masters in that respect, a straightforward character, some would say brusque, and the passing years hadn't altered that part of his personality.

Ros watched as Macklyn brought a small toy truck out

from his pocket and for a moment she just stared at it before looking, puzzled, back at him.

'Don't you recognise it?'

Ros, cautiously, took the offering, turning it first to one side, then the other, still failing to grasp the significance it quite clearly possessed for her remaining parent.

'It's from the old yard.'

From somewhere an image began to form, Ros being taken as a small child to a large, open space full of lorries and vans all belching white smoke as they spluttered into life, her father striding through it all, holding his small daughter's hand in his, barking instructions all the while, a colossus, the master of all he surveyed or so he seemed to her back then.

'The local council did a sales push, signed up lots of local businesses at the time, you wouldn't remember it, you were too little but I thought you might remember this, I brought one home one day, just like it, and you grabbed it out of my hand, ran upstairs with it to your room.'

Macklyn faltered as Ros still didn't reply.

'Wouldn't stop playing with it for days.'

Ros moved to the communal front door, her father following, absolutely no reciprocal memory returning for her. Macklyn might have been talking about one of the fictional biographies she'd create for a client who needed to be reinvented, the same cover story that had been created for the inhabitants of the graves she'd just left behind.

'I saw it on the internet, some trader was getting rid of this big collection, I don't know why I even stopped on the page, but all of a sudden there it was, in amongst all the Dinky lorries and Corgi cars, one of my trucks painted in our old livery.'

Ros punched in the key code and led her father up the single flight of stairs to her apartment.

'You can't see the name now, that's rubbed off, but everything else is exactly the same.'

Macklyn kept talking as Ros fished in her bag for her keys.

'I sent him a message asking if I could buy just that one piece, but he said no, it was a job lot or nothing. It was ridiculous really, I didn't want forty toy cars and lorries and I told him that, but there wasn't any choice, it was either take them all or don't take any.'

Then, as Ros paused at the door, still fumbling for her keys, Macklyn fell silent.

'Anyway – .'

Ros turned, looked at him, her father suddenly becoming hesitant, already half-turning away.

'Aren't you coming in?'

Macklyn didn't reply directly, just nodded, tentatively, back at the small toy again.

'Stupid really.'

Ros kept staring after him as he moved away down the stairs. Then she looked back at the toy truck still in her hand.

Later that afternoon, Ros seated herself on the small balcony that wrapped round the south-facing exterior of her apartment but which was never blessed by the sun thanks to the larger, more upmarket, apartments crowding it on all sides. Ros stared at the toy truck again, willing memories, any memory, to return; but none came.

Then Ros placed the toy truck on the table before her, looked out over the thin strip of water below towards those more upmarket apartments on the opposite bank all of which very definitely attracted the sun, her mind now running, not on the gift, but the donor.

At the age of five, Ros's world had literally exploded in front of her eyes as her eldest sister, Braith, was gunned down inches from her in a case of mistaken identity that had condemned her and what remained of her forever-fractured family to life in the protection programme.

Then, in her late teens and while she was still living inside that programme, she'd made the decision, a decision she still didn't totally understand, to become a protection officer herself.

But maybe the fact she didn't understand it was the whole point. Maybe, by doing all she'd done that day she was taking the first step in trying to comprehend all that had happened to her. Perhaps, by journeying through similar experiences played out in the lives of others, she might come to understand her own. The problem, the ever-present problem, was that it still didn't feel like any kind of first step at all.

Ros looked down again onto the water below and let her mind drift back to her father. It had been drummed into them for so long now that all that had happened before had to be forgotten, was part of a past that was gone. So to hear him talking so freely about a memory from that past was more than a little worrying.

If it was a memory at all, of course. And now Ros began to feel even more uneasy. Because it was possible that all this was some sort of invention, a memory he'd convinced himself they might share but which was actually no memory at all. Macklyn, or the man who had been Macklyn, was getting on now. And the shocks to the system he'd endured over the previous years had been severe in the extreme.

The old man, in short, might be losing his mind.

Ros looked at the toy truck on the table before her for a moment longer, another thought, almost disloyal, assailing her, a thought she tried to dismiss but couldn't.

Then again, that might be no bad thing.

7

'WE'VE PUT HIM in the Marriott, he's in one of the suites on the tenth floor.'

Conor consulted his notes. Ros and Conor were back in their offices, a nondescript former retail unit on a piece of blasted wasteland just off the link road leading out from the capital towards Newport and, beyond, to the English border.

'Room 162.'

Ros, barely listening, was looking out of the window. A large sign outside their unit, Mega-Bed Sale, bore testimony to its former occupants and their long-failed business. The sign had remained in place for all the years Ros had worked there and for the simplest of reasons. No-one had ever bothered to take it down. The first 'e' was missing and had been for years and for the simplest of reasons too. No-one had ever thought to replace it.

Inside, on the first floor, the former retail space had been divided into a succession of small offices. On the second floor a rather more exalted space had been created for Ros's immediate senior officer, Jukes, first name Edward – although Ros only discovered that by accident one day when, temporarily alone in that second floor space, she'd answered his office phone to his wife.

To everyone else in the unit he was simply, Jukes. No-one knew too much about him and the reason for that was simple as well. No-one had ever cared enough to find out.

With Ros still lost in thought at the window, Conor continued.

'We've taken the two rooms to either side and there's CCTV

covering the corridor. The tech boys have also taken a feed into the suite itself. We'll move him out to one of the safe houses on the coast in a day or so, but with Murder Squad wanting another debrief we thought it best to keep him close for now.'

On the other side of his oversized desk, Jukes nodded, bestowing his blessing on Conor's résumé of the arrangements. The safe house on the coast was like them all, unremarkable. The Marriott was typical of the brand, home to a floating population of corporate business types making it, like the safe house on the coast, perfect for its present purpose.

Conor paused, looking up from his notes, growing more and more curious about this new client by the minute. He still knew next to nothing about him, a few grisly details culled from a scenes-of-crime report aside.

Who, exactly, was Leon and how had he ended up in Amsterdam?

What had triggered the sort of alarm bells that provoked the previous day's flight across from the Dutch capital and Leon's immediate return to the city of his birth?

Conor had tried asking but Masters had always been at Ros's elbow, forestalling by his presence, as well as his habitually-forbidding manner, any attempt. Meaning Conor wasn't only just curious now. Conor was growing uneasy too.

One half-glance across at the still-silent Ros told him she was feeling exactly the same.

Leon looked out of his hotel window, having managed no sleep at all the previous night. He leant his pounding head against the large floor to ceiling window that boasted, according to the in-house brochure he'd found in one of the bedside drawers, panoramic views of a city he never wanted to see again over a retail development that hadn't even been planned the last time he'd been there.

All the time Leon willed himself not to look across that same retail development towards a huddled collection of roofs in the near-distance.

Leon concentrated on the street below instead, desperately trying to interest himself in the shoppers down in the pedestrianised precinct, weaving in and out of tables already being placed outside various fast-food outlets.

Leon watched a tramp being sick in the doorway of a sex shop. A nearby waitress remonstrated with him, ineffectually, before she headed back inside one of the nearby units. Briefly, Leon wondered if there was anyone down there he'd recognise or who might recognise him in turn. Then, without realising he was doing so, he turned slightly, shifted position a little and only a little, but it was enough.

Now Leon wasn't looking down. Now he was looking across at the roof of a building some few hundred metres to the east.

There was nothing particularly remarkable about that one roof to mark it out from the others surrounding it on all sides. But Leon's eye was drawn to it instantly. And while Leon had no idea what business the present-day building now housed, he knew the core activity it used to host.

Briefly – and it was displacement activity he knew – Leon struggled to concentrate on at least some of all that Ros had said to him the previous evening, although he'd heard it all before, years before in fact when he was first taken into the protection programme. Like then, Ros had her department bible in hand, like then she'd listed the various criteria for admission to that programme, the different boxes that needed to be ticked and specific agreements secured in order to activate the new care Ros and her department proposed to offer him.

The all-too-familiar questions swam through the edge of Leon's consciousness.

Does he feel his life is at sufficient risk that he needs this level of protection and is he prepared for the measures that might need to be employed to offer the same?

Leon had just given a simple nod by way of a response.

Does he undertake that that there will be no direct communication between himself and relatives or friends who are not included in the protection programme?

Leon had little difficulty in nodding his agreement to that one too.

Upon entering the programme, does the witness agree to co-operate fully and to fully disclose all personal history?

And then, almost involuntarily, Leon looked beyond the roof of that building some few hundred metres to the east, towards an alleyway.

'Oceana and Soda are just about the only ones left now. But back then almost any space you could find was being turned into some sort of club and catering for all sorts too, garage, hip-hop, house, grunge.'

Ros paused at the latest in an ever-lengthening plethora of traffic lights.

'Didn't matter what you were into, in one small square mile around St Mary Street, you'd find it.'

As they waited, Ros looked across at a new Arts Centre marooned on a traffic island in the middle of a dual carriageway, all the while looking out on a very different landscape instead.

'At the time the whole city was being talked up as the new Manchester. Every club that opened was about to become the new Hacienda.'

Conor jerked forward in his seat as the lights changed to green and Ros selected third rather than first, the engine fighting to make up speed as the wheels scrabbled to maintain traction. Conor suffered through every desperate revolution. Ros didn't even notice.

'Leon and Joey had always been what you might call competitive. There wasn't much between them in terms of age, a couple of years if that, so I suppose it was inevitable really. From their early teens they'd been in the same schools, drunk in the same bars and clubs.'

Ros hesitated.

'Hit on the same girls.'

Conor looked at her, registering the hesitation.

Conor was a Cardiff boy himself or a Butetown boy to be more precise, as he always told anyone interested enough to listen. But he'd been in London doing his initial training in the Met when Leon and his brother Joey had held sway in his home city.

Conor still made the occasional trip home back then to see his old mother before her encroaching dementia would finally render such excursions not only pointless but too painful as well, but that aside, his home city was history as far as he was concerned. So he'd been unaware that, as well as being mainstays of the local club scene, the two brothers had been of considerable interest to the local police as well.

Maybe that was inevitable. All manner and type of characters were drawn, moth-like, to them at the time, all manner and types of substances traded in and around their fast-expanding premises. But then the boys began dabbling in another burgeoning market too.

It was a new trade that was something of a natural fit. They came across a lot of stunning young girls during the course of their working week as well as a number of hot young boys. So the clubs began to be used for filming of the adult variety in the downtime between club nights.

None of it was exactly illegal. But then rumours began to

spread about some harder-than-usual offerings as the boys branched out into the S&M and bondage scene, all of which meant they became of even more interest.

In truth, they were still relatively small fry. But they were seen as a possible Trojan Horse, allowing access to something infinitely larger in scale. Officers at the time had just become aware of much darker corners of the web, subterranean sites that hosted all manner of abuse. Leon and his brother were already being courted by some of its leading practitioners, and while the brothers may have been unaware of the nature of this new business themselves – there was some doubt – the police were not.

Roman Edwards, the new murder victim, had been one of the leading lights beckoning the boys towards the dark back then.

And a decision had been made. If the police backed off, just monitored their growing involvement instead, they could journey with the unaware brothers. Keep invisible pace with them on a silent voyage of discovery.

But then, and all of a sudden as far as the rest of the world was concerned, Leon and Joey disappeared. They vanished from the club scene overnight, their businesses closed down, their former premises taken over by wannabes, most of whom failed in weeks. Rumours circulated, including hints of a somewhat implausible-sounding underworld vendetta causing problems for the formerly high-flying brothers, but no-one seemed to have too many hard facts regarding what had actually happened to them.

Conor looked down at the original scenes-of-crime photos, a visual record that, up to that point, had been held in the most restricted of files. He looked again at Joey's dead body on the floor, at his throat slashed almost from ear to ear. And tried not to look at the bloodied figure on the bed.

At the time of their joint disappearance, most casual

acquaintances in Conor's home city believed that the brothers had simply burnt brightly and briefly and had then, apparently, burnt themselves out.

Conor looked down at the bodies in the photographs once again as Ros drew closer to the city centre, the redbrick edifice of the Marriott now looming into view.

Only there was, quite clearly, rather more to it than that.

In the basement of the redbrick building ahead of Ros and Conor, the only light in the large hotel kitchen came from overhead strips. More light did spill sporadically, almost violently, from a door that smashed open with metronome regularity as a small army of waiters ferried food from the steaming kitchen to the various restaurants, bars and function rooms above. But that aside, most of the kitchen's perennially sweating inhabitants spent their working days and nights cocooned in a miasma of swirling steam.

All in all interludes such as this, as the head chef silently reflected, were a welcome relief.

The new female recruit had arrived that morning. She'd been sourced by some employment agency he imagined or had been recommended by some employee or other. He didn't know, and the lofty head chef was certainly not going to waste any of his precious time finding out. She was an extra pair of hands. That was all that mattered.

But before those extra pair of hands could be put to work in earnest there was the simple matter of the initiation test. All kitchens had them, all kitchens the head chef had worked in anyway. From the start of his career, he'd watched different chefs welcome new members of staff in many different ways and with wildly different outcomes as those new recruits either rose to their respective challenges or fell, miserably, by the wayside.

The former were marked out as ones to watch, potential

nuggets to be nurtured, even cherished if they proved particularly promising or useful.

The latter were immediately identified as dross to be discarded, perhaps even before the end of their first shift.

The head chef eyed the new female recruit. Usually he had some inkling into which camp a fresh face might fall, but he had to confess he had absolutely no idea in her case.

The head chef summoned the new recruit to his side. In front of him on a preparation table was a plate heaped high with various cold cuts and salads, sourced from different countries and regions, including yard long beans, krupuk and asinan, alongside the more traditional beetroot and chickpeas. The first task was simple; to identify as many as possible either by sight or taste. By such means the head chef would know immediately just how sophisticated a palate he was dealing with here.

Across the kitchen, other graduates of the same initiation test stole quick, sideways, glances at the latest inductee. Waiters paused, briefly, as she sifted the plate in front of her, inspecting, assessing, the head chef standing close by her side.

The new female recruit had done reasonably well so far. Four out of six ingredients had been correctly identified, but as she parted a heaped serving of radicchio, one item now seemed to give her pause for thought.

Across the kitchen, an uncharacteristic hush suddenly descended. Some of the kitchen workers actually held their breath. They'd witnessed many different reactions from many different employees at this stage of the initiation test and, like the head chef, were none too sure just what to expect from this one.

Ten storeys above, Leon was still looking across at the distant alleyway, still lost in his involuntary memories.

There'd been the usual sibling rivalry for weeks. There always was when it came to Leon and Joey. But this was different, perhaps because of the prize on offer.

Clare was special. Very special. And both boys had put an extra-special effort into their joint pursuit.

But Joey had won. And the alley Leon was now looking at was where Clare had finally made her choice, had finally succumbed to Joey's evermore insistent advances.

For his part, Leon had been left with the consolation prize, in this case Clare's friend, Toya, and he understood the rules. He would have fulfilled his duties, as his brother was enthusiastically and vocally fulfilling his just a few metres away, Clare's dress hitched up above her waist, one languid leg wrapped round his brother's thrusting arse.

But Toya, as she made only too clear, had never been interested in charity and particularly not a charity-fuck and that's all it would have been and she knew that and Leon knew it too. So she just kissed him, lightly, on the cheek and with one piece of parting advice which he really should have taken – telling him not to be a bad loser – had returned to the club.

And Leon had followed, but not before looking back at Joey, his large frame completely obscuring the girl that Leon now wanted, of course, more than ever.

And in that moment, in the instant before he turned back into the club itself, Leon made a silent vow, a vow he'd come to regret more than anything he'd regretted before or since.

Joey may have won the battle.

But Leon intended to win the war.

Ten storeys below, the new female recruit stared, impassive, down at the nine-inch penis hidden underneath the red radicchio.

She kept staring, equally impassive, as the chef gave his penis a slight shake, and asked her if she could hazard a guess as to the meat she was now inspecting? The new female recruit remained stock-still as the head chef next nodded down at his flaccid member and asked if she'd like to undertake a taste test?

Across the kitchen, laughter rolled as waiters turned back to their trays and sous-chefs returned to their hotplates and ovens. The loudest laughter came from the males. The women smiled too, their smiles perhaps slightly more forced. At the preparation table the head chef smiled too as he tucked his penis back inside his trademark houndstooth pants.

By his side, the new female recruit remained still which was a welcome change from some other raw recruits who'd run, sobbing and screaming, towards the nearest exit. All in all, the head chef reflected as he returned to check on a now-bubbling sauce, this one looked like someone he could work with.

The new female recruit, still calm and cool, cleared away the salad. She endured the cheers and catcalls from her fellow workers with what seemed like good grace. Then she turned to begin her actual work that evening which was to help prepare the few room service orders that were already beginning to trickle in, lowly work admittedly, but if she could deal with that as coolly and calmly as she'd dealt with everything else then the signs, as the head chef now reflected too, really were looking promising.

The owner of the outsize penis in the houndstooth pants bent back to his sauce. The rest of the kitchen staff, that evening's cabaret concluded, returned to their own tasks. The new female recruit picked up the first of the trickle of room service orders, sifting them until she found the one she wanted for the new guest in one of the suites on the very top floor of the hotel.

Room 162.

Meanwhile, the occupant of Room 162 was still looking across at that one small alleyway, more pictures flashing now in front of Leon's eyes.

It was a full five years after that coupling in the alley. Clare and Joey had been married for four of those years, the birth of their daughter, Donna, prompting the actual wedding.

Leon's own affair with Clare had begun just six months after that.

Joey had gone away on a business trip. Leon couldn't now remember where. Maybe it was with Roman, he was around a lot at the time. Together with Clare, Leon had taken the young Donna to a local riding school. They'd watched while the instructor fitted her with her helmet and body protector. Then a small pony had been brought into the sawdust-strewn arena along with a selection of larger horses for the older riders.

They'd all formed up in a makeshift ring and, at a signal from the instructor, the lead horse led the procession away. As Donna proudly flicked her whip to spur her small mount into action, an equally proud Clare had taken Leon's hand. The eyes of similar couples all around them were on that slow-moving procession and no-one else saw the gesture. But as ever, and as with any touch from Clare, Leon felt as if his hand had just turned molten.

Then, suddenly, disaster threatened. Donna's horse strayed, momentarily close, too close, to the larger horse in front and the front horse gave an idle-looking kick back towards the following pony's face by way of a warning. The kick didn't connect but the pony suddenly reared up, dislodging the little girl, sending her crashing down to the ground under the hooves of other horses approaching from behind.

For a moment it was as if the whole world had stood still. All Leon could hear was his own blood suddenly roaring inside his head, pounding against his eardrums, so he could only begin to imagine what Clare must have been feeling. At any moment he expected her to race across that arena towards her fallen daughter. At any moment he expected to find himself following close behind.

But Clare did nothing, save grip his hand so tightly it felt like his fingers were now being crushed in a vice. And Leon took his lead from her and did nothing too. He didn't even feel the pain from his compressed fingers till later. All the while the panicky instructor was moving towards the small rider, visions of career-ending lawsuits probably flashing before her eyes.

Which was when, calmly, matter-of-factly almost, Donna stood up, adjusted her helmet which had twisted a little, picked up her riding crop and remounted her pony.

The instructor risked a quick glance back at the small girl's mother and was rewarded by the slightest of nods from the watching Clare. Then the instructor called for the horses and riders, who'd all paused at the spectacle, all similarly fearful of a potential casualty, to resume their circuit of the arena.

Back in the present day, Leon turned back from the floor-to-ceiling windows of his suite, tears starting in his eyes, aware they'd probably be captured by a bemused technician on the ever-present CCTV feed, but he just couldn't help it.

Because what Leon had felt, coursing through his body as Clare gripped his hand, was love, her love for her daughter and it was the most magnificent kind of love too, not the kind of love that would have propelled a panicky parent straight into that pack of waiting horses to scoop a precious daughter up into her arms, vowing all the while that she'd never, in her life, return to such a place as that.

Love that would cripple her in other words.

Emasculate her.

Deny her the clear lesson Donna seemed to have instantly absorbed, that in anything she did there was always going to be danger and the important thing was not to shy away but deal with it as it came along, making herself stronger each time she did so, as she already appeared stronger now, flicking her whip evermore confidently as her pony moved on beneath her.

And Clare did all that while her body quite clearly ached to do the opposite. And all that told Leon that Clare truly loved her daughter and not with the cloying, self-serving, affection he'd seen meted out from weak-willed parents of uncertain resolve. This was a lioness protecting her cub, equipping her with the sort of experiences that would guarantee her survival.

Leon stood stock-still in the centre of the suite as, from outside, he heard the elevator ping, signalling a new arrival on the floor outside.

Which made all that happened later all the more impossible to understand.

Outside the suite, Conor followed Ros out of the elevator, Conor finishing his speed scanning of his file as he did so. Ros paused as, from the service elevator, a waiter approached, a room service order in hand, but Conor hardly saw him.

No-one knew exactly when Joey had found out about Leon's affair with his wife, as the entries in Conor's file made clear. It was most probably sometime on the night of the double killing. All they did know was that Clare had been the object of his murderous intentions but Toya, her hapless friend, had attempted to divert Joey, had tried to pacify him, calm him down, only it hadn't worked.

Unable to find Clare, unable to find out from Toya where she was and frustrated beyond reason by Toya's efforts to protect her friend, he'd vented all his deranged anger on her instead.

Clare had struggled with her grief and guilt for no more than twenty-four hours. Then she'd visited the stable block in the mansion she'd shared with Joey. According to forensics, Clare had first concentrated her efforts on the family horses, burning down the stables that housed them as as they roared, tethered and terrified, in their stalls.

Then, having destroyed her prized horses and assorted ponies, Clare had next turned her attention to Donna. At first, on finding the fragmented, charred remains of Donna's DNA at various locations in the burnt-out house, the scenes-of-crime officers had wondered if she'd been simply burnt alive too.

But then traces of a drug had been found, Thorazine, a neuroleptic substance that had once flooded mental hospitals in the US and UK. Thorazine achieved, chemically, all that a lobotomy accomplished surgically in destroying all functioning of the frontal lobes of the brain. On being injected the patients, or victims as they came to be seen, quickly became human vegetables, a paralysed body in a chemical straitjacket with no mind or personality.

Having first sedated her in that way, Clare had then killed her with a further lethal injection. Then Donna's body had also been consumed by the flames.

Clare hadn't died in the fire. Clare, who was by then an arsonist and a murderer, had killed herself with a single shot to the head from a gun Joey had kept for his personal protection.

Ahead of Conor, Ros now signed the room service chit and he followed her inside the suite, Leon's food under a metal cloche in her hand.

As Conor did so, he took one last look at the original scenes-of-crime photographs and at Toya's slashed body on the bed.

Then he looked at the slumped figure of Joey on the floor to her side.

And Conor wondered just how crazed and how jealous you had to be to inflict that sort of damage on another human being.

Later that night and with all food service concluded, a janitor walked from the rear of the hotel to a local housing shelter. It was a journey that Joaquin Alejandro, the well-meaning janitor, made at the end of every shift, and a journey eagerly anticipated by all waiting inside.

As usual, Joaquin, an émigré from Venezuela, handed out a whole pile of leftover food from various room service orders that had been picked at by over-fussy diners, but tonight there was a real prize. The current inhabitant of one of the largest suites in the hotel hadn't even lifted the cloche on his room service delivery.

The Venezuelan janitor, his good deed for the day completed, left a few moments later just as one of the shelter's guests bit, hungrily, into the untouched burger that had been reheated for him by one of the volunteers.

For a moment, as he bit into the centre and encountered something hard, he kept on chewing, believing it to be just a piece of gristle, although the warm rush of blood that began pouring from his mouth really should have told him he'd bitten on something a little more sinister than that.

In fact he'd split one of the glass shards that had been concealed inside, now making it even easier to ingest, although even then only one half of that shard actually went down into his gullet.

As he spat the rest of the burger out of his mouth, he realised what he'd done and started to cough, putting his fingers down his throat, hoping to vomit up all he'd just swallowed, but it was too late.

The next thing he knew yet more blood started spewing from his mouth as the jagged shard sliced into his windpipe.

Down in the bowels of the Marriott, the head chef, now at the end of his shift, looked at another salad freshly prepared by the new female recruit. She'd made it for him before she went off shift. The head chef picked up the large kebab lying on top of the salad leaves and smiled at the obvious reference back to that evening's initiation test for which there seemed to be – and pardoning the pun – no hard feelings.

The head chef bit into the kebab, noting with approval the liberal use of seasoning and spices. As he chewed, he relived the cool stare of the new recruit as she'd looked up during that earlier initiation test and met his eyes. His penis started to thicken, always a sure sign that a new acquaintance really was worth cultivating despite the fact that he now seemed to have encountered a piece of gristle in amongst the otherwise tasty meat.

The head chef chewed a moment longer, then stopped abruptly, a cold feeling now beginning to creep into his stomach as small red drops began to drip from his lips.

Ten storeys above, Leon, finally, dropped off to sleep.

8

B Y FIVE-FORTY THAT night everyone who'd shown an interest, which in this case comprised just about every single one of Jamie's workmates, was in place.

Some more cynically-minded souls might have said those men would have watched the test card if there was still such a thing. The days and nights were long on a rig and any kind of diversion was always seized on. But Jamie looked round the packed room and smiled. Because there was another reason why each and every one of those men were attending that evening.

OK, some of them may now be estranged from their former families, indeed a majority of them seemed to be from the little they'd let slip, but all could remember happier times when they were not. All could remember moments when they'd also watched as a first word was cajoled from an offspring, when a first tentative step was taken across a floor. And bets had already been taken on the nature of the floor show that Jamie and the rest of his workmates were to enjoy that evening.

So it wasn't just a case of any old port in a storm, and a quite literal storm at that if the wind and rain outside were anything to go by. Tonight's entertainment would hopefully conjure memories of happier times for the rest of the men on that rig too.

Jamie had tried calling the flat earlier in the day just to make sure the show was still going ahead as planned, but he'd hit the answerphone each time he'd tried on both the landline and Kim's mobile. He'd left his usual messages, a little more puzzled now than previously.

And that puzzlement deepened as the magic hour approached. Jamie could understand Kim taking Aron out for a walk during the day, to visit the shops, or enjoy some late sun in the park, but he'd really have expected her to be home by now, with just a few moments to go before curtain-up.

Assuming that the curtain was still going up, of course. Assuming there hadn't been some fault on the line, some failure of the connection from the rig to the shore.

So Jamie, now growing more than a little nervous, had logged on at the allotted time, taking advantage of the five-minute window that had been sanctioned by the rig manager. Strictly speaking the main computer wasn't to be used for personal use, but that same rig manager knew they all had to rub along together in occasionally-trying circumstances, so he also knew it paid to cut his workforce the occasional small amount of slack.

But that same rig manager was actually now hovering in the doorway too and even though he would never have admitted it, least of all to himself, that wasn't just to make sure precious oil company property came to no harm. Jamie knew from their previous exchanges that his own son was now thirty and, courtesy of the family rift that had seen the rig manager taking employment in the North Sea in the first place, he hadn't spoken to him in over ten years. But it was only too obvious that he still remembered days when even the thought of him would cause his chest to almost burst with pride.

Kim's visitor straightened up from her latest inspection of the camera, then bent down next to Kim herself.

And for the second time since that blinding explosion of light had bleached the whole world white, turning that world inside out as it did so, there was actual physical contact.

Because the woman was now taking her arm.

Kim still couldn't see the woman's face. She just stared instead at a small bag that now came into view and then, a moment later, at a bottle of clear liquid as that also materialised before her. She didn't know what it was but it smelt – Kim didn't know how else to describe it – medical in some way, sharp and clean.

Then the woman must have reached into her bag again because now she brought out some cotton wool and, tearing off a small piece, dipped it into the fluid before rubbing it into Kim's arm.

Then she picked up a syringe.

And Kim's mind began to race.

What the hell was she doing now?

What fresh torment was in store for her?

Kim had already been rendered totally immobile by the last drug, so what was this one going to do to her, for fuck's sake?

A moment later she felt the contents of the syringe wash into her arm. For another moment again she feared complete oblivion, her world suddenly lurching into darkness, perhaps forever; but then the opposite happened and Kim, almost weeping now with ridiculous gratitude, felt something resembling feeling actually begin to return to her limbs.

And it wasn't just her wishful imagination, she could definitely feel her fingers again and then she found she could lift first one and then another of those fingers too. At the same time a distant sensation of pins and needles began to course along the back of her hand as she flexed that as well.

Kim stared at the bowed head of the woman still bent by her side, her face still averted, concentrating it seemed on injecting the very last drops of the contents of the syringe into her patient.

Kim's mind kept racing. Had she decoded Kim's silent appeal

after all? Had she taken pity on her and on Aron? Was this bizarre game, whatever it might be, whatever the point of it might have been, was it now actually coming to an end?

Not that Kim wasted too much time speculating on motives, twisted or otherwise. All she could think about was Aron. With feeling returning all the while, with warmth beginning to flow along her arms and legs, all she could think about and all she wanted to think about was simple.

Within a few moments and a very few moments too given the sensations she was starting to experience, she was going to be able to reach out to her son, was going to be able to pick him up and, finally, offer him the comfort and succour they both so desperately craved.

Kim tried to raise her arm, but she wasn't strong enough yet, her muscles still unsure of their new freedom. She couldn't quite make her arm reach as far as she needed and so she paused, flexing her fingers again, willing herself to stay calm for just a few more moments and then, surely, she'd be able to reach out fully.

And for those few moments, with all her attention focused on her recovering limbs, she almost forgot that the woman was there, but she wasn't going to be allowed to ignore her for too much longer.

Still distracted, still concentrating only on her recovering strength, willing her arms and legs back to life all the while, Kim suddenly realised that the woman had picked up the small camera again. Then she brought the viewfinder up to her face and made some adjustment, maybe to the lens or to some setting or other.

But it was only a temporary distraction as Kim turned all her attention back onto Aron again. Just a few more seconds and then she'd be able to do it, she knew she would, she'd be able to reach out, scoop up her son.

Which was when, out of the corner of her eye, Kim saw the woman put down the camera and pick up another syringe.

Then Kim watched as she picked up some more cotton wool and approached once again.

Back on the rig, Jamie – in a reflex response – clapped his hands together as the pictures on the screen finally flickered into life and as he saw the inside of his small flat. For a moment the images on screen shook as if Kim was adjusting the focus on a hand-held camera, but then the picture came back again, pin-sharp, which was when he saw him.

Aron.

In his buggy.

Fast asleep.

Which was, he had to admit, something of a puzzle. A cheer had sounded around the room as the first image, that of the room and the baby, had appeared but those cheers then faded much as Jamie's smile as the camera moved in, closer all the time now, on the small and silent infant.

At the same time, and with a definite hush now falling around the room, Jamie realised that Aron wasn't sleeping as he normally slept. In fact he didn't look how he normally looked at all, either sleeping or awake.

And as Jamie kept staring at the screen, the camera swung away from his baby and now he saw Kim, but she wasn't operating the camera as he'd expected; she was just lying on the floor a metre or so away from Aron and at first he thought she was asleep too but, and like Aron, she didn't seem to be sleeping in the way he'd have expected either, he could see that the moment the camera zoomed in on her eyes.

Suddenly, a new thought flashed through his fast-overheating brain. Because if Kim was on the floor, then who the fuck was holding that camera?

But then he had something else to think about. Because now he could see that Kim's eyes were almost dancing inside her head, flickering constantly in what looked like absolute terror and he could also see that her eyes were fixed on one point and one point only and that was Aron, still just that metre or so away from her and whom he could now see again, only this time he was actually reflected in his partner's eyeballs.

And then, reflected in those eyeballs too, Jamie now saw a figure, albeit indistinct, little more than a moving shape; he couldn't even make out if it was a woman or a slightly-built man.

And, with the room now deathly quiet behind him, with all eyes on the pictures on the screen, Jamie saw that same figure approach Aron and he watched the figure reach out, almost tenderly, and close his baby's eyes with their outstretched fingers.

And then Jamie felt rather than saw something explode in Kim's eyes as Aron's eyes stayed closed and the infant remained still.

At which point Jamie did what Kim could not do right now.

Jamie screamed out loud.

The ending was actually something of an anticlimax, but maybe endings always were.

Maybe journey's end always felt more than a little flat.

Kim's visitor cleared and packed away all her recording equipment at the same time as checking there was nothing left in that small flat that could be traced back to her.

Aside from the infant of course.

And the young woman, but she already looked as if she'd lost her mind by now anyway.

Kim's visitor let herself out of the flat, treading her way back down the landing and stairs, her nose wrinkling at the slightly musty smell coming from the old and more-than-threadbare carpet under her feet. Then she moved out onto the small step that led down to the pavement and closed the communal front door, making sure to deadlock it behind her.

Then Kim's visitor walked on, becoming swallowed up as she did so in the moving crush that surged, day-in, day-out beneath Kim and Jamie's first-floor window, passing students heading for the nearby college, girls in summer dresses and boys in slogan-emblazoned T-shirts and cropped shorts, before pausing at the traffic lights in the company of a female Asian Big Issue seller heading for her habitual spot just outside the college entrance itself.

As Kim's visitor did so, and with Kim herself now in the extremities of what would soon be near-certifiable insanity and with Jamie some hundreds of miles away in a paroxysm of impotent bewilderment and grief, their baby opened his eyes.

PART TWO

THE SHORT CON

9

W ITH KEZIA SILENTLY studying the shelf of DVDs behind her, Ros checked round the small sitting room as casually as she could.

The intention, as with all they were doing right now, was to make everything seem as normal and everyday as possible. Which was a totally doomed endeavour of course given everything that had happened to Ros's new charge, but as Jukes had pointed out on more than one occasion with regard to more lost souls than they could both now possibly remember, what else were they supposed to do?

The same tactic had to be employed with every client irrespective of age or recent experience. They had to give the impression that life was going on as normal. The client in question – or witness to use the term most commonly employed by those outside the Protection Unit – might be feeling as if they'd just stepped straight into the final reel of some horror movie, but from that point on all they were experiencing, all the dislocation they were enduring, was to be the new norm. And if Ros and the rest of her team couldn't do a great deal to make that any better, the very least they could do was not make it worse.

So Kezia had the shelf-full of DVDs she was currently studying – mostly standard family fare – and some colouring books as well, although maybe she'd already moved beyond such innocent distractions if her now-haunted eyes were anything to go by.

Outside in the small garden there was a plastic swing and slide and a cheap bouncy castle sourced from some supermarket a few weeks before on special offer. Kezia had so far shown little interest in that either but, as it had so far defeated the combined efforts of just about everyone in the unit to inflate it, perhaps that didn't matter much anyway.

But Ros had still dutifully pointed out the various distractions provided to help pass the time. All the time, Kezia simply stared ahead, not seeing anything, taking in even less.

And Ros knew why. Because Kezia was now looking out on a world she never knew existed. Perhaps the young girl already understood that, perhaps she didn't, but this was how she was going to live from this point on irrespective of anything Ros could do; a half-existence suspended between a life to which she could never return and one she would never fully embrace.

Ros looked at Kezia and, suddenly becoming aware of her new protector's eyes on her, the small child now picked out a DVD. If that signified a breakthrough of any sort then Ros would have felt more than heartened, but Kezia was just going through the motions and they both knew it. Taking refuge in activity, any sort of activity, in a doomed attempt to forget.

Ros kept looking at Kezia, who was about to be called by a different name and who was also about to begin the process of memorising and absorbing a new life story.

No-one in her current department knew about Ros's past. To the best of her knowledge no-one in any other police department, save for a handful of people at the highest level of clearance, knew that she herself had been brought up in the same programme she now oversaw, or that she was still actually living under the same sort of protection herself. The level of threat, still extant for all she and the remaining member of her family knew, made that an all-too-necessary precaution.

Ros kept looking at the young girl, wondering how she was going to cope, knowing all the time that she was actually asking a very different question of course.

And it wasn't the only question Ros was asking right now either.

Ros parked her car in a small car park just a few metres away from a single-storey purpose-built building nestling off the local high street. A petrol station was sited opposite, a couple of fast-food outlets a few doors along.

Nothing outside the anonymous-looking building gave any indication as to what went on inside. It wasn't the sort of place that advertised what might be called its wares, but then it had never needed to. Word of mouth had always been enough.

Ros pressed the entry buzzer, waited a moment for the security guard inside to recognise her, then pushed against the door as an answering buzzer sounded in turn. Ros moved past the guard, ignored the constant adult DVD feed playing on the first of the TV monitors above his desk and headed on into the changing room.

That changing room was communal for obvious reasons. Given the nature of the club and all that happened there, there was little point in segregating the sexes. Ros opened the first locker she found, quickly shrugged off her clothes and wrapped herself in the large white robe hanging inside.

Dimly she was aware of a couple of other people in the same changing room, all performing the same ritual but she didn't take any notice. They, similarly, didn't take any notice of her. Locking the door, she put the key into the pocket of her robe, moved through a small bar where a florid barman, always red-faced and always perspiring or so it seemed to her, was munching on a large pizza spread out before him, just delivered from one of the fast-food outlets further along the street.

A door led off the bar to a corridor and, by that door, a stranger hovered. Ros hadn't seen him before, was sure she'd have noticed him if she had. The stranger in question was black and young-looking, although he was probably in his mid-to-late twenties, around Ros's age. He also sported one of the club's regulation white robes, although his was open to the waist and displaying a firm torso, with no hint of the man boobs that drooped from the chest of the sweating barman currently shovelling pizza inside a mouth that more resembled a cavern.

But it wasn't how he looked that caught Ros's attention. It never was with any one. It was more his manner instead.

The stranger was still. There was no other word to describe him. He didn't even look at the flashing images on at least two further TV screens dotted around the bar, or even seem to hear the sounds of couples – or possibly threesomes – or maybe even foursomes – from the cubicles lining the corridor beyond.

Ros glanced at the still stranger, briefly, as she moved past, noting with approval that he didn't glance back at her. Then Ros treaded along the corridor past, first, those cubicles and then the showers to the first of two giant Jacuzzis, communal again for the same obvious reasons, contenting herself with a silent promise along the way.

Maybe later.

Then, before she slipped inside the Jacuzzi and allowed the warm waters to enfold her, Ros paused as she saw a couple, regulars this time, standing together under one of the showers.

Ros had seen them before. She'd witnessed the same scene before as well. If it had been taking place anywhere else a clear assault would be taking place, perhaps worse. There was a barely-controlled ferocity to all Ros was witnessing now that bordered on the psychopathic. Anywhere else, the victim would have been screaming at the top of her voice, desperately pleading for help.

Here, in the club, all was silent. And the young woman's eyes were closed, not in some desperate attempt to blot out all that was happening to her, but in seeming ecstasy instead. She seemed to be positively welcoming the savage attentions of her companion who was plunging first two fingers, then four and then his whole fist deep inside her, opening her up wider and wider all the time.

The male reserved this special kind of attention exclusively for his partner. No-one else had ever been invited or permitted to join them. Everything might take place in full view of anyone who happened to be in the club at the time, but neither sought or encouraged any outside participation.

The man had the look of a public school boy about him. There was just something about the floppy sweep of the hair, the supercilious cut of the nose. The girl was mixed race and stunning. She looked younger than him and by a good few years, but there appeared to be nothing unequal about the relationship from all Ros could see.

Most of their time together was spent in the man pleasuring the girl, albeit in this most unusual of ways. Ros had never seen his attentions reciprocated, although she shuddered to think what form they might take given the treatment he meted out to her. Maybe that would be too strong even for the hardy souls that trailed through these doors. Or maybe all that took place in one of the cubicles instead.

Those cubicles, just a few metres away, had doors attached to the outside, constructed in two sections, an upper and a lower, and club rules were simple. If any part of those double doors were closed then the inhabitants of the cubicle at the time wanted and were guaranteed privacy. Ros had seen the young couple disappear in there from time to time so maybe that was where any reciprocal attention took place. But they always closed the doors behind them, for which relief Ros always silently intoned heartfelt thanks.

As the water from the oversized shower pounded down on the two lovers, Ros turned her back on the bizarre ritual. She closed her eyes for a moment as her body slipped further under the warmer water of the Jacuzzi before opening them again, which was when she saw it.

Or rather, when she sensed it.

And felt the colours prickling against her eyes, feeling her spirits rise as they did so.

Ros looked out across the corridor as, reflected in the streaks of water trickling into the drainage channel from the showers, she now saw the glitterball.

On club nights or party nights, nights she rarely attended, the glitterball would spin ceaselessly, coloured lights assailing every inch of the dance floor and beyond, illuminating the coupling bodies, flashing lights shimmering amongst the sweat. Now the glitterball was barely turning at all, but lights still danced along the corridors and cubicles.

Ros stared up at it, as entranced as ever. She'd no idea why those objects fascinated her like they did. It wasn't as if they transported her back to any happier or more innocent times, conjuring memories of fondly-remembered lovers or the like. Hers had never been the more usual teenage rites of passage. But the glitterball still worked its magic every time.

Ros settled back in the water, luxuriating now in the ceaseless bubbles, which was when something else happened.

Because while Ros intended to empty her mind of everything – the club, the still, black, stranger, the stunning, mixed race, girl, now fast approaching her climax if the sounds from just a couple of metres away were anything to go by – even her beloved glitterball; she suddenly found she couldn't.

Somewhat to Ros's quiet concern she found her mind drifting back to her trip to Amsterdam, to her pilgrimage to the Begijnhof; and to Hendrix.

There was a stillness about him too. That same sense Ros just had as she passed the stranger in the bar of a life lived slightly apart.

But then Ros put him out of mind once more, some instinct again telling her that Hendrix was a potential complication and she really didn't want any of those in an already-complicated life. That wasn't a matter of choice, that was – and always would be – necessity.

Besides, Ros had come to the club tonight to allow her mind to drift on another matter and another officer altogether.

And to ponder the question that had been gnawing away at her more and more both on her way out to Amsterdam and on her return.

What wasn't she being told?

And why?

'It doesn't actually make sense, does it?'

Four hours earlier, a frustrated Jukes had stared across the desk at Ros, frustrated not simply because Ros, somewhat characteristically, wasn't taking any notice of a single thing he was saying right now. Jukes was also frustrated because he'd allotted this one all-too-brief period of his always-too-busy day to private matters.

Strictly private, strictly personal matters.

Not that he let Ros know that.

'A man finds out his wife has been having an affair.'

Jukes remained silent.

'And yes, OK, there's a twist, Joey also finds out that this affair was actually with his own brother which presumably explains why he turned into that one-man killing machine and why he tortured Toya like that, to find out if she knew where Clare or Leon was, we don't know now, never will.'

Jukes interrupted.

'Your point?'

'Two points.'

Jukes sighed, inwardly.

He had a feeling there'd be more than one.

'Why was it all hushed up in the first place?'

'That was explained to you at the time.'

'At the time, I'd only just joined the department. This was just about my first case, all I was concerned about was getting Leon out of the country and settling him in Amsterdam.'

'Doing your job in other words. Dealing with your own concerns and issues.'

Jukes's message was clear. In other words, stop poking your nose into the concerns and issues of others. But Ros, somewhat characteristically again, just rode on.

'And, yes, it was an unusually brutal killing, but so was Lynette White and all those details were put out there.'

Jukes didn't respond. Lynette White was a Cardiff prostitute whose head had been virtually severed from her shoulders in a frenzied knife attack by a deranged punter. And everything that happened to her, as Jukes would have been forced to concede, had been reported in almost forensic detail by the press at the time.

'But it's like some sort of blanket was thrown over all this. No-one could know anything about it, nothing could get out.'

Jukes struggled to sound patient.

'Which was explained at the time as well, there's a lot of sick people out there, we circulate those sort of details and who knows what might have happened, someone might have decided to match it, blow for blow, a killing like that could have gone viral.'

'In other words, there was the fear of a copycat killing.'

Jukes fell silent, her point all too clear.

Ros shook her head, frustrated. She wasn't going to get any further with this line of thought and she could see it.

'Point Two. Why was Leon actually taken into the programme at all?'

Jukes stared back up at her, frowning now.

'I don't understand.'

'We take clients in when they're at risk. Or when they're being prepared to testify at trial. The risk to Leon was from his brother, but his brother was dead. And Leon wasn't being prepared for any trial either, there was never going to be any prosecution in this case – had Joey lived then yes, but he hadn't. Toya had seen to that, so it was like Leon was taken in for no real reason.'

Jukes just maintained his hardball stare. The same sort of stare Ros knew would have greeted any attempt on her part to ask Masters the very same questions. Questions to which, for whatever reason, Masters also didn't want to supply an answer.

'With Leon resettled and out of the way, with the first killing closed down, then OK, maybe none of this would have mattered, but now there's this second killing and now we've got Kezia too, now she's caught up in whatever's going on here.'

Jukes just maintained his stare, his silent instruction clear.

Drop this and drop this now.

Ros rode on.

'So do you know or are you not being told? And if you do know, don't I have a right to know too? I'm Kezia's handler. And if you don't know, don't you think we should find out?'

Jukes spoke very clearly, very deliberately.

'There were good and clear operational reasons for keeping the Joey and Toya killings quiet all those years ago.'

'Which were?'

Jukes continued, same deliberate tone.

'Good and clear operational reasons which were none of your concern then and none of which are yours now.'

Jukes hunched closer over his outsize desk.

'You have a job to do, DS Gilet, a task to perform.'

'And how am I supposed to do that if I don't actually know what the fuck's going on?'

'Resettle Kezia as you previously resettled Leon, so why don't you go and do that, go and do that job, go and execute that task and stop bothering me and the rest of my department with your half-arsed ramblings, if not downright fevered, fucking, imaginings.'

For a moment longer there was silence as Ros eyed Jukes who eyed her back. Then Ros – taking that as an indication their exchange was at an end – turned, walked away, collected her car from the small car park in front of the unit offices and headed for the club.

As Ros drove away, Jukes stood and locked the door. Then he turned back to his computer. For the next few minutes at least there could be no more interruptions.

It was time for those strictly private, strictly personal, matters at last.

A year or so before, DCI Jukes had followed a young girl on a train. Every Tuesday evening he'd fallen in step behind her as she'd taken the same trip a few stops down a local branch line to a private music lesson.

Jukes had seen her quite by chance as he walked onto the station concourse one afternoon. He'd still no idea what it was about her that had first caught his eye but once she did that was it. He may have been a forty-something career cop, she may have been a schoolgirl who couldn't have been much older than fifteen or so, but he simply couldn't get her out of his head.

Jukes glanced at his computer monitor but, as yet, there was nothing. No alert signalling the arrival of the email he'd been eagerly anticipating all day.

On each and every one of those train trips, Jukes watched the young girl as he'd previously watched others before her, wondering if she would be the one, if finally he'd cross the line and actually make some kind of move this time.

Then the girl had looked at him, he was sure she had. And it wasn't just a look either, there was something else in that sideways glance across a train carriage, some kind of challenge, the ghost of an invitation behind those hooded eyes. And so he'd decided to make that move on their very next trip together and had planned, down to the last detail, exactly how he was going to do it.

There'd been a lot of stories in the press at the time about men in positions of power and influence becoming caught up in sex scandals. The police were putting a lot of effort into investigating historic claims of abuse. The truth was that if they'd put even a fraction of the effort they were currently expending into investigating the original allegations at the time, the world would have been a far better place for countless more victims, but that was hardly the issue as far as Jukes was concerned.

Jukes was going to enlist the young girl's support. He'd be careful not to say her music teacher was actually involved in anything, but he would still appreciate a private chat with her about the lessons he conducted.

Jukes didn't know if she'd see through the subterfuge. He didn't know if she'd actually care. There seemed to be a waywardness about this particular girl which was one of the reasons he'd been attracted to her in the first place. Despite her advantaged background, as the private music lessons more than suggested, she looked like Jukes's very favourite sort of female irrespective of age or social class.

She looked, quite simply, like a dirty girl.

Then the alert on his computer sounded. Jukes stilled in his seat as his eyes swivelled to the screen, a name prominently displayed in the subject header of the incoming email, a coded message telling a dry-mouthed Jukes that he'd done it.

He'd actually managed to trace her at last.

One day before he'd planned to make his move, a previous case that had enmeshed his department involving a rogue cop and a psychopathic Ukrainian, ended in Jukes being hospitalised. By the time he returned to active duty the girl in question had stopped making her regular journeys. For the whole of the past year he'd made discreet, if evermore strenuous efforts to find out where she might live but had drawn a complete blank, which was hardly surprising as he didn't even have a name and, until his recent brainwave, no clear route to finding one.

But a week ago he'd finally managed to get police clearance for the home of the music teacher to be surreptitiously searched during his absence on a short holiday. Jukes had used the same cover story he'd intended to use on the girl, and his vaguely-bewildered colleagues had acquiesced, albeit grudgingly, to his request. They'd received no untoward reports about the music teacher themselves. But Jukes seemed to have picked something up, so they acted.

Jukes made sure he was present throughout the whole search. While light-fingered techies well-practised in covering their tracks investigated the music teacher's computer and internet history, Jukes leafed through the hard copy files relating to his private pupils, which is where he'd found her name.

The email that had just been delivered to a private account on his laptop and which originated from a very discreet enquiry agent would now contain her current address.

With trembling fingers, Jukes opened the email, scanning the contents, feeling his stomach tense as he read that the girl and her family had emigrated some six months before to enable the father, an IT consultant apparently, to take up a secondment at the head office of his employer just outside Phoenix.

Jukes looked out of his window, another dream decaying into dust before his eyes, another trawl on a lonely railway platform for yet another vulnerable target now before him.

And nothing now to distract him from the demons that had just been resurrected by Ros.

Demons which, despite all Jukes's stout denials, were all too present and all too active.

Ros rested her head on the side of the Jacuzzi, closed her eyes for a moment, then opened them again to see the glitterball now reflecting a new colour across the gleaming floor as the mixed race girl dabbed with paper towels at the thin trickle of blood which had escaped from the inside of her now-torn vagina.

Ros kept staring at the blood-red streaks of light flashing in front of her, Jukes's stern instruction to leave this alone still ringing in her ears, that instruction already comprehensively dismissed.

Ros stood, letting the warm water run off her naked body back into the Jacuzzi for a moment, then retrieved her robe and retraced her steps along the corridor, passing a seating area in front of another giant DVD screen, before moving on through the bar. The couple from the showers were also heading for the changing room, the public schoolboy-type leading the way, the mixed race girl following. If she was suffering any ill-effects from the attentions of his crazed fingers she wasn't showing it.

In the bar itself, a middle-aged man was coupling with an older woman on a circular rug spread out on the floor. Ros had seen her a few times before. She had the look of a kindly old headmistress about her, sensible hair cropped short around the ears. She usually arrived at the club clad in a pair of sturdy shoes. As the man pumped away inside her, another woman, the man's more usual companion, his wife or so Ros had always assumed, leant down and began tickling, idly, his exposed balls.

The still black stranger was now nowhere to be seen.

Ros changed, let herself out of the anonymous entrance and made for her car which was when, at the bottom of her bag, her work mobile pulsed with a new client alert.

Briefly, Ros felt grateful for an excuse to bury herself in some new distraction from the Kezia case, if only temporarily.

The problem being that this was to turn out to be no distraction at all.

10.

Conor's wife, Francesca, knew what all his work colleagues, both past and present, thought of her. On the rare occasions she'd been persuaded to go along to one of her husband's always-excruciating Christmas parties in his days in Murder Squad, the general attitude towards her had always been clear.

Francesca didn't fit in. She wasn't one of them. She appeared, and with good reason as she herself would have been the first to admit, to be a cut above in some way, a badge which – privately anyway – she'd always worn with pride.

Francesca had simply never got on with Conor's old colleagues, particularly his senior officer in that department, the tall and rangy DCI known to all and sundry as Masters. If it hadn't been for the official police pass hanging round his neck – secured with, of all things, a Bentley lanyard for God's sake – she'd probably have marked him down as one of the more venal villains whose exploits Conor would occasionally relate across the supper table as he wound down at the end of a particularly long and trying day. To this day Francesca was very much in two minds as to whether the head of the local Murder Squad didn't occasionally dabble in darker arts for the other side.

But then came Conor's transfer to the Protection Unit which, initially at least, she'd welcomed. But over the last year or so she'd begun to wonder if he hadn't gone from the proverbial frying pan to something much more inflammable.

At least in Murder Squad there were clear divisions. There were criminals and there were victims, even if the courts, to her husband's habitual exasperation, couldn't always agree which was which. But his investigations back then followed a familiar, even time-honoured, pattern. There was a crime or a situation, there was an investigation and there was a conclusion. Sometimes that conclusion was satisfactory, sometimes not, but there was an ending of a sort, at least.

Which was exactly the same as her work in the hospital. Some patients needed a period of fairly intense aftercare post-surgery, but her work was usually concluded once those patients were wheeled away from the operating table, the occasional check-up aside. In other words, there was a situation followed by an investigation followed by a conclusion there too. Boxes were ticked and tasks completed, hopefully more or less successfully.

But Conor's new job didn't seem to involve any kind of boxes, ticked or otherwise. And it didn't seem to involve any sort of investigation either. In fact, and from all Francesca could see, he actually went out of his way not to know too many details of the cases that came his way, claiming it made things simpler.

There didn't seem anything all that simple about it to Francesca. And the new characters her husband now encountered didn't exactly seem simple souls either. Francesca was well aware that Conor used to mix with some seriously damaged individuals in the days when his job entailed taking them off the streets and locking them away, hopefully forever. But now he didn't lock anyone away. Now, and as he had done an hour or so ago, he sometimes brought them home instead.

Conor had let himself into their apartment with a young woman. Or, more accurately, with what looked like the shell of a young woman who was currently sitting in their kitchen. The young woman in question wasn't looking at anything or anyone and just seemed to be the latest in a long line of what had always appeared to Francesca to be the walking dead.

After fixing herself a coffee, Francesca had moved out of that kitchen as quickly as she could. As with most of her husband's clients, she had no idea why the young woman was sitting there and something was already telling her that she really didn't want to know either.

But then Francesca paused – and how she was going to regret that uncharacteristic moment of indecision.

Then Francesca looked back into the room.

Conor had been handed the file by Jukes an hour earlier. He was just about to leave for home. Ros had left a couple of hours previously after being closeted with Jukes in his office for an exchange that didn't seem to have ended all that well if the expression on her face as she came back out again was anything to go by.

Conor read the name on the front of the file. The surname had been removed as a precaution to disguise the real identity of the client inside, so all Conor had to go on was the new client's Christian name.

Kim.

After scanning the first few pages, he'd taken a seat opposite the young woman herself and stared into a pair of eyes that stared back in turn at nothing. Kim, indeed, didn't even seem to take in the fact that Conor was there.

All that had happened in this particular case had been easy enough to establish given the near-documentary record left behind by the perpetrator. Far from concealing their tracks, whoever had inflicted this period of extended and gruesome torture seemed to have gone out of their way to provide chapter and verse on its every twisted moment.

And twisted it truly was, a wondering Conor now reflected. How else could you describe living through days in which a mother believed she was watching the slow death of her infant only for the whole charade to be revealed as just that? A smoke and mirrors deception?

But why stage that deception in the first place? If the purpose had been to tip Kim into virtual insanity, it had been accomplished, but who would want to do that?

And why record it in such forensic a fashion too?

And why leave that dubious testament behind for the police to find?

Like most cops, Conor had come across torturers who'd filmed their crimes, but they usually kept those records for their own pleasure, to be pored over later, often and lovingly, a constant reminder of their extraordinary achievement, in their eyes at least.

So had this testament been left to taunt someone in some way?

But again, who and why?

Conor kept looking at the silent Kim. One thing was already clear from everything he'd just read. They weren't going to be able to count on any assistance from Kim's partner who was also identified in the file by just his Christian name of Jamie. Kim's mental scars might run deep but Jamie seemed to have equally deep physical scars of his own to contend with now too.

In the aftermath of the now-notorious DVD viewing at his place of work, and still believing at the time that his young son was dead, a hysterical Jamie had demanded that a helicopter be brought out to fly him home as in there and then, that minute, with no delay.

Refusing to listen to his rig manager's pleas that to arrange a facility like that at such short notice was impossible, Jamie had attempted to launch one of the rig's own emergency boats to pilot himself back to shore. A North Sea wave had smashed the small craft against one of the giant metal supports, smashing Jamie against it too. For a time, as he was being treated in the makeshift rig hospital and later, in the larger hospital in

Aberdeen, it had been touch and go whether Kim would have a genuine funeral to face.

So for now only Kim could help them. But she'd remained in the same catatonic state of deep shock she'd been in ever since officers, alerted by her evermore hysterical husband, had broken down her door and discovered her and her baby. Kim was still immobilised by the drugs that had been used to sedate her, but her child was in the good health he'd actually enjoyed all through the illusion of his ordeal, even if by then he'd been in some quite serious need of a change of nappy.

But even when Kim had been shown the healthy infant it had made no difference. It was as if her mind could not accept the evidence in front of her eyes. She simply refused to believe it had all been an elaborate hoax, perhaps because by then all hope had been extinguished beyond the point of no return. What Kim had endured simply seemed to have blasted her apart, obliterated all reason.

But Conor was still going to have to make an attempt at some kind of connection. And so, in an attempt to usher in some kind of normality at least and in the absence of Ros, Conor took her home.

Later, Francesca could at least say she'd tried. In fact, in many different ways she'd been trying for the whole of the last year and with good reason.

Conor and herself had endured something of a bad patch a year ago, had been on the edge of splitting up in fact. If pressed at the time, Francesca would have put it all down to the strain of his new job as well the ever-constant demands of her always busy lifestyle, but they both knew it was more than that.

As far as Conor was concerned, Francesca knew that some of his private activities during that period didn't bear too close an investigation. He had some serious debts back then, not helped by several incautious attempts to gamble his way out of it all.

But Francesca also knew she bore some responsibility for all that as well. Because, and in his own doomed way, Conor had been trying to keep up with his high-flying, high-earning wife.

Francesca also knew she was at fault in other ways too. Because during that same time, she'd become embroiled in an unwise and much-regretted relationship with a fellow consultant.

Both Conor and Francesca had pulled themselves out of the mire that was threatening to swamp them. She still didn't know exactly how Conor had managed it. He didn't seem to have gone to any of the payday loan sharks that seemed to be proliferating back then, and thank heavens for that not-so-small mercy.

But Francesca had caught snatches of the odd, late-night, phone call and she had gleaned enough from a few overheard exchanges to understand that his former senior officer – the decidedly-strange Masters – appeared to have had some hand in resolving his problems. And Masters seemed to have done all that in exchange for some operational, if unspecified, favour that Conor had managed to do for him.

Francesca had also heard the odd, muttered, reference to another officer now invalided out of the force. Conor's silence about the circumstances behind that enforced retirement seemed to be part of that same deal.

But Francesca didn't enquire too deeply. Because if she had, then Conor might have taken too keen an interest in a trip she and her fellow-consultant had made to a certain gastro-hotel in southern Spain around the same time.

They'd gone as part of a group. Somehow, and she still wasn't quite sure exactly how, it had all ended up at midnight in something akin to a mass orgy in the hotel's celebrated outdoor pool, a pool that meandered through the gardens with several private enclaves along the way.

Francesca couldn't absolutely swear she'd had sex with her companion that night, on account of not being able to totally swear at the time what country she was in or century she was inhabiting. The recreational substance of choice provided at dinner, a strictly unofficial accompaniment to the hotel's universally-renowned tasting menu, had well and truly seen to that.

But something had happened and she knew it. And it was a lapse and a lack of control she now deeply regretted.

It could have been the final nail in the marital coffin, but when she returned she found Conor actually beginning to get his life back on track. And slowly, through a combination of joint effort and mutual self-deception, their lives began to return to what they had been previously, the lives she'd imagined for them both when they'd first met. So trying to involve herself in his work seemed part of that same healing process even if neither of them, openly at least, ever acknowledged there'd been anything to heal in the first place.

Which was why, when Francesca saw that Conor had taken a break to make a phone call and that the strange, silent, young woman was momentarily alone in their kitchen, she decided to extend the hand of friendship.

Why not, Francesca reasoned?

Where was the harm in that?

In fact, Conor was wrong about Kim. She appeared to him to be locked in some sort of unreachable trance. But somewhere deep down, so deep Kim was almost unaware of it herself, connections were starting to be made.

There'd been nothing for the past week. It was as if a light had indeed extinguished inside her as she saw that same light flicker into nothing in her small son's eyes. And no-one could now tell her that Aron was still alive, that it had all been some kind of trick, she even distrusted the crying infant they'd tried presenting to her as a desperate last resort. Nothing, in short, could now convince her she hadn't seen what she knew she'd seen with her own eyes.

Perhaps because she simply couldn't rid herself of that image. The image of her dying son. It was as if it had been seared on her eyeballs and now there simply wasn't room for anything else.

But now, sitting in an unfamiliar apartment with people she didn't know, something was starting to stir and it was the slim, elegant, woman who'd suddenly appeared in her vision, not the burly man who'd been there previously, that was prompting it.

There was just something in the way the slim, elegant, woman's arm moved in front of her. As it did so, an image suddenly flashed through Kim's mind, a distant memory returning. It was unfocused, not even a proper image for now, just something telling her – or trying to tell her – something.

The memory was from a long time before, from her old home and her old life. A visitor had called, which was unusual in itself. Her always secretive ex-husband hadn't told her much about the visitor at the time, he'd just made some reference to an old friend from the past.

But when a curious Kim had tried to press him on just who this visitor was and why she was calling in on them in their detached executive residence with its gravel drive and ornamental fountain, that had been the first time he'd hit her; so Kim didn't ask again.

Kim kept staring at the far wall of the unfamiliar kitchen, more and more of that same picture, that distant memory, forming all the while. There was something in the way that visitor also swung her arm as she walked past the window as Kim looked out from inside the house. Graceful, like a dancer.

And something in the way that arm moved connected with another image, the arm moving in front of her eyes much more recently.

The arm reaching down in front of her to adjust the settings on a camera, a hand holding a syringe.

And then, as Kim tried to concentrate on that elusive image, as she allowed it to creep into her mind's eye hoping thereby to flesh it out some more, she suddenly realised that, for just a moment since everything had happened, for just one moment since that blinding light had bleached the whole world white, she'd actually thought of something else apart from Aron.

And that sudden realisation swamped her. And the guilt instantly closed her down.

Then Kim looked up and saw the woman who'd unwittingly provoked all that.

Conor was in the next room liaising with Jukes. The choice of a safe house for this particular witness was fast becoming a matter of heated debate in the department. Given how the fragile Kim presented and given all that had happened to her, some were already making dark mutterings about secure units and psychiatric wards.

And, for not the first time, Conor was regretting the absence of Ros. She was no miracle worker. Like the rest of the department she may not have made much headway with this most uncommunicative of witnesses at the start. But she usually made some sort of connection. For reasons Conor still didn't quite understand, she just seemed to have the knack.

On the other end of the line, Jukes was listing a choice of likely locations. As he did so, Conor was leafing through Kim's case notes. Then Jukes settled on a choice of two main possibilities and, ever the politician protecting his back, asked Conor his opinion.

But Conor wasn't listening.

Because Conor had just come across a note towards the end of Kim's file.

A note that had, quite literally, stopped him in his tracks.

With Conor still on the phone to Jukes in the next room, Francesca leant close to Kim. The young woman was perched on the edge of one of their kitchen stools, which seemed appropriate somehow. Because in some strange way the young woman seemed perched on the edge of everything right now, as if nowhere could she be sure of finding any sort of foothold.

All Francesca wanted to do was ask if she wanted a coffee or perhaps some snack or maybe a magazine while she waited for Conor to finish his phone call to his creep of a DCI.

As Francesca bent down to her, she and Kim were momentarily at eye level and suddenly Francesca saw her own reflection in Kim's fixed eyes. Which was when she saw something else in those staring eyes too.

It was impossible she knew, but afterwards she would swear she saw a brilliant white flash somehow ignite behind her eyeballs.

Francesca stared, suddenly transfixed, but she didn't have too much time to take in the strange phenomenon. Because a second later the young woman's fingernails snaked out and started scrabbling at Francesca's eyes.

Francesca fell back onto the expensive Italian tiles that crisscrossed the kitchen floor, Kim following her down as she crashed onto her back. A second or so later, Francesca's whole world had shrunk down to one literally blinding sensation and, her surgeon's brain clearly operating even in these extraordinary circumstances, to one stomach-wrenching realisation as well.

Because the young woman who seemed perched not just on the edge of a kitchen stool but of life itself, seemed intent on just one objective and that was gouging out Francesca's eyeballs. Already, in the few seconds since the attack had started, the young woman's fingernails had managed to get some sort of hold in her left cavity and she was pressing harder and harder all the time, trying to physically flip out the eye itself, while at the same time the fingers of her other hand attempted to inflict the same treatment on her right eyeball.

The medical term for the procedure Kim was attempting was enucleation. A skilled surgeon would have kept Francesca's eyelids apart while pushing the eyeball aside, seeking the orbital muscles that held it in its socket before locating and slicing the sinew.

Kim's method was more brutal but just as effective.

Francesca screamed, ever louder, as Kim's thumbs scrabbled for a grip between the bridge of her nose and the side of her eye socket. It could only have lasted moments although to Francesca, perhaps understandably, it all seemed rather longer.

Then, just behind the young woman, the door burst open and Conor dashed in from the next room, alerted by his wife's screams. A moment later he'd bundled Kim away from the shocked Francesca and into a corner where she closed her arms around her head and then simply shook, soundlessly.

Francesca was lifted to her feet by a panicked Conor who made a swift call to the emergency services. Five minutes later, courtesy of an extra-rapid response team, Francesca was being helped into an ambulance and taken to the A&E department of her very own hospital for a colleague to assess the extent of the damage their visitor had just inflicted.

As it turned out, that damage hadn't quite been the catastrophe it promised. One of Francesca's eyeballs, the left, had suffered some quite considerable bruising but would heal within a month or so. The other eye, thanks to Conor and his swift intervention, was unharmed. No physical scars would endure, but for months afterwards Francesca would wake up from a fitful sleep to find herself shaking in fear, her body back on that kitchen floor, the young woman's fingernails that had now turned into talons in Francesca's nightmares, scrabbling for their hold in her eyes.

In particularly acute and extended versions of the same nightmare, she actually felt all light in her universe suddenly extinguish and a black hole replace it, as first one eyeball popped out and then another as her tormenter gouged away.

That nightmare fear wasn't totally without foundation of course. Because Francesca knew, with absolute certainty, that if Conor hadn't intervened as speedily as he had, then that young woman would have achieved all she'd intended that day. The ambushed Francesca would have simply been too shocked by the sudden and single-minded ferocity of the attack to prevent it.

Francesca's eyes would have been gouged from their sockets by those talon-like nails. Then, the macabre mission executed, Francesca would have been left to stumble around their gleaming designer kitchen, blood streaming from those now-vacated sockets while the young woman squeezed her extracted eyeballs into a gory pulp on their Italian-tiled floor.

11.

W ITH THE LAST of the evening light fading fast, Ros drove
along a newly-built feeder road. Trucks thundered along
beside her, most making for ports to the east, drivers on the
Continental run racing to catch ferries.

The ceaseless movement of trade. It was a trade that had
positively defined her father before the murder of Ros's sister,
Braith, after which his former trade was denied him. Then he
became a figure adrift, a man excluded.

Only according to the alert that Jukes had passed onto her,
completely unaware of its ultra-sensitive nature or so Ros fervently
hoped, her father seemed to have forgotten that simple fact.

It had been a routine notification. The unit received them
all the time, reports of this person who should have been inside
the programme but was not, that person who should have been
observing the rules of memorandum agreed on their admission
but who were quite obviously testing the boundaries, straying
into parts of the country they'd sworn never again in their lives
to frequent.

It seemed so easy to most of them at the start. To some indeed
it appeared like an enticing fantasy.

What would it be like, how would it feel, what would you do,
if you were given the chance to start all over again?

To leave everything you'd ever known behind?

Slough the trappings of the past and emerge on the other
side completely reinvented as someone totally new?

Some embraced it with something approaching intoxication
and no wonder. Currently enduring a present-day nightmare, all
they'd be craving, more than anything, was for that nightmare

to end. So the prospect of having it erased, sometimes at the literal stroke of a pen, was heady.

The reality, of course, was very different. Because most of those same people almost always had massive trouble in jettisoning all they'd ever known, in turning their backs on the people and places that had been their whole world up until then.

And sometimes it was something tiny that provided the tipping point. Some illness that had suddenly afflicted a favourite old aunt. A small family celebration from which they were excluded and all of a sudden it became too much. The event itself may not have actually been all that important, but it became a touchstone. And, eventually, they did what so many had done before and would do again. They decided they could stand the separation no longer and returned.

Just as her father seemed to have done.

To the best of Ros's knowledge he'd never done it before because he knew the risks, still real after all this time. Risks that had been drummed into him and Ros over and over again. A contract had been taken out on their family twenty years before and, so far as anyone knew, that contract was still active.

And yes, they'd had that slightly strange conversation outside her apartment those few days before, but while he'd talked about the past he didn't seem to have actually been near any of his old haunts. None of the usual alarms that would have sounded had done so.

If Macklyn had even been tempted, there'd been no evidence of that either. But now he quite clearly had been tempted. And that morning he'd equally obviously given into that temptation. Because one of those alarms triggered by one of those routine checks had just sounded loud and clear.

'Some old man, it's probably nothing, maybe he's just wandering a bit too close to where he shouldn't be.'

Jukes checked the file in front of him as he talked to Ros, not even referring to their exchange of a few hours previously and not all that interested in this new case either in truth. This one was so cold it was bordering on the frozen.

'Maybe he doesn't even know where he is, he's a fair old age.'

Jukes exhaled a slightly irritated breath. They could really do without this sort of thing in these days of straitened budgets and stretched resources.

'Still a Category A though.'

And Jukes had handed the file over to Ros. Initially, Ros had been inclined to take about as much notice of this as Jukes, Category A or otherwise.

Until she realised just where the old man had been spotted.

And just who he was.

Which was when she immediately took personal charge of this new sighting, leaving Conor to deal with another client who'd just been taken into the programme.

A client that, unbeknown to her, Conor then decided to take home.

Half an hour later, Ros parked her car and looked round, momentarily disorientated. This small market town on the English/Welsh border didn't hold the associations for her it would have for her father. Ros had left the town at the age of five and had never lived there since. But she did retain some sketchy memories. What she definitely didn't remember was an outsize petrol station complete with adjoining mini-market where an old, semi-industrial lorry yard once stood.

Ros looked round some more. She knew the place would have changed, but still couldn't take in for a moment the extent to which all the old landmarks seemed to have completely vanished. The sheds that used to house all the units had disappeared. The wasteland that used to surround them had been landscaped and now surrounded a newly-built supermarket instead. In the near distance she could hear the muffled, ever-present, roar of a recently-constructed dual carriageway in place of the single lane road that had previously been there.

Ros looked round some more, latching onto one familiar landmark at least. An old pub, a firm favourite of the drivers who at one time had colonised the whole area, still clung defiantly to existence by the side of one of the link roads to a newly-constructed road junction. A few tables had been placed outside for those brave or uncaring souls who wanted to imbibe exhaust fumes along with their drinks.

But it was an anachronism, out of place and out of time. Much like the figure currently sitting on a small bank of grass a few metres down from the entrance to that new-build supermarket, a patrol car parked close by, two bewildered-looking traffic cops standing next to him.

All they'd done was send in the old man's details after a spooked service station receptionist had spotted him hanging around for over an hour on the other side of the forecourt. The next thing the patrol cops knew, they'd been told to stay where they were and to keep the harmless-looking old man where he was until other officers were contacted. They had absolutely no idea why they had to do that or who those other officers would turn out to be, and the arriving Ros didn't enlighten them any further. She just flashed her warrant card and told them she'd be taking over now.

As the cops somewhat thankfully departed, Ros settled herself next to her father. For a few moments she couldn't be absolutely sure he was even aware anyone was with him, let alone who she was. He just kept looking out over the former site of the business he'd established and had then built up into one of the area's leading employers. Until one totally routine afternoon when he'd been escorted from the premises by two plain-clothes officers who wouldn't even tell him why.

And then, when they had told him, Macklyn really wished they hadn't.

Macklyn looked at her and Ros waited, wondering what would come next? More of the same sort of thing she'd had in that car park outside her apartment? Some more rambling recollections of times past, an extended reference to old colleagues she'd probably never met and could not, in any event, possibly be expected to remember?

But none of that happened. Macklyn just kept looking at her almost as if he wasn't seeing her at all.

Almost as if he was looking at someone else.

Ten minutes later his daughter was driving him away, one thought only in Macklyn's mind.

Was she now, he wondered, one of them? Had his own daughter crossed over to what he now regarded as the other side?

Macklyn knew Ros had gone into the police, of course. He knew she'd joined a specialist unit of some description, but exactly what that unit was she'd never said. He had his suspicions it might be the very unit that had acted almost as a surrogate parent to her from childhood, but didn't know for sure.

He could have asked her of course, but he never had. Both he and Ros had learnt over the years not to probe too deeply into anything the other did, each only too aware of the dangers. Curiosity, as the old proverb had it, killed the cat. And many others besides.

But from time to time he did wonder if Ros now did to others what had been done to him? Role play, some of them had called it in a phrase so divorced from anything he regarded as reality it was almost laughable. In later years he'd watch children acting out make-believe fantasies in school playgrounds, and if there was any connection between those innocent pastimes and all that had happened to him and his family he'd always failed to spot it.

Because they just piled it on back then. Pressure, more pressure, and then even more again. In those days, the days they'd all inhabited no-man's-land as he'd always silently termed it, it simply never stopped.

'You're not who you were.'

'You can never be that person again.'

'You're not the person you're going to be either, not yet anyway, that's what this is all about, that's why I'm here and that's why we're going to go over this time and time again until it becomes second nature.'

Then there'd been a pause.

'No, that's not right, it can't be second nature, it's got to be your nature, the one and only because there is no first or second, not any more, just this.'

Macklyn had tried mounting some sort of feeble protest, at least at the start.

'It can't work, how can it? There's records, documents, if I say I used to live in that house, on that street, all anyone has to do is check and they'll know that's not true.'

But Macklyn's companion shook his head.

'Everything will match. Everything will check out. That's our job and believe me, we're good at it.'

'What about my passport?'

'Your passport, your driving licence, your marriage certificate.'

Then that same companion had leant forward, bringing his face ever closer to Macklyn's.

'As for all your old documents, they'll all be erased. Hospital records, electoral registers, bank accounts, credit cards, you name it, everything that used to be there, it's gone.'

Macklyn kept looking out of the window as Ros drove on, registering the last of the former, familiar, landmarks now being left behind. All that had been hard enough to take in. But what came next was even more so.

'You can't hesitate, not for a second, when someone asks you your name, where you come from, what you do, what football team you support, what you voted in the last election, when's your birthday, your wife's birthday, what you prefer for Sunday lunch, pork, lamb or beef.'

Instinctively, he'd come straight out with it.

'Lamb.'

His companion had stared at him for a long moment, then picked up his pen, made a note on the file in front of him, a look of mild disappointment on his face now, the kind of look a parent might bestow on an errant child.

'That's something else we're going to have to change.'

And Macklyn had tried to be a good student. There'd been a powerful incentive to do so after all. Even if he couldn't give a fig about his own safety, there was the welfare of his wife and surviving daughter to consider. And even in his darkest and most nihilistic moments, living a new life that seemed no life at all, just an echo of a life that once meant something, he still couldn't contemplate the prospect of some fresh tragedy happening to them.

And so he'd learnt it all. He'd memorised the primer. He'd become word perfect in a fiction that, he'd been assured time and again, had to become reality.

But there'd been a price.

Macklyn had never told anyone in the protection programme about the headaches. Using his new name and assumed identity he did consult a doctor once who'd diagnosed them as migraines.

He wasn't the doctor that Macklyn had been told to consult, accessed via the number he'd also been told to call in case of any problems. This was a locum in a drop-in centre and Macklyn's visit had been made on a whim. His headaches had been getting worse lately and they were now being accompanied by pulsing lights in front of his eyes, lights that almost seemed to score the waves of pain coursing, virtually continually, across his temples.

The doctor had run through all the usual triggers. Had he developed a food or drink allergy? Had he recently adopted a change of diet? Had he suddenly become exposed to a new and unfamiliar working environment? But none of those hypothetical diagnoses had even remotely ticked any boxes.

But then it happened. Suddenly it all clicked into place. And Macklyn had managed that all by himself when the increasingly bewildered doctor had asked him to try and describe the physical sensation and Macklyn told him it was like being split in two.

And that was it. All of a sudden he had it. In fact Macklyn was surprised he hadn't thought of it before.

Because he was, of course. The person he'd been, the person who'd come into the world, who'd grown his herbs in his small garden and who preferred lamb to pork or beef, that person had now been eclipsed by this new one, the lie he'd adopted to keep living a life he no longer understood.

No wonder he felt as if there were two souls fighting for the same space inside his head. No wonder he felt as if his head was splitting as each protested the other's inevitably-warring presence.

Macklyn walked away from the drop-in centre with a small bottle of pills and dropped them in a nearby bin. They wouldn't do any good and he knew it. Only one thing would make any difference now.

Macklyn toyed with the idea for weeks but was too scared to do anything about it, to take that forbidden first step. He still hadn't said anything to the unit quack about it either. If he had then for all he knew he might have ended up strapped to some hospital bed somewhere, hooked up to electrodes, his brain blasted with electricity, medically erasing all that the former brain-washing had been meant to achieve.

Then, one night, the pain had become intolerable. And, finally, he'd acted. He'd left his small car behind – in his distressed state he really didn't trust himself to drive. Then he'd taken a local train to a small country station and then a bus to a locale he hadn't visited for more than twenty years – but a destination he hadn't stopped thinking about for a single day.

And that's all it had taken. That was all that was needed, just a few moments sitting there. It didn't matter that everything had changed; he still recognised where at least some of the old landmarks had been and the basic geography of the site was more or less intact. And as Macklyn looked out on the site of his former transport yard, his migraine ebbed away. Those two warring sides of his brain seemed to resolve themselves and the reason was simple.

Who Macklyn was – and who he'd always be despite other people's insistence that he was someone else – that person was back. The man they'd tried to erase had not been erased, the soul they'd sought to deny still endured. Macklyn could almost physically feel him returning.

Not that, once again, he'd said any of that to anyone. And not that he intended to say it to the small, slight, protection officer currently driving him away. She may have been his daughter but she was like all the rest of them as far as he was concerned. All she wanted to do was kill the man he really was.

Macklyn stared out at a now-unfamiliar landscape and felt the beginnings of that old and all-too-familiar pressure beginning to build up once again inside his skull.

A short while before, sitting amongst the ghosts of his old haunts, his head had been clear. Now he felt like he was drowning once more, stepping back into a sea of treacle.

And so the lesson was clear. No matter what that small, slight, protection officer by his side might say to him, he had to keep going back. He had to keep returning to meet again the man he used to be. Even though he'd been spotted once it didn't mean he'd be spotted again and anyway it didn't matter because his head was already splitting.

Like a drug addict denied his substance of choice, he was already suffering the first of the withdrawal symptoms.

And all Macklyn could think about, all he would dream about indeed from that moment on, was the next hit.

Ros returned to the office to find a note waiting for her. Conor was still at the hospital with Francesca, but he'd managed to have the file he'd been studying before the attack couriered over.

Ros looked at a photo on the front. A young woman who meant nothing to her stared back at her. The young woman was identified only by her Christian name which also meant nothing.

Then Ros opened the file and read the passage that had been highlighted by Conor.

Then, and like Conor before her, Ros just kept staring.

Then Ros raised her head and looked out of the window, her father now forgotten, even more questions now dancing before her eyes.

'**G**UV.'

    Two hours earlier, as Ros was approaching her father and as Conor was rushing Francesca into A&E, Masters had stared at his new recruit as he approached along a corridor, a file in hand, a quizzical expression on his face.

Masters hadn't quite worked out Hendrix as yet, perhaps because he didn't fit the usual mould. His previous helpmate, the unfortunate Donovan Banks, had been a lot easier to assess. He was a self-centred, grasping, greedy little shit who overstepped the mark on one occasion more than was good for his health, and that health had suffered quite catastrophically as a result. The occasional report on the station grapevine confirmed that he was still confined to the wheelchair that would almost certainly host his broken body to the largely-unlamented day he died.

But if Hendrix was cut from a similar cloth he was keeping it well concealed. So far he hadn't stepped out of line at all in fact. Whether that betokened an officer totally devoid of personality or one who was taking considerable pains to conceal it, Masters hadn't yet been able to decide.

But he would.

'Picked this up from the duty log about an hour ago.'

Masters stared at the file in Hendrix's outstretched hand, making no move to take it. Hendrix hesitated, then retracted the file, beginning the résumé that was quite obviously expected instead.

'Hospital admission, late last night from a homeless shelter just off the Broadway. Single male, internal injuries consistent with swallowing slivers of glass. At the moment he's in intensive care, it's touch and go by all accounts.'

Masters stared back at him, his face expressionless but the message clear enough anyway.

So what?

Hendrix sifted the papers in the file, extracted another item from the same night's log.

'The weird thing is that a chef from the Marriott was admitted an hour or so later with exactly the same injuries. Insides sliced into ribbons. The same triage nurse assessed both patients, she alerted the consultant, he alerted us.'

Masters's expression remained the same, the silent message unaltered.

Hendrix hesitated again.

'It could be coincidence. A punter in a shelter on the end of some sort of reprisal for something, a chef who really should have washed his salad a bit better.'

Hendrix paused once more.

'But according to the consultant who opened up the shelter punter, his last meal was a bit on the exotic side, definitely a cut above what he'd have expected to find in the gut of a casualty like that with no fixed abode. So he makes some enquiries and finds that the punter in question had just eaten some food brought in by a Good Samaritan from a local hotel.'

Hendrix paused.

'The Marriott.'

Hendrix hesitated again.

'One plate of food with one unusual condiment, fair enough. That could be an accident. But two totally different plates of food? Served to two totally different punters? And according to the triage nurse, just before he went under the knife the chef from the Marriott was ranting and raving about some young woman they'd just taken on to help out with room service who seemed to have disappeared.'

Hendrix held Masters's stare.

'If it wasn't the Marriott, if it wasn't last night, if we didn't have Leon in there, I probably wouldn't have thought anything about it.'

Masters kept looking at him as Hendrix tailed off. Then he reached out, took the file from his junior officer's hand, still without saying a word.

Then he screwed the file up into a tight ball before dropping it into a nearby bin.

Then Masters turned and, still without saying a word to the now-staring Hendrix, exited the building.

A few moments later, Masters gazed out, unseeing, from the driver's seat of his car which, typically for Masters, was no ordinary run-about but a silver Bentley, the Continental GT Speed.

Masters kept staring through the windscreen. Had these been normal circumstances and had Masters been any normal sort of DCI, his junior officer should now be basking in the glow of a congratulatory slap on the back for employing his initiative, not left on a corridor staring at a balled-up collection of paper wondering what the hell he'd done wrong.

Fleetingly, as he started his car and felt the engine detonate into life in front of him, Masters reflected that a couple more encounters such as those and he really should start getting the measure of a man who might just be the kind of officer he'd been searching for these last few years.

Or he'd have destroyed another promising young cop along the way.

Time would tell.

Then Masters selected a gear and moved out through the

gates towards the feeder road that would take him into the city, rather weightier matters now in mind.

Joaquin Alejandro, the émigré from Venezuela, was a hard-working man. As well as his night shift as a hotel janitor, he also put in a few hours at a very different sort of establishment a mile or so away during the day.

This establishment had been set up by a local chancer called Keith Walker who used to run a fly-posting outfit until a rival one moved in and macheted off his arm when he'd protested their unwanted presence. Keith took the hint and decided to find a different way of earning a living before he lost any more limbs. A retail unit on City Road, nestled in between two car dealerships, was vacant at the time and Keith, using his one remaining good arm, turned it from an emporium specialising in bankrupt kitchen stock into a brothel.

Not that his new establishment was actually called that. Euphemisms like 'Massage' and 'Sauna' were blazoned across the outside instead. But once inside the nature of the new business was pretty difficult to mistake. The hardcore porn stills tacked up on the walls were one clue. The coked-up young female Albanians sitting around the waiting room dressed only in tight skirts, bras and crotchless panties were another.

Joaquin wasn't a visible presence. He was simply there as hired muscle in case any trouble kicked off. So far he'd had an easy time of it, but all that was about to change as a decidedly-upmarket car pulled up outside and a large, well-dressed, man materialised in the doorway. The receptionist started intoning the list of attractions currently on offer along with the relevant prices, all subtly inflated given that the new arrival was quite obviously loaded, but she hadn't managed to get beyond the third or fourth item on the laminated tick sheet in front of her before he'd moved past her into the room at the rear and closed the door.

Joaquin looked up at Masters, warily. Then Masters flashed his warrant card and Joaquin felt himself growing warier still. He'd only been in the UK a relatively short time but he'd already developed a healthy respect for the forces of law and order. From all he could see, things seemed to be the same here as in his home town of Caigua. Those who enforced the rules had no need to observe them.

From the other side of a thin partition wall a slow rhythmic thumping began as one of the early afternoon punters made the acquaintance of one of Keith's stable of not-so-lovelies. Joaquin barely registered it. All he could see was a pair of eyes staring at him and a growing feeling that he was in trouble, a suspicion that hardened into conviction as the owner of those same staring eyes grabbed him by the shoulders, lifted him off his feet before aiming him, head first, towards the top of an old steel filing cabinet.

Joaquin threw up one hand to stave off the collision and felt a bone splinter in his wrist as he did so. Now on the floor, he felt his attacker lean close to him. Joaquin listened as that attacker swiftly took him back to the previous evening, his shift in a local hotel, his act of charity at the end of the night in spiriting some excess food along to a local shelter and the absolute necessity of his remembering exactly where one particular item on that list had come from.

As it happened, Masters really hadn't needed to indulge in any of his trademark aids to memory, on this occasion involving heads, broken wrist bones and steel filing cabinets. Joaquin remembered only too well that untouched metal cloche and its appetising contents. The problem being he couldn't quite remember the number of the room on the order, at least not straightaway.

So Masters picked Joaquin up, spun him around a hundred and eighty degrees until he was facing the partition wall, the thumping sounding evermore urgent now on the other side. Joaquin wracked his brains some more, mentally counting off the numbers on the doors as he retraced his journey from that service elevator along the carpeted corridor, but then he had another and more immediate journey to contemplate as Masters hurled him straight at the thin partition wall. Joaquin crashed through the plasterboard a second later, collapsing on top of the punter who didn't even break stride.

The coked-up Albanian in the now removed regulation bra and short skirt, but with the crotchless panties still in place, did stare, blearily, at the sudden apparition that had landed, complete with broken pieces of plasterboard onto her now-climaxing punter, but the punter himself just moaned, made a couple of final thrusts and was still.

Masters leant close to the dazed Joaquin who had now completed his mental roll call of room numbers and who just hoped, more than anything he'd hoped for in his life before, that he'd remembered correctly.

'162.'

Joaquin gasped, still spread-eagled on the punter who was still straddling the prone Albanian whore.

'Room 162.'

Masters nodded, grimly.

He had a feeling it might be.

Then Masters turned and headed back outside. He unlocked his car, ignoring a nearby and sour-looking traffic rat who'd been pondering issuing a ticket. One look at the vehicle's owner and the traffic rat in question forgot all about the automotive equivalent of penis envy and moved on.

Inside the car, Masters stared, unseeing, at the dash in front of him for a moment.

Briefly, the demons that had been before Jukes's eyes earlier that same day flashed before Masters's eyes too.

Past demons that seemed, indeed, to have returned to the present.

Then Masters focused on his phone.

More than two hundred miles away, the woman was carrying a large stick. Viewed through hostile eyes it could be described as an offensive weapon, but the pink tassels stapled to the top, not to mention the bright yellow dots painted on the woman's cheeks, went some way to ameliorating any overt threat.

On any more normal street and in any other more normal company she'd have stood out, but on all sides several other women were dressed in a similar fashion. And as the beleaguered security guards watched her and her new companions approach, their hearts sank.

Those guards, by and large, had never even heard of fracking before being recruited. But they'd been given a quick crash course when they first arrived on site and it all sounded simple enough to their admittedly-uncurious ears.

The company that now paid their wages believed that trillions of cubic feet of something called shale gas was under the very soil on which they now stood, and they wished to extract it. To do so they intended to drill down into the earth and direct a high-pressure water mixture at the rocks to release the gas inside.

Which all sounded a little like the old-fashioned mining industry to them. Something valuable was under the earth's surface. In the case of that old-fashioned mining industry it had been coal, now it was some sort of gas. And what was down there now needed to be brought to the surface for the greater benefit of the wider public.

The term given to it all sounded a bit odd admittedly but,

that vaguely obscene description aside, most of those guards really couldn't see what was wrong.

But the group currently approaching the gates believed there was something very much wrong and they'd spent the last few weeks advising them of that fact in their own idiosyncratic and, it had be conceded, rather effective way.

First, the group had told them they were concerned about the huge amounts of water that needed to be transported to sites such as this and the significant environmental cost involved.

Second, they were concerned the potentially carcinogenic chemicals that were used in the process might escape, contaminating not only the groundwater around the site but the innumerable small streams and water courses that crisscrossed it as well, spreading those same potentially carcinogenic chemicals even further afield.

Thirdly, they were worried that the whole fracking process could cause earth tremors by rendering the site inherently unstable. To back up their claims they pointed to two small earthquakes that had already hit a couple of towns in the north of England following similar activity.

And, finally, they alleged that fracking was simply a way of distracting their employers and the Government from investing in renewable sources of energy and encouraging continued reliance on fossil fuels, something most environmental campaigners, and not just themselves, vehemently opposed.

It had all provoked heated debate on both sides. It had also provoked some quite violent demonstrations in the recent past with other more hardline environmental groups, all of whom the security guards could deal with. That was a world they understood. Most of the guards were culled from the various services, with the Army the most fertile recruiting ground. They weren't exactly shy when it came to getting up close and personal with the more traditional opposition they encountered.

But how do you get up close and personal with a bunch of female clowns?

The group had been formed a few months previously. Their intention was to use street theatre as a tool of dissent and they'd attracted a lot of publicity so far, as a largely-amused media proved only too willing to film some of its more extreme stunts which included staging sit-ins with nothing more offensive in the way of weapons than giant lollipops.

But there was a more serious side to it all as the fracking company understood only too well. Because, by such non-violent means, they were getting their message across more effectively than the combined efforts of all the other hardline protestors had managed so far, making them of special interest to the local police and the wider security forces.

And of extra interest to one member of those security forces who, just a short time previously, had stared in rapt adoration as a legend in her field received a commemorative plaque, but who was now carrying what her group described as a tickling stick, and was starting to brush the tassels, almost lovingly, across the broad shoulders and bulging biceps of the nearest guard.

Smiling all the while, Anya's fellow protestors started to do the same. A couple of the guards tried to look fierce and forbidding but it really wasn't easy with a posse of female clowns tickling them, and it didn't help that a couple of passing children, on their way home from school, now paused to watch the impromptu show too.

Then Anya felt her mobile pulse in the pocket of her baggy trousers, a mobile that was always kept fully charged but which, up to that moment, had never received a call.

Anya kept gently tickling her guard, not one muscle on her face betraying her, but inside her stomach was churning violently.

Because only one person would be contacting her on this particular number and via this particular mobile.

And that one person would only be contacting her in the most extreme of circumstances.

Anya kept tickling as another of the guards now approached, making a half-hearted attempt to grab her stick, earning him a remonstrating brush with the gaily-coloured tassels and a ragged cheer from the watching children in turn.

Anya kept tickling, her body engaged on the task in hand, her mind now working overtime.

Masters returned to his office some thirty minutes after extracting the information he'd been seeking in his trademark way from the well-meaning and charitably-minded Joaquin, who wouldn't be quite so well-meaning or charitably-minded from that point on.

Then Masters opened up an email, marked at the highest level of priority from his opposite number in the Protection Unit and which seemed to have something to do with a badly traumatised young woman.

And then, as he read on and like Ros and Conor before him, Masters just stared at the screen.

Then Masters remained hunched over his monitor, those past demons now circling ever closer it seemed.

I N THE NINETEENTH century Cardiff was one of the UK's three major ports, rubbing shoulders, metaphorically speaking at least, with Liverpool and London. At the same time – three clearly being the magic number back then – the Norwegian merchant fleet was also the third largest in the world.

The area around the docks at the time, the old Tiger Bay, made sure it serviced the physical needs of its visiting seamen from Norway in the time-honoured manner as a vibrant red-light district ushered itself into existence. But the spiritual needs of those same servicemen were also serviced by an organisation called the Norwegian Church Abroad, part of the Church of Norway. They built a dedicated place of worship in 1868 on land between the East and West Docks donated by a local benefactor, the Marquis of Bute.

But then trade in the docks declined. Shipping began to abandon Cardiff as a destination of choice, not only as other ports vied for its business but as other forms of transport such as air freight came to the fore, at which point it seemed the building would suffer a sad and lingering fall into inevitable ruin.

But the local community determined otherwise. They formed a trust and, in collaboration with a Norwegian support group in Bergen, raised a quarter of a million pounds for its preservation. With that money, the church was dismantled and stored with all its remaining original features preserved, including the pulpit and central chandelier.

Then came the acquisitive Eighties and land reclamation became the new buzzword. And as the old Isle of Dogs, one hundred and fifty miles or so to the east, fast became the new Canary Wharf, so the old docks in Cardiff was similarly reborn.

With money now positively washing through the formerly blasted wasteland, reassembly of the old church began in a new location, but this time with some modern-day additions. An art gallery was included in an attempt to make the new venture pay its way as was a coffee shop, which was where Ros accosted Jukes the very next morning.

The file passed on by Conor hadn't given Ros too many sweet dreams. And by the look on Jukes's face that morning it hadn't exactly wafted her immediate senior officer into an undisturbed slumber either. And while Ros hadn't received too many answers to her previous questions, it didn't mean she wasn't going to ask some new ones.

'So first, we have a copycat killing.'

Jukes, currently enjoying – or trying to enjoy – his breakfast, eyed Ros heavily.

'Every detail of the modern-day re-creation is arranged to match the original.'

Jukes kept eyeing her, his appetite fading fast.

'A few days ago, we take in the victim of a totally different and, in one sense, even sicker crime. There appears to be no link between the two and no reason to suspect one.'

Ros stared at Jukes.

'But what do we find?'

Jukes remained silent but Ros could see it in his eyes. It was only too obvious that exactly the same questions, concerns and doubts were assailing him right now too.

'Our new witness, Kim, the victim of one of the sickest head-fucks it's possible to imagine and whose head is now probably permanently fucked as a result, is closely related to our first young witness, Kezia, whose head is now probably also permanently fucked by stumbling across that copy-cat killing.'

Ros nodded down at the file on her lap and the note in that file highlighted by Conor, Ros still as rocked by all this as she was the previous evening.

Their new charge, Kim, had previously been married to the new murder victim, Roman Edwards.

Their other new charge, Kezia, was Kim's stepdaughter.

Jukes tried to maintain his usual poker face but it was being held in place by duct tape. Outside, a water taxi, pulling up opposite, was now discharging day-trippers and the occasional commuter onto the unmarked terminus, some heading across the Bay, some heading for the converted church itself and Jukes tried to interest himself in them, failing miserably.

Ros kept staring at him all the while.

'So we've not only got one sick murder and another equally sick head-fuck. It's the same family that's been targeted in both.'

Ros should have paused as the waitress, a bustling, fussy woman in her fifties now approached, setting down a coffee, a tea and a tray of biscuits that hadn't been requested.

But she didn't.

'We've now got two clients in the programme.'

Jukes shot a warning glance at her but Ros was beyond such simple warnings now.

'And we're still no nearer finding out what the fuck's going on here or what we're up against.'

Jukes nodded at the startled waitress who didn't need a second invitation to melt away.

'Or at least I'm not.'

Jukes just maintained his trademark silence.

Leon was bored. There was no other way of putting it. And not only was he bored, Leon was irritated too. So far as he could see his handlers seemed to have run out of ideas.

How else do you explain this latest waste of time?

Leon just about understood why he had to leave his new life in Amsterdam. But it was a reluctant acceptance. It was the second time he'd had to take flight from a former home in under a decade and no more welcome the second time round than the first.

Leon looked out of the window as he shifted on the rear seat of the unmarked police car. But what was the point of this new interview? And after this one, what then? Would there be another and then another? Was this going to happen on a daily basis from now on, was he going to be seated in front of the same old officers to answer the same old questions over and over again? What purpose was that going to serve?

He'd said as much to the copper called Hendrix the previous evening when he'd called him on the untraceable mobile he'd been given to tell him he'd be collected that morning. But Hendrix hadn't replied. Partly, as Leon suspected, that was because Hendrix had been told not to engage with him too openly. Mainly, as Leon also suspected, it was because Hendrix didn't have a clue what was actually happening here either.

And the driver of the unmarked car quite clearly didn't know anything, so there was little point in asking him.

So all Leon could do was settle back in his seat and wait for journey's end.

Meanwhile, Hendrix himself arranged two high-backed chairs, one placed opposite the other on either side of a small desk. Then he checked the tape machine was working. Then he checked his watch. Just ten minutes before the man for whom all these preparations were being made would arrive.

The man who'd actually be conducting the upcoming interview wasn't there as yet.

Hendrix just assumed that Masters was preparing for it all somewhere close by.

'Let's make a start, shall we?'

Masters smiled, quickly, at Leon. Then he nodded behind them both, a silent signal directed towards a figure that couldn't be seen.

And now Leon was fast becoming rather more disturbed than bored.

Nothing about this new interview was as Leon expected. For a start it wasn't taking place in an interview room or indeed in any sort of police station at all. A few moments earlier, the driver of the unmarked car had deposited Leon on a pavement outside what was quite clearly a derelict building. Masters had been waiting and had offered only the barest of nods as a greeting before opening a door half-hidden in a wall before ushering Leon inside.

Picking their way over fallen pieces of masonry and the occasional piece of rotten plasterboard, they'd made their way into what had once obviously been a rather ornate, if small, cinema. Little remained of the original interior save for a few rows of seats at the front, their upholstery ruptured, foam spilling out from inside like uncoiled intestines, but before them was a decayed, but still-functioning, screen.

As Leon was about to discover.

Light struggled to illuminate the interior as wooden boards had been hammered in place over the original windows, only pencil beams of brightness illuminating the general gloom. Motes of dust flickered everywhere.

Leon stared at Masters but then, suddenly, the screen in front of them stuttered, then pulsed, into life.

Previously he'd hardly taken it in. When the screen was dark it had merged in with the blackness all around the rest of the auditorium, but now it had illuminated, albeit with just a diffused bank of light at present, it dominated everything, making it virtually impossible to tear one's eyes away.

Which, as Leon was also to discover, was rather the point.

For his part, Masters hadn't viewed the images that were about to appear in their entirety. He'd given a copy of the tape to a particularly strong-stomached techie in a local post-production facility. The images had been edited down into what that same techie had termed a Greatest Hits version, a sally Masters hadn't even dignified with a response.

The techie in question was also the restorer of the old cinema in which they were currently encamped and was, at present, feeding that tape into a large, old-fashioned projector.

The idea for this most unusual of interviews had come to Masters – as had most of his best ideas – at his regular weekly retreat. Every Tuesday evening Masters attended a local chess club. He'd first become interested in the ancient game courtesy of a frustrated Grandmaster in his old school who'd never made the grade professionally and had turned to earning his crust as a maths teacher. Masters had been something of a protégé at one time and the failed Grandmaster in question had once harboured hopes of fulfilling his own destiny via his promising pupil.

But then Masters discovered something much more interesting to occupy him, namely the criminal mind. For a short period it was a close-run thing whether Masters would spend his life studying the phenomena or embracing it, but then he joined his local police force.

The police gained an unconventional, if brilliant, recruit. The criminal world lost something of a potential legend.

The chess club was composed of a ragbag collection of life's casualties, all of whom shared a keen interest not only in the Four Knights Game and the King's Indian Defence, but also in any burning matter of the moment and were only too ready to debate the same.

As they had done the previous evening when Masters had initiated a very particular discussion knowing he had this interview the following day.

Leon stared at the screen and, for the first few moments and up on the screen anyway, it was now much as he'd expected.

First, he saw that room again, that totally nondescript room which made all that had happened there all the more horrifying somehow. If it had been some sort of torture chamber or some kind of dungeon then there might have been some sort of emotional preparation for all that had taken place inside.

Once again, and courtesy of the scenes-of-crime photographer who must have had to force himself to focus on the horror of all he was filming, Leon saw the blood on the walls and then the corpse, almost unrecognisable as either male or female, lying on the bed. Then he saw again the second figure on the floor.

But these were all images he'd seen before. The same images he'd stared at in that Amsterdam coffee house. He hadn't understood the reason for that viewing and, for the life of him, couldn't understand the point of this one either or why the hell it was taking place in these strangest of surroundings.

But then, suddenly, there was a different image. Now he was in a completely different room, a much smaller room and unlike the image it had just replaced, the image he was viewing now was pin-sharp, the camera rock-steady, meaning it was presumably on some sort of stand.

Leon looked across at Masters, now seated beside him on another of the ruptured chairs.

'What's this?'

Masters didn't reply, just nodded behind him once again towards the still-unseen projectionist. And now sound faded up as well, although Leon couldn't make out what he was actually hearing at first.

Then he realised it was breathing, although he couldn't work out where it was coming from. All he could see was a small baby, strapped in some kind of buggy. The baby seemed to be sleeping and no-one else seemed to be in the room.

But then the breathing sounded louder and now it was more ragged and urgent. For a moment Leon wondered if it had been added on in some kind of edit. But then the camera changed angle slightly and a pair of eyes filled the screen, a woman's eyes, nothing else.

Masters started speaking.

'The images are time and date stamped. As you'll see, we're accelerating them, combining timescales, merging one hour into the next, one day into the following. In truth, there's not a lot of development in story terms anyway so I think a little dramatic licence is permitted, don't you?'

Leon stared back at Masters, more and more lost. What the fuck was he talking about? But Masters was now leaning forward as if to inspect the pictures up on the screen more closely, although those images were already dominating the whole of that ruined auditorium anyway, almost seeming to suck the air out of the surrounding walls.

Leon's unwilling eyes looked, reluctantly, back at the screen. Then he realised that – and presumably courtesy of the time lapse – the infant's cheeks were now more sunken, his eyes more hollow, his nearly inaudible breathing also more shallow than it had been even just a few moments before.

'Is he ill?'

Leon stared, uncomprehending, up at the screen. Why was he being shown images of a clearly poorly baby for fuck's sake?

'He's dying.'

Not strictly true of course, as Masters reflected, but in the circumstances he felt a little further dramatic licence was justified.

Anyway, the images currently before them had certainly fooled the mother. And from the look on his face they seemed to be fooling Leon now too.

'From this point to the end was something like two days in real time. We've rather conflated events as I said, but to capture all the key moments in the deterioration you're about to witness, we're still looking at roughly another hour or so. It's difficult to know which is worse, to watch the whole thing in real time as the mother was forced to do or to view these edited lowlights as I suppose you'd have to call them.'

Then Masters paused, looked sideways at his charge who wasn't looking at him now.

Leon was simply staring at all that was taking place up on that screen.

The experiment had first been conducted in Princeton, as Masters had explained to his chess club the previous evening. A carefully selected cross-section of volunteers had each been shown an image. The image was of a woman falling from a high building, her arms outstretched, her legs splayed, hands frantically scrabbling for a grip that would now quite clearly be denied her.

It was unclear from the simple, if shocking, image alone whether the woman had been pushed or was committing suicide. But that wasn't actually the point. The point was that while most who viewed the image fixed, naturally enough, on the woman herself, a significant number inserted other images into their later recollection of it all.

But why would they do that, Masters had wondered to

his regular companions? That image on its own had to be striking enough. Why add to or embellish it? And why insert images that weren't even there?

The answer, so the instigators of the Princeton experiment believed, was simple. Because they wanted to transform the image into something more palatable to the eye. Something easier to absorb. So they focused on a person in a nearby doorway or a sign above a coffee shop or a passing taxi. Or they inserted other images entirely, a man walking a dog, a police officer directing traffic, neither of whom was present in the original picture.

A significant proportion of the participants, in other words, had become adept, either consciously or unconsciously, in filtering out images they simply didn't want to see, transforming the image between sight and memory, creating a sort of visual defence mechanism along the way.

But Masters had always relished breaking down defences.

'Does the brain get used to the images over time?'

Masters patrolled the ruined auditorium in front of a still-staring Leon.

'It didn't for the mother, of course, we know that, she's well and truly lost all reason now, but for the dispassionate observer?'

Outside that auditorium all now seemed completely silent, Leon suddenly realised. All the usual human, and occasionally sub-human, traffic passing out on the street seemed to have faded below consciousness. Nothing existed. Just this decayed former pleasure palace with its still-functioning screen playing out, or so Leon believed, the last few moments in the life of a murdered innocent.

'Is it the same process that operates, as some allege, with

hard-core pornography? The more extreme examples one views, the more inured one becomes to it all?'

Leon, unwilling eyes still fixed on the screen, cut across.

'Turn it off.'

Masters didn't even seem to hear him.

'Meaning you need even more extreme images the next time round to produce the same sort of thrill?'

Leon stood, made for the door behind. He probably knew it would be locked, but he yanked down on the handle anyway. It didn't give a millimetre.

That much he half-expected. What he didn't expect was the pair of strong hands that now grabbed him by the shoulders and spun him round so he was staring into the most chilling pair of eyes he'd ever seen, eyes that seemed to have seen everything, done everything, eyes that would do so again.

'All that young woman sees when she looks into anyone's eyes right now is her baby. He's all she watched for days, the most precious life she'll ever know slipping away in front of her and that image is imprinted now.'

On the screen behind Masters, the small child seemed to be sinking fast. Dates and times flashed across the screen, time ticking down much in the manner of a referee intoning a count over a fallen boxer.

'Now comes what might be called a refinement, although most reasonably-minded onlookers would probably term it an abomination.'

On the screen, the camera suddenly shifted and the young mother finally came more into focus. Her body was still immobile, her limbs frozen in what seemed to be some kind of locked-in torment. But her mind was still active because those eyes never stopped moving, flashing from side to side inside their sockets, pupils dilated in a terror that was all the more powerful as it wasn't accompanied by the scream that was only too obviously reverberating inside her head.

By the locked door, Leon, still in the same frozen state, waited for the camera to shift once more, for the baby to once again fill the screen, but the camera remained on the mother, on her wildly staring eyes and, a moment later, as the angle widened and more and more of her face became visible, Leon began to understand why.

Masters continued, ignoring Leon's eyes which were widening all the while now in turn.

'I've been taking some soundings amongst those rather more expert in these matters than myself, and the consensus is that this next shot is something of a masterstroke. In fact if this were a film, the general feeling is it would merit serious consideration for some sort of award for cinematography because the camera operator, whoever he or she might be, really has captured a most arresting image.'

On-screen that image was still pin-sharp, the only soundtrack the accompanying adult's breathing now sounding louder all the while.

'The death of an infant reflected all the while in a mother's eyes.'

A totally rocked Leon kept staring up at the screen as Masters's words, almost-honeyed now in their soft seduction, maintained their mendacious trickle.

'Perhaps a wider audience had already tuned in by now. The orchestrator of this particular homage to hell might have circulated details of it on some website set up specifically for that one purpose and closed down immediately afterwards. But if there was a wider audience, if that was the point of all this, we don't know and probably never will.'

Masters paused.

'We do know one member of that audience though.'

Right on cue a small window opened at the bottom of the screen. Now, incongruously, Leon was watching a small group of men in some other room altogether, the walls painted a functional grey, most of the men dressed in overalls, some hard hats lying on a few tables to their side.

Masters nodded at one staring face in amongst all the others.

'The father's the figure in the centre of the secondary screen. He'd tuned in to video-link with his partner, to say hello to his child and in doing so he'd set up the sort of two-way communication you see day-in, day-out via the likes of Skype. Meaning that for the final moments of this bizarre entertainment its instigator had assembled a particularly macabre framing device, two souls, both helpless in their own way, witnessing the end of a life they'd jointly created.'

Masters kept his eyes fixed on Leon.

'And you know her? Don't you, Leon?'

And suddenly, as he kept talking and as more and more of Kim's face was revealed to the trapped and staring Leon, Masters could see it.

Leon hadn't shifted position, all his attention still seemingly concentrated on the screen in front of them, but something had changed inside and that was nothing to do with the mayhem erupting in one small corner of the screen as a father disintegrated into emotional overload, and it was nothing to do with the single eyeball that now dominated the main screen, tears pooling inside, a mother in the most intense kind of mourning.

Something else was happening inside Leon.

Leon was starting to crack.

An evermore frustrated Ros had left minutes before.

Jukes remained, still looking out over the water.

Jukes did sympathise with Ros in a sense. If he'd been in

her position and was in possession of just the small amount of information that she'd been blessed or cursed with, depending on one's point of view, he'd probably have felt exactly the same.

He'd actually rather liked to have told her exactly what she wanted to know. But he couldn't. He couldn't tell Ros – and especially Ros – anything about it.

Jukes couldn't tell anyone in fact and he knew Masters felt exactly the same. So Jukes could only hope the interview he'd just sanctioned – an interview Ros knew nothing about and which he assumed Masters was conducting right now – would provide some sort of breakthrough.

For all their sakes.

'He came to see me.'

'Who did?'

A gasping Leon wasn't wasting time in any more denials and not just because Masters was rapidly cleaning him out, drilling down ever deeper into all he'd been trying to conceal, but because relief was starting to wash over him now too.

Relief at finally getting all this out in the open. Or at least part of it. Handing on the baton to hopefully-wiser souls who could maybe make sense of it all, because he hadn't even been able to start.

'Roman.'

'A man you'd told us you'd had no contact with, had no idea where he lived or what he was doing.'

Leon nodded, uncaring, past all that now.

'He said he needed money. He said something about some deal going wrong, I didn't know what, I wasn't really listening. It was totally out of order, him contacting me like that. How had he got hold of me for one thing, no-one was supposed to know where I was, you know that, absolutely fucking no-one.'

Briefly, Leon stared, belligerently, back at Masters who didn't reply, just extracted a slim DVD from a bag before him before sliding it across.

Leon looked at it, his heart sinking as he did so.

Masters had just handed him one of his own DVDs. The offering in question was never going to achieve anything like wide circulation, but it had still sold reasonably respectably. On the cover were some of the amateur performers Leon had indulged in their more or less sad little fantasies in his previous life in Amsterdam. And, in the background, small but clearly visible, was a headshot of Leon himself, the indulgent facilitator.

Leon kept looking at the DVD cover, Masters's point all too clear. Given the business he'd established in his new life on the Continent, there were plenty of ways an interested party from his old life could have traced him. Especially one as determined as Roman.

'What did you say to him?'

Leon tore reluctant eyes away from the self-incriminating DVD and focused back on Masters.

'I told him to fuck off.'

'And he did?'

Masters eyed him.

'He just nodded, wished you well, told you to look him up the next time you were back in town and caught the next flight home?'

Leon struggled.

'Not exactly.'

Masters kept eyeing him, grim.

Somehow he didn't think so.

'He started making all these threats, said he could make things difficult for me, really difficult, that there was someone out there, someone who knew what had happened, someone who would be really interested to know where I was now and what I was doing, someone I really wouldn't want taking any sort of interest in me at all.'

Masters stared at him, intent, getting closer all the while now to the real matter of the moment.

Someone?

'Who?'

But Leon just shook his head, helpless.

'I just thought he was pissing in the wind. He'd had a lucky break, had traced me somehow and spotted a chance to make some easy money. He wouldn't even tell me who this new face was for fuck's sake and I thought there was a good reason for that too, because there wasn't one, because it was all just one great big fucking con.'

Masters opened the file on his lap again, slid a large, full-colour, close-up of the dead Roman across to him.

'But someone did know.'

Leon stared down again at the grotesque image.

'Didn't they?'

And this time Leon didn't flinch as he stared at the image again.

'Someone knew exactly what had happened and that same someone knew exactly how it happened as well and we can't rule out the possibility that someone knew why. Until we know who this someone is, we're really not going to know for sure are we?'

An anguished Leon cut across again.

'I thought it was just a fucking scam. There wasn't anyone left, you know that, there was just the two of us, just me and Roman.'

Involuntarily, Leon's eyes flickered down to the image of his former and now-fallen companion again, the expression on his face saying it all.

A few days ago there were two.

Leon kept looking at the still photo of the dead Roman.

Now there was one.

And now Leon felt as if his heart was going to burst out of his ribcage it was pounding so much.

'What is all this? What's happening? For fuck's sake, you saw what – .'

Then Leon stopped, abrupt.

Masters eyed him.

'I saw, what?'

Masters leant closer.

'I saw what happened to Roman, yes, I certainly saw that. But you were about to say something else, weren't you Leon?'

Leon didn't reply as Masters repeated Leon's last, half-completed sentence, Leon's words cut short.

'You saw – what. That's what you said. You saw what – and then you stopped. So what were you going to say? I saw what he did to him? What she did to him? What they did to him?'

Then Masters fairly spat in Leon's face.

'What else aren't you telling me, Leon?'

Masters spat at him again, great globs of spittle now splattering him.

'What else is hidden away inside that twisted fucking apology of a mind of yours?'

But Leon just kept staring back, Masters's spittle mixing now with his own sweat, making his face glow, translucent.

After leaving Jukes, Ros had returned to her apartment. With the Kim and Kezia case files in hand she'd gone out onto the balcony of her small apartment where she'd remained for the next two hours. But it wasn't going to make any difference. She could have stayed there for the next two days and it wouldn't unlock anything. Her deliberate attempt to empty her mind of everything, to let her unconscious roam, unfettered and unshackled, wasn't going to produce any fresh insights into the two related cases that were totally consuming her right now; or answer the questions that were going round and round inside her head in the same never ending circle.

Who targeted Kim?

And why?

Who targeted Kezia?

And, again, why?

Leading to the single, biggest, question of all.

What the hell does Ros do now to make sure her two new, badly-damaged, witnesses aren't damaged any further?

One thing was now clear if nothing else. She wasn't going to be able to count on any help from either her immediate senior officer or his opposite number in Murder Squad when it came to supplying anything in the way of answers.

Ros stood, quit her balcony and let herself out of her apartment, heading out onto a bank following the line of the old restored waterway. A few joggers passed her as she passed, in turn, a couple of fishermen; then Ros slowed.

Up ahead another sole figure hovered. This figure wasn't clad in running gear and he wasn't a fisherman either. Something also told Ros he'd been waiting there for some time and that he'd have waited for some time to come as well.

Hendrix looked at Ros as she approached. For a moment neither spoke.

Hendrix had spent the last few hours in a police interview room waiting for an interview that was never going to take place, but he didn't tell Ros that. He could have taken it up with Masters, but he wasn't going to do that either. He wasn't that self-deluded or that much of a masochist.

Hendrix just looked out over the water instead, then back at the motionless Ros. Then he started speaking. And for a moment it was like listening to the voice that had been sounding inside Ros's own head for the last few days.

'What if that had been the whole point?'

Ros looked back at him.

'What if Kezia had been meant to find her father's body? Just like Donna all those years before?'

Hendrix looked back at her.

'What if it had all been planned that way?'

Ros just kept looking back at him.

Masters left the cinema and settled himself back on the white leather seat of his Bentley, Leon dismissed, someone else in Masters's mind now.

Someone maybe better equipped to provide what he needed more than anything, and what Jukes was also praying for right now too.

That breakthrough.

Some answers to a totally unexpected – and unwanted – puzzle.

Masters shifted slightly in his seat, his eyes alighting again on the in-car phone fitted to the side of the dashboard.

Masters paused a moment as he computed options, pondered possibilities.

Then he reached out and picked up the handset.

14.

O N THE FRIDAY night following the fracking demo, Anya loaded a small van with a couple of spades, a Kaiser blade, a pair of secateurs and two pairs of shears. By their side she stacked some compost and a couple of bags of fertiliser.

It was a well-rehearsed routine. The job she was about to undertake was also a regular engagement, involving the clearing of leaves and other fallen debris from the garden of a large house some thirty or so miles away, although this time she'd also been asked to dig out an old flowerbed that had apparently gone to seed.

This time too, Anya was taking another member of the activist group to help out. It was an offer of part-time work that had been gratefully accepted, its recipient unaware it was all part of the usual tradecraft. The more members of Anya's new group who witnessed her at her work, the more likely they would be to trust her.

Anya and her new helper met the elderly owner of the large house and indulgently endured her rambling recollections of living there as a small child before the Second World War. Then her new helper worked alongside Anya, enthusiastically at first, increasingly less so as the backbreaking day had worn on until, to her companion's clear relief, Anya had told her it was time to pack up.

Anya had loaded her implements back in her van, reasonably confident that companion wouldn't volunteer for another shift too quickly.

Meanwhile, and after watching her two visitors leave and waving after them all the way down the winding drive, the old lady in question locked up the rambling old house that hadn't actually been lived in for the last thirty years and returned to her own small semi-detached house where she reflected, with warm satisfaction, on her enduring ability to play some sort of role for her former and still-beloved employers.

That crumbling old ruin didn't quite match the glamour of some of the more exotic postings she'd journeyed to in the past, but when the call came, as it had done the previous evening, she liked to think she could still play her part.

But as the old lady settled in front of her TV for the evening she, briefly, wondered. Despite a whole day floating in and out of their company as she brought them drinks and sandwiches, she still had absolutely no idea which of the two women she'd entertained that day had actually been one of their own.

Which was obviously a very good thing. Because if the young woman in question could fool someone with as many years experience as herself, then the outfit to which she'd dedicated her former working life really did seem to be in safe hands.

Two hours later, after Anya had finished her backbreaking shift and with the old lady long settled back in her cosy house with a cup of hot chocolate and her equally cosy memories, Anya had swung her small van back in through the gates after dropping her exhausted companion off at their squat.

The true professional, to the tips of her muddied fingertips, she'd spent the intervening period unpacking her implements and the next hour cleaning and oiling them. Then she'd returned to the large, rambling house to retrieve the set of secateurs her apologetic part-time companion seemed to have left behind.

The secateurs had been a subterfuge, misplaced by Anya herself, just in case anyone from the group checked up on her. Given the man she was about to meet, it was never, ever, a good idea to become complacent.

Anya pulled up on the drive, and made for a locked garden shed at the end of the lawn. She used the key given to her by the kindly old lady to open the door before closing it behind her.

Then Anya turned to face Masters who hadn't wasted any time. Partly that was down to a natural reluctance to spend any longer than was absolutely necessary in close proximity to garden refuse. The nearest Masters ever wanted to get to any sort of countryside was looking down on a small patch of Green Park from the lofty heights of his sixth-floor weekend retreat in upmarket St James.

But mainly, and as Anya was about to discover, it was because they had little time to lose.

'We need to get you out.'

Anya nodded, prompt, eager even. She'd been expecting this ever since she joined the department; would indeed have been disappointed had this call to arms not come. She always knew that at some time she'd have to execute an exit strategy from the group she'd spent the last year or so infiltrating, and it really wasn't going to present too much of a problem.

As part of her ongoing cover, she'd already absented herself on numerous occasions in the past, apparently to visit an old and sick mother. Another elderly lady had been provided to play the part, just in case any of her new friends in her new life should decide to accompany her on one of those visits. So if her old Mum died and she went off to sort out her affairs, that shouldn't strike anyone as peculiar.

Swiftly, Anya and Masters ran through the pre-arranged timescale, honing the fine details until both were satisfied, including when and where she'd receive the phone call, how long she'd need to clear up any outstanding matters, both work and personal. Then Anya looked at him again, this time even more eagerly.

So much for the past. Now for the future and, as she thought about it, Anya felt a delicious thrill begin deep inside. Something in Masters's tone and manner was telling Anya this – whatever this was – was going to be big.

And she was right.

Anya's next assignment was going to be different to anything anyone had ever attempted before.

Swiftly again, partly because the refuse stacked around the shed really was now beginning to ripen, but mainly because this was the most dangerous part of any operation – the few necessary moments when a mark in the field was in contact with their handler – Masters ran through the main points of Anya's new mission.

Up to now the name of Anya's game had been infiltration. But what Anya was about to do was more than that. Masters didn't quite know what to call it, although no description would ever be applied to it anyway as no record of any of it would ever exist.

If pressed, then Masters supposed insinuation might be a rather more accurate term to employ. And, when Anya heard some of the details of her new assignment, she could see exactly what Masters meant.

But there was a complication which again wasn't unusual. Each and every case threw up its own challenges and dangers. But this was going to be more than usually challenging and dangerous.

It sounded like an oxymoron, but the complication was simple. The exit strategy. What could they put in place in this case? Put simply, once in, how the hell would Anya get out? Subterfuges, such as the one they were about to execute involving the death of a much-loved mother, were hardly going to be fit for purpose here.

And it wasn't just the personal danger posed to Anya. Unless they handled all this carefully there was a real danger of it blowing up in their faces and that, as Masters made clear, could never be allowed to happen. It wasn't just the fate of an individual officer that was at stake here.

Anya waited, but Masters didn't say any more. In strict contrast to all their previous meetings, no further explanation followed. This time, Masters simply departed as quickly as he'd arrived.

Leaving Anya to work out her exit strategy for herself.

One hour later, Anya returned to her squat. For the next couple of days, while her mind wrestled her new challenge in the future, she worked on more fine details of her exit strategy in the present. What they had was adequate but Anya, being Anya, wanted more.

To supplement her earnings in the difficult winter months, Anya worked part-time in a local garden centre, helping out on the tills as well as doing odd-jobs and general maintenance. Anya had complained loudly and volubly in the past at the poor pay and the long hours. She'd strayed, dangerously close, to being sacked on more than one occasion but over the next couple of days the patience of the long-suffering manager snapped and Anya was out.

That came as little surprise to her companions back in the squat. The only surprise was that it hadn't happened sooner. But what happened next was rather more disquieting.

A day later, Anya received the pre-arranged phone call about her mother. Consummate actress that she was, she played her response to perfection. Anya went quiet, very quiet. A few friends tried to offer words of comfort but Anya didn't even seem to register they were there. She just went out into the night to be alone, so they assumed, with her grief. She returned a couple of hours later with her van full of various high-value items all stolen from her now-former employer.

As well as the various garden tools and implements, Anya's haul included the most expensive item the garden centre had ever stocked, a life-size bronze fox retailing at just under a thousand pounds.

Before her astonished companions could do or say very much, Anya was on the phone to a mutual contact who'd helped them out in the past. An hour or so later the items in question had been moved on in exchange for a pay-out that Anya immediately donated to the movement. Two hours later still, and a good hour or so before the long-suffering manager of the garden centre would open up for the day and discover they'd suffered a break-in, Anya was gone.

It might have seemed madness to most, but to Anya's companions in the squat it was curiously understandable. Anya had always been wilful, headstrong even. It didn't come as any sort of surprise to anyone that the combination of the bad news from the nursing home and her recent sacking seemed to have tipped her over the edge.

It was all part of the same meticulously-planned deception of course. At one and the same time Anya had set up yet another reason to leave the group and put in place a further reason why she could never return. When the manager of the garden centre reported the thefts to the police, the prime suspect had to be the employee he'd sacked just a day or so previously, a disgruntled employee who would certainly know her way around the fairly primitive security system they employed.

It was all part of the same lesson which had been drummed into them from the start too. Getting out – and getting out properly – was at least as important as getting in. Having won the confidence of a group of activists, it was essential that confidence wasn't shattered by an over-clumsy withdrawal. Suspicion breeds and spreads and it wouldn't just infect

Anya's own group but others. So it was essential that Anya's new comrades in the movement continued to believe, totally, in the credibility of her alter ego.

Meanwhile, and making sure the gesture could not be traced back to him and his department, Masters reimbursed the garden centre for its stolen stock.

But all the time she worked on and then executed one exit strategy, all that dominated Anya's thinking was another. Anya crossed the Channel, drove down through France to enjoy some Spanish sun, then back into Italy, thinking all the time.

Anya checked into a converted monastery on the Adriatic coast. The building towered over an ancient town to one side and the wide expanse of the sea on the other. The former monastery, now a cheap hotel, played host to a church which was still packed each Sunday as townspeople struggled their way up the steep path from the town below to worship.

Anya watched a family dressed in what would be called their Sunday best back in the UK. The family in question, like most in the town, were of the extended variety; a mother, father, children, grandparents, an elderly aunt or two.

From her small window across the courtyard, Anya watched them head into the church and, an hour or so later, emerge again into the blazing sunlight, pausing to talk to other worshippers before making their way back down the hill again.

And, all of a sudden, Anya had it. All of a sudden it was as if someone had laid it all out before her.

Suddenly she knew exactly what she had to do.

At lunchtime the next day, Anya made a call from a public phone box down on the quayside in the old town. Behind her was a small restaurant which was hosting a conference of academics from the UK. Anya, tradecraft honed as ever, had checked out each and every one of them as she heard the familiar accents. Not one familiar face hove into view.

Anya's call was short and to the point.

Masters didn't waste any words either.

A day later Anya queued along with delegates from the same conference who all hurried across the tarmac to a waiting budget flight once the boarding signal illuminated. Anya let them speed ahead. They were all going to arrive at the same time anyway.

Anya landed in the UK a few hours later. Carrying only hand luggage she caught the shuttle into London and then a train on to a halt in the Cotswolds. She took a taxi to a small hotel that boasted private, cottage-style, accommodation to the rear of the main building, complete with its own rear garden that opened onto a quiet lane.

Anya made her way inside in the middle of the afternoon when the picture-postcard village was bustling with tourists, making her arrival as anonymous as possible. An amateur would have made an entrance in the early hours at a time when the rest of the village was still asleep. Only one pair of eyes might have seen her but that person would have wondered about that visitor for the rest of the day.

Once again, Anya didn't waste any time. Quickly and clearly she laid out all she'd been working on as far as her new exit strategy was concerned.

Masters didn't say a word throughout the whole exchange. They'd scarcely even exchanged a simple greeting. And then, when Anya finished, he just looked at her for a moment that seemed to stretch time.

Momentarily, Anya wondered if she'd overplayed her hand, but that wasn't the reason for Masters's sudden and uncharacteristic silence. Masters was silent because he simply couldn't speak. And he couldn't speak because, and not for the first or last time, his new protégée had quite simply taken his breath away.

In a career that had seen Masters pull a few white-hot strokes himself, this was volcanic even for him.

Masters had run a few good operatives in the past. He'd run a few stellar operatives indeed such as Jack Ryan, the tattooed skinhead with the Union Jack-bedecked boots. But Anya had just taken this into a different league. Even the likes of legendary luminaries like Jack Ryan were well and truly going to fade into forgotten folklore once this operative's future exploits began circulating around the department's grapevine.

Not that Masters said any of that of course. Masters just nodded, a silent acknowledgement of approval, then handed Anya a file.

Anya extracted various documents and photographs. She turned one over in particular and looked at a headshot of a man. He didn't exactly boast film star looks but there was very definitely something about the eyes as he stared back at the camera.

Then Anya turned the photo over and read the name on the other side, looking back at the man himself again a moment later.

She'd never met a Leon before.

MACKLYN WAS, OF course, a grown man with all the usual, associated, freedoms.

The right to go where he wanted, whenever he wanted and to see whomsoever he wished – time, money and inclination permitting.

And, in his case, certain legal constraints.

Occasionally Ros did wonder what her father did with his free time, but for most of the year it wasn't really an issue. Because, and after a period of considerable and enforced idleness, Macklyn had retrained some years before and now held a post as a primary school teacher.

It had all been arranged easily enough. His references and past employment history, all immaculately prepared by a unit much like Ros's, ensured there were no puzzling gaps in his past to give any head teacher or board of governors cause for concern. So as far as his new employers were concerned, Macklyn had previously been employed as a minor civil servant who'd spent thirty or so fairly unremarkable years toiling in local government. A succession of spending cuts had left him redundant at an age too young to happily contemplate retirement. The chance sighting of a notice on the wall of a local library had alerted him to a shortage of male applicants for primary school teaching posts and he'd applied.

That chance sighting of the notice on the library wall was actually true. Which was usual. The protection officers who'd constructed the fiction that was now Macklyn tried, as did all similar protection officers, to retain some fact in amongst the invention. The closer a resemblance that 'legend' – to use the official phrase – bore to an actual life, the easier it was to memorise and the more convincing it always then sounded in the retelling.

As for the rest, they had little choice but to invent. What else could they have said? That, some years previously, Macklyn's eldest daughter had been killed in front of his youngest daughter and wife, her head almost literally removed from her shoulders by a gunshot in the hallway of their old home?

That it had all been a tragic mix-up, that she'd been mistaken for another of his daughters by an organisation hellbent on revenge against that daughter's new husband?

That in the almost literal blink of an eye, his life and the life of his family had gone from a reality they all knew and understood to something that only too quickly came to resemble an enduring nightmare?

Perhaps understandably that part of Macklyn's past had been excised from all but the most classified of official records.

But it had turned out to be a totally justifiable deception. Macklyn not only enjoyed his new job, he was good at it too. To his new colleagues he was always going to be something of a minor mystery admittedly; he didn't ever go along to the usual Friday night winding-down sessions in the local pub, for example. But for the most part he was as pleasant and equable with them as he was professional and adept in the classroom, so nobody was all that concerned about one small deficiency in the sociability stakes.

Much like Ros, his new colleagues didn't have much of an idea what he did during the holidays either. They probably imagined him pottering about in a small garden or on some local allotment somewhere. He'd made some vague reference in a staff meeting once to a collection of herbs of which he seemed rather proud, but had then fallen silent as if illogically embarrassed by the admission which was actually quite endearing.

Macklyn wasn't embarrassed at all of course. He was just frightened and had taken refuge in near-silence for the rest of the day in case he made a similar slip.

Because now and again he'd do it. He just couldn't help himself. From time to time he'd automatically refer back to the life he'd once lived. The herb collection to which he'd referred was indeed once his pride and joy, but that was at his old house, before the virtual decapitation of one of his daughters. But thankfully, just as in that instance, Macklyn usually caught himself before any real damage was done. Staying away from the pub on a Friday afternoon when, in reality, he'd have loved to join his colleagues was another sensible precaution.

If those new colleagues had discovered how he actually filled his free time they'd probably have been more amused than anything else. Because what Macklyn did was simple. It was what he was about to do that very day in fact, as he retrieved his grey mackintosh from a coat hook he'd sourced on the internet, a coat hook much like the one that used to hang on the inside door of his old office, before slipping out of his small house and getting into his nondescript saloon.

Macklyn travelled the country visiting a succession of destinations, although most of his fellow-travellers would regard them more as stopping-off points than anything else. Because Macklyn visited motorway service stations.

Macklyn still remembered the opening of virtually every one. The first of them had opened at the same time as he established his business and they were all Macklyn and most of his truckers were talking about back then.

They'd begun as a simple accident prevention measure of course. The civil servants of the day didn't want drivers just pulling up anywhere they chose on the new high-speed highways as if they were still on some country lane somewhere.

But if the new service stations began as a pragmatic response to a problem, the solution soon went far beyond the strictly practical, which was mainly due to those newly-issued franchises being taken up by genuine visionaries.

Design guru Terence Conran, no less, styled a fish restaurant at Leicester Forest East where waitresses in sailor suits sashayed amongst classic wooden furniture, while the newly-opened service station at Forton paid more than a nod to the burgeoning airline industry with its elevated views across the hills to Blackpool. The sundeck there famously, and in a sighting reported directly to Macklyn himself by one of his breathless drivers, once played host to the Beatles grabbing a quick cuppa after a local gig.

Trowell Services featured a mock-historical tableau based on Robin Hood and his Merry Men complete with fibreglass trees, jousting knights and an old oak banqueting hall, while at the other end of the taste scale, Membury paid homage to the Scandinavian Expressionists with its sweeping, corrugated-steel roof and wall-to-wall double glazing beneath its cavernous dining gallery.

Another notable designer, Patrick Gwynne, the genius behind the soon-to-be demolished Serpentine Restaurant in Hyde Park, conceived of his addition to the canon at Burtonwood as two copper spires that had apparently touched down on the bleak moorlands surrounding the Lancashire mill towns. But perhaps the most bizarrely wonderful creation of that whole period was at Washington-Birtley where motorists were invited to marvel at a fully-automated microwave kitchen service as they traded travellers' tales with a team of mini-skirted hostesses surfing effortlessly along psychedelic carpets.

In the early years of his new business Macklyn would visit them all as would most of his drivers, often within a day or so of their opening, helping rate each new offering in an unofficial league table compiled by his secretary back at the yard.

Macklyn also witnessed successive governments lose interest in the whole notion of providing facilities for motorists, mourning along with the rest of the yard as anonymous conglomerates moved in to reshape the original designs, and as innovation and flair were swept away, being replaced by wipe-clean surfaces more redolent of a budget café.

None encapsulated that depressing trend more than Farthing Corner which Sydney Clough had assembled in a style best described as sub-Festival of Britain, but which had been so remodified over the years that all its original design characteristics had been completely lost.

But long before that happened, Macklyn and his fellow-disciples had discovered a rather humbler, but just as appealing, attraction. A new breed of outlet sprang up which may only have been an old breed in new clothes, but it was a change of apparel that made all the difference.

Because just off those motorways, within a mile at the most of an exit if the vendor in question was particularly astute, variations on the old greasy spoons began to appear.

Sometimes they were housed in Portakabins, sometimes in renovated cottages, sometimes in snack bars literally bolted on to the side of garage workshops. One, in the Midlands, boasted a river running next to it, meaning that those so-inclined could pick up a takeaway from the counter and head out for an hour's fishing on the nearby bank or even unpack a small dinghy and chill out for a while on the water.

Another old favourite, sited just outside Bawtry, offered showers and an all-day carvery long before the larger chains jumped on that particular bandwagon.

But for Macklyn, the absolute ultimate stop was on one of the bleakest roads in the country, the much-feared Snake Pass between Manchester and Sheffield, often the first route to be closed by snow, turning the outlet into more of a refuge than a staging post. It had been run by two sisters for as long as Macklyn could remember, siblings who boasted the remarkable facility of remembering every trucker by name, meaning he'd never, in his life, ever step through that particular door again of course.

But Macklyn didn't need to actually head inside any of them. Just passing by would instantly soothe, if not totally alleviate, his otherwise ever-present migraines. Simply by staring out at them from his car window he felt as if he was ridding himself of everything he'd become and was somehow returning, full circle, to all he used to be.

But today he was making a visit to a new truck stop he'd come across by chance as he was driving up through mid-Wales, pulling out onto a small straight after a series of near-suicidal bends just north of Knighton. There used to be an old van parked up in the lay-by knocking out the regulation bacon baps and tea, but now there was a more permanent structure, painted dark green to blend in with the forest behind perhaps, along with an awning so any resting trucker could enjoy the occasional blast of sunshine.

Macklyn pulled up outside, making his usual mental note of the livery on the side of the two trucks also parked on the small concourse. He didn't recognise either of them.

Heading inside, he paused at the door, another reflex response, conducting a final check before venturing any further. Again, no familiar faces appeared before him, although even if there were he doubted there'd be many who'd recognise him. In the last twenty years Macklyn had changed greatly, and it wasn't just the years, as the old saying went, it was the mileage and there'd been plenty of that.

Macklyn moved up to the counter and ordered a tea from a

young girl, took a laminated menu from a display by the side of the till and moved across to a far table well away from the door or the front windows; habit imbued over the years again melding seamlessly into a now-automatic routine.

As he did so, Macklyn was completely unaware of the pair of eyes watching him all the while.

It had been a long time. A lot of water had flowed under all sorts of bridges since they'd last met. And as he glanced across, idly at first but then more intently, at the figure hesitating in the doorway he wondered, momentarily, if his memory was playing tricks on him.

If this actually was the man from all those decades before?

But as he studied him more closely, he became more sure. And something, some instinct or probably some much more venal impulse, was already telling him to keep his head down, to keep looking at the paper that was spread out on the table in front of him, to not pay the new arrival any undue notice in case he registered the attention, turned round and headed away again.

Because something – and again he didn't quite know what, perhaps that same instinct again – told him that's exactly what would happen if this particular visitor felt a pair of even mildly-curious eyes settle on him for even a fraction too long.

But then, as the new arrival somewhat tentatively crossed the floor to the counter, he had a second moment of doubt. Because there'd never been anything even remotely tentative about the man he remembered from all those years before. That man always seemed so sure and certain about everything. This modern-day version almost seemed to be apologising for being there, even for ordering a drink.

But with the new arrival's back now turned to him, Aidan,

the owner of those watching and hooded eyes, studied him more openly and as he did so he knew he was right.

It was him, he was sure it was.

Aidan would hardly be likely to forget him after all.

Macklyn seated himself at the table, rested his mug on the obligatory wipe-clean surface.

And, for a moment, he didn't look at the menu or at the paper left by the table's previous occupant, now heard outside in the small yard trying to coax his grumbling engine into life.

Macklyn just permitted himself another of his small but cherished rituals instead.

It only took a moment. If anyone noticed – the girl behind the counter, the odd fellow diner dotted around the functional but spotless room – they might imagine he was just resting his eyes after a long drive.

But Macklyn wasn't. He was closing his eyes to savour all the more intently the sensation of being in a place that felt like home.

A home he thought he'd said a permanent goodbye to a couple of decades before.

The past was also very much on Aidan's mind now too. Or, more accurately, one very specific moment from that past.

It had been one of the most extraordinary days of Aidan's life. He hadn't been working in Macklyn's transport yard long, although long enough to work out how he might execute the odd little scam. Nothing too spectacular and nothing, hopefully, that would excite too much interest from the powers-that-be or at least the sole and only power there was back then.

Aidan's fellow drivers had assured him that their boss had been round the block so many times there wasn't any sort of scam he didn't know about and, more importantly, wouldn't sniff out the moment any misguided employee might even daydream about carrying out.

But Aidan had always had a high opinion of himself. Or at least a curious faith that his sins would remain undetected. Looking back, it was a faith that had probably been forged that very day, which was why he was more inclined than most to remember the figure who'd just turned away from the counter, mug of tea in hand, before moving across to a far table overlooked by no other and far away from any window.

It had only been a small supplement to earnings that were on the generous side anyway. Macklyn treated his drivers well and Aidan hadn't really needed the money at all, but when a friend of a friend had mentioned some items that needed transporting, and when he realised that he had the means to do so if he simply invented some traffic problem that would delay his return to the depot by a couple of hours, the temptation was too much to resist.

It had actually taken a little longer than he'd planned. But none of the other drivers remarked on his absence when he returned, so he thought he'd got away with it.

But then there'd come the call to go and see the boss from that snooty secretary of his, the one who'd been with Macklyn ever since he'd started and who seemed to share her employer's near-telepathic power to sniff out something hidden.

Or maybe that was just his guilty conscience. Maybe she hadn't stared at him that fraction too long as she delivered the summons, but Aidan was instantly nervous.

And the way the rest of the drivers began humming the 'Funeral March' as he started walking towards the depot office didn't exactly soothe those nerves either.

Aidan wasn't aware of the car pulling up behind him as he approached the office door. All he was aware of were the pair of eyes he could now quite clearly see watching him every step of the way and they weren't the eyes of that snooty secretary either, they were the eyes of the boss.

Aidan moved on into the office, all his former confidence draining from him as Macklyn moved into the reception area and fixed him with the sort of stare that told Aidan, more eloquently than words could ever have managed, that he really was a dead man walking right now.

And then it happened.

Aidan couldn't exactly call it deliverance from above, given that it actually came from behind, but that's still how it felt. Like some sort of divine intervention. Because two men now came into the office and before anyone had time to do anything, even say anything almost, they frogmarched his now-staring boss back inside his office while Aidan was escorted into the snooty secretary's office along with the secretary herself who now didn't look snooty at all, who just looked scared.

And she looked even more so when the same two men reappeared a few moments later and escorted their boss towards the door and a waiting car to be driven away with the whole of his workforce now looking on.

Aidan still remembered the secretary asking one of the passing men when he'd be back, they had wages to make up, invoices to prepare and he well remembered also the curt response.

He won't be back.

Then the door slammed behind the three men, leaving Aidan and the snooty secretary and the rest of the workforce still staring after them.

Over the days and weeks that followed they quickly realised that all those tight-lipped visitors had said that day was true. Macklyn never came back. No-one in that yard ever heard from him again and no-one ever found out what had happened to him either.

A short time later the firm was wound up. Everyone who worked there received a generous settlement and Aidan shared in that pay out too after coming within a missed heartbeat of being sacked.

All of which put something of a spring in his step. And so, when he got his next job as caretaker at a private school and there'd been that inquiry, he'd looked to the skies again, drawn strength from the way he'd cheated what had seemed his certain fate once before and decided he could do so again.

And so he looked that headmaster and the rest of those governors full in the face and told them that the pupil was lying, that Aidan hadn't laid a finger on him and that if anyone even dared to repeat such a wounding allegation outside that room then he'd have absolutely no choice but to sue.

It hadn't been that difficult to bring off because Aidan had actually been quite genuinely outraged. He wasn't about to tell them but the boy in question had definitely led him on. Aidan knew he'd welcomed the fondling of his unformed genitals, even if his equally-unformed mind wouldn't permit him to admit it. Aidan could see through those wails of genuine-sounding anguish. Deep down the boy wanted all that Aidan did to him and Aidan was more than happy to oblige.

The upshot was that it never came to any sort of court case, civil or criminal. The school just did what so many similar schools did, at the time anyway. They suggested to the boy that he might care to consider whether all he alleged had happened had actually happened in exactly the way he'd reported it. At the same time they requested, gently but firmly, that Aidan might look for a position in some other school, given a certain difficulty he may have with one pupil and his family from hereon in, along with a rather attractive lump sum offered by way of an inducement.

Time and again since then Aidan had transgressed in one

way or another, more often than not with other unformed bodies and immature minds. But he still hadn't been found out and he traced it all back to that single stroke of good fortune in that depot office. He'd come to see all that happened that day almost as a blessing.

So by rights he should really now march across to that far table and shake Macklyn's hand, for by now he was absolutely convinced that the rather stooped figure currently hunched over that laminated menu and his former employer were one and the same.

But Aidan didn't. Because Aidan didn't now just glimpse a former, if totally unknowing and unaware, benefactor. Aidan also spotted an opportunity.

From time to time he had pondered the events of that life-changing day, had wondered, like the snooty secretary and the rest of the workforce in all probability, just what had been behind it all. Macklyn had fallen foul of a pretty heavy-duty police investigation, there was no doubt of that. Those two visitors hadn't exactly called to discuss a few traffic offences.

So what had Macklyn done?

What crime or crimes had he committed?

And now the man who could answer those tantalising questions had just dropped into his lap.

Aidan turned and looked out onto the small car park, searching for and fairly quickly alighting upon the car that had brought Macklyn to that newly-opened truck stop in the first place.

LATER THAT EVENING and with the skies now dark, a completely different car pulled up a short distance down the street.

From the vantage point of the driver, the whole row of houses along that terrace could now be seen, but there was only one house that was of interest.

A dim illumination ghosted the shielded pane of a first-floor window with extra-thick curtains draped across. Those curtains were indistinguishable from others in similar windows up and down the same street, but they would have been especially ordered and fitted by specialists so no detail of the room it concealed could be seen.

The driver settled in her seat wondering if by just sitting there the young girl inside would be able to sense her. And, if so, would she derive comfort from that?

Because she'd need comfort right now. She'd need comfort and she'd need reassurance, and that was what these silent vigils were all about. Messages exchanged through the ether between two damaged souls.

The driver looked up at the first-floor window. If only she could talk to her. Then she could tell her that she was going to be able to make it through all this, that she wasn't alone, that she'd never be alone from that point on because that's what this was all about in the end.

Help.

Fellow-feeling.

The hand of support extended from one to another.

It had been extended to her and now it was her turn to do the same. To pick up the baton, and not just in this way either.

The driver's eyes narrowed, her lips tightening now.

Then the driver looked back along the terrace. Which was why it had become so important to perform this ritual, to drive down this one street at least once during the evenings Kezia was inside.

There was an element of risk of course, but she'd always taken care to use different hire cars and to vary the passing times too, and she always dressed differently as well. So, if anyone was looking out of one of those windows they'd see, on one night, a student-type at the wheel of a small run-about, the next, a business-type in a smart suit in a different car completely.

As chameleons went she was one of the best, but then again, she'd had a good tutor.

The driver waited a few more moments, still lost in her silent communion. Then, slowly, she started the engine and began to move away, approaching the house as she did so, slowing for the sleeping policeman the local council had installed just outside.

This was actually the moment she relished the most, actually passing the front door of the house, being the closest she could possibly be to the small child inside while remaining undetected.

Then, suddenly, light flooded the interior of her car. For a moment the driver stilled, bewildered, then she realised. Someone had opened the front door of the safe house just as her car was passing and light from the hall was now spilling across the pavement into the street, a jagged streak of yellow creating a flare that had made her, briefly, all-too-visible.

Instinctively, the driver glanced towards the sudden source of light, saw the burly male protection officer she'd seen there once or twice before, alternating with the slim young woman. He was framed in the doorway now, a couple of empty milk bottles in hand.

Briefly there was eye contact. For perhaps a nanosecond,

two strangers registered each other's presence, but maybe it was good there was that sort of contact, the driver reflected. Maybe it would have been simply too suspicious had there been no reaction from inside that passing car at all.

The burly male turned back into the small hallway, the bottles now deposited on the step as the driver, casually, selected a higher gear and drove on.

THE NEXT MORNING Ros walked through the wide streets of the new Bay, Kezia, silent as ever, by her side.

Excursions of this sort weren't exactly encouraged, but neither were they forbidden. The life of any protected witness resembled a pressure cooker and every now and again a release simply had to be found. Even witnesses at the highest level of risk needed to do something ordinary and everyday from time to time, if only to touch base with normal life again.

It was a life to which they'd, hopefully, return. But even if they didn't there was no point in keeping a client locked up in a room for months on end, seeing no-one and going nowhere. They weren't the ones in prison even if their time in the care of the protection programme occasionally felt like a never-ending incarceration.

Just ahead, in the basin outside the Millennium Centre, a film crew was setting up for a scene for some TV or film drama and Ros slowed to take a look. Several other spectators were already milling round. The scene seemed to be little more than an establishing shot of some description, just an actor walking towards a door while speaking a few lines into a mobile phone. Ordinarily, Ros would have walked on within moments, but Kezia suddenly seemed interested and so they lingered.

Up to then Ros had struggled to find anything that would engage the attention of their young witness for more than a moment. Books, TV programmes and DVDs had all been tried at different times. All had been rejected.

Ros looked out across the basin towards the swooping roof of the centre itself, branded as beautiful by some, as an eyesore by others, as the director made his last-minute preparations. Then she looked back at Kezia who was still not moving, just staring as the director called for a preliminary walkthrough. The eyes of all the watching spectators, including Ros's eyes, automatically followed the actor as he left one mark, mobile in hand, and walked to another, a couple of extras passing him, talking and smiling as they did so.

But then Ros realised that not all eyes were following him. Kezia didn't even seem to register the actor who'd now reached his second mark and was looking back, anxiously, at the director to see if he'd mastered the art of walking and talking at the same time.

All Kezia seemed to be looking at was the cameraman by the side of the director who was currently peering into his lens, committing the scene everyone else had just watched to celluloid memory.

'It's not a bouncy castle.'

One hour later, Ros and Kezia arrived back at the terraced safe house to be met by a harassed and sweating Conor, an electrical inflator pump in hand.

Conor nodded towards the rear door, lowering his aggrieved voice for the sake of Ros's young charge.

'I plugged this into it, turned it on, next thing I know it's not going up, it's going fucking sideways.'

Ros followed Conor's look. Out in the garden the small patch of lawn had now vanished, replaced by what looked like a totally random, interlocking series of plastic tunnels.

'It's some sort of kid's obstacle course. The labels must have got mixed up in the shop or something.'

Suppressing a grin, Ros moved past Conor and headed outside. Kezia joined her, pausing by the entrance to one of the tunnels. Now she was closer, Ros could see that there were six, all coiled into different shapes before feeding into an enclosed central space where, presumably, any intrepid child who'd braved the journey could celebrate.

Ros kept watching Kezia, expecting her at any moment to turn back inside the house, but she didn't. Kezia just stared at the apparition that had literally popped up in front of them.

And, suddenly, there it was. An expression Ros recognised only too well. An expression that had crept across her own face at times when she was growing up too.

Ros had also felt, back then, as if she didn't have the right to feel like Kezia was feeling right now, that she'd forfeited it somehow courtesy of all that had happened, even though none of it was even remotely her fault.

But out in a school playground or in a park, watching other children on swings and slides, she'd suddenly forget all that had happened, all that had fractured her world. She'd forget about a sister who was no longer there and parents who no longer smiled. For that one moment she'd become what she was deep down. A child again.

And that explained the look on Kezia's face right now too. Because no matter how apart from the rest of the world Ros felt back then and how much of a stranger in some strange land Kezia felt now, all Ros wanted to do back then and all Kezia quite clearly wanted to do right now, was play.

And, suddenly, and with a bewildered Conor staring at her, Ros dropped to her knees and started inching her way through one of the plastic tunnels.

As she did so Ros heard a muffled explosion of laughter from behind as Conor eyed the now-bulging tunnel. They were actually designed for children under the age of eight, so this was going to be a squeeze even for the ultra-slight Ros. But then Conor realised he wasn't the only one watching her progress.

All of a sudden Kezia dropped to her knees too, dipped her head inside the opening of another of the tunnels and also began inching her way along, slowly at first but gaining speed all the time as her shoulders and knees found grip, catching up on Ros as she did so.

From the adjacent tunnel Ros felt the whole structure shaking as Kezia advanced, gaining on her all the while. Ros redoubled her efforts to reach the open space in the centre before Kezia, who was now speeding up as she also registered the sudden spurt in Ros's progress.

All the while, from outside, Conor yelled encouragement, urging on both Ros and Kezia in their impromptu race to the middle.

The wriggling Ros urged her shoulders and knees on. Kezia did the same. Ros was fighting for breath now but Kezia wasn't. And from Kezia there now came a sound neither Ros or Conor had heard from her before and which neither had expected to hear either. Because for the first time since she'd been taken into the programme, Kezia was laughing.

And, for a moment, as she heard the young girl in the adjacent tube, Ros felt a new warmth wash through her. Courtesy of a mislabelled child's toy they actually seemed to have made some sort of connection at last.

Kezia was now ahead of her and for a moment Ros contemplated ceding her the victory. But the small girl deserved better than that and Ros, literally, kicked on. Kezia registered the sudden movement and did the same. From outside, Conor's yells were becoming evermore animated, Ros and Kezia now absolutely neck and neck. A gasping Ros poked her head out from her tunnel into the central space, only for a human cannonball to explode out of the tunnel next to her as Kezia tumbled onto the grass just a second or so before Ros hurled herself down onto it too. For the next few moments a helpless Kezia and Ros did nothing, could do nothing, apart from lie there and laugh and laugh and laugh.

For the next two hours Ros and Kezia played in the Perspex bubble. Via a flap in the roof, Conor delivered a makeshift picnic along with some pens, paper, a sketchpad and an iPad. Kezia sketched a surprisingly accurate reconstruction of the scene they'd encountered back in the Bay that morning, framed from the perspective of the cameraman. Ros used the iPad to create a crudely animated version of her comically wriggling progress through that plastic tunnel. Then they'd both tucked into the rolls and fruit that had been delivered by Conor.

Barely a word was exchanged. None were needed. Maybe both Ros and Kezia knew they'd break some sort of spell if they spoke, and so they didn't. They just remained seated on the grass, enclosed in a Perspex bubble, the rest of the world excluded.

Later that afternoon Ros retreated back along the tunnel. She could have used the flap that opened above the central space, but it would have felt like cheating somehow. Kezia wanted to stay and sketch some more, so Ros returned with a small battery-powered lamp to illuminate any developing gloom. It also meant Kezia would be visible from the kitchen window all the time although Ros didn't tell her that. That same spell again.

For the next hour Ros remained at the kitchen table, ostensibly catching up on paperwork, stealing regular glances out towards the bubble where Kezia could be seen, still hunched over her sketchpad.

Only Ros wasn't catching up on any sort of paperwork. Ros was coming – or was trying to come – to some decisions instead.

Ros hadn't responded to Hendrix out on the bank of that restored waterway. She'd just stared at him for a moment and then turned away. Hendrix hadn't followed and they hadn't referred to that exchange on the couple of occasions their paths had crossed since. He'd just left her alone to think about all he'd said – and all he didn't say – which was what, finally, she was now doing.

And the more she thought about it the more inclined she was to wonder whether maybe Jukes was right. Was this – any of it – actually any of her concern? Ros and her colleagues were never supposed to get involved in the details of any case that involved their clients anyway. Ros's job and the job of the rest of her colleagues in the unit was simple, to keep those clients safe. The whys and wherefores of whatever crime they'd witnessed simply wasn't their remit.

But it was always difficult, if impossible, not to become involved of course. Every one of the people Ros took into the programme may have been different, but all were alike in one way too. They were all usually scared. Scared of what they'd seen or what they'd done and definitely scared of the consequences. They were also living lives of extreme dislocation, be that at their own hands or at the hands of others. Inevitably, a connection began to form between client and handler. How could it not?

And in Kezia's case there was an additional complication, of course. Because when she looked at Kezia, Ros was looking at a mirror image of her past self. Looking at Kezia, Ros was once again a terrified young girl living in a world she didn't recognise or understand. Ros returned once more to being a young girl who'd seen things no person of any age should ever see.

So maybe this was what Ros should be pouring her energies into, afternoons like these. An afternoon when a young girl who had absolutely no reason to ever laugh again did so. An afternoon when she forgot about everything aside from winning a race through a plastic tunnel and tumbling out onto a patch of damp grass the victor.

Yes, Ros still had all those questions racing through her head and, yes, they were still the same questions she'd previously asked Jukes.

Who'd targeted Roman Edwards and why arrange his murder to so closely resemble the previous murder of Toya James?

Why had Masters been so keen to airbrush that original murder from all records?

And why had that cruellest of deceptions been played on that other innocent soul in all this, the young mother, Kim? It had to have been because of her past connection to the murdered Roman, but what part did that play in whatever Byzantine scenario was being acted out here?

But maybe none of that mattered, at least so far as Ros was concerned. Maybe this was what mattered the most. Simply staying close to Kezia. Letting her know there was a world out there where people still played and raced along plastic tunnels and had picnics at the end of it all.

And maybe the silence she'd maintained so far should be her only answer to Hendrix. He'd made an implicit offer to her that day that the two of them work together on this in some way and they both knew that – but maybe she should just let that lie. Anything else might open up a whole other can of worms.

Because what was actually behind that offer and his approach in the first place? A simple, if coded, appeal for help from an officer also frustrated beyond measure by the actions of his senior officer and recognising in Ros a kindred spirit? Or something else? Something Ros hadn't as yet discovered and which perhaps she wouldn't want to discover either?

An hour or so later, and with Conor about to leave for home, Ros finally stood. She cast one last, regretful, glance out into the garden, registered the light that was just beginning to fade as afternoon crept into evening. Then she went out into the garden to bring Kezia back inside. She'd left it to the last possible moment as it was, knowing this would definitely now break that spell, just hoping the damage wouldn't be too terminal. Today had been a milestone of sorts and Ros was desperate not to spoil it.

Kezia was still hunched over her sketchpad as Ros approached and, briefly, an alarm sounded. Because Kezia had been in that exact same position just a few moments before as well.

Ros looked at the overhead flap which was slightly raised. A second later Ros yanked it open and stared down.

Kezia's sketchpad was still on the grass.

Her iPad was still there too as were the pens and paper, as was the remains of the picnic Conor had provided a few hours before.

But in place of Kezia, there was now a child's mannequin.

Kezia herself was gone.

PART THREE

THE HOME RUN

18.

A FTER WHAT EVEN Jukes would have had to concede was a travesty of an interview with Masters, Leon had been moved to a safe house forty miles down the coast.

Ros had been made aware of the move, but was still unaware of the interview or at least so Jukes fervently hoped. He really didn't want any more interrupted breakfasts. For his part, Leon had been told he wouldn't be facing any further interviews in the foreseeable future at least, which was true so far as Jukes knew. So all Leon had to do now was relax.

In truth, Jukes couldn't care less what Leon did. He could throw himself off one of the nearby cliffs, the head of the local Protection Unit would barely have noticed. Only one thing mattered now to Jukes.

Masters, it seemed, hadn't made any sort of breakthrough with Leon or at least none that made any real difference.

Meaning this new nightmare – or, more accurately, this return of an old nightmare – was still going on.

At that time in the morning there were only the surfers to keep him company and none of them took any notice of the silent figure moving past them on the beach. All their hungry attention was fixed on the water, not the shore.

So for those few hours, before the first of the families arrived and the bistro-style café squatting on the shingle at the head of the beach opened its large glass doors for business, there was mainly just Leon, moving from one headland to the next before doubling back and repeating the same solo journey all over again.

Various large houses were dotted around the headland, along with a newly-constructed block of upmarket apartments but, as most had their curtains drawn at that time in the morning, Leon was pretty sure he wouldn't attract any attention from them either.

Leon paused for a moment, looked out at the surfers, now plunging into the waves and as he did so, and from years before, pictures began to form, memories of other walks on beaches similar to this near to his and Joey's old home, walks conducted, not only in the company of his dead brother, but their father too.

One beach he recalled in particular was studded solely with pebbles, not a single piece of sand to be found along the whole of its three-mile length but it was the beach he'd always remember the most clearly. Because, one day, the three of them had stood on those pebbles in stunned awe as a small school of dolphins suddenly appeared before them, playing in the bay.

Leon could still remember holding his breath in case that almost mystical, otherworldly, sight vanished before his eyes.

Both boys had badgered their father to take them back there at exactly the same time the next day and the day after too, just in case that visit had been part of some regular ritual and they'd see their exotic visitors again. And, in the company of their indulgent father, they'd duly returned, but those visitors never did.

But that sharpest of memories still endured, and it was all Leon saw now as he looked beyond the surfers swimming ever further out in the bay. Two small boys, hand in hand with a protective parent, both scanning the horizon as they offered up a silent and heartfelt prayer.

Leon reached the end of the beach, turned, and began the return journey across to the opposite headland taking care not to tread in his own footsteps still visible in the sand. Someone had once told him it was unlucky and in the bad luck stakes he really didn't want any more.

But then, as Leon kept walking, another image swam before his eyes, not of a beach this time but the steepest path he'd ever seen in his life, leading himself, the young Joey and his father down a hillside on the Llŷn Peninsula to a former quarrying village that had been declared dead decades before. An entire community had once lived there but then the local, sole, employer had ceased operation and the small collection of rented houses they'd abandoned had fallen into disrepair.

Then some charity had taken an interest in the now-ghostly locale, involving in turn the local council who'd managed to access some obscure grant from Brussels. With that in place more funds had then been sourced to restore the dilapidated houses and turn the whole site into a tourist attraction.

Slowly, and thanks to a new visitor centre and a café, people began walking down that steep path again, heading once more into a formerly-forgotten village and gradually the village began to return from the dead.

Leon, Joey and their father had been among the very first visitors. They'd spent a whole morning exploring before making their way along a neighbouring beach that hadn't been accessed by human feet for longer than the boys' respective lifetimes although they still, sadly, didn't see any dolphins.

They'd all stood for a moment on a small headland looking out to sea, a vast expanse of water in front, the steepest of hills all around. Then Leon and his brother had spent the rest of the day exploring shallow pools accessible only from the cliffs, their father watching over them all the while.

Back in the present day Leon walked on, still taking care not to tread in footsteps that were being erased in any event by the incoming tide which was now on the turn.

Leon knew why those images were now returning. He knew

why he was now remembering dolphins and lost villages and all those other childhood memories he'd previously believed had gone forever. Because he felt, back then, as if nothing could harm him. He felt cosseted, enfolded in some cocoon that nothing and no-one could penetrate. Leon, quite simply, felt safe.

Too late he'd realise that all those simple childhood memories were really doing was relaxing him, insinuating their way under his habitual guard, allowing rather more corrosive memories and even more corrosive images to usher themselves inside.

Leon had now reached the opposite headland and made to turn back once again. Ahead, he could now see a sole waitress opening up the bistro-type café, getting ready for the day. Behind her, he could see the small house that was now his home, nestled in the shadows of the larger houses and upmarket apartments that crowded the surrounding hills, curtains now beginning to open in a few of them, residents looking forward to whatever the day ahead might hold.

Leon should have walked on. He should have walked back along the beach again, taking care once more not to tread in his own footsteps. But Leon didn't. Leon paused on the sand instead.

Around him, the wind blowing in from the west began to pick up, promising some good sport that morning for the surfers. But Leon didn't notice the wind and he didn't feel the drop in temperature either. Leon just remained there for a moment longer, then struck out along the beach again, not even seeing his previous footsteps. A slow chill began to creep over him and that was nothing to do with the quickening westerly now blowing in.

Because ever since Leon had stumbled out of that disused cinema, his eyes aching from the horrors he'd witnessed, other pictures had been slowly forming inside his head. Pictures he'd banished years before, vowing never to revisit them and he hadn't, not in all that time. But now Masters seemed to have unlocked some sort of unholy Pandora's box.

Leon stared, unseeing, out across the sea.

Did Masters know?

Was that what that sick interlude was really all about?

Did he, somehow, know?

But how could he?

How could anyone?

And now Leon didn't even see the surfers or the waitress or even the few other early walkers who were now coming down on to the sand from those large houses and upmarket apartments with their children and dogs.

Leon moved on again, unaware he was walking faster now, picking up speed as the pictures forming inside his head gathered momentum, those pictures coming thick and fast, dancing before him as surely as if he'd been transported back in time.

Now he didn't even look down or make his usual mental note to avoid stepping in the evidence of his previous journey lest he offend the gods and bring their wrath down on his bowed head. Perhaps he'd simply forgotten. Or perhaps something was already telling Leon that he was moving way beyond any help those gods could render him right now.

Streaks of sunlight, glinting through the fast-travelling clouds above, were now burnishing the sand, staining it a ghostly pink, then red before the more familiar yellow blush returned once more. But again Leon didn't even see it. Across the bay, a couple of the surfers emerging from the water paused as they registered the more determined strides of the sole walker, where previously he'd been dismissed as just another dreamer on a picture-postcard shore.

Leon kept on walking until he reached the far headland once again and then, as the surfers plunged back in the sea, riding the new waves whipped in by the winds, he didn't do what he'd done on every other morning since he'd arrived at that small seaside house; this time Leon didn't turn back.

Leon rounded the headland and walked on instead.

And as he did so, and as if to hasten him on his way, the first of those new pictures flashed again before his eyes.

All those years earlier, Leon had paused in the doorway, totally unable to take in what he was seeing.

For that moment he just stared at the body on the bed, unidentified for now but almost literally unidentifiable anyway, a body that may have been clinging on to what still passed for life, but whose soul had quite clearly already passed over to the other side.

The man standing over the female body also seemed to have made something of a similar journey. He was no longer recognisable as human and certainly didn't look as if he possessed a soul. For a moment Leon didn't even realise he was actually looking at his own brother. The effects of Joey's handiwork, all too visible on the body in front of him, seemed to have twisted him inside out in much the same way as his victim, as if he'd become a mirror image of the monster he himself had just created.

Briefly, some last vestige of a survival instinct kicked in as the slashed and mutilated figure on the bed registered a dim shadow at the door. And now something flashed in those eyes.

Had help arrived at last?

Those eyes then flickered past her persecutor in a last desperate appeal, Joey in turn wheeling round, blood dripping from his hands and, as he did so, Leon suddenly realised.

It was Toya.

For God's sake that creature on the bed was Clare's best friend, Toya.

The sparky young girl who'd refused to be the consolation prize while Leon's brother plucked the peach, the friend who'd smiled up at him as she'd told Leon to go fuck himself instead because no way on God's earth was she going to become some sort of makeshift fantasy while he salivated over the real deal.

Only Toya wasn't anywhere near anything that could even remotely be called God's earth right now. Toya was in a very different place.

By the bed, Joey had already forgotten all about her. Now Joey was looking at a far more potent quarry and fleetingly, even in the midst of everything, Leon felt a quick stab of sympathy for the hapless Toya. Even in death, or near-death at least, she'd still just been a bit-part player in an unfolding tableau, a single step along the road to what was always going to be the main event, at least so far as his crazed brother was concerned.

Joey had been looking for both Leon and Clare for the whole of that evening and his brother knew why. One single, hysterical, phone call from Joey's wife had been enough to alert him that their affair had been uncovered and that Joey was now on the warpath. Clare had used that actual word as she'd yelled at him down the phone, and it looked as if it wasn't just hyperbole on her part.

For a moment, wild thoughts flashed through Leon's mind as his brother kept staring at him.

Had some weird sort of dislocation happened inside that obviously-deranged head of his?

Had Joey seen Toya and somehow seen his wife?

Or Leon?

Had Joey's frenzied stabbing of Toya been some strange sort of transference, visiting on the perennial substitute the barbarity he'd intended to inflict on Leon himself?

Then Joey took a step towards him.

And Leon began to concentrate on rather more practical matters instead.

Forty miles away from Leon's seaside home, and as Leon himself rounded the headland at the end of his early morning walk, Conor was doing a frantic trawl through CCTV footage, desperately trying to spot the person or persons still unknown who'd somehow spirited a young child away from a walled garden in a secure house under the very eyes of two officers deputed with keeping her safe.

Jukes was liaising with Masters and Hendrix, spreading the CCTV net ever wider.

Ros was on the same mission too, but she wasn't studying CCTV tapes. Ros was settling herself opposite a silent young woman in a private room in a secure psychiatric ward instead, and was beginning the first of a series of gentle questions.

'Did Roman have any visitors in the time you were with him? Especially in the last year or so, anyone out of the ordinary, anyone you hadn't seen before?'

But all Ros was getting was silence. Kim might have been looking back at Ros but her eyes were still fixed on one object and one only and that was nothing to do with past partners or present interrogators.

All Kim was still seeing was her small son.

By Kim's side, Jamie broke in, adding what he could to the pitifully small pool of current knowledge.

'I worked there for months.'

Jamie, still quite clearly recovering from his own more visible injuries, shook his head.

'I can't remember anyone calling in the whole of that time. No-one even seemed to phone.'

Jamie shrugged, helpless.

216

'He lived like a hermit, just him, his daughter and Kim in that great big house. I always thought that was part of the problem, the whole place felt like some kind of prison.'

Jamie paused, a dim memory returning.

'A doctor called once. To drop off some drugs or something, I think. I know Kim tried asking what he wanted them for. I heard her when I was working out in the greenhouse.'

Then Jamie paused, the memory of the sharp crack that had greeted that totally innocent enquiry, still quite clearly haunting him.

'Apart from that, nothing.'

Ros kept looking at the silent, seemingly-unaware Kim, an all-too-familiar instinct stirring inside.

Most children took the world around them on face value, believing what they were told. For as long as she could remember, Ros had been assured of the opposite. Nothing was to be taken on face value. Everything and everyone had to be questioned, no matter who they were or how unimportant anything they might be saying. Danger lurked around every corner and she could never, ever, let down her guard.

Others had crumbled under that constant pressure and Ros had supervised some of them in her new calling. She'd watched the slow, and sometimes not slow, disintegration of entire personalities as they tried to maintain a fiction they themselves could never believe.

What had probably saved Ros back then was her youth. At the time she'd entered the protection programme she'd taken it as the norm. When she finally realised it wasn't the way most people lived it made no difference. This was life as she knew it and would know it from that moment on, and with no previous yardstick against which that new life might be judged, she hadn't wasted any effort in regret for times past.

But what it had left her with was a highly-developed antennae and Ros knew that somewhere inside Kim was some sort of key to all this. There was something Kim had seen or heard that would not only lead them to her own persecutor, but to a killer and then to an explanation of what was behind the two linked crimes.

Not to mention the present whereabouts of one small, missing, vulnerable girl.

But for now and with no other avenues open to her, Ros decided to renew her acquaintance with a former star of the professional wrestling ring, and to indulge in a little breaking and entering as well.

Two hours after rounding that headland following his latest morning walk, Leon was telling himself to get a grip, just get a grip for fuck's sake.

He'd done this so many times before. It had been a familiar routine for the first few years of what had become his new life. In those early days, when he'd first settled in Amsterdam, he'd followed a virtually identical army of more or less bored hotel porters as they led him down a whole array of endless corridors lined on all sides by identical doors differentiated only by ascending or descending numbers.

And he'd done all he was doing now too. He'd hovered behind each and every one of those porters as they'd used the ubiquitous credit-card-sized pass key to open the door to his room or occasionally, in the older or more upmarket establishments, an old-fashioned key.

And he'd done all he was doing right now too as he looked round and affected disappointment.

'It's looking over the front.'

The porter nodded, cautious, much like his forebears had all done as well.

'These are our best rooms.'

'Only I was hoping for a room at the back.'

The porter looked back at him, puzzled and with good reason. The rear of the hotel looked out over a two-lane dual carriageway and a retail park. The front boasted views of the waterfront. The porter's face said it all. He'd never known anyone express a preference for the former over the latter.

Leon smiled, half-apologetically.

'I'm agoraphobic. Open spaces, they sort of freak me out.'

Leon smiled again, evermore apologetically.

'Can you see if I could be moved?'

The porter hesitated, but only for a moment. This was a hotel that prided itself on its in-house training.

'Of course.'

The porter placed Leon's bag on the bed and headed back to reception. Leon waited till he'd gone, then crossed to the window and forgot all about fears of open spaces and distant vistas as he surveyed other guests arriving and departing a few storeys below. Nothing seemed out of the ordinary. No-one scanning the windows above.

Within a few moments the bedside phone rang and a receptionist assured Leon they could accommodate his request and that the porter would be returning in the next few moments with a new key.

Five minutes later, Leon was in a considerably smaller room than the one he'd been previously assigned. He barely noticed. He didn't take in the restricted view out of the window looking down onto the dual carriageway or the retail park either. The switch of room had reassured him on one count at least. If anyone of malevolent intent had been following him for the last couple of hours and had somehow found out in advance the room he was occupying, that last-minute switch should prevent any direct attempt to get to him.

Leon seated himself on the small bed, stared at the door. He knew he was taking unnecessary precautions but he just couldn't help it. Even when he'd been resettled in Amsterdam he'd always felt as if Ros and the rest of her department were still somehow at his side and they were in a sense. Even then he'd always been just a single phone call away from the sort of help he'd come to take for granted.

Now Leon had placed himself rather more than a phone call away from all that. And it was unsettling him more than he'd expected.

Leon rested his head on the window again, still not seeing anything outside. Because all he was seeing now were those pictures from years before.

Pictures he'd banished for so long, trickling in now past his defences.

Joey stared at Leon, one brother facing the other across a blood-drenched floor. And Leon knew he was now in one shitload of trouble.

Physically, Leon and Joey had always been evenly matched. From childhood their frequent physical spats usually ended in stalemate, but that night was going to be different and Leon knew it. Something had taken over inside Joey, something that would prevail no matter what, and Leon knew he had only seconds, perhaps less, to act.

It was only afterwards that Leon would fill in the blanks. It was only later he'd realise that Joey must have inflicted those appalling injuries on Toya with the large boning knife he'd then discarded on the floor.

It was only later he realised that he himself must have swooped down as his brother had approached and had scooped up that same knife. Everything happened so quickly it was as if he didn't have time to think, for his brain to catch up with all his body was doing.

That boning knife was still stained with Toya's fast-drying blood but now fresh blood saturated the blade as Leon lashed out with the weapon, slashing his brother's throat with a single movement as he approached, almost severing his windpipe.

Joey collapsed by the side of the bed, choking horribly, his death rattle bouncing off walls that had already seen more than their fair share of horror that night.

Still by the door, Leon slowly lowered the boning knife, not even daring to look at his brother and the damage he'd just inflicted.

Leon just looked at the figure on the bed instead.

Driving back to the Protection Unit offices, Ros stared out of the window at a sea of faces passing her on all sides. The first of the year's rugby internationals was being played that evening and the streets, as ever, were buzzing.

But all Ros saw now was a quite different face, the face of yet another soul she'd ultimately failed to keep safe; a young woman known to the world as Gina Bell.

Gina had been born in Longsight, one of the blasted boroughs, along with Ardwick, Beswick, Clayton and Gorton, that made up the former slums of east Manchester. At the age of twelve she'd dropped out of a school that had little interest in keeping her anyway and even less in taking her back, and she became a member of one of the area's most feared street gangs known locally as Mara Salvatrucha, named in honour of an equally violent street gang in America.

In the first year of what she clearly regarded as an honoured inclusion, Gina was handed round various gang members as a prize and had borne two of them a child each by the time she was fifteen. She also played a full part in the various robberies, shootings and stabbings that had been the trademark way the city's home-grown Mara Salvatrucha earned its daily crust.

But then Gina began to tire of it all. Ros always found it difficult to square the notion of burn-out with a girl who was still, legally at least, a child, but that seemed to sum up what happened. Or maybe some latent maternal instinct kicked in and she decided she just wanted a better life for herself and her two children. No-one now would ever know.

Gina was arrested on a relatively minor count, car theft in her case. In exchange for leniency and for her children not being taken into care, Gina gave the police chapter and verse on those robberies, shootings and stabbings carried out by her now-former associates the length and breadth of her home city and beyond.

She also volunteered first-hand information on the operations of those former associates and agreed to become a key witness in an upcoming murder trial in which one of her former boyfriends, and the father of one of her children, was the sole defendant.

Ros had taken her into the protection programme and immediately moved her hundreds of miles south. Gina had been provided with the usual new name and social security number and for the first few weeks all had been normal enough. But Ros could almost see the agitation building inside her new charge.

Maybe it was the isolation. Maybe it was suddenly being apart from a gang that had become more like a family. Or maybe it was a pure and simple yearning for places and people she'd left behind, a phenomenon that, in her home country, Ros had heard described as hiraeth which was sometimes and erroneously called homesickness, but which was so much more than that; an overpowering desire for all that a soul was now separated from, impossible to describe to those who'd never experienced it, equally impossible to ignore or deny for those who had.

Ros moved on as the crush of people in front of her momentarily parted. But Ros was still only seeing that one face.

Ros didn't know to this day whether the security of the programme had been breached or whether Gina had made contact with her former friends and lovers herself. All Ros knew for sure was that on a sunny June morning, Gina walked out of the safe accommodation that had been provided for her, boarded a train with her two children and returned to a city which had always been her home, and to a gang who'd promised, on their honour and on the honour of their mothers, fathers, brothers and sisters, that she was forgiven for all she'd done, that the slate had been wiped clean.

As had happened now with Kezia, Ros then lost track of her. For more than forty-eight hours Gina completely disappeared and for that same period of time the rest of the gang members vanished also.

Gina was found two days later. Her children were still with her. It had been difficult to assess who'd been killed first, although the police pathologist was fairly sure it was her children, and probably in full view of their mother who would have been forced to watch.

Gina herself had been hanged, although she'd been tortured first as evidenced by the sixteen stab wounds to her chest and neck. The gang comprised sixteen in number. Each of them would have been deputed the task of making as savage an incision as they could without actually killing her.

Then Gina's body and the bodies of her two children had been dumped at the front entrance of the school that had washed its hands of her those few years before.

The school caretaker, arriving late that day for work, had phoned the local police immediately after stumbling upon the grim discovery, but by the time the emergency services had arrived the tableau had already been captured on at least a hundred or so mobile phones as more and more pupils arrived behind him. Within moments those images were catapulting around the internet as the gang members no doubt intended.

No-one betrayed the gang again. Membership increased exponentially over the next couple of years as well. The murder trial that was to involve Gina as a witness collapsed.

Ros had suffered a familiar feeling throughout the whole of that period, a feeling she could only describe as a nameless sense of dread.

It was the exact same feeling she'd experienced in her early days of caring for that other soon-to-be-lost family, the Kincaids. That sense of disaster lurking around every corner, just waiting to ambush her every unwary tread.

But the strangest thing was that she wasn't feeling any of that now. No internal alarm was now sounding as it always had in the past.

And the even stranger thing was that it hadn't from the very start, from the moment they realised Kezia had been taken. As all hell had broken loose all around them, as police, local and national, had been mobilised to trace a missing child at clear risk, Ros hadn't felt her stomach twisting into cramps as it had done so many times before.

Ros, in short, didn't register danger.

She wasn't sensing that Kezia was in danger now either.

And she didn't understand why.

Half an hour after his extended and circuitous check-in at the hotel, Leon visited a large and recently-opened department store.

The store was like them all, a repository for middle-range designers to peddle watered-down designs. But the major attraction for Leon didn't lie in the merchandise but in the switchback escalators lined with mirrors and situated in the very centre of the building.

Again, it used to be second nature. Two or three times a day in the first few months of his new life, he'd avail himself of similar facilities in his adopted city too, double-checking all the while that he didn't spot the same face in more than the one location.

Before he'd left the hotel, he'd noticed a young woman talking into a mobile in the lobby. The woman was most probably a young professional judging by her dress, in the city on some trade visit or other, an impression bolstered by a reference he caught as passed by to a company called, he thought, Burton or possibly Bourbon Biscuits.

Then, as he'd walked into the mall a short time later, he'd seen a perspiring man in his mid-thirties standing by another escalator, carrying a plastic carrier bag in one hand, scratching his balding head with the other.

The man was probably just another overweight shopper pausing to ponder his next purchase but Leon was taking absolutely no chances. Ros had called it dry cleaning when she'd first coached Leon in these strange practices, more usually associated with spooks of the type that haunt opposite banks of the Thames. But the same routines and procedures held sway for protected witnesses as well it seemed.

If the woman visiting Burton or Bourbon Biscuits suddenly appeared on the opposite escalator in the department store, that might not be an issue. She could have taken a totally innocent detour on her way to a business meeting. But if, later again, she was sitting a few feet away in a coffee shop while he turned away from the counter with his morning espresso, then he very definitely had a problem.

Leon rode the escalator to the second floor and then up to the third. The fact that the escalators were not only mirrored but were sited in the middle of the building permitted another seemingly-innocent check to be made as, on at least two occasions, Leon was able to make an apparent wrong turn into some other part of the store, only to double-back as he realised his mistake, allowing him to check on the arriving escalator for any sort of tail.

Dimly, Leon remembered how he'd felt when he'd first done all this. It had actually felt mildly intoxicating at the time, as if he'd suddenly become a spy engaged on some top-secret mission.

But maybe that intoxication derived again from the knowledge that at any time he could make a call for help to a number that would always be answered within two or three rings. And then Ros, or an officer dispatched by Ros, would be on their way.

Now there was no number and no help. And now he just felt terrified. And if he had spotted the woman from Burton or Bourbon Biscuits or the sweating man with the carrier bag, Leon couldn't have guaranteed he wouldn't have simply hunched down in the middle of that department store and howled.

But on this day anyway there was nothing.

No faces he'd memorised suddenly reappearing before him.

Just other faces instead.

Leon approached the bed.

The man-made atrocity that had been Toya, that was still – just – Toya looked back up at him.

Later, Leon would wonder. Had he summoned help right there, right then, could some medical miracle have taken place, would some enterprising surgeon really have been able, despite her injuries, to save her?

Looking down into those eyes, Leon could sense not only that same question but the silent plea that he at least try. At some point in that evening's torture, Toya must have truly prayed for death, but she wasn't doing that now. All of a sudden Toya had been offered hope where previously she'd believed all hope had been extinguished, seen a potential saviour where she'd been sure none would appear. And now she was latching onto Leon with all her fragile might, beseeching him to help, for pity's sake, help her.

Leon looked back at his brother, his choking sobs now becoming less frequent as blood pooled out underneath him on the floor.

Then Leon glanced back at Toya again, but Leon wasn't really looking at her any longer. Because something had taken over inside Leon now, some atavistic instinct, one thought inside his head and one only, and that was his own survival.

And that instinct was telling him that his survival and that of the formerly-sparky young girl he was staring at were fast becoming mutually exclusive.

It was a simple calculation. Summon help and it might make no difference. Toya might already be well beyond all help anyway. Do nothing, and Toya would very definitely die, a death that hopefully for her sake would come soon.

But if she were to live, even for a short time, there was always the possibility she'd say something, tell a paramedic or a police officer enough for them to piece together what had actually happened in that room and the part Leon had just played in it all.

But were Toya to die before anyone could reach her, then those cops and paramedics would have to piece together the sequence of events for themselves. And Leon looked round, not even seeing his dying brother now, not even listening to his death rattle as he desperately tried to suck in air as more blood gushed from his slashed throat.

There'd be no evidence that anyone else had been in that

room. Leon would make sure of it. Meaning there'd be only one logical conclusion that anyone could reach. At some point, Toya had somehow managed to clasp her dying hand onto the handle of the boning knife that had already been used to such devastating effect on her own body.

Then, summoning a strength she could not reasonably have been expected to possess, Toya must have lashed out, catching Joey across the throat.

Then she'd died, all the while listening to her attacker die too.

It was a no-brainer of course. And while Leon might have briefly computed other, more humanitarian options, there was only one he was ever going to take that night and he knew it.

So Leon stood by Toya's body on that bed and, in some small gesture of kinship at least, looked down into the eyes of his former friend and maintained that eye contact until the light finally flickered inside them and was still.

All the time he kept telling himself this was simple. Survive or die. Kill or be killed. Leon had chosen life over death, life for himself over the death of his brother and Toya. And if he'd just left there and then, the moment he'd made his decision, then everything would have been fine. But Leon hadn't. He'd remained in that room, some last spark of humanity still extant, keeping company with Toya's terror, not wanting to abandon her totally to the abyss.

Behind Leon, Joey died. Toya herself died a few moments later. And as she did so, Leon sensed something. Even years later, he couldn't pin down exactly what it was; it certainly wasn't a sound or a change in the light, it was just something in the way the atoms in that room suddenly seemed to rearrange themselves.

Leon, half-hesitating, turned to see the young Donna

standing at the door, her eyes staring back, unblinking, into his own.

Ros let herself into Jukes's office.

Jukes himself was still with Masters and Hendrix in Murder Squad. Conor was still trawling through CCTV footage from the cameras covering each end of the street on which the safe house was sited.

Meaning Ros, for now, was alone.

Ros opened the first in a series of files on Jukes's computer, cross-checking dates and entries. Most of these files would be duplicated on her own computer, relating to ongoing clients in current protection programmes. But somewhere in the files before her was information that would not be duplicated, that would be for Jukes's eyes only.

And, right now, for Ros's eyes too.

But then, as she negotiated passwords and surfed deeper into evermore sensitive files, Ros paused, puzzled, as she now came across one file in particular, accessed once again by a password it had taken her some time to crack.

This file didn't seem to be related to a work matter at all. It had as its subject a teenage girl recently emigrated to Arizona. Ros read some more, then copied the file onto a memory stick. It wasn't, strictly speaking, germane to Ros's present inquiry. But it might become useful ammunition in some future inquiry to come.

Then Ros paused again as she came across a rather more relevant file from years before, the transcript of an interview conducted just a matter of weeks after Ros herself had first joined the unit, one of the very first interviews that Jukes had conducted with Leon, in fact.

Much of it was familiar, some of it was not. Some of that original interview had been censored, some left intact; but as Ros read on one phrase of Leon's, one repeated insistence, began to hammer round and round inside her brain, that same antennae once again at work, telling her that this was significant in some way.

Then Ros stilled as she saw a list of additional files to the side of the same screen.

And, in amongst them, another – and quite different – file.

As Ros was reading the contents of that different file, Leon quit the department store, riding down those same mirrored escalators. Then he walked up a pedestrianised precinct before pausing for a few moments outside the entrance to a large block of new-build apartments.

Opposite was a large church, open for coffee and afternoon tea according to a sign he was reading as he studied, in turn, every passing face at the same time.

Leon had found the apartment on an accommodation website. Even in the short time he'd been there, Leon had realised that a hotel with its constant flux of arriving and departing guests was simply going to be too wearing on his nerves.

Using the same tradecraft he'd employed so far, he'd used a false name and email address to make contact with the accommodation agency. The deposit that had been requested was going to be taken from a credit card he'd applied for using a name invented for that one single transaction. The debit would be collected from a bank account he'd set up on-line which would be liquidated once the single charge had been settled.

The bank account and the credit card were registered to the same address in a city some three hundred miles to the north, an address that sounded as if it was an ordinary house on an ordinary street but which would prove, should anyone be so minded to investigate, to be an accommodation listing.

All of which was, once again, probably totally unnecessary. As were the similar precautions Leon set in train when the short and rotund agent looking after the rented apartment met him a few moments later before escorting him into what would be his home for the next few days.

Leon followed the agent around the apartment as he made his usual checks on the electricity and water meters, making sure he was by his side all the time, double-checking that his guide wasn't, at the same time, planting any bugs.

Then, and only then, as the door closed behind his unwanted companion, did Leon begin to feel at least halfway safe.

Across the pedestrianised walkway and inside that church serving coffees and teas, the woman seated at a small wooden table sipped her coffee from a chipped mug handed to her by a waiter who looked and acted as if he had special needs.

That wasn't an unkind judgement on her part of his professional abilities. The church was staffed by volunteers cared for by a local charity.

Still sipping her coffee, the woman kept watch as the rotund letting agent came back out of the apartment block. She kept watching as he extracted a file from his briefcase before scanning the street for the arrival of yet another short-term tenant.

Deliberately, because the woman was good, she kept her eyes at street level all the while, making sure she didn't look up once at the windows of the apartments sited above the various retail outlets before her. If her quarry was looking down onto the street it would be the first thing he'd be looking for, a pair of eyes raised upwards, searching for a mark, perhaps unable to resist speculating which apartment he was in right now.

The woman had actually been quite impressed with the tradecraft this mark had demonstrated. She'd watched, amused, but with a grudging respect as he'd completed his various, circuitous, perambulations earlier in the day. For an amateur, she had to concede, he really wasn't that bad.

Or maybe he was just desperate.

The problem being that whether he was desperate or not he was still very definitely an amateur.

Opposite, in one of the apartments, the blinds in a window suddenly twitched, presumably as a resident looked out. That same blind remained half-parted for a few more moments during which the woman at the rickety wooden table kept sipping her coffee and kept her eyes firmly fixed on the street. She couldn't be absolutely sure it was the blinds in Leon's rented apartment but the last thing she was going to do was look up and check.

Dimly, on the very edge of her vision, she was aware of those same blinds moving one final time before they stilled.

And all the time the woman, watching but not watching, sipped her coffee.

Back inside the apartment, Leon hunched down on the floor and now he did what he'd wanted to do for days. What he would have done earlier if he'd seen the woman from Bourbon or Burton Biscuits or the overweight male.

Leon howled soundlessly.

And all the time he did so, the same question raced around inside his head.

Did someone know?

All that Roman had come to tell him that day, was all that true?

But who could know? There was one direct witness to it all admittedly in Donna, but she was dead herself less than twenty-four hours later.

And even if Donna had told Clare, even if the small child

had confided in her mother all she saw in that room that night, within that same twenty-four hour period, Clare would be dead too.

A raw Leon shook his head. So many questions. So many ghosts from a past he thought was dead.

Leon remained on the floor of the rented apartment, silent screams echoing inside again, drowning out – or trying to drown out – everything else.

But not quite everything.

Because, suddenly, Leon opened his eyes and stared down the small hallway.

Someone was opening the door.

18.

I<small>T HAD BEEN</small> a frustrating couple of weeks for Aidan.

He'd imagined it would be easy to trace the elusive Macklyn. Not that it would have been easy for most people, but Aidan had never counted himself amongst that unfortunate breed. Most members of the public, for example, wouldn't have access to a police officer who could trace vehicle registration numbers for them.

Aidan and his police contact, Don, had once been leading lights in the same paedophile ring. Back then, Don had been only too willing to provide Aidan with the occasional favour in return for his activities not coming to the attention of his employers. In those circumstances the occasional titbit of information seemed a small price to pay.

But now there was a complication. Don had recently turned thirty and with a seemingly-successful marriage to his name and counting two small children as amongst life's blessings too, Don had come to regard his former dalliance with underage boys as some people view a brush with drugs in their youth. Something regrettable and regretted, an early lapse of judgement to be consigned to history.

Don believed he rather broke the mould in that respect. In one of the more excruciatingly uncomfortable afternoons of his life, Don had once attended a lecture given by a well-respected and high-ranking female police officer regarding the character and make-up of the typical paedophile.

In the company of dozens of his colleagues he'd listened as the incidence of paedophile activity in old age was compared to the incidence of rape. He'd studied the charts she'd handed out which demonstrated beyond any doubt that rapists tended to tire of their compulsion, as attested by the crime figures recording such activity. Rape, as he read, was almost statistically non-existent amongst eighty year olds for example.

But paedophile activity simply never stopped. It didn't seem to matter what age the perpetrator might be or how enfeebled they might become; they all seemed to look at small children in exactly the same way.

More than once during the course of that lecture and the question and answer session that followed, Don had wanted to stand up and challenge the rather terrifying female cop. He'd have loved to point out that there were definitely exceptions to that seemingly all-encompassing rule, but as he would have had to cite himself as an example, Don, perhaps wisely, decided to keep that to himself.

But the fact remained that for the last three years, ever since the birth of his first child and the subsequent birth of his second, Don had bucked a seemingly-inevitable trend. He was, in his own eyes anyway, living proof that a man could emerge from the other side of an admittedly-unsavoury predilection to become a well-balanced and useful member of society.

Don had even joined the local church where he'd risen through an unofficial hierarchy to become the head bell-ringer, a duty that was only entrusted to a very select few as he'd proudly pointed out to any of his colleagues who cared to listen. Not too many did, but he still pointed it out anyway.

So when Aidan turned up completely out of the blue and made his fresh request for some new piece of inside information, a resolute Don simply refused. Aidan might have been able to exert pressure at one time courtesy of Don's youthful indiscretions but – and as he stoutly maintained to Aidan – those indiscretions were very much part of his past.

And the following Sunday, Don rang his local church bells with even more gusto than usual.

A few days after those church bells rang out, Don's eldest son Michael celebrated his third birthday.

Up to then the family had marked those kinds of milestones with small, low-key, celebrations. But Michael had recently started in the local nursery and now he had a small collection of friends, all of whom seemed to celebrate their birthdays with rather more pomp and ceremony.

Some parents hired halls in the local leisure centre, others squired small parties of excited children to a local amusement park, while one had even arranged a themed event in a local chain eatery complete with a professional children's entertainer.

One of Don's own colleagues had even arranged for a party of breathless youngsters to spend half an hour with a specialist police driver sampling the delights of the local force's skid pan.

And so Don had bowed to the inevitable, although even then he didn't go in for quite such extravagances. He was still only a lowly PC after all, albeit with dreams of passing his sergeant's exams one day. So Don, praying for good weather, bought a paddling pool complete with slide.

Don's wife, Susan, prepared a minor feast packed with all the goodies small boys and girls might like, all researched with her characteristic thoroughness. Her mother had divorced when Susan was quite small, having made an unfortunate marriage to a feckless partner, and Susan still couldn't quite believe her luck in landing a good man with a steady job.

Meanwhile, a smiling Don watched as the first of the arriving small children dashed off to change into their costumes.

Aidan made his appearance twenty minutes later. To say that it was a shock for Don was an understatement. Aidan had not been invited, although the man himself seemed pretty confident he wouldn't be turned away.

Not when Don saw Aidan's youthful companion at his side, the totally angelic-looking, blond-haired five year old he'd brought along with him.

The five year old was the youngest child of Aidan's habitually-stressed sister who had absolutely no hesitation in agreeing to his offer to take her small boy off her hands for the afternoon. The small boy himself also had no hesitation in agreeing to attend a birthday party, even if he didn't actually know the birthday boy. The pool and the slide were all that mattered. And the sweets and the cakes.

Don intercepted the smiling Aidan as he approached across the small lawn. Pasting on a strained smile himself, he had intended to get rid of the interlopers at all speed until the face of the smallest interloper looked up at him, and Don felt as if he'd suddenly been hit by a thunderbolt.

Because all of a sudden there it was again, that uncontrollable shake in his stomach, the sudden and devastating dryness in his gullet, a thirst no simple drink could slake. Suddenly, it was back, only now it felt more intense than ever as if the monster that had suddenly awakened had been gathering strength in the years it had lain dormant, like some mythical, terrifying, beast from a child's fairytale.

Only this wasn't a fairytale. This was real. This young boy whose name Don didn't even know yet was real too. As was that dryness in his throat which now felt as if it was spreading through the rest of his body.

Don turned away, and for a moment he was still doing all he'd been doing just a few moments before.

Don was still standing in the rear garden of his suburban house in the company of a group of indulgently-smiling parents watching as a small group of children splashed around in an inflatable pool.

By his side his wife had already started handing out the first of the day's treats to evermore excited children, one of which was their very own birthday boy.

Across the lawn a couple of well-respected elders from his local church, including the head verger and his wife, were setting out chairs, getting ready for some game later on.

Everything was as it had been, but everything had changed.

The world kept on turning, but Don's world had shuddered to a stop.

Don turned back once more. Now, he almost didn't feel as if he was there at all. He also didn't feel as if he was the person he'd been just moments before either. Now he just stared across at that one young boy in amongst all the other boys and girls, and all he could think about was how to get that one boy alone for the few moments he needed to do what he now knew he had to do.

A short distance away, the knowing Aidan recognised only too clearly the look on Don's face. Alone of all the other party guests, Aidan was well aware what that look meant and was also only too well aware that with his young companion at his side, Aidan was now going to easily achieve what had formerly been denied him.

Aidan looked across at his young charge, now changed into the swimming trunks Aidan had brought with them, joining his new friends in the paddling pool.

And Aidan was already wondering what other advantages

this gift might bring him, before nature ruined what God created by making small boys grow old.

Post, as in actual post, meaning a direct communication and not some generic mail-out, was unusual.

Macklyn received junk mail in abundance, of course. Adverts for double glazing, exhortations to carry out this or that home improvement, invitations to donate to various local and national charities, most of the latter arriving, somewhat bizarrely he'd always thought, with greeting cards or pens engraved with the name of the charity of choice.

But then, one day, there'd been something different and it had sent shivers down his spine. Because as he opened the envelope Macklyn found a whole row of small, neatly-printed, address labels inside, all inscribed with his own name and address.

It didn't matter that it wasn't his actual name, the fact was that someone seemed to know who he was or at least seemed to know the name of the man he'd become. And that bombshell caused him to withdraw completely for a while, to draw the curtains tight and not to venture out, not even to the local shops for the whole of the following week. For a man used to living a life of strict anonymity, to have even his assumed name suddenly become public property in that way sent him into a blind panic.

Then, a week or so later, he'd cautiously ventured out to dump some rubbish and had spotted the postman delivering a similar-looking letter to the house next door.

Macklyn had steered a hopefully innocent-sounding conversation onto the topic of the threatening item of post only to realise that there was no reason to feel threatened at all. Most householders on that street could apparently paper the walls with similar examples of freebie merchandising. Macklyn had returned inside, placed the neatly printed labels in the bin and put the whole thing down to his habitual paranoia.

But that morning there'd actually been post. And this was real post, as Macklyn in common with most of his generation would term it.

And as Macklyn opened the thin envelope on the kitchen table and scanned the contents, he felt his heart begin to race.

A day or so earlier, after duly receiving the information he'd requested from Don, Aidan had looked around the small room in mounting frustration.

Aidan had kept watch on the address he'd been given for most of the day and had finally been rewarded by the sight of Macklyn, car keys in hand, getting into and driving away in the anonymous saloon that Aidan had first seen outside that rural truck stop.

At the same time, Aidan's five-year-old nephew was being driven down to the coast in Don's car for an afternoon's fishing, or so Aidan's still stressed and barely-listening sister had been assured.

Aidan didn't see too much risk. The small boy was unlikely to remember too much about what was going to happen that afternoon and even if he did, Aidan was pretty certain he could persuade him to keep quiet. Aidan could be very persuasive when it came to making small children do his bidding. He'd had a lot of practice over the years.

What concerned Aidan rather more was the suspicion that it could all have been a complete waste of time. Because Macklyn's home was proving something of a big disappointment.

Aidan was on the lookout for something to give him a momentary advantage in some way. He could hardly, after all, simply march up to Macklyn in the street and slap him on the back as a long-lost friend. For a start, they weren't and never had been. And, even if Macklyn did recognise him, he'd hardly recall Aidan as a much-missed model employee. So Aidan needed something else, something to broker a connection.

Aidan looked round, growing more and more agitated by the second. Because there was nothing, no photos on display, no family mementos concealed in any drawers. There were a couple of books out on a table awaiting return to some local library but they were just standard fare, generic Grisham or Archer, either genuine or imitators.

Aidan opened a small fridge, turning away in disgust from the one small carton of semi-skimmed milk inside. Macklyn seemed to be more of a shadow than a living, breathing, human being.

Don't say Aidan's luck was actually beginning to run out at last? Would this be the one catch that somehow managed to squirm itself away from him?

Which was when Aidan saw it. Half-hidden away on a shelf, just behind an ashtray that didn't look as if it had ever seen any use. A small, toy truck. A small truck painted in what looked like a curiously familiar livery.

Aidan picked up the toy, making a careful note of its place on the shelf as he did so. It would be replaced, like every object he'd examined, exactly as he'd found it.

Aidan turned the toy over in his hand, nothing stamped underneath to hint at its provenance. But as he held that small toy, Aidan began to be assailed by the same sensations that had so overwhelmed his former employer when he saw it advertised on that website that day.

Aidan also began to hear the sounds and smells of the lorry yard as the various trucks and vans started up for the day. Once again he relived the habitual shouts, greetings and even the full-blooded curses that would float across that same yard as various drivers set off.

Then Aidan saw a letter tucked underneath the nearby ashtray and, carefully again, he extracted and opened it, scanning what was quite obviously an invoice along with a handwritten note from what must have been the vendor apologising for his not being able to split the collection as requested.

Aidan looked at the address on the invoice. Then he looked back at the toy truck in his hand and then Aidan started to smile.

Maybe his much-fabled good luck hadn't run out after all.

A RMED WITH THE information sourced from Jukes's files – and feeling that even if she still hadn't any actual answers, she was at least beginning to ask more of the right questions – Ros arrived in London.

Ros took the tube from Paddington to Baker Street, then made her way via the Jubilee Line to Canary Wharf, but there Ros paused. She now had a choice of the overland DLR or the river clipper. The former was quicker and cheaper, the latter slow and more expensive. Ros hesitated above the steps that would take her down to the river embarkation point, then looked back at the wide causeway that would lead her to the train station. Then she descended the steps, waited almost fifteen minutes for the clipper to hove into view from central London before arriving at the pier in Greenwich a good thirty minutes after the train would have deposited her just moments from the newly-restored Cutty Sark.

But the delay actually suited Ros as she was now feeling nervous. Mentally she'd been preparing herself for this ever since she started her journey earlier that morning. Now it was upon her, she seemed to need just a few minutes more.

From the pier, Ros cut up the main street, the great parks of Greenwich in front of her. Ros passed an old-fashioned pie-and-mash shop she'd promised herself she'd visit at different times in the past, but not today. Right now, food was just about the last thing on her mind.

Before the entrance to the park that led, via a tortuous climb, to the Royal Observatory, Ros took a right turn, skirted a museum devoted to, of all things, decorative fans, and headed on into a small churchyard. A quick search amongst the simple headstones ended with Ros standing stock-still in front of one in particular. A headstone marking a resting place she'd never, in her life, expected to find.

Ros's trawl through Jukes's files the previous evening had struck gold in more ways than one, because next to the details of Leon's case was another. This second case dated from years before Leon's, and little action had been taken in respect of these clients for almost the whole of that time.

There'd been little need. A couple of the people involved had died and the remaining clients seemed to have lived relatively anonymous lives since they were first taken into the protection programme. Their actual identities were concealed even from Jukes, being identified only by a code, although some details of the lives they were now living had been reasonably well annotated.

So it was that Ros had accessed another sight of the official records that were held on her and the rest of her family.

The majority of it was fairly anodyne stuff. In the case of her father there was his current address along with his National Insurance and passport numbers. In her case, Ros was relieved to see that those details had been removed years previously when she herself had joined the protection programme in her new incarnation as protector rather than one of the protected. Neither Jukes nor anyone else could possibly now make the connection between that former client and herself.

The file had been updated with the last stray sighting of Macklyn in a place he really should not have been – one of the reasons the file had been retrieved in the first place, Ros assumed. But then Ros had found herself staring at another entry, not as recent as the Macklyn sighting, but still dating from the last two years.

It noted the removal of the remains of one of the family's

children from her original burial place in Kent to a site in Greenwich, after the original graveyard had been demolished to make way for a new ring road.

There'd been some protests at the demolition, but not too many. The old graveyard was one of the protection programme's locations of choice for the disposal of bodies whose real identities were lost in time, meaning it was largely populated by real-life ghosts.

Ros stood before the grave of her dead sister, Braith. She wasn't called Braith on the headstone of course. Ros didn't really take in the new name she'd been given. She just stood in silent tribute to a young woman who'd opened a door one day to see a gun pointing back at her and whose last act in life was to move, instinctively, to protect the young girl standing behind.

Ros felt her body give a slight shudder as she remembered the deafening blast that had sounded around their small hall, and the flailing arms of her sister as she crashed back down onto the floor, blood and brains spraying from an entry wound that virtually destroyed her skull, staining the wallpaper all the way up to their first-floor landing before trickling, snail-like, back down onto the carpeted stairs.

Ros had no way of knowing whether that attack on her sister would have been followed by a second attack on her too. It seemed incredible that it would, she was only a five-year-old child at the time. But one thing Ros had learnt over the intervening years was not to count on simple humanity from the people who'd targeted her family back then and who, so far as Ros knew, were still targeting them now.

The man – now dead too – who'd visited all that devastation on their formerly-unexceptional family had upset some maniacally dangerous and determined characters. Those characters were to wait almost twenty years before they finally found and eliminated him. So there was no expectation amongst any of the officers who'd dealt with their case at the time that they'd have hesitated, for even a moment, when it came to the murder of a small girl.

Ros was lucky. But then Braith had made sure of it. She'd moved in front of her small sister, blocking the gunman's path. She'd bought Ros a vital few seconds and Braith's assassin had decided to content himself with just the one, almost literal, scalp that day, probably reassuring himself that he could and would return any time he chose.

Ros kept standing for a moment in silent tribute to a sister she barely remembered, but to whom she owed her life.

But then, as she did so, another lost soul swam before her eyes. The subject of the second of her missions that day.

Braith's world had been destroyed in an instant, but even then her only instinct had been to protect the small child behind her.

But Clare, Joey's wife, had done the opposite. Clare's world had also been destroyed, in her case by her husband's discovery of her affair with Leon and the murderous rampage that had precipitated. But then Clare had taken the life of her small child along with her own.

Only according to the original interviews with Leon, interviews Ros had read the previous evening, Leon had simply never accepted it. At the time Leon's interviewing officers had just put it down to shock, but now Ros was beginning to wonder.

Ros looked back at her lost sister's grave and gave the silent thanks she'd wanted to give for the last twenty years, standing in still-silent tribute for a few moments longer.

Then Ros turned and walked away.

Back in Cardiff, the rotund letting agent was not happy and, in the absence of the short-term tenant he really wanted to blame, was venting his spleen on the two police officers who also seemed to have a bone to pick with him.

'Look at the place, just look at it for fuck's sake.'

Which was exactly what a silent Masters was doing.

'What was he thinking of?'

Which was exactly what Masters was wondering too.

As the agent ranted and raved, Masters looked round some more. The apartment seemed, as the now-sweating letting agent was volubly pointing out, to have hosted one hell of a party. Chairs had been smashed, the walls had great chunks gouged out of them and the kitchen had been totally trashed.

Across the small hall, Hendrix was checking out the bedroom and bathroom but something was telling Masters it was likely to be the same story there too.

'The deposit isn't even going to begin to cover all this and now you lot are looking for him too, so what the fuck's going on here, is he some kind of nutter or something?'

Hendrix came back into the living room, gave a slight shake of his head. All Leon's personal effects had been removed, including his clothes. Aside from the damage, and that was considerable, the flat had been completely swept clean.

The letting agent fumed on, sweating more as he did so, his blood pressure rocketing now to danger levels if the pink spots on his cheeks were anything to go by.

'If he's been let out of somewhere when he shouldn't have been, then I want to know because someone's got to pay for this and I don't see why it should be me.'

Masters moved to the window, looked down at the CCTV camera covering the front of the building. At Masters's insistence, it had taken an increasingly whey-faced operative more than sixteen solid hours of continual checking before the initial sighting of Leon had been made.

It had taken Masters and Hendrix sixteen minutes to check which of the apartments in the complex had been recently let and by whom and a further six minutes to appropriate the keys, but it had still been too little too late. Leon had already gone.

Masters looked across at a church opposite as, behind him, the letting agent risked a further escalation in his blood pressure by beginning a written checklist of the damage.

The problem being that while some quite serious activity had obviously taken place inside the apartment, there was no sign of a forced entry from the outside. The front door of the apartment was undamaged, as was the lock. The communal corridor was still in the pristine state in which it had been left by the cleaners that very morning. Which was a puzzle to add to an already-existing conundrum.

But all of a sudden there was another complication added into the mix.

'And he'd been told about the sub-letting clause too, so what the fuck was that all about?'

Masters had been looking at the holes in the wall, trying to assess whether the indentations could approximate to the dimensions of a human head. Now he looked back at the letting agent.

'Girlfriends popping in, fair enough. Book an escort for the night, no sweat. But this is a one-signature let, everything's priced for that: gas, electric, the lot, but according to the neighbours she was here more than he was.'

Masters and Hendrix kept staring at him.

Ten minutes later the two officers were down in the basement with the concierge responsible for the whole block.

The concierge's duties included delivering the internal mail, replacing lost keys, supervising disputes over underground parking spaces and liaising with various contractors as they carried out minor and occasionally major repairs. As such, he was the resident eyes and ears and was now confirming all the stressed letting agent had just told them.

'I thought she was the tenant to be honest.'

The concierge shrugged.

'Hardly saw him at all.'

Masters and Hendrix stared at an upmarket motorbike still parked in its allotted bay in the underground garage, the chariot of choice, apparently, for the female in question.

A quick check had already established it was stolen from another part of the city several days before, its principal attraction already only too clear. The woman – whoever she was and whatever she was doing there – could then park the bike and travel up to the apartment with her helmet still in place. When she'd left that same apartment her helmet would still be clamped on her head as the few random CCTV images they'd manage to source thus far had confirmed, rendering recognition impossible.

Meaning they had no idea what Leon was doing in that apartment.

They had no idea how the damage to that apartment had been caused.

And they had no idea who he might have shared that apartment with either, be that willingly or unwillingly.

Or at least one of the officers in that underground garage had no idea.

Hendrix looked across at Masters as he continued his interrogation of the concierge, one thought running almost constantly now through his head.

Because Masters hadn't really seemed surprised by any of this. His eyes had widened slightly as he'd taken in the scale of the damage in Leon's rented apartment. But where Hendrix had been totally bewildered, there was almost a resignation in Masters's eyes as he stared at it all.

Hendrix looked at the stolen motorbike and felt a familiar frustration building inside. He absolutely hated being kept in the dark on anything, loathed being out of any loop. And he knew Ros felt exactly the same.

So why hadn't she responded to him out on that riverbank that day? Why had she just studied him with those cool eyes of hers, then turned and walked on?

And why hadn't she followed all that up in any way, either by calling to take him up on all he'd said or reporting his approach to Masters?

From Greenwich, Ros took the river clipper back to central London. She disembarked at Embankment, cutting up Northumberland Avenue and across Trafalgar Square. She walked through the gift shop of the National Portrait Gallery a few moments later, heading into one of the display areas on the ground floor before joining a six-foot seven-inch apparition dressed, that afternoon, in an all-cream suit set off with pale suede cowboy boots.

Eddie Faulkner was sitting alone, which wasn't unusual. One look at his forbidding frame and idiosyncratic dress sense and most people steered a wide berth. Occasionally some boozed-up male, usually on a night out, would try to give him grief, almost always to try and impress a girlfriend, but they'd only ever do it the once. The girlfriends didn't usually hang around too long either.

Eddie used to be a star of the old-style wrestling ring. At one time, in terms of audience appeal, he'd been up there with genuine greats such as the Royal Brothers and Johnny Saint. Most of those former stars had quickly faded once they'd hung up their leopard-skin leotards, but Eddie's star had risen to heights he could only have dreamt of in his days in the grunt and groan game.

Initially, and like so many of his contemporaries, Eddie had gone into security, standing guard on the door at nightclubs or forming part of a human barricade at various public events. But Eddie had always been an inquisitive, if not ambitious, type and he'd started talking to some of the men as well as the occasional woman who now dispensed his daily bread. That included one woman who could have been a wrestler herself, given her name of Linzi Lake. Linzi had inherited a security business from her late father and she'd asked for Eddie's help in cracking an attempted sting by a competitor.

Eddie discovered he had a nose for sniffing out treachery and used his size fifteen Chelsea boots to kick out not only the competitor but some of the woman's own staff who were also on the payroll of that competitor and looking to bring down her business from within.

Linzi, in turn, discovered true love.

Eddie and Linzi married six months later. From that point on, as well as running their joint business, he'd been used by various organizations, including the local police, to gather information which would otherwise remain hidden from official view.

No-one asked how he sourced that information. That didn't matter. Eddie always got results. That was all that did.

Ros seated herself next to him, staring out at the faces now in front of them. This particular exhibition charted the progress of various child actors from precocious stardom to oblivion. Previous exhibitions they'd enjoyed had featured a roll call of Great Train Robbers. Another – Ros's favourite – had featured Eddie himself in a photographic tribute to the demigods of the profession he'd once graced.

'So who is it this time?'

As she'd done on many other occasions in the past, Ros just slid a photo across to her companion who picked it up, studied it.

'And what's he done?'

'I don't know.'

Eddie nodded. Too many answers and he'd have been worried. That was his job.

'I found that photograph and his name in a file last night.'

Ros looked over Eddie's shoulder, studied the lean skinhead featured in the photo, his arms decorated with tattoos, feet clad in Union Jack-bedecked boots.

'His name's Ryan. Jack Ryan. He's something to do with a murder that took place a few years ago. Or he might have something to do with a copycat murder that took place a week or so ago, or he might have something to do with both, I don't know.'

Ros paused.

'There's also a woman's name alongside his. Just a Christian name this time, Jen. Again, I don't know who she is, maybe someone he's involved with, someone he shouldn't be involved with.'

Ros paused again.

'All I do know is that photo and his name was in the file. And I want to know why.'

Eddie studied the photo some more and the expression on his face said it all. Something about the face, the pose – not to mention the boots – was sounding some sort of warning bell.

Ros looked at him.

'What?'

'I don't know.'

Eddie struggled for a moment as Ros kept looking at him. Maybe all those years performing all those pantomime falls had given Eddie a sixth sense when it came to this sort of thing. Or maybe, as Ros had always suspected, he was just very, very bright.

'He looks fake.'

Ros didn't need to relax, but as she looked out past the crowds streaming in to pay tribute to fallen idols, she did anyway. With Eddie, she'd always felt on the surest of ground. And she'd just had the confirmation she really didn't need, that once again she could leave this part of her new quest in the safest of hands.

Ros kept looking out past the crowds milling around on all sides of them. Something told her it was going to be a very different story with the person she had to see next.

ONE WEEK AFTER his son's third birthday party, Don was press-ganged into another strange endeavour.

Most previous favours he'd performed for Aidan had usually involved the supply of information sourced from inside his own police headquarters. Standard fare in other words, but occasionally there was something more curious, like today.

For the life of him Don couldn't see how his posing as a toy collector and selling on some small trucks and vans to some other, more aged, collector he had to meet in a three-star hotel could possibly help Aidan, but the truth was he didn't really care.

All he cared about was the small boy Aidan had brought to that birthday party, a boy he'd already got to know on a day out, although not yet in the sense he craved. Then he'd just contented himself with building bridges as they fished a local river. But every time the picture of that flaxen-haired child wafted before his eyes, he was transported to a very different place with very different matters in mind.

The hotel was on the link road running out from Newport and up into the Valleys. Don settled himself on the sagging armchair in the open-plan reception area, watched as harassed business-types checked in around him, made a mental note not to avail himself of the buffet lunch he could see being laid out for the benefit of several elderly men and women now shuffling towards it.

Then he looked down at the table and tried to look at least a little interested in the contents of the small boxes he'd been deputed to bring along and deliver that day, just in case one of those elderly men suddenly turned out to be, not a diner, but his contact.

Five minutes later and with the still-shuffling procession now making their hesitant selections, a shadow fell across Don as a figure he hadn't expected approached.

The man certainly looked elderly, but in a curious way he was actually quite difficult to age. It was as if he'd been prematurely aged somehow. His face betrayed the ravages of advancing years – or possibly something else – but his frame still seemed strong, his handshake firm and manly.

And Don grew evermore puzzled. Because his new companion might have been blessed with that strong frame and that firm and manly handshake, but in all other respects he was completely and totally nondescript, there was simply no other way to describe him.

He was even dressed anonymously. A V-neck jumper over a check shirt and tie, comfortable loafers and neatly-pressed Marks and Spencer trousers that would probably still be called slacks by the sixty-something in question.

And yet, there was something else to him and Don could sense it. Not that he was going to find out. His new companion, as well as being so seemingly unremarkable as to almost make him remarkable if that made any sense, was also determinedly taciturn. Any attempt at small talk on Don's part was met with an almost total stonewall. All his visitor's interest and attention was on one thing and one thing only, and that was the collection of toy trucks Don had brought with him, one of which he now handed over for inspection.

Which was when the most astonishing thing happened. Don had never been the poetic type but if he'd possessed the language to describe the strange phenomenon he now suddenly witnessed, he'd have compared it to some kind of chrysalis opening up before him. All of a sudden a new life force seemed to infuse the strange and withdrawn man who'd shuffled in just those few moments before and all it had taken was the simple unpacking of a box and the extraction of a single toy truck.

His visitor's back, previously stooped, seemed to straighten and the years seemed to fall away from his face, and for a moment Don spotted a younger and quite different man instead.

Not that Don could have known it, but it wasn't the first time such a transformation had taken place inside Macklyn. And all it had taken was one single letter from, apparently, the original seller of Macklyn's previous toy truck.

The seller in question, it seemed, had remembered Macklyn's keen interest in toy vehicles painted in that one particular livery. And by chance he'd just taken in a collection from a recently-deceased enthusiast who seemed to have specialised in the esoteric and the unusual. The upshot was he had a collection of six trucks and vans all painted in that exact livery and all, apparently, forming a complete collection.

Sitting at his small table in his kitchen, Macklyn wracked his brains. He remembered the one promotion that had been done by a toy manufacturer in co-operation with the local council back then, but he really couldn't remember anything like a complete collection. Then again, maybe all that had been done in that period after his departure when his company had limped on for a short time while its assets were disposed of and the workforce resettled.

Not that fine details like the whys and wherefores bothered him that much anyway. Because ever since he'd opened that letter that morning he hadn't had any sort of headache or migraine or anything else that useless quack of a doctor had called it. He was feeling better than he'd felt for months, if not years. And once he'd replied to the email address on the letter and agreed to the suggested meeting with his unexpected benefactor, he felt even better.

Macklyn brought out the single toy truck he'd acquired so far. He turned it over in his hand, wondering if, unlike this one, the logo was still intact on some of the others? With six more trucks and vans on offer, there had to be a good chance.

Then Macklyn looked out of the window. He knew it was more than a little ridiculous. He was a grown man excited beyond words at the thought of acquiring a toy collection. But it was more than that of course. And as Macklyn's mind now drifted back onto the collector, the man who'd taken the trouble to contact him and to let him know about this new acquisition, he felt another unaccustomed emotion now too.

Macklyn had little to thank anyone for over the previous twenty or so years. But now Macklyn felt a positive surge of gratitude.

Back in the three-star hotel, Don leant forward across the chipped and stained low table that separated him from his visitor.

'So are they a present?'

But Macklyn hardly seemed to hear him. All his attention was fixed on the toy truck in his hand, his mind on the five other packages also containing similar toys and all painted in the same livery and all, apparently, back in Don's room.

'For a grandson, maybe?'

Macklyn looked up at Don and, just for a moment, Don now saw something else in his eyes. And now he did have the vocabulary to describe the emotion he could read there because it was an emotion Don understood only too well.

Don saw need, but he saw more than that too.

Don saw simple, naked, desire.

And Don hunched closer, growing evermore intrigued by the minute.

'Or did you have something like these when you were a kid, have they got sentimental value or something?'

And, equally suddenly again, it was like a switch had been thrown. At the same time the prematurely-aged man's back adopted its more habitual stoop. The younger and quite different man who'd peeked, all-too-briefly, from under the older incarnation vanished, and Don was left once again with the sixty-something in the V-neck jumper and check shirt and tie and the Marks and Spencer trousers he probably still called slacks.

'I'll take them.'

It was virtually all the old man had said since he'd first walked in. At the same time, he took some cash out from an old wallet extracted from the inside pocket of his coat and placed the correct and exact sum of money for the small collection down on the table. Don hesitated, but he quite clearly wasn't going to get any more out of his visitor, so Don just checked the money and told the old man to come with him to his room where he was storing the rest.

Macklyn stood, taking out a recycled carrier bag from his coat pocket – M&S – what else? He placed the sample toy inside, then followed Don past the swing doors and along the corridor to a standard room on the ground floor.

21.

R OS CUT ACROSS Haymarket and, turning her back on the thronged thoroughfare of Piccadilly, crisscrossed her way through the back streets of St James where she paused by the London Library.

As she always did whenever she was there, Ros moved into the reception area and stood for a moment, drinking in a place that almost rivalled her Amsterdam retreat for spiritual appeal. If Ros didn't live in the Welsh capital rather than the English one, and if she'd been on the sort of pay grade that would permit such indulgences, she'd have taken out a lifetime membership on the spot. But Ros didn't, so that was that.

Ros remained for a few moments. As ever, no-one bothered her or asked her what she was doing. She could have stayed longer but while those metaphorical woods were, as always, wonderfully dark and deep, she still had all those promises to keep. And so Ros retraced her steps a moment or so later and headed back outside, but not before helping herself to a complimentary bookmark and embossed carrier bag from the reception desk.

A few minutes later after once again crisscrossing various alleys and lanes, Ros was looking up at the elegant façade of an upmarket apartment block just a few metres down from The Ritz.

At the reception desk she asked a concierge she'd seen before on her sole previous visit, and who always seemed to be smiling, to announce her arrival to one of the block's long-term residents. The concierge checked a sheet before him. The resident's silver Bentley was in the garage, the concierge had valet-parked it himself after giving it the obligatory valet clean of course. All he had to do was check the man himself was up in his park-view apartment and whether it was convenient for him to receive an unexpected visitor. The concierge did so – still smiling all the while – and Masters, albeit after a moment's hesitation, told the concierge to show Ros up.

Travelling in the mirrored elevator, and not for the first time, Ros allowed her mind to drift briefly and wonderingly on the personal circumstances of a man who maintained this sort of opulent accommodation as a weekend retreat.

Then the doors opened onto a carpeted corridor and Masters stood facing her. So, to Ros's surprise, did Jukes. But she didn't waste any time in wondering why. More pressing matters took over instead.

'She wouldn't have done it.'

Masters stared at Ros as, now in his apartment and taking a leaf out of his own book, she plunged straight in. If he'd been surprised by her unexpected appearance on his doorstep he hadn't, one momentary hesitation aside, shown it. And if Masters was surprised by her opening gambit, he wasn't showing it either.

'It's all Leon kept saying. When he was first interviewed. The same thing over and over.'

Ros nodded back at Masters who maintained his unblinking stare. Minor details such as how the hell Ros had accessed that interview in the first place didn't arise. That was strictly restricted material but Masters gave that the same consideration as Ros had just given to his living arrangements. He could have asked but he wouldn't have been told the truth. And it was hardly the matter of the moment anyway.

With a silent Jukes looking on, Ros handed Masters a print-out of selected sections of Leon's original interviews, highlighting the passages where the stunned and rambling Leon had repeated himself time and again.

In some strange, almost elemental, way Leon had understood everything else. His brother's crazed attack. The torture inflicted on Toya who'd desperately tried to bar his way to his wife.

Much of what Joey did that night was beyond all reason and all understanding, but Leon could still connect with it in some way.

But the one detail with which Leon could never connect, which he could never understand as he made clear over and over again in those initial interviews, was the killing of her daughter, Donna, by Clare.

Leon understood Clare's guilt. He understood that she was a woman tormented by demons, appalled by the unexpected consequences of her actions. Or, more accurately, hers and Leon's actions.

And yes, he understood she was looking for a way out and if she'd taken that way out, alone, if they'd found her body at the bottom of some cliff somewhere or slumped on a floor beside a bottle of pills, then Leon would have accepted it without a second thought.

But she didn't do that, she killed Donna too, and so Leon kept repeating the same anguished, impotent mantra, almost as if he was trying to deny it had even happened at all.

At which point in her initial reading of the files, Ros had looked up from the transcripts and had looked out of the window of her first-floor apartment, down onto the small bank where she'd met Hendrix those few days before.

And she'd paused at exactly the same point in her re-reading of it all the following day, looking out on fields and farms and wide rivers and small streams as she made the train journey that had brought her to this most opulent of settings, the same feeling growing inside all the while.

Back then, everyone had put it down to simple shock, to events too painful to even begin to absorb. Masters had even made a note to that effect in the margin of the restricted file.

But now, years later, standing in the hallway of his upmarket apartment with a distant view of Green Park glimpsed via the floor-to-ceiling window in front of her, Ros saw something else. For the first time in all the years she'd known him, Ros actually witnessed something cross Masters's face, and from the look on Jukes's face he seemed to have seen it too.

Ros had seen anger there, and many times too. She'd actually seen grief once at the scene of a particularly vicious double-killing of one of his officers and his wife. But what she was seeing now was something she never expected to see from the likes of a man such as Masters. Because what Ros was seeing now was regret.

Ros pressed on.

'And Kim – what happened to her – the one thing none of us could understand was why? Why would someone go to all those lengths to make her think her baby was dying when it simply wasn't true?'

Ros kept staring at the still-silent Masters.

'But what if that wasn't the point? What if it was nothing to do with her, not really? Yes, she was targeted because of her connection to Roman but what if someone was trying to tell us something else?'

Masters kept staring back.

'Kim thought her baby was dead but he wasn't. Just like we're supposed to think someone else is dead but maybe that's the whole point, maybe she isn't either.'

Masters just kept staring at her. In truth, he wasn't surprised Ros had worked it out. If he had to put money on anyone doing so, it would have been her. Not that it made a great deal of difference.

And, finally, he spoke.

'Donna was her masterpiece. Her living legacy if you like. Her passport to immortality. Leon was right, Clare would never have killed her.'

Ros kept looking at him.

'And she didn't?'

Masters, with Jukes still silent at his side, just kept looking back at her, the expression on their faces Ros's all-too-eloquent reply.

2 2 .

ALL MACKLYN SAW was a flash. And, for a moment, some memory of an event he himself hadn't experienced but still lived with day-in, day-out, was suddenly before his eyes.

Another blinding flash. A world drained of colour as a bullet smashed into his eldest daughter's brain, her body crashing to the floor of their small hallway a moment later.

Then Macklyn realised he wasn't being fired at by any sort of gun. He was just being photographed, over and over again, by a figure standing in the room he'd just entered and that same figure was talking now too, although Macklyn couldn't really take in what he was saying, at least at first.

Behind Macklyn, Don picked up the camera Aidan had now placed back on the table and began taking photographs himself.

'We know, Macklyn, don't even try denying it, it's out there, it's taken a while, but now it really is.'

Macklyn still wasn't really taking in the words. At least not their meaning. He was just taking in the name.

Macklyn.

This man, this stranger, was calling him by his actual name, a name he hadn't used for so many years now and which hadn't been used by anyone else in all those years either, a name that absolutely no-one else was supposed to know.

All the time more flashes illuminated the room, capturing more and more images of Macklyn's bewildered face.

'You've been lucky, so lucky, but this is it, this is the end of the line, the day that luck of yours finally runs out.'

Macklyn could now see the small collection of toy trucks and vans on the table, the object of his visit that day, or so Macklyn had fondly imagined.

'But then again – .'

And now the man's expression shifted, something more calculating stealing into his eyes. And again, out of nowhere, another memory returned to the staring Macklyn.

He was back to the day of the shooting again, to the day his life and the life of his family changed forever. But this memory wasn't of that family, this memory was of a face still just out of reach.

The owner of those calculating eyes nodded at him.

'It's not completely out there yet. So far, I know, and my friend here knows.'

Aidan nodded at Don, the camera still in his hand, now shooting pictures of the wallpaper just behind Macklyn's head. Don had no idea what Aidan was talking about and no real idea why he was taking these photographs either, but he didn't care. There was only one thing on his mind and that was his promised liaison with Aidan's small nephew later that afternoon, so he just kept snapping away, playing his full part in whatever was supposed to be happening here.

Moving closer, Aidan nodded at Macklyn.

'And you know, Macklyn, but so far as I can see that's it. Three people in the world who know, and one of them's not going to say anything is he? Well, why would you? You've had a lot of practice keeping quiet all these years.'

Aidan nodded across at Don who fired off another series of snaps.

'And my friend here could probably be persuaded to keep quiet; he doesn't know you after all, so why should he say anything?'

Aidan shook his head, almost sadly.

'But I don't look at it like that, I'm not so easily persuaded.'

And, suddenly, Macklyn had him. As if out of the ether, he saw a figure walking towards his office back in his old transport yard, Macklyn watching him every step of the way, almost seeing the thought processes going on in what he'd always suspected was a devious little brain, wondering how easily his new employer would swallow a story he must have known himself was deeply unconvincing.

But he'd obviously been prepared to give it a go which was the clearest possible evidence not only of that devious little brain, but of his rank stupidity as well.

Back in the present, Aidan was now extracting the unresisting Macklyn's wallet from his coat and was flipping through it, finding nothing aside from a few banknotes, little more than sixty pounds in total, but taking it nevertheless.

Then Aidan nodded at Don, a silent signal that his part in the proceedings was over and Don didn't need a second invitation to head away. Don took a few extra snaps, then left the two men to their business, whatever that might be. Don still didn't know or care.

Aidan looked back at Macklyn. He didn't want Don to discover the sort of money he now had in mind. Don might get ideas. The one thing Aidan had learnt from an early age was that you really couldn't trust anyone.

'A thousand tomorrow. At this time tomorrow. Then a thousand the day after. Same time again. By the end of the week I want ten. Another ten thousand the week after that. Then we'll see where we are.'

Then Aidan paused as he contemplated the seemingly-broken figure before him, shaking his head as he did so, almost sadly again.

'It catches up, Macklyn, it always does. It takes a little longer with some than others, but it always catches up and this isn't so bad, is it? A few grand just to keep everything quiet, everything under wraps, a few small little payments and then it all goes away again.'

Aidan picked up one of the toy trucks on the table.

'No.'

It was all the man who had once been Macklyn said. The only word he'd uttered from the moment Aidan had all-but imprisoned him in that anonymous hotel room.

And Aidan smiled. He'd just been handed his one little bit of extra leverage on a plate.

Aidan scooped the rest of the small collection back into the pocket of his coat.

'You get one of these each time I come back too. And each time I do come back everything I know gets that little bit harder to remember. And the last time I call, the last time you give me the last of my money, that's the moment it all gets wiped.'

Which wasn't going to be all that difficult, as Aidan silently reflected. Despite all his bluster, he still didn't actually know what Macklyn had done or why Macklyn had suddenly vanished from their lives like that.

'Same time tomorrow.'

Then the door closed behind Aidan and he was gone.

But Macklyn didn't even look after Aidan and he didn't even register the closing door. All he was looking at was the table which was now empty, his precious collection of toy trucks and vans all painted in the livery of his old transport company gone.

Macklyn slowly seated himself at the table and stared at the space where the collection had been.

As Aidan walked past the last of the elderly diners making their lunch choices, he was computing numbers.

A hundred grand had been his initial estimate and he saw no reason to revise that downwards now.

Aidan had spent a lot of time doing the sums. He'd factored in the likely value of the transport business, making a fairly conservative estimate regarding what Macklyn might actually own and what he might have leased. All that had been guesswork as Aidan would have been the first to concede, but he had been able to estimate what Macklyn's rather nice semi-detached house would have been worth back then. All he'd had to do was scroll back through the pages of various property-listing sites on the internet to see the price similar houses in the same area had sold for around the time his former employer had so mysteriously disappeared.

Aidan exited the hotel, crossed a small car park and headed up onto a nearby feeder road where he stood in line for a bus which arrived a few moments later.

Then Aidan boarded the bus and looked back at the hotel as it drove away, the first of the elderly diners now emerging after their buffet. And as the bus turned a corner ahead, Aidan felt the small toys he'd brought out with him chink, reassuringly, in his pocket.

One hour earlier, standing in Masters's upmarket London apartment, Ros had actually felt a sudden stab of fear.

All Ros had begun to suspect was true.

Donna was alive.

Clare hadn't killed her daughter in that inferno.

That story was a fiction invented by officers keen to rescue something from the wreckage the young girl's life had become. Then she'd been reinvented, just as Ros herself had been. The intention was that maybe then she'd be set free from all that had happened in an attempt, however hopeful, to give her some sort of normal upbringing.

Which was when Ros had felt that sudden stab of fear. Because she was now on the trail of a young woman just like herself. She was trying to trace another woman whose past had been hidden from general view. And if Ros could do that with Donna, then could someone, at some time, do the same with her?

Not that Ros shared that with Masters. Or with Jukes. Or revealed her sudden and strictly private fear.

More immediate matters were concerning her right now.

'Donna has no connection with what happened to Roman.'

Ros stared back at Masters in disbelief.

'Despite the fact that she didn't die in the fire?'

Masters just rode on.

'Donna's been tracked, forensically, ever since. Tabs have been kept on her every movement. Anyway, all that was only a few years ago, do the maths, does any of this even remotely look like the work of a teenager to you?'

Ros stared back at him again, the expression on her face her only too eloquent reply.

Why not?

Masters stared back, cheeks mottling.

'So what are you saying, that we're in the middle of some crazy vendetta, what the fuck would be the point? And why target Roman of all people?'

Masters maintained his stout denials for the next half-hour. By his side, Jukes stayed silent, although the silence from her senior officer was already telling Ros all she needed to know. This wasn't just a trademark desire on the part of Murder Squad not to share any more information than was absolutely necessary. This was something else. Something even her own senior officer wasn't going to share with her, even now, when she'd got so close, through fair means or foul, to finding out what was actually going on. As well as trying to find out what might have happened to two missing clients.

An evermore frustrated Ros turned to go. This was fast turning into the same old story. On almost every case she could ever remember, small details were unwillingly dripped through to her by officers who clearly viewed her questions, if not her very existence, as a major irritant. So maybe it was now up to Ros to connect some more of those dots herself.

Which was when Jukes finally spoke.

As Ros opened the door, Jukes told her to close it. Then he nodded across at Masters and suggested, with far more passion and vehemence than Ros had ever heard him employ in the past, that he explain exactly why Donna could not possibly have played any part in the butchery they'd all witnessed.

2 3 .

ONE HOUR AFTER Aidan boarded his bus, Macklyn also exited the hotel.

Macklyn already knew that he couldn't do what he'd done so many times in the past. He couldn't just make a simple phone call and ask his handlers in the protection programme to sort this out for him.

If he did he'd open up a real hornets' nest. Maybe then he'd have to tell them about the headaches and they'd insist they be investigated and then he'd be in the middle of it all again. Some new system would enmesh him. He'd be turned back into what he'd become all those years ago, a shapeless void to be prodded into whatever form others determined; which was an intolerable prospect given the advances he believed he'd made in the last few months. The thought of once more losing the small control he'd started to exercise over a life that – for so long – had been dictated by others simply defeated him.

So now he had to think, as in think for himself. Which was only what he used to do a hundred times a day all those years previously of course – encounter a problem, think of a solution, then translate that into action.

Now he'd encountered Stage One, the problem. Next he had to complete Stage Two, the solution. Then he had to execute Stage Three.

Macklyn crossed the car park and unlocked his car, which was parked at the top of a shallow incline tucked in among a whole line of similar saloons. And all the time he couldn't help reflecting how strange it was that this particular individual had now provoked all this.

Because, in one sense, Aidan – Macklyn had now remembered his name – was the most vital link back to the world he still mourned. His was the last face he had seen, the last employee he remembered as he was driven out of his yard that day, staring out at him from the inside of an office he was destined never to see again.

As he started the engine and drove his nondescript saloon home, Macklyn repeated the words as if they were a mantra.

Problem.

Solution.

Action.

The three words that had carried him through most of the business problems he'd encountered in the past. The rituals he'd applied to each minute of a usually frantic working day. Sometimes the problems were large, sometimes not. Sometimes the solutions were obvious, sometimes not. But whatever the nature of the problem or the solution, he always acted. Macklyn had been proud of that. Whatever happened, he always did something.

Macklyn still had no idea how Aidan had traced him. That was one mystery. What exactly he was referring to by Macklyn's secret – that was an even bigger one. Aidan had been vague, or maybe Macklyn's recollection was hazy.

Aidan certainly didn't mention Braith, he knew that. And he didn't mention any other member of his family.

But in a sense it didn't really matter what he'd said of course. The rather more salient point was the fact that the nightmare scenario had actually happened. A hundred thousand times Macklyn had imagined himself passing a shop, coming out of a park, pausing to look at some truck that was trundling past on a nearby road and out of nowhere a voice would say it.

'Hello, Macklyn.'

The greeting would be flecked by surprise, if not downright

astonishment. And hot on the heels would come all the questions he feared.

What had happened to him?

Where had he been?

Why did he drop out of all their lives so suddenly like that?

Come for a drink, old friend, tell all.

And, in the first few years of his new life anyway, Macklyn wouldn't have been able to guarantee he wouldn't do exactly that. Already the headaches were beginning. The thought of sitting in some pub somewhere and unburdening himself to some kindly-disposed old acquaintance was overpoweringly seductive.

Macklyn hated everything about his new life, but he hated the stasis more than anything else. That sense of being suspended between one life and another and inhabiting neither. It was easy enough for Ros, she'd only been a small child when Braith was killed. She had almost no experiences or memories behind her and so nothing to be reconciled with the experiences or memories to come. Or at least so Macklyn assumed, he'd never actually asked her. It had been like so many things in both their lives from the moment of that shooting onwards; something they simply never spoke about.

But then, as he returned home, slipping out of his grey mackintosh and hanging it on his prized, office-style coat hook, the strangest thing began to happen.

Once again he repeated the words.

Problem.

Solution.

Action.

And, as he did so, all his former, previous, panic began to fade. Desperation began to mutate into something actually resembling hope. Because if he could really do all that, think of a solution to his present problem, alone and unaided, and then translate that into action, then maybe Macklyn really could start getting close again to the man he used to be. The man he used to see reflected in the eyes of others.

And so, and as a first step, Macklyn did what he'd always done back then. He emptied his mind of everything. And, operating now more on instinct than conscious thought, Macklyn took out the original small truck he'd bought along with all the others and laid them out on the kitchen table before him, one by one.

Instantly, he was transported back to his own little kingdom where he'd once, indeed, been king.

Macklyn remained seated in front of his collection of toy trucks and vans for the next two hours, not even touching them at first, just smelling again in his mind the diesel fumes from the engines as they started up in the mornings, hearing again the banging of doors and the crashing of pallets as deliveries were loaded inside. He heard his own voice from back then too, barking remonstrations at any late arrivals.

Then Macklyn reached out and lined up the toy trucks and vans as if they were preparing to leave the depot, concentrating on the task with all the seriousness of a small boy, moving them round, swopping positions as, first, a van left and then came back to the depot, then a larger truck and then another before, finally, they all returned home.

24.

ALL ROS, MASTERS and Jukes could hear was a persistent wheezing from a hospital ventilator.

All they could smell was the stench of disinfectant and the promise of death.

And all Ros was now focusing on was a feeding line that, along with the wheezing ventilator, was keeping the immobile patient before them alive.

But maybe that description rather more than dignified all they were looking at right now. Because Ros was actually starting to think Roman Edwards's fate might have constituted some sort of blessed release. Ros looked again at the young girl on the bed. Anything, surely, had to be better than this.

Masters also stood in silent tribute to the young woman for a moment. Then he moved outside to the corridor, Jukes following a second later. Ros lingered a moment or so longer before moving to the bed and standing next to the young woman herself, looking down at her.

This was Donna.

Clare's daughter, Donna.

She'd been rechristened something else of course, as Ros had been. But this was still Donna, no matter what name she'd next been given. A girl who'd been stripped of one life and then had another thrust upon her, only to have that ripped from her too.

Atrocities abound as Ros knew only too well, crimes were committed each and every day, and she'd come across more than her fair share in both her professional and personal life, but this blanked everything out for her right now.

At that moment, her heart almost literally bled.

Then Ros too turned and joined her colleagues out in the corridor.

'Her name's now Maureen, shortened at her own request to Mo.'

Masters stared, unseeing, down the corridor, filling in more and more of the blanks along the way.

'She worked in the local housing department. Amongst the houses on their books were a couple of our very own safe houses. We've no idea if that's connected to what happened to her but, as the security of none of those houses has been subsequently breached, it seems unlikely. The simple fact seems to be she just came across a maniac.'

Masters shook his head, sounding and feeling at a genuine loss now.

'Maybe she wouldn't do what he wanted. Maybe she did and he didn't like how she did it, we simply don't know. All we do know is that at some point in an evening that, according to all the girls in her office, was a first date she was hugely excited about, he slipped something into her drink.'

Masters paused as the door swung open and one of the nurses moved past them before heading down the corridor, the recently-vacated contents of her patient's bowel in a small bag in her hand. He then resumed.

'He probably intended to render her more pliable for whatever he had in mind. In fact he grossly over-estimated the dosage. In the bedroom stakes he'd have been better off visiting the local morgue. She's been in that state since the night of the attack and, according to the doctors, will remain in that state for the rest of what they're still calling her life but which any reasonable person would probably describe as a living hell.'

Jukes picked up where Masters left off, as Masters fell silent and looked at the closed door before them again.

'We've checked each and every one of the safe houses. We've kept watch on every one ever since she was found in that lay-by that night. Different witnesses at different levels of risk have passed through without even the hint of a problem.'

Masters cut in again as another of the nurses returned, moving back into Mo's room to begin another round of routine checks, his mind heading off on what seemed to be a tangent.

Or at least what Ros hoped was a tangent.

'Maybe it's some kind of occupational hazard or something and that's why she agreed to meet that man that night. Maybe all the usual checks and balances are missing somehow and that's the real legacy of something like that. Your life gets fucked up at too early an age and no matter all the measures put in place to protect you, for the rest of your life that's it, you're a fuck-up too.'

Ros forced herself to keep staring at Masters, to not let her eyes betray her even fractionally, knowing he'd recognise and pursue any sign of weakness until he found out what was behind it.

But in any event Masters didn't even glance at Ros. He was still just staring at the door before them, now closed once again.

'But whatever's happened here, whatever was in her attacker's mind, whatever she should have done or not done, it doesn't matter too much now, does it?'

As the doors closed behind her visitors, the young woman on the bed reflected on something quite extraordinary.

The men who'd just visited her did all she'd have expected them to do which was all most visitors did these days. They'd looked everywhere and anywhere apart from at her.

But her female visitor had actually looked into her eyes. And she'd held that look too. None of the nurses did that and nor did the doctors, aside from the occasional checks they'd make on her motor responses.

She knew why, of course. It was incredibly difficult to maintain eye contact with an unflinching stare. Some had tried but had broken away within seconds, the experience too embarrassingly intimate somehow.

But that female visitor hadn't looked away. She'd stared deep into her eyes, almost as if she was trying to look behind them in some way. And then she'd felt herself doing the same. Looking up into her visitor's eyes as if she might see some sense to all that had happened to her in there. Perhaps her visitor was doing the same.

There was only one other recent visitor who'd ever done that, but they'd had a special connection since childhood so maybe that wasn't too surprising.

She'd even felt her face trying to break into a smile when he'd looked down at her, just as she used to do when she was a little girl and he used to parade up and down in front of her in those outsize boots of his, hand-painted in the colours of the Union Jack.

2 5 .

E VERYWHERE ROS LOOKED, all she could see were naked men. Most were crowded round open doors leading to rooms in which there was a bed and nothing else. Sometimes there wasn't even a bed, just a mattress thrown down, carelessly, on the uncarpeted floor.

Most of the men were playing with themselves, kneading and stretching penises in their hands as they focused on the action taking place inside those rooms, awaiting their turn. Ros moved amongst them, ignoring all the open stares, definitely ignoring all the accompanying silent invitations realising, too late, that she'd forgotten.

Tonight was party night.

For six nights of the week the club catered for a strictly private guest list. Membership was composed of like-minded souls like Ros, individuals who wanted company when they chose it and on their own terms, with liaisons accepted or rejected as those individuals saw fit. It was a lifestyle that suited some and would alienate many.

It suited Ros.

That was all that mattered.

Usually Ros avoided party nights like the plague. It wasn't just the different kind of men they attracted; there was always the possibility that one of her colleagues, out on some stag night perhaps, might decide to look in. It might have sounded curious given the all-too-public nature of the couplings that often took place under those low ceilings and dimmed lights, but Ros was a woman who valued her privacy.

But a quick glance around the current gaggle of men reassured her on that count at least. Most crowding those corridors that night were middle aged and gone to seed, coaxing more or less unwilling penises into life beneath overhanging rolls of fat. The vast majority of Ros's colleagues, both in Murder Squad and the Protection Unit, were finely-honed young bucks who would probably have seen this sort of event as a badge of dishonour, a recognition they would not want to acknowledge that they'd reached the stage in life that when it came to sex they had to pay for it.

Ros slipped off the robe that had covered her all through her walk amongst that sea of wobbling flesh, illuminated all the while by the glitterball now revolving at full speed, and slipped into the always-warm, always-bubbling water of the outsize Jacuzzi. On the way she'd briefly glimpsed the interior of one of the rooms and seen two of the women who'd been deputed to entertain the queueing punters that night.

One of them – the older, curiously – just looked bewildered, but the younger one seemed more composed. One man was rolling away having just climaxed inside her, another man was slipping on a condom ready to do the same. Briefly, Ros heard her aside to the night's organiser that maybe they should rig up some sort of electronic reader of the kind she'd seen in her local supermarket, alerting customers when it was time to be served.

Man Number Four, to Woman Number One.

Man Number Three, to Woman Number Two.

Then the next man in line climbed on top of her, fumbling fingers trying to locate the point of entry before the young woman took pity on him and took hold of his half-erect penis to guide it inside.

Ros settled back into the water and dismissed the waiting men and the lives they'd all abandoned that made this a more attractive alternative. Then she let her mind drift on the investigative dead end that turned out to be Donna.

Or was it?

Masters took the old road out of the city, stopping at a seafood restaurant just outside the faux-designer town of Cowbridge.

Once inside he stared at a steaming pile of mussels before demolishing the bottle of wine he'd ordered with it instead.

The hovering waiter debated whether to approach, then decided against it. Something in Masters's demeanour told him he didn't want either company or conversation. By the look on his face he'd already had enough of the former. And as far as the latter was concerned, he seemed to be having a thousand different conversations all by himself anyway.

The restaurant closed at eleven. Masters was the last diner, if you could so describe a man who hadn't touched a single morsel of food, although the waiter had spared the feelings of the occasionally-temperamental chef by disposing of it directly into the bins at the rear of the restaurant rather than delivering his untouched plates back to the kitchen.

Then, to their relief, Masters had left. At one point in the evening they wondered if he intended simply sitting there till the lunchtime service the next day.

Masters drove his Bentley down to a deserted beach, illuminated only by moonlight. No homes overlooked this stretch of shoreline. Masters exited his car, stared out across the sea and tried to do what he'd failed to do all evening, and for longer than that in truth.

All Masters had said to Ros was true. Once the decision had been made to protect and resettle Donna, disseminating the fiction regarding her fate at the same time, he'd kept track of her. He'd dropped into her life at regular intervals over the years, albeit always silently and leaving no trace. He'd journeyed with her through most of the major events of those years – a change of school – a first trip abroad to visit relatives that were, strictly speaking, not her own – wondering, all the time, if and when any problems might occur.

But none had. The event that stopped her world all those years before didn't seem to impinge on the world that had been created to replace it. Donna seemed to be a success story in short, which made all that happened to her all the harder to take.

The attack on her had actually hit Masters harder than he expected. But then there were other things to think about, such as the copycat murder of Roman and the return of Leon. All of which ushered in the fear that all that had happened to Donna hadn't been quite so random as it had seemed at the time. But, despite poring over it obsessively both then and since, Masters still hadn't been able to come up with any connection between that and the resurrection of the case that had killed her father and mother.

However minutely he examined it, all that had happened to Donna just seemed a cruel twist of what some would call fate.

Lying in her Jacuzzi, Ros let her mind drift back again.

Earlier that day, Ros had stood outside a ruin of a house. Makeshift security barricades surrounded it on all sides along with a plethora of signs, both old and new, warning any potential intruders that the structure they were viewing was inherently unstable and in imminent danger of collapse.

Which was obvious enough. One non-load bearing wall had already fractured, a giant crack clearly visible in the brickwork and more cracks were opening up next to an estate agent's For Sale sign, a clear testament to hope over experience.

The sign was leaning to its side and had quite clearly been there a long time. The whole place had, equally clearly, been unvisited by the agent in question for most of that time too. Further evidence, if any were needed, that little effort was being made to market this most difficult of properties.

And no wonder. It wasn't just the expense involved in clearing the site of its former structures, it was the fact that any prospective purchaser would quite reasonably want to know how such a formerly-grand property came to be in such a sorry state in the first place.

Ros looked across at the old stable block, the seat of the original fire that had then claimed the rest of the property, now just rubble.

And, once they heard the answer, most prospective purchasers would probably have run a mile.

Then Ros had looked to her side at Hendrix.

Ros had called him a few hours before and asked to meet him there. As earlier, out on that river bank, neither spoke for a moment. Then Ros handed him a copy of the same file containing the same name she'd previously handed to Eddie.

Hendrix looked at it but didn't open it.

'So what's this?'

'The reason I called.'

'Finally.'

Ros let that lie.

'I don't know who he is. I do know his name. Jack Ryan. I know what he looks like or looked like anyway, there's a picture in the file.'

Hendrix opened the file and looked at the same picture Eddie had studied of the tattooed skinhead sporting Union Jack-bedecked boots.

'All I know is, he's something to do with all this. Because of something he did or didn't do, like I said, I don't know.'

Ros nodded at the file again.

'I found it among Jukes's files. It was buried deep, classified, need to know. Somewhere in Masters's files there's the same name. The same photo. With maybe some more detail.'

Ros didn't say any more. She didn't need to. Hendrix didn't ask any more questions. He didn't need to either.

Hendrix just remained a moment longer, looking at the photograph before him, before looking up again at the ruin of a house.

Then Hendrix turned and left.

Back in the club, Ros stretched out some more, ignoring all the different sounds emanating from all the different rooms and cubicles on the other side of the small corridor and bar.

Ros knew why she was doing this, why she was risking career and possible prosecution by delving into issues that were, strictly speaking and as Jukes had made only too clear, none of her concern.

The still-missing Kezia, not to mention the shocked and catatonic Kim, justified everything in her mind.

But Ros still didn't know why Hendrix was doing this.

All she did know was that at some stage she really was going to have to find out.

Back on the beach, Masters turned away from the sea, opened his driver's door and seated himself back inside. Then he powered up the engine, the headlights illuminating automatically, playing on a low harbour wall some fifty metres or so ahead.

The engine in front of Masters settled into its trademark low grumble. The lights on the dash imparted to his staring features a spectral glow. For the next few moments his mind remained a thousand lifetimes distant from anywhere he was at present.

Then, without warning, a hand snaked from the rear of the car. Before Masters had a chance to even begin to react, that same hand clamped itself around his throat, constricting his windpipe, cutting off his breathing. Masters's eyes searched, wildly, in the rear-view mirror but he could see no-one. Whoever had secreted themselves in the surprisingly roomy rear seats of his car was obviously determined to remain hidden from view. Masters couldn't even get anything like a clear sight of the hand that was currently attempting to end this evening's tortured inquest on his part either.

And, from the way the grip kept tightening and tightening, end much else besides.

Masters flung his head from side to side but the hand didn't slacken for a moment. Now lights were beginning to appear in front of Masters's eyes and they weren't the warning lights on the dash display. His brain was being starved of oxygen and those lights were warnings of a very different nature.

The owner of the hand still hadn't spoken. No instruction had been conveyed. Masters had no idea if he was being choked into unconsciousness or whether his attacker really did have something more permanent in mind. He also had no desire to simply wait and see.

Masters stared ahead, conserving the last of his energies now, not dissipating them by any clearly-useless further efforts to dislodge the pincer-like fingers. His eyes focused instead on the gear selector on the central console.

Masters flicked his fingers, selecting Drive on the control in front of him. The park brake had already been de-selected when Masters first fired the six-litre, twin-turbo engine into life. Masters tried to focus on the rear-view mirror again but now the lights in front of his eyes were changing colour all the time, the dots and dashes elongating as if he were on some crazy hallucinogenic trip. Masters had seconds and he knew it.

The manufacturers of Masters's mechanised behemoth claimed for their creation a nought to sixty time of just over four seconds. Masters depressed the accelerator, hard, the car rocketing from a standing start. By the time the bonnet smashed into the low harbour wall ahead, those manufacturer's claims had been comprehensively vindicated.

The car howled to an involuntary, protesting, halt. A second later Masters lost the fragile hold on consciousness to which he'd been clinging.

The hand around his throat hadn't slackened once. The ride might only have lasted a few seconds but there hadn't been a hint of the panicked reaction Masters had hoped to provoke.

For the whole of that short ride that hand had just kept constricting his windpipe and, if anything, its grip had grown tighter and tighter.

PART FOUR

ENDGAME

26.

EARLY THE NEXT morning and with Masters's Bentley still embedded in that harbour wall, Eddie made contact with Ros.

While Ros had travelled via the London Library to Masters's upmarket bolt hole in St James, Eddie had made a very different journey down to a new-build apartment block on the Isle of Dogs. The apartment was sited next to an old-fashioned boozer, the exterior of which was draped from floor to roof in the flag of St George.

Given the redevelopment taking place on all sides, the pub was fast becoming stuck in a time warp, unlike the occupant of the new-build. This was one man who was definitely moving with the times.

'This particular little beaut is tiny, look, just take a look, little more than the length of a small finger, right? So it can be attached to anything that moves – a bag, a mobile, a baby buggy, whatever you want.'

Eddie's new companion was, by now, almost salivating.

'Once it's on the move it records every journey courtesy of signals – listen to this Mr E – just listen! – from twenty-four satellites orbiting the Earth. It's got an internal computer on board – actually on fucking board – which tells you where it is within two and a half metres every second.'

Eddie struggled to look interested.

It wasn't easy.

'And the best bit of all is you don't only find out where your mark is, you can even work out where they stopped and for how long.'

The box was opened, its contents upended, eager fingers demonstrating more delights inside.

'It's powered by a tiny battery, look, little bigger than a pinhead. And it comes with a magnet mount which is water resistant. It'll record up to a hundred hours of data, will stop when the mark stops, when they're asleep, taking a shower or chilling out in front of the tele.'

Eddie looked behind Brendan at a figure hovering a few metres away.

Or even, and as in this case he reflected, taking time out from being urinated on by a thickset rent boy.

Eddie and Brendan were in the roof garden of the new-build. A planted birch hedge afforded some privacy from the immediate neighbours, a man-made barrier rendered all too necessary given some of the more extreme activities Brendan indulged in during his downtime from being CEO of a small but thriving local electronics company.

Brendan hadn't always been in this game. A few years previously he'd run a small business importing pet food from dubious sources in what used to be called the Balkans. He would have remained a more or less unsuccessful small importer of ever dodgier pet food as well had it not been for a certain stroke of luck.

Brendan's rented warehouse boasted a private car park. As that stroke of luck would have it, the car park was a short drive away from the local red-light district and overlooked by no near neighbours. Aside from Brendan that is, but as he was usually away from his struggling office and in the local pub draped in the flag of St George by early evening, the working girls of the area had free rein.

One single blockage first alerted him to what was happening when his office lights went out at night. A call to the council to clear his blocked drain resulted in a bewildering exchange with the amused drainage contractor and an even more bewildering question.

Could Brendan please tell the contractor what he was on and could the contractor please get some of the same?

Which was when Brendan looked into the contents of the industrial waste skip that the private contractor had sucked from the drain outside his rear door and saw hundreds and hundreds of used condoms swimming inside.

Brendan, to the drainage contractor's disappointment, didn't have anything like the active sex life evidenced by all those condoms. In fact, Brendan didn't have a sex life at all which made them all the more of a puzzle. But a few hours later – by keeping watch from his darkened and seemingly-empty office – he cracked that particular mystery quickly enough.

Which was when Brendan had his idea. He could have marched out there and told the various working girls to get the fuck away and stop blocking up his drains and they probably would have done. For a while at least. Then, when he'd slipped back into his usual routine propping up the bar in his local boozer, they'd probably slip back into their usual routine, allowing their many and varied punters to slip back inside them too.

It started as just strictly private entertainment. There was a CCTV camera covering the car park but Brendan had never bothered accessing any of the images it recorded as he had precious little inside his small warehouse that anyone was likely to steal.

But he soon realised he had a fairly spectacular floor-show on which to feast his eyes. Some of the encounters he watched were a bit blurred and indistinct but most were clear enough, particularly when the arriving cars were a little on the small side and the occupants a little on the large. Then the working girl, or girls in the case of some greedy punters, would perform their duties either by the side of those cars or even on the bonnet, giving the increasingly dry-mouthed Brendan the sort of entertainment that very definitely beat anything on offer in his local pub.

It also involved Brendan in some additional and not insignificant expense as his consumption of paper towels and tissues shot up to something approaching record levels.

But then he spotted another opportunity, namely a way of exploiting this private entertainment by turning it into something a bit more public. Brendan wasn't to know it, and the two men had never and would never meet, but across the Channel in Amsterdam Leon had previously come to much the same conclusion.

But in truth neither man was that much of an original thinker anyway. Brendan's local newsagent had always told him that the biggest selling wank mag was something called Readers Wives. Even the most cursory trawl on the internet told the same story. Punters loved watching everyday girls fucking the most everyday sorts of blokes in the most ordinary of circumstances. And if they were doing all that unaware that they were being watched, then that was very definitely the cherry on the icing.

Brendan was one week away from being closed down by his landlord when he uploaded the first images from his CCTV tapes. Two days later he had to upgrade his server as he was getting so many hits. Each hit was only generating him a matter of a penny or so at a time, but once those hits began to hit the high hundred thousands, and once he began to receive enquiries from a couple of DVD labels wanting to know if they could do some sort of deal, Brendan decided it was time to move out of imported pet food from what used to be called the Balkans, much to the relief of the long-suffering canine population of his home patch and their even more long-suffering owners.

Eddie had first come across Brendan a few months after his business had gone viral. He'd been asked by Ros to keep tabs on a client of hers at the time, the daughter of a middle-aged prostitute who was being inculcated into the dubious pleasures of her mother's precarious profession. The mother was well past her sell-by date and the daughter no oil painting, but they were, genuinely, mother and daughter, and some punters seemed to get off on that.

The problem being that people the mother and daughter had never met seemed to be getting off on it too, because one day they saw themselves on the internet pleasuring some punter in a certain car park they used that was far away, or so they'd fondly imagined, from prying eyes.

Eddie paid Brendan a visit of care, nothing heavy, just a reminder that the daughter in question had connections. He left it at that, not explaining that those connections involved the only copper he'd ever trusted, which was the reason he put the services of his security company at her disposal from time to time.

But while he was there, Eddie had also taken a look around Brendan's business, quickly realising the specialist surveillance he offered might be useful in the future and so it proved. The more Eddie got to know Brendan personally, the more he disliked him, but the more he appreciated his professional expertise. Expertise that was about to come in useful once again.

Eddie pocketed the small, portable, bug just as the rent boy those few metres away straightened up from gulping down the latest in a long line of glasses of cold water. Then the rent boy nodded at Brendan, a clear, if silent, signal that he was ready to try and squeeze out some more piss.

Eddie turned away as the rent boy took out his penis and held it a few inches away from Brendan's face. And as Eddie opened the apartment door to let himself out, he just heard the first, half-strangled, moans of pleasure as a thin stream of urine was coaxed out of the rent boy's dick and began splashing over Brendan's face and into Brendan's ecstatic open mouth.

As he journeyed down in the small elevator, Eddie did reflect on some of the characters he had to deal with in his new calling and gave a small, inner shudder. But the device Eddie had just taken away more than made up for it and he was pretty sure Ros would feel the same.

One hour after receiving his early-morning phone call, Ros met Eddie on the first floor of the Castle Arcade, one of the most beautiful of the city's winding indoor thoroughfares, although how much longer any of those arcades would endure was a moot point with the modern abominations of out-of-town retail parks threatening their existence.

Ros whiled away her waiting time in another endangered species, the best second-hand book shop for miles around, then nodded at a six-foot seven-inch apparition, clad that day in a mustard suit and maroon Stetson boots as he walked along the gangway toward her. In Dallas, he'd have fitted in perfectly, in the Welsh capital less so, but whatever passers-by might have been thinking they kept any opinions firmly to themselves.

Eddie handed Ros a computer print-out, once again not wasting any time.

'Jack Ryan is – or was – a cop.'

'A what?'

Ros stared at the image Eddie had just handed her, the tattooed skinhead with the Union Jack-bedecked boots once more staring back at her.

'He was part of a specialist unit. What they call a deep swimmer. He'd been out in the field for years and he was good by all accounts. Very good. None of the groups or activists he infiltrated back then suspected a thing, and most don't from all I can see.'

Ros looked again at the tattooed skinhead staring out from the photo before her.

No wonder.

'Right now, he's in Scotland. An old country manor hotel not far from Perth. The Government used it to house asylum seekers at one time, but now it's used as a secure unit for problems they need to hide away.'

'And how long's he been there?'

'In that unit, less than a year. Before that he was shunted all over the place. Before that he kept disappearing. No-one seemed to know where he was or what he was doing. Then he had some kind of breakdown. Again, no-one seems to know why.'

Eddie shrugged.

'Maybe he just cracked. Living all those lies for all those years – has to take its toll I suppose.'

Ros kept quiet, her poker face expressionless.

If Eddie noticed he didn't show it.

'With Ryan in that sort of state they couldn't take the risk he'd go public with all he used to do, so they tried some new treatments which weren't really treatments at all. Good old-fashioned electric shock therapy they'd have called it in days gone by, but it did what it said on the tin. Now your man just sits in a corner and dribbles.'

Eddie paused, looking down on a party of excited Japanese tourists all of whom were experiencing orgasms, so it seemed, at the sight of a small retail unit below selling decorative buttons.

Then Eddie slid another piece of paper and some more photographs across to Ros. As well as his information, Eddie always supplied a corroborating explanation as to how he'd sourced it. In this case, that had been via the device acquired from Brendan which had been every bit as effective as the excitable entrepreneur claimed.

With it, Eddie had carried out some discreet surveillance on a less than discreet Home Office official who, so rumour had it, indulged in the local S&M scene in a dormitory town on the English south coast. That wouldn't have been so embarrassing in itself had he not also been married to a high-profile television newsreader. Exposure might not still have been quite so catastrophic if the newsreader hadn't taken to participating in the same scene, albeit with the security of a face mask to match her husband's leather gimp, as the photographs Eddie had just handed to Ros made clear. With two careers on the line, not to mention hundreds of thousands of pounds a year in joint salaries, the Minister in question had no problem in agreeing to a trade, leading Eddie to his quarry in Scotland along the way.

'Jack Ryan's the classic basket case fuck-up. And just in case anyone was playing any games or planting any false trails, I flew up there late last night, took a look for myself.'

Eddie paused, looked at Ros.

'So that's who he is. That's what he used to do.'

Eddie glanced at the silent Ros.

'But something's telling me it's not exactly helping you all that much?'

Ros didn't answer. She didn't need to. Eddie, as sharp as ever, was right. She now knew who Jack Ryan was and she now knew his recent and not-so-recent history too.

But how all that fitted in to the present-day murder of Roman Edwards, the present-day mental torture of Kim, not to mention the present-day disappearance of Leon and Kezia, Ros still had no idea.

Ros was still a long way from connecting up those dots.

As Eddie was coming to the end of his briefing on the first floor of the Castle Arcade, a dog walker came across the wreckage of a Bentley embedded in a remote section of his local harbour wall.

The uneasy dog walker stared for a moment at the unexpected sight before him, the metal still faintly ticking. The dog walker had something of a weak stomach and a fear of blood. He knew, in the interests of simple humanity if nothing else, that he had to see if there was anyone injured inside but really wished he didn't have to.

But then he steeled himself and approached, his dog barking at the car all the while.

A moment later the dog walker squinted, albeit with one half-closed eye, through the driver's side window, relaxing as he saw the driver's seat was empty. A quick check confirmed the other seats were unoccupied too.

Then the dog walker took out his mobile. Presumably whoever had crashed the upmarket car had quit the scene soon after the accident. Maybe they were joyriders and they'd destroyed this rather lovely looking vehicle for fun. But that wasn't his business.

The dog walker had already done part of his civic duty by checking for casualties.

Now he completed it by calling the local police.

Hendrix let himself into Masters's office at almost exactly the same time the local police in Cowbridge received a call about a crashed Bentley.

So far, no-one in the Squad had seen or heard from Masters that morning. That wasn't unusual. No-one had any idea if he was even in Cardiff or out of the city altogether in his weekend retreat which was rumoured to be in some impossibly expensive district of central London. Once again, that lack of knowledge concerning the present whereabouts of the head of Hendrix's department was hardly unusual either.

But none of that mattered. All that did was that Hendrix

had a brief window of opportunity. How brief that might be he had no idea, which meant he had no time to lose.

Like Ros, Hendrix had no real idea what he was looking for. But at least, and courtesy of the Castle Arcade briefing from Eddie which had been relayed on to Hendrix a few moments before by Ros, there was now more in the way of flesh on the bone. Jack Ryan was still the only name in the frame, but at least now they had his present whereabouts as well as who he was and what he did, or at least what he used to do. If Hendrix could cross-reference that information with any similar references in Masters's files, it might throw up something new. It was a long shot, but it was better than nothing which, as Ros had also pointed out just a few moments before, was pretty well all they still had at present.

Hendrix suspected he wouldn't get beyond first base. He suspected Ros felt the same. And both Hendrix and Ros would have been right, in normal circumstances anyway.

Just in case anyone had ever felt inclined to probe into the background of a name that Masters, for very good reasons, wanted to keep hidden from general view, there was a safeguard built into the system Hendrix was currently attempting to access.

Not even Masters could eradicate Jack Ryan's very existence. But he'd made sure he'd know the moment anyone became interested in him. Unknown to anyone who might be running data checks of that kind, there was a silent trigger on every file relating to the former undercover operative, meaning Masters would receive an automatic alert.

That alert could be nothing to worry about of course. The file in question could have been caught up in a more general trawl for some quite innocent purpose altogether. One alert in the past had been triggered by an over-enthusiastic amateur genealogist, a retired taxidermist of all things, who'd been rudely awakened early one morning by two members of the security services dispatched by Masters and masquerading as armed intruders.

To the considerable bewilderment and alarm of the amateur genealogist, the tight-lipped intruders had cleared his small flat of everything of value as well as everything that was not, including the much-prized family tree on which he'd been labouring for the last few years and which had triggered the ultimately innocent alert in the first place.

All that research was now destined to be lost as most of it wasn't properly backed up as the anguished retired taxidermist made clear to his unwelcome visitors, but as those same representatives of the security services masquerading as armed intruders would have taken all back-up files and memory sticks as well, it really wouldn't have made too much difference.

So Masters may not have been too worried – initially at least – when this new alert suddenly flashed up, copied to his private laptop. But when he read the name of the originator of the new request, Masters would have grown rather more concerned. But as Masters was in no position right now to read anything at all, no action was taken.

And, to his surprise, Hendrix found himself journeying ever further into files he'd never expected to be able to access.

As Hendrix settled to his study, a uniformed PC pulled up by the crashed Bentley. The impatient dog walker was still there at the PC's request, although he was released a few moments later to continue his much-delayed morning stroll.

The PC radioed in the details of the car, including its registration number and chassis number which was still visible through the car windscreen. That had remained intact despite the severe damage sustained to the rest of the front of the vehicle, a testimony to good old British workmanship as the PC reflected, even if the good old British car company in question was now actually owned by Volkswagen.

While he waited for the details to be cross-checked and the name of the registered owner to be relayed back to him, the PC also reflected on the strange choice of interior colour scheme. The PC, who was something of a petrol head, would have expected the cream leather that complemented the silver exterior very nicely. He hadn't expected the red carpets, though. They really didn't go in his opinion.

Then the PC took a closer look at those carpets.

And felt his stomach begin to clench.

At around the same time Ros received a call back from Hendrix.

Masters still hadn't arrived for work but he was expected any moment. But Hendrix had managed to add another name into the mix at least. Or, at least, provide more detail on an existing name.

Hendrix had located the equally mysterious Jen.

Ros jotted down the details on a pad in front of her.

Then Ros cut the call, told Conor she was going out for a while and left the unit offices.

One hour later Ros walked into the reception area of a private hospital some forty miles down the coast to the west.

Ros gave her name to the receptionist and took a seat. Neatly stacked on a table in front of her was a pile of upmarket monthly magazines, each one in pristine condition. No well-thumbed copies of gossip mags featuring celebrities from daytime television here.

'Ms Gilet?'

A honeyed voice insinuated its way in through Ros's ears. She looked up to see the smiling receptionist who'd now levitated from the reception desk to her side.

'Doctor Rahman will see you now.'

As Ros made to follow, the receptionist straightened magazines that hadn't been looked at since the last time they'd been restacked. Then Ros followed her down an expensively-carpeted corridor with discreet solid teak doors lining each side.

The receptionist delivered Ros into an oak-lined consulting room. Ros produced her official accreditation and two minutes later Doctor Rahman was opening one of the solid teak doors leading off the expensively-carpeted corridor she'd passed a short while before.

Inside, Ros saw the woman referred to in the Jack Ryan file as Jen. Ros now knew that Jen had met and fallen in love with him. She was who she claimed to be. The man she met and fell in love with, was anything but.

Ros still had no idea how all this connected to the murder of Roman, to the persecution of Kim, or to the disappearance of Leon or Kezia. All she knew was that somewhere here there must be some kind of link and, by association, some kind of answer. She also knew she was fast running out of time to find it.

From a comfortable armchair on the other side of the room, Jen looked back at her new visitor. Jen seemed young, her eyes clear and untroubled. Only the slight shake of her hands as she repositioned herself to gain a better view of Ros gave a hint as to anything amiss.

But one glance at her case notes told a very different story. And even the most cursory of glances across at the bedside table and the almost-embarrassing concoction of pills and potions that kept her on just about the right side of sanity would have told any visitor the same story as well.

Jen had met Ryan, not as a tattooed skinhead, but in his next incarnation as an animal rights activist. Jen was a fellow activist in the same group. Ryan had befriended her straightaway because she'd been perfect fodder according to the case notes sourced by Hendrix. Young, insecure, her parents divorcing when she was still a child, Jen was almost painfully seeking a place in the world. Her disturbed education meant she wasn't destined for any glittering career and her already highly-developed inferiority complex militated against any late flowering of latent talent too.

Jen, in short, was heading for as miserable an adult life as the one she'd already suffered in childhood. She'd only joined the animal rights group as a way of making friends, and the fact she was already being treated with amused condescension by most in the group suggested she wasn't going to be too successful in that either.

Then along came Ryan.

According, again, to the initial notes Hendrix had accessed, Ryan seemed to have devoted to Jen the kind of attention she'd never, in her life, experienced before, meaning he not only acquired an adoring acolyte, he gave her a mission. From being a barely-tolerated volunteer, Jen became one of the key cogs in the activist machine. Under Ryan's almost messianic-like tutelage she rose quickly through the ranks, desperate to match her new lover's drive and commitment. For the first time in her life Jen not only had a relationship but the place in the world she'd always craved. Life, quite simply, could not get better.

But once Jen was hooked, Ryan's mood swings started. The undercover cop had found out all he needed to know about her group by now and it was time, as his handlers had told him, to move on. Soon, Jen simply didn't know where she was with him. Then came his sudden announcement one day that he just had to get away, that he felt as if he was suffocating in some way.

Which all seemed like perfect tradecraft, from the little Ros understood of this hidden world. What happened next was anything but.

Did Ryan overplay his hand, Ros wondered? Or had something else happened? He was supposed to be upset at the thought of leaving a woman he'd, apparently, fallen in love with, and who'd fallen in love with him – that all added credibility to the same carefully-created picture, making the inevitable withdrawal messy and therefore real.

But Jen read more into it than that. She sensed that Ryan still loved her perhaps, as Ros now reflected, because he did.

Whether that conviction had led to Jen's breakdown, Ros didn't know. There were massive gaps in the initial notes Hendrix had so far managed to access. How exactly she'd ended up in this facility was one such gap and Doctor Rahman wouldn't be able to help Ros with that. All he knew was that one day she'd been presented at his door by a tight-lipped member of Her Majesty's Police Force, an institution who'd picked up the tab for her treatment ever since.

Ros looked at the still-silent Jen. But she was still the only link back to Ryan they'd found so far, the only link to a man who seemed to be closely linked to the murders of Toya and Joey and possibly that of Roman Edwards too.

Ros leant close to the seated Jen, looked into Jen's eyes much as she'd previously looked into Donna's and Kim's eyes as well. In those eyes she'd seen nothing, no spark of recognition and nothing that might hint at any kind of connection, let alone anything that might have promised any kind of enlightenment.

But there was something in Jen's eyes, Ros could see it. But whatever it was, it was going to remain there because Jen just stared back at her and didn't speak a single word.

'We send regular reports to the department.'

Ros looked up at Doctor Rahman. She'd almost forgotten he

was there. The doctor had now finished his routine annotation of Jen's file and was replacing some sheets of paper to the existing bundle appended to the end of her bed.

'There's little change as you can see, but we try.'

Doctor Rahman had made little secret of his surprise at Ros's visit. Jen had so far been abandoned twice to his certain knowledge and with devastating effect both times. The first seemed to be by a man responsible in some way at least for her current condition, the second by the government body who seemed to have sanctioned it. As far as Doctor Rahman could see, Jen was now an unwanted irrelevance and an embarrassment, and for the life of him he couldn't see why this further visit from a representative of the organisation responsible for all that was even taking place.

Ros looked back at Jen. Ros didn't understand it either. That was, partly at least, the whole point of all this.

Back in the harbour, the first of the investigating plain-clothes officers had now confirmed that the carpets of the crashed Bentley had definitely not left the factory in that strange shade of red.

Just to make sure, one of the officers had managed to lever himself at least part-way inside the now-compressed cabin to check, but it was obvious enough in truth, even from outside. Those deep pile carpets were stained in blood.

At the same time it was established that the registered owner of the crashed vehicle was actually the head of the local Murder Squad.

At which point all hell broke loose.

Ten minutes later, an evermore frustrated Ros walked back along the expensively-carpeted corridor with Doctor Rahman. Ahead, the automatic doors almost seemed to tense as they anticipated their approach, and maybe they did. Maybe, somewhere, some sensor had already been activated.

Ros paused, looked at her silent companion, Ros now growing increasingly desperate and no wonder. She'd got precisely nothing from this visit and even less from Jen herself.

'Has anyone ever visited?'

Doctor Rahman's response was prompt and positive and was exactly the answer Ros would have expected.

'No-one.'

'In all the time she's been here?'

'Not a soul.'

And the doctor's face said it all. In his opinion that was part of his patient's problem although he assumed, shrewdly enough, that the police might not share that view.

'We've tried to compensate in other ways of course. She's allowed out whenever she wants for example, sometimes she even goes away on small trips, some supervised, some not.'

Doctor Rahman shrugged.

'But it doesn't seem to make much difference. She always returns in much the same state as she left. In much the same state you've seen right now.'

But then Doctor Rahman paused as Ros took a step towards the automatic door which did now glide open in front of her.

'There was a name she mentioned once. An old colleague of her ex-boyfriend's I think. Someone she'd seen on one of her trips away from the facility – or maybe someone she'd just remembered – I honestly can't quite recall.'

Ros looked out beyond the plate-glass automatic door onto a distant road, then back at the doctor, a faint suspicion now stirring.

'Was he called Masters?'

'He?'

The doctor shook his head.

'This officer was female.'

Ros stared out through the open door again, yet another blind alley opening up in front of her.

'I don't think Jen ever mentioned a surname. It might be in some file somewhere if you want me to check. We write everything down.'

'It doesn't matter.'

Ros smiled, quickly, moved away.

'Jen just called her Clare.'

Which was when Ros stopped in the doorway and looked back at him.

27.

A IDAN DIDN'T BOTHER with anything so superfluous as a greeting. He just gave a single curt nod as Macklyn stepped back from the door to let his unwelcome, if not entirely unexpected, visitor inside.

And, despite everything, Macklyn almost smiled.

It had been his tactic when dealing with potentially difficult encounters too. Macklyn had never wasted time then either, had just nodded his head at whomsoever was before him, usually some truculent trucker, the silent instruction all-too-clear.

Right.

We're here.

Let's get on with it.

Macklyn had now remembered more about Aidan. He'd not only placed him as the distrusted former employee he'd been on the verge of sacking on what turned out to be his last day in work, he'd now remembered just what Aidan had done to incur his wrath. He could even remember the actual run Aidan had been on, as well as the vehicle he'd used that day.

For his part, Aidan just remained silent. It had worked as a tactic in the past. Let the silence fester. It was a tactic that worked particularly well with targets under the age of puberty.

In fact, and if Aidan had eyes to see it, he'd have realised that silence was probably the very worst tactic he could employ right now. Because it was allowing all those pictures now forming in Macklyn's head all the more space to breathe.

Aidan finally made to speak, but suddenly Macklyn cut across. And what came out of Macklyn's mouth was a question he hardly knew was in his mind, a question that had been delayed some twenty years in the asking, but which now came out with all the original force he would have mustered that day too.

'Where the fuck had you been?'

A rocked Aidan stared at the old man before him, the expression on his face saying it all.

What was he talking about?

But Macklyn was rolling on.

'That was a two-hour job, maximum, two and a half if those roadworks on the other side of the Rec were still up, which they weren't because I checked, and that's if you'd really taken your time.'

Macklyn leant closer to the staring Aidan.

'You didn't have a break scheduled because I'd checked that too, in fact you weren't due your next one till you got back to the yard, so maybe you can tell me how that simple little run hadn't taken you two hours or two and a half, max, it had taken you four – four hours – so I'm asking you again, where the fuck had you been?'

And, suddenly, Aidan realised what Macklyn was talking about as memories of that last trip he'd made in Macklyn's employ came back to him too. Aidan hadn't experienced any of his employer's famed righteous anger that day. Events had well and truly overtaken them but, and incredibly, he seemed to be on the receiving end of it now.

'Let me tell you, shall I?'

And now Macklyn started pacing which was another of his usual tactics when it came to these sort of encounters, much in the manner of a prowling animal, well aware how disorientating it was, how a trucker's eyes would swivel to follow him as he moved around the office, putting that trucker off-balance, unsure what was coming next, even from which direction.

'You were moonlighting. You were using my van, my diesel,

my time, the time I pay you for, to do a mate's job, cash in hand, no questions asked, only now I've got a question.'

Macklyn stopped, abruptly, shot out a hand.

'Where's my money?'

Aidan just kept staring back, no words actually finding their way from brain to mouth.

'Which you've obviously pocketed as your money, but which actually is mine seeing as you earned it in my time, using my van, my diesel, in the time which I'm already paying you for anyway, so come on, let's have it.'

And for a moment, as he kept staring at his suddenly fierce interlocutor, Aidan was actually back in that office, back inside his young man's body, trying to look as if he could handle whatever life might throw at him, only too painfully aware he could not.

'I didn't – .'

Then Aidan stopped, some semblance of reality crashing back in at last.

What the fuck was he doing? For a moment he was actually going to engage with the sad old loon, was actually going to dignify his rantings with some kind of a response.

Not that any similar semblance of present reality seemed to be crashing in on Macklyn right now. From all the staring Aidan could see he was still away in Neverland.

'You didn't what? Didn't use my van, didn't use my diesel, well let's take a look shall we, that run you did would be a hundred miles, give or take, definitely not much more than that, so let's see what the tachograph says, let's see how many miles over the hundred you've done this morning and then let's add that to what you owe me for all that extra diesel not to mention all that extra wear and tear.'

And, finally, Aidan cut across.

'What the fuck is this?'

Aidan stared at Macklyn who suddenly ground to a halt. And, slowly, and to Aidan's relief, Macklyn seemed to focus on the man actually before him as opposed to the man who'd been there two decades before.

Aidan leant closer.

'Aren't you missing something here? I don't work for you, you don't employ me, there is no fucking van and there is no money. All that's gone and it all went, you stupid, pathetic, sick old bastard, the day the police came calling and put you away for doing this.'

Aidan took out a pile of papers from the bag he'd brought with him, laid them down on the table, papers he'd intended to lay out before Macklyn five minutes earlier.

It was, as Aidan would have been the first to admit, something of a punt. He was trusting his much-prized good luck once again. But he'd remembered yard gossip about these newspaper stories at the time and the more he'd thought about it the more he reckoned this had to be it.

For his part, Macklyn just stared at the headlines from decades before, all of which, so his stunned scanning told him, had something to do with the arrest of some local child abusers.

Aidan eyed him, more and more convinced from Macklyn's sudden silence that he'd struck gold. Aidan had taken a special interest in this story for reasons of his own. Several local men had been picked up in connection with it and, the more he thought about it, the coincidence of all that happening at the same time as Macklyn's enforced removal from his place of work and his former life was simply too great. This had to be the secret Macklyn had been concealing all these years.

Aidan gave Macklyn a moment or two longer to let the incontrovertible evidence of his past sins confront him. And as he did so he fully expected Macklyn to shrink back into his former stooped and wizened shell.

But Macklyn didn't, and he didn't because all that had happened a few moments before was still coursing through him. He might have been momentarily quietened, but Macklyn was far from cowed. And that was because he'd just finally experienced something he hadn't experienced for over twenty years. Macklyn had just assumed some sort of control where for so long he'd been impotent, meekly accepting instruction from others.

And something else was happening now too which was the principal reason for his temporary inability to speak.

Macklyn was in shock.

Whatever else he might have expected, he'd never expected this. Whatever story he imagined his former employees had been told about his sudden disappearance he'd never, in his wildest imaginings, believed it would be anything like the story currently screaming out at him from the pages of a photocopied newspaper from years ago.

Macklyn had felt waves of panicked nausea wash over him in the past, particularly when he'd relived, inside, the circumstances of Braith's brutal murder.

He remembered another particularly acute attack when he was trying to play with the girl he and his wife had christened Cara, but who had then become another creature completely called Ros. His wife had sent him out in the small garden of their latest house to push her round on her bike. Idly, his mind elsewhere as it always was in those days, Macklyn had glanced down at the handlebars and felt his stomach turn liquid.

None of them had seen any harm in the small child bringing her bike from her old home and life to her new. But it wasn't only harmful, it could have been disastrous. Because at some stage in the weeks or months before, the young girl had scratched her name, her actual birth name, into the steel handlebar. So if anyone had wanted to find out who she really was and, by association, who they all were too, all they'd had to do was read the name their daughter had so obligingly supplied.

All that had precipitated yet another house move, yet another change of identity but that horror, at least, had passed.

Macklyn kept looking down at the newspaper reports before him, less sure this fresh horror would fade so easily.

Aidan eyed him all the time, gratified on two counts. First, he'd definitely shut the old man up. But secondly, his suspicions really did seem to have been bang on the money as Macklyn's expression now seemed to confirm.

Which meant – and not the first time since he'd renewed his acquaintance with his former employer – Aidan had managed to get something spectacularly wrong. But this mistake was going to cost him more than most.

Because all Macklyn could see right now was red. It was a phenomenon he'd read about in the pages of books but always thought it was some sort of construct, a storyteller's device. It had become a cliché in the kind of thriller fiction he'd tried to immerse himself in at one time, that red mist that descends on a formerly rational individual when they're in the grip of an overwhelming emotion, a grip that tightens all the time.

Dimly, Macklyn was aware of Aidan bringing something else out from the small bag he'd brought with him. Focusing a little more clearly, Macklyn saw it was one of the toy trucks he'd been promised, his reward for handing over the first instalment of money Aidan quite clearly believed he was due, in return for keeping quiet about offences that Macklyn hadn't committed.

Aidan rolled on, all his former self-satisfaction restored now, infusing his each and every word.

'So let's get real, shall we? I don't know what kind of life you've built for yourself since all that, what your new neighbours think about you, where they think you came from, why you're here.'

Aidan tapped the photocopied pieces of paper.

'But I'm pretty sure they don't know about this. And I can't imagine what they'd do if they did.'

Then Aidan spread his arms wide, mock-supplicatory.

'But it can stay that way. There's no need for anyone to know anything. You can go back to whatever do you day-in, day-out, play with your toys, play with yourself or play with some little kid who's come in off the street to look at your collection if that's what this is really all about.'

Aidan nodded smugly at the sole truck he'd just placed on the table, making a mental note at the same time to keep back a couple for himself. Aidan hadn't actually used anything like that to lure any of his youthful victims, but he had used sweets and comics and even on one occasion a recently-acquired stray puppy. Now he might just have added another enticement to the arsenal.

Macklyn kept looking at him. Had this conversation taken place twenty years previously, Aidan would have been in no doubt as to the danger he was currently courting. Then, Macklyn had no need to dissemble, to hide feelings and emotions, but now it had become second nature to do so which was the reason why, on the surface anyway, he looked much as he always did.

Macklyn had only ever really lost it the once back then. And on that occasion it had left one of his fitters short of three of his teeth after he'd squared up to Macklyn after a late return to work from the nearby pub. It was the first time any of his employees had dared raise even a finger to Macklyn. But it would be the last.

Macklyn looked into Aidan's sneering eyes. And, for that moment, he saw a living, breathing embodiment of all that had gone wrong in his life since the day they'd last stood face to face. For all those years Macklyn had craved some sort of revenge for all that had happened to him and to his family. Now he craved no longer.

Macklyn grabbed the sole toy truck that Aidan had placed on the table. Aidan was just about to tell him that wasn't the deal, he was supposed to hand over the money first. But – and much like the hapless fitter from all those years before – Aidan suddenly had something else to think about.

Macklyn balled his fist around the metal toy, fashioning it into a makeshift knuckleduster. Then he lashed out, smashing it into Aidan's face, flattening Aidan's nostrils against his cheeks as the bone splintered, fracturing one of his eye sockets at the same time.

But the force of the blow didn't only rearrange Aidan's features, obliterating at the same time his sneering smile. It also cannoned him back towards the door which was when a second and even more lacerating agony assaulted him. Aidan's nerves hardly seemed to have caught up with the first blow, and were actually destined never to do so which was a blessing in a sense, although whether the coat hook Macklyn had sourced from the internet driving into the base of his neck from behind before embedding itself in his throat could be called a blessing was something of a moot point.

There was just one more second of consciousness. One second when an impaled Aidan stared at Macklyn as he tried to pull his head away, but only succeeded in driving the coat hook further into the back of his neck as he skewered the tip ever deeper inside.

In front of him Macklyn could actually now see the hook becoming faintly visible at the front of his throat.

Then Aidan's head dipped slightly and his arms and legs became slack. He let out a great rasping sound from deep inside his ruptured windpipe and then just hung there, impaled on the coat hook that so resembled the one that used to hang on the inside door of Macklyn's old office, swinging gently from side to side.

314

2 8 .

A T AROUND THE same time, down in the harbour, a tow truck was starting to retrieve the smashed Bentley. At the same time too, phones were beginning to ring off the hook at the Murder Squad offices and in Masters's weekend retreat in St James. But of Masters himself there was still no trace.

In blissful ignorance of all that was happening elsewhere, Jukes was leaving his office. It was hardly his usual time to leave, but no-one paid too much notice. No-one ever did.

When Jukes first indulged himself on these sorts of days away his mind used to play tricks. Was that person looking at him that little bit strangely? Was there an edge to the way that person had bid him goodbye? Some would call it a heightened awareness. Others would call it an old-fashioned guilty conscience.

But today Jukes just strode out and unlocked the family saloon parked in its usual slot at the rear of the former retail unit that still lacked the first 'e' in its Mega-Bed Sale sign and was now, from what Jukes could see, in imminent danger of losing the 'B' as well. Then he drove the few miles along the feeder road to the satellite rail station that connected to the main line and bought his ticket.

His quarry this time wasn't the girl with the music case of course. She'd now been consigned to that achingly-familiar graveyard of missed opportunity. But he'd learnt his lesson from all that and the target this time was a girl he'd researched in advance.

Jukes knew where she lived, where she went to school, where her parents worked and how she spent each weekday night between four and six p.m. It had all, ultra-conveniently, been included in a report in one of the local papers, along with a picture of the girl in question; a vision that suddenly stopped his breathing for a while or at least it felt that way.

Jukes didn't even take in at first the achievement that had merited the newspaper report. All he knew was he could sit at his desk and drink in the teenage sensation in front of him for hours.

But he was determined not to let history repeat itself and so he researched with impeccable thoroughness the establishment she attended and the proud gymnastic trainer who'd been behind her local success. Then he decided to have one practice run at the next step, a single train journey taken in her company, just to make sure the reality lived up to the image, and then he'd make his approach.

Two days previously he'd done his dry run, and the girl really was every bit as special as her photograph promised. In fact she was even better, as the photographer couldn't capture the way she moved. There was something gamine in the shake of her hips, the coltish appeal of a young foal.

Jukes decided to use the same approach as last time. He'd approach the girl, show her his warrant card, explain that his force were investigating possible claims of abuse by other young girls against the adult responsible for overseeing her training, while stressing that at this stage they were just making discreet enquiries.

Jukes hoped his simple request for assistance might build some kind of bridge. And it meant, if later challenged, that he could just deny the whole incident as, in procedural terms, the whole thing was total bollocks of course.

Jukes wasn't contemplating any violent sexual assault. Rape wasn't the object. Sex with a minor certainly was of course, although exactly how he was going to achieve that he still wasn't too sure. But a highly-charged exchange between an impressionable young girl and an authority figure that focused directly on the issue of sex had to be a decent starting point.

Or indecent, depending on one's point of view.

And from Jukes's point of view the more grossly indecent the better.

The train pulled towards the platform and Jukes felt his mouth begin to go dry. In one of the forward carriages, he just caught sight of the luxuriant curls of the young girl in question and moved, as casually as his feet would allow, towards her.

Only now his mind did seem to be playing tricks on him. Because there seemed to be something in the way the guard on the train was looking at him as he held open the door, as well as a similar something in the way the young woman operating the on-board catering trolley glanced his way now too. Something quizzical. Wary even.

But then Jukes dismissed all that. Having come within a matter of feet of his latest quarry, Jukes wasn't about to let idle fancy stand in his way. Jukes grasped the handle of the train carriage door, but then stopped as the figure of the guard blocked his way.

'Could I see your ticket, sir?'

Jukes looked beyond him at the girl just a few seats away. What the hell was he talking about? Tickets were checked on the train, not at the door to the carriage. This was a guard, not some bouncer barring the entrance to a nightclub.

'And some identification if you would too, sir?'

And now Jukes really did feel as if he'd entered some sort of parallel universe. Identification? Since when had he ever been asked for that on a simple train journey? Those few feet ahead, the girl turned slightly, alerted by the delay in restarting the journey. For a moment Jukes caught a glimpse of the eyes framed in rolling curls of hair that had so transfixed him when he first saw them in that photograph.

Making all this even more intensely irritating.

Jukes looked back at the guard.

'Is there a problem?'

'If you could just show me your ticket and some ID?'

A late straggler dashed up the platform and opened the second of the carriage doors that opened into the compartment. The guard didn't even give him a passing glance. For an agonised moment, Jukes watched as the new arrival dithered, checking out the exact seat Jukes had mentally allotted himself; one row behind his quarry and to the side so he might catch her face in half-profile, perhaps even drink in some distant echo of any scent. Then, to Jukes's blessed relief, the new arrival saw a discarded paper on another seat and chose that instead.

Jukes looked back at the guard, a sudden fury gripping him.

'Why do you want to see my ticket?'

Jukes gestured at the late arrival.

'You didn't ask for his.'

Up ahead, the young woman operating the catering trolley was now leaning close to the girl herself, whispering in her ear and the girl stood, collected her few possessions and stuffed them in a bag.

'If this is some sort of stupid exercise – .'

Then Jukes paused again as the girl followed the young woman out of the carriage, passing the staring Jukes, heading for a nearby waiting room, Jukes's eyes following her every inch of the way.

The guard broke in again.

'Let's do this in the waiting room, shall we, sir?'

And now Jukes lost all interest in boarding the train. Now he just followed the guard back along the platform towards a room that also was about to host the girl with the curls. And as he did so, his mind computed all sorts of options for this most unusual of starts to what should have been a routine train journey.

Maybe this was some sort of security spot check – and as that thought flashed through Jukes's mind he felt his spirits start to soar. Because if he and the girl had been picked out in that way there'd be an instant bond. They could chat in that waiting room quite naturally as fellow-travellers caught up in an uncommon experience.

This might actually work out even better than his original plan. Now Jukes had any number of witnesses to testify that his first contact with the girl with the curls had happened by complete chance.

The guard opened the door to the waiting room. Jukes looked inside, trying to disguise his eagerness. At the far end, the young woman operating the catering trolley was momentarily blocking his view to the girl, but then she moved and Jukes suddenly felt a roaring in his ears as Ros looked back at him instead.

Ros nodded at the woman who melted away, following the guard who'd also retreated. From outside, Jukes heard the distant blast of a whistle. The girl with the curls was nowhere to be seen. She'd presumably been escorted back onto the train after her brief disembarkation.

Dimly again, Jukes became aware of Ros telling him that Masters had disappeared and that his car had just been found abandoned in some remote coastal spot, badly damaged as a result of a high-speed frontal impact. A large quantity of blood had been found inside which had already been identified as Masters's blood group. Traces of another person's blood had also been found, but the identity of that other person was, as yet, unknown.

Jukes kept listening, still barely taking any of it in, as Ros also pointed out that Masters had made many enemies over the years, but the fact this had happened so soon after the murder of Roman, the persecution of Kim and the disappearance of

Kezia and Leon made it inconceivable this wasn't linked to that case.

Jukes nodded, mechanically, finding it hard to disagree with any of that. But all the time his mind was grappling with a rather more thorny issue than the apparent disappearance of a man he'd often wished would just vanish anyway.

Ros had acted totally correctly in informing him of this latest development as quickly as possible. She hadn't allowed the fact he'd turned off his mobiles, both work and personal, and hadn't told anyone of his movements that day to deter her, meaning she'd demonstrated considerable and commendable initiative as well.

The issue that rather more concerned him, and which made him feel sick to the pit of his stomach, was how she knew which train he'd targeted that afternoon and why she'd chosen that particular girl as bait for him to follow, Pied-Piper style, away from the platform and into the waiting room where this confidential briefing could take place.

Jukes looked at Ros, her clear eyes looking back at him and, as he did so, he felt the last vestige of any sure ground on which he might still be standing slowly, but surely, begin to shift.

But if Jukes was feeling vulnerable right now, Masters was feeling even more so.

Slowly, Masters felt consciousness return but – some innate survival instinct at work – he didn't reveal that immediately. He was actually aware of nothing at the moment, where he was, how he'd got there, he didn't even remember the car crash at first.

But something inside him still powerfully registered danger. Maybe because danger had been all-too-present before he'd lapsed into unconsciousness.

Gradually, his eyes still closed, Masters's memory began to supply pictures; a deserted seafood restaurant – an untouched meal – a couple of nervous, hovering, waiters – a late night car ride. All the time his mind crept up on the night's main event.

Then Masters stiffened slightly as he recalled what, in all probability, would be the last ride of his beloved Bentley. The force at which the car hit that wall suggested the damage would probably be pretty terminal. Instinctively, his eyes still closed, Masters checked out the damage to his own body, but he could feel all his limbs and his mind was clearly still working normally too.

So why couldn't he move?

29.

J UKES HAD MADE an instant and – in his eyes at least – an
ultra-simple calculation.

Jukes knew that the contents of certain classified files, if
seen by the wrong eyes, could spell the end of their careers
for several high-ranking police officers.

Jukes also knew that the contents of those same files,
should they ever become public, would cause maximum
embarrassment to the force as a whole.

But Jukes was also painfully aware that not to give Ros the
information she was now demanding risked his own extra-
curricular activities in and around rail stations becoming
exposed to public view.

Ros, he knew, would make sure of it.

So Jukes had returned to the Protection Unit's office and
had duly handed over to her files that had been kept from Ros
ever since she joined the department, including the transcript
of a phone call that had kick-started the whole sorry sequence
of events in the first place.

Events that had then enmeshed Leon and Joey and Toya
and Clare.

Events that seemed to have enmeshed Kezia, her father
Roman, and his ex-wife Kim as well.

Two hours later, Ros was back on the balcony of her small
apartment and as she scanned the files and read the transcript
of the telephone call, it happened again.

Ros turned into that silent, invisible, empathetic ghost
once more.

Previously, Ros had journeyed with two uniformed officers as they entered a bedroom that more resembled an abattoir. Now, and courtesy of the file Jukes had just handed her, she was travelling with Joey, just before his discovery of Clare's affair with his brother.

It all happened on a totally normal day. Joey had been about to go home. But before leaving the club and heading away, Joey had played back some answerphone messages on his mobile.

Only one message didn't seem to make any sense, in fact it didn't seem to be a message at all.

Ros imagined a puzzled Joey about to erase the message, but then he must have heard the sound of the police radio in the background. Maybe he realised straightaway he was listening in to an exchange between a couple of police officers, maybe he didn't. That didn't matter. All that mattered was that Joey had kept listening.

Maybe, initially anyway, it was amused curiosity that kept him on the line. Like most people, Joey had probably heard tales of official frequencies being hijacked by mobile devices, and Joey must have assumed that's what was happening here. His mobile – or maybe even his whole network – had suddenly been granted access to all areas so far as the local constabulary was concerned. Some screw-up had taken place in cyberspace somewhere and their lines of communication had somehow crossed with his.

A male voice that Joey didn't recognise was talking about some photographs that had been supplied in the last couple of days, and that same male voice was making it clear to his caller that they needed more. What they had was good, but if they could get anything better that would be a real bonus.

Which was when Joey heard the second voice waft down the line, a female voice this time, responding to the male.

And realised just who it was.

Back in the unit offices those two hours previously, Ros had stared at Jukes, Ros still trying to get her head round all this.

'So Jack Ryan wasn't a sole operator?'

Jukes shook his head.

'Far from it. There was quite a collection of them back then. Different types, different personalities, but Ryan was definitely the star.'

Jukes paused.

'Or at least he was.'

Jukes paused again.

'Until someone else came along.'

Back in her apartment, Ros sifted through some more of the transcripts.

Once again the sequence of events, as best the police at the time could track them, had been transcribed. Once again, Ros, the empathetic, invisible ghost, travelled with Joey through each and every twist and turn.

The transcripts made clear that Joey had then returned home and had gone through all the numbers on Clare's mobile. Most he'd have recognised immediately as friends or mutual acquaintances.

But a couple of numbers he wouldn't have recognised. One he called from a public phone box in a nearby village which yielded nothing, his call just ringing out.

The second number yielded some sort of contact, but the male voice on the other end of the line just wanted to know who he was and how the hell he'd got that number? He sounded aggressive and something else besides.

Panicked perhaps.

Then the call had been cut.

Ros read on. From Joey's own phone records they knew that Joey had next contacted a private detective who'd run a trace on both mysterious numbers. The private detective couldn't help with any names, but he did supply a location for one of them, a rundown office block somewhere in Cathays. He also supplied the name of the Government body who maintained it.

Ros stared out over the water, the last step in the reconstruction of Joey's movements now before her.

From his credit card records and armed with the information from the private detective, they knew that Joey had next applied to the Family Records Office at Myddleton Street in north London. The details he'd requested had been dispatched to him the next day.

Ros kept staring out over the water, trying to put herself again in Joey's place, her imagination totally failing her now and no wonder.

How could she?

How could anyone?

It was betrayal of course, but not the normal sort of betrayal Joey must have considered from time to time. Like most husbands, he'd probably wondered whether his beautiful wife would ever wake up one morning with the feeling she'd made the wrong choice in marrying him and whether she'd ever act on it if she did.

Previously it would have been something of a nightmare scenario. But now, staring at a document that had just stalled the revolving heavens, he'd probably have welcomed it with open arms.

Because how do you deal with the undeniable fact that the one person you trust most in the whole world doesn't actually exist?

Back in the unit offices, Ros had kept staring at Jukes, all those dots finally beginning to connect.

And, as Jukes just kept looking back at her, Ros felt her world somersault, much as Joey's must have done all those years before.

Clare – Joey's wife – the mother of his child – wasn't actually Clare.

Her name was Anya.

Clare wasn't a wild child Joey had entrapped.

She was a cop who'd ensnared him.

Ros, finally, found her voice.

'And Leon? What was that all about?'

Jukes paused, struggling as he did so, reluctant – even now – to put any of this into actual words. Then he took a deep breath.

'Leon was her exit strategy.'

Ros kept staring at him.

'From what we understand it was her intention from the start. Begin an affair with Leon while she was still married to Joey. Play one brother off against the other. Then, when it was time to get out, she'd make sure their affair came to light. Once it did, she'd have every reason in the world to get the hell out of there. Slip out of sight of them both, never to return.'

Ros now had a million more questions hammering away inside her head, but above everything, one thought, one question, took precedence over all the others, as it must have done for Joey when he made that same, shattering, bombshell discovery too.

Donna.

His child.

His and Clare's child, the child they'd created together, the child they'd dedicated themselves to raising. A living, breathing, human being.

Or was she?

Because what was Donna in the end? What was her real role in what Joey must have come to see as a macabre charade?

A daughter to be doted on as Joey doubtless did?

Or a price that had to be paid for Clare?

Ros looked past Jukes, stared unseeing out of the window.

She'd got it all so, so wrong hadn't she? It wasn't the discovery of the affair that had sent Joey into his crazed and murderous madness at all.

Slowly, Masters opened his eyes. He stared up at a single ceiling light shining down at him, momentarily blinding his sight. Masters closed, then opened his eyes again, narrowing focus, shading and protecting his vision.

Turning his head slowly again from right to left, he could see that he was naked and tethered by each hand and foot to what looked like a hospital gurney but which could also be a massage treatment table.

Masters let his head sink back, one thought and one only now in his mind.

Masters had seen this exact same scenario before.

Twice before in fact.

The first time with Toya James.

The second time with Roman Edwards.

Back in the unit offices, Ros looked at Jukes again. And from the expression on her face, Jukes knew exactly what she was thinking.

As well as the next question she was just about to ask.

'Clare – Anya – whatever the fuck her name was – .'

Jukes cut across.

'She's dead.'

'Like Donna, you mean?'

Jukes cut across again, impatient.

'What happened with Donna was artifice. Pretence. Much as we pretend, day-in, day-out, with our clients.'

Jukes slid a scenes-of-crime photo across the table towards Ros. A woman stared back at her. Her body was badly burnt, but her face was still recognisable.

'Just as a safeguard, her body was exhumed when you were with Masters in Amsterdam, collecting Leon. It's why I stayed behind. DNA samples were taken, matched to the ones we already have. There's no doubt, absolutely none at all, Clare killed herself after setting fire to her house.'

Ros kept staring down at the photograph of the corpse in front of her as Jukes nodded at her.

'Whoever did all that to Roman and to his ex-wife, whoever's behind the disappearance of Leon and Kezia, it wasn't Clare.'

Ros kept looking at the scenes-of-crime photo. And once more she felt as if she was locked inside some real-life game of snakes and ladders.

One step forward, two back.

But something else was prowling into her already over-crowded thoughts now too.

'How the hell has he done it?'

'Who?'

'Masters.'

Jukes didn't reply as Ros looked at him, wonderingly.

'This was his old department, right? Clare – Anya – whatever – she was one of his marks? This was probably all sanctioned by him for fuck's sake.'

Jukes still didn't reply but the expression on his face said it all.

Ros just kept looking at him.

'So right from the start of all this he's been putting out

fires. Yes, he's been trying to find out who killed Roman – but all the time he's been desperate that no-one really finds out why.'

The silence in Jukes's office just grew and grew.

Masters was still strapped to the bed which might have been a hospital gurney and which might have been a massage treatment table.

All he could think right now was who, who, who?

Which was when the door opened and Masters had his answer.

It was only the briefest of flashes he caught of the figure that had just come in.

But Masters was finally face to face with his persecutor.

ONE HOUR LATER and Ros met Conor and Hendrix outside Leon and Joey's old club, the site of the original killing of Toya James.

Hendrix had already put in a call for back-up from specialist officers. Conor had already checked with the local utility company who'd previously supplied power to the property. The site had been derelict for months, the whole area slated for the usual sort of redevelopment that had already colonised many of the surrounding streets. Wall-to-wall new-build apartments destined to be ripped down in turn when the developers had pocketed the tax breaks.

But it was a redevelopment that wasn't due to start for another few months as the property company sign affixed to the wall made clear. So it was something of a puzzle to the local utility company to find power was currently being consumed somewhere in the bowels of that building. They had no idea why or what that power was being used for.

Neither did Ros.

But it wasn't a mystery that was going to be solved by the simple expedient of opening the front door and taking a look. That door was barred and bolted.

Hendrix returned to them, having now checked the rear of the building as well. The door and windows back there had been bolted and barred just as efficiently too.

Masters hadn't seen him since. But he was still there, he was sure of it.

And Masters's mind now raced back over the previous few weeks, desperately trying to square circles all the while.

Leon's denials that he knew nothing of Roman's murder had been prompt back in that coffee shop, and his shocked manner had been convincing ever since, particularly in the disused cinema.

But maybe he'd just been a far better actor than they'd given him credit for. In the early days in the protection programme Masters knew that Ros had despaired of ever making Leon's new character and persona even halfway convincing, given the shattered sham of a man he'd been back then.

But Leon had improved. The last few years were ample evidence of that. He'd convinced everyone in his new world of his assumed identity for all those years, meaning he'd had a lot of practice looking people in the eyes, his expression rock-steady as he assured them of a sincerity he'd never possessed.

Masters's eyes flicked from side to side, trying to catch a second glimpse of the man he'd seen, albeit fleetingly, a few moments before, his mind racing on all the while.

So had they all fallen headlong into what, in retrospect, would turn out to be an all-too-obvious trap?

With wide open arms?

Had they brought Leon back to find a solution, only to discover he was actually the problem?

Outside, the first of the specialist officers summoned by Hendrix, including a police marksman, had now arrived. They didn't know why they were there or what they were doing. Neither, at that stage, did Ros, Hendrix or Conor, not for certain anyway. The situation was complicated by the fact that this was only one of the possibilities being investigated by the local force in connection with Masters's disappearance. And no-one could be sure this was the right one either.

Then Conor returned to Ros, an iPad in hand. Conor had now made contact with the property company in charge of the upcoming redevelopment and had been emailed plans of the proposed new properties. And it seemed that while the apartments were new, they were taking advantage of the original infrastructure and services.

Including, as Conor now pointed out, the air conditioning shaft.

Ros looked at the tiny space detailed on the plans in front of her. Then Ros made the same mental calculations everyone else seemed to be making right now too from the expressions on their faces.

If they could just get someone down there they'd have a pair of eyes and ears inside. At least that way they'd know if Masters was actually in there or not, and then they could get some proper back-up. At the moment and with all those other possibilities being investigated at the same time, resources were being spread far and wide.

But of the small group currently huddled outside that building, there was only one of them who could possibly even contemplate accessing that sort of restricted space, and it wasn't the burly Conor or the tall Hendrix or any of the other officers.

Meanwhile, and as Ros, Hendrix and Conor debated options outside Leon and Joey's old club, Jukes left his office and made for his family saloon again, aware that he should probably now keep a low profile for a while. Jukes hadn't survived this far in his career without knowing when to disappear. He'd swum with some large sharks in his time and had outlived most of them. As he intended to do again.

Jukes started his engine, intending to drive home and then maybe go off for a small solo break somewhere, just till the dust settled.

Which was when he saw her. Not the girl on the train of course, that would have been too much to ask. But very definitely another lost, young-looking female standing on the street outside the unit offices.

Jukes hesitated a moment. As he did so, the girl looked his way and in that split-second moment Jukes made his decision, feeling his spirits lift as he did so. Maybe he could rescue something from this disaster of a day at least.

So Jukes drove the short distance across the road towards her and then he did what any other kindly-disposed older gentleman would have done in similar circumstances.

Jukes depressed his electric window and asked the lost and vulnerable-looking young female if she was all right?

Ros, now beginning to inch her way along the shaft, stilled as she suddenly suffered an involuntary recall.

For an instant, another slight, slim, figure flashed before her eyes, a fellow officer burnt alive in a similar enclosed space in circumstances no-one had ever investigated too deeply, mainly because Masters had once again choked off all efforts to do so.

That fellow officer had been immolated in a refuse shaft that had been transformed into a makeshift inferno. And, for another moment, Ros remained still, hoping against hope that the sudden recall owed more to paranoia than prescience.

Then Ros pressed on, that other, equally slight figure from the past now firmly banished. So Ros knew, when she smelt it, that her mind wasn't playing tricks on her.

It wasn't smoke she could smell now or burning flesh, but it was something equally incendiary in its own way.

Something metallic with a distinctive tang right at the heart of it, brittle somehow.

Ros could smell blood.

Back on the street, Conor was now liaising with evermore hard-pressed techies back in police HQ, checking for any evidence of internet feeds, cables, cameras, wireless connections, anything.

If part of the purpose of the Kim persecution was to spread the images of what was supposed to be happening to Aron far and wide – and maybe for the same audience, Leon, Joey and Roman used to target in those dark corners of the net – then maybe this was more of the same.

But so far they hadn't found a thing.

Meanwhile, Hendrix was downloading more and more of the files he'd sourced from Masters's computer, searching for something, anything, that might give them some new lead.

Then Hendrix paused.

Back in the ventilation shaft, Ros paused again too.

The old club may have been derelict, but that didn't mean it was unoccupied. Ros had already come face to face with a succession of staring eyes as resident rats investigated the new presence among them.

Some of the bolder examples held her stare for a moment, perhaps wondering if she was trapped and they could begin an unexpected feast. Then Ros's eyes had flashed back at them and they'd scurried away, running underneath her on at least two occasions, touching her momentarily before they wriggled on, leaving a silent scream echoing inside Ros's head.

She'd also seen something else too, something that loomed in front of her and this time Ros had no idea what it was. Momentarily, she feared a snake of some description as yellow eyes blinked at her, once.

But then, equally suddenly, the apparition vanished, leaving a now panting Ros telling herself that her mind was playing tricks, that it was just a figment of her imagination, knowing she had to convince herself of that even if she knew it was not.

Then Ros moved on, her arms still clamped tight by the walls of the shaft, sucking in her stomach, squeezing herself into the smallest possible shape.

Which was when, suddenly, she saw him.

Masters.

Lying in a basement room on some sort of bed, conscious, but strapped down.

Ros looked round, stopping again as she did so. Because slumped across the room, she also now saw Leon. Or, at least, the man who had been Leon. Leon was conscious too, but from the expression on his vacant, staring, horribly-shocked face as he lay on the floor, he looked as if he really didn't want to be.

Then Ros felt rather than heard her mobile pulse in her pocket.

Ros looked at the trapped Masters, the human wreck that was now Leon. Then, manoeuvring her fingers carefully, she answered.

Hendrix's voice came down the line.

'It's a set-up.'

Ros kept looking at the two men before her, the two decoys.

'I know.'

It had taken Jack Ryan a long time to find the main man. The actual commander of his old unit. Consummate political survivor that he seemed to be, Jukes had concealed himself behind other more natural front men back then including, among others, Masters.

But Jack had got there in the end.

And so, now, had someone else.

Seated in Jukes's family saloon, Jen glanced to her side at Jukes himself, hot tears starting to flow as she thought of her former boyfriend, a man who'd dared to come in from the shadows and who was now a shell.

Jen kept looking back at Jukes. So carrying on his fight was the very least she could do. It may not have been a battle Jack had planned to fight. He'd always promised the pair of them a quiet life from that point on. But Jack, the lovely sweet Jack, had always had a soft spot for innocents. Maybe that was why he'd been attracted to her in the first place. So it was inevitable that what happened to Donna would hit him hard.

And it was equally inevitable that he'd want to exact some kind of retribution for all that too.

Take some sort of revenge.

Jen looked at the blood-drenched knife in her lap. The knife that had killed Roman Edwards and had now killed Jukes if the sound of silence in that family saloon was anything to go by.

Then Jen brought the same knife up to her own throat.

31.

MASTERS DIDN'T SPEAK for the whole of the journey.
Masters shouldn't even have been out of hospital yet given his injuries. The advice from his doctors had been crystal clear on that count. Masters needed an extended period of rest and recuperation to recover from his near-catastrophic car crash. Masters had ignored both his injuries and the advice.

Ros didn't even know where they were going at first. Then they pulled up outside a large, brick wall in a small part of the old docks that had escaped gentrification so far. A door set into the brick wall still bore faint traces of scenes-of-crime tape.

And now Ros didn't need to ask where they were. Behind that door, one of the worst atrocities ever witnessed in the city had taken place, the torture and murder of a police officer, his wife and their unborn child. Ros and Masters had discovered their bodies.

'I thought it was over.'

Masters looked out at the door through the windscreen of the unmarked car he'd appropriated from the police pound for this trip.

By his side Ros stared at the same door, reluctant memories returning all the while.

'Clare had died, Donna had been taken care of, as best we could anyway.'

Masters tailed off for a moment, even now the attack suffered by the tragic Donna still ambushing him.

'The unit was disbanded, exit strategies executed, every officer was recalled back to their original units or assigned new ones, no-one any the wiser.'

Ros looked at him. In the case of Masters, the story everyone in Murder Squad had been told was that there'd been some trouble with Masters's previous posting, a vague reference to a problem with one of his team.

Jukes's arrival in the Protection Unit hadn't really required an explanation. Everyone assumed it was just another unremarkable appointment in an otherwise unremarkable career.

How wrong they were.

Masters looked back at her.

'But no matter how badly everything turned out back then, it's over now.'

Ros turned back to that anonymous door set in the large brick wall. She understood only too well now the point of this trip and all that Masters was saying to her.

Everyone just keeps quiet – and it wouldn't be too difficult to do that in truth. So far as Clare was concerned – Ros couldn't now think of her by any other name – the same story as before was still out there. To the majority of the dwindling number of souls who'd once known her, or known of her, Clare was a good-time girl who'd played the most dangerous of games by having a relationship with two volatile brothers at the same time. Her best friend had paid the initial price for her actions and she'd paid the rest at her own hands.

That was the story that had been fed to the wider world and, presumably, the story that had even been fed back to the small family she still had left, although as the committed young woman had quite clearly prided herself on a virtually-total immersion in a new life and the excising of an old, Ros doubted if she'd ever indulged in too many old-style family reunions anyway.

The death of Jukes would be put down to the unfortunate killing of an officer on duty. His and Ros's department dealt with a lot of seriously damaged souls. The usual professions of regret would be expressed of course, but it wouldn't really strike anyone as all that extraordinary that one of those souls seemed to have snapped.

The copycat murder of Roman would be consigned to the back of some filing cabinet somewhere, a mysterious incident destined never to be resolved. Along with another invisible alert put on the file in case any overly-zealous cop in future decided it all merited a closer look, in which case some senior officer somewhere would have a quiet word.

Ros kept looking out of the window at that door set in the large brick wall. Like Masters, Ros could never rid herself of all they'd encountered behind that door that day. But Masters was telling her to do what they'd done then, to move on, to not make waves.

They'd both kept quiet about consequences before.

They could do so again.

Later that same afternoon Ros was with Hendrix in a restaurant down in the Bay, a distant view of the Senedd across the water, a mini iPad in place of a menu in front of them.

Ros took a moment to remember Donna and the last meal she'd enjoyed in that same location. Then she stared out over the water, another emotional – and physical – casualty now before her instead.

With Masters hospitalised, Hendrix had found out more about Jen from files accessed from his senior officer's private laptop. He'd sent those new files along to Ros the previous evening. Once again, none of it had made for easy reading.

'So what do we do?'

Within moments of settling in front of their iPads, undisturbed by any hovering waiters, Hendrix cut straight to the main matter of the moment, but Ros didn't reply.

For now, Ros was still locked in the middle of all-matters Jen, those final entries in the case notes on Jack Ryan and his former lover swimming before her eyes.

One week after Ryan had walked out on her, a postcard had arrived for Jen from her former lover. From the notes annotated in the margins of the files Ros had read the previous evening, that seemed usual enough. Ryan was supposed to maintain some sort of contact for a limited period after his exit – again, it made that exit all the more real somehow. The postcard was stamped with a Greek postmark and the next day Jen booked a budget flight out there to begin her search for him.

In fact, the postcard had been forwarded onto a member of the Greek police force from Ryan's new posting in Haywards Heath, meaning Jen was destined for a fruitless few weeks haunting the sorts of bars and harbours a man like Ryan – or the man she believed to be Ryan – might frequent. She plundered her meagre savings to finance the trip and soon ran out of cash. That wasn't such a problem back then as she was hardly eating anyway and her weight plummeted. Jen was soon sleeping rough under the stars.

Meanwhile, and with Jen now on her doomed quest in Greece, Ryan had returned to his original and long-suffering family from whom he'd been living apart – the odd weekend and family holiday aside – for the previous three years.

Ryan's wife had accepted the unusual arrangement as short-term pain for long-term gain. The agreement always was that he'd return from his mystery posting with a sack-load of money in the way of bonus payments to begin the sort of accelerated career path that meant they wouldn't have to worry about college fees for their two young boys who were just about to start secondary school.

They both knew that living together again was going to

involve a period of adjustment, and so it proved. Like many undercover operatives before him, Ryan found settling to one life – where previously he'd juggled two – to be difficult, but in his case it seemed to have been compounded by strong feelings of guilt towards, and continuing attraction for, the woman he'd abandoned.

In an increasingly desperate attempt to shore up what was fast becoming an evermore fractured marriage, Ryan suggested a family holiday in a small village in the west of Wales, a part of the world he'd always loved. He'd seen the village in question from the window of a small train that travelled on the other side of an estuary inlet. Picture-postcard cottages hugged a wide expanse of beach, a ruined castle that looked vaguely Norman in origin towering above them. The local council had recently paid to have floodlights installed and at night the base of the old castle was bathed in light that gave it an almost mystical look.

Meanwhile, Jen was hitchhiking home, suffering the attentions of first one sexual predator and then another. She fought off the first but wasn't so lucky with the second. She arrived back in a bad way and was immediately dispatched to a women's refuge by one of her concerned former colleagues.

On her arrival at the refuge it was quickly decided she needed a complete rest and change of scene, and the refuge had just had a stroke of luck in that respect. They'd recently hooked up with a retreat run by some ex-hippies who had a spare room in their crumbling old mansion.

Two days later, Jen found herself on a small train heading west but she didn't even notice the small village on the other side of the estuary or the castle that towered above it, even with its locally-famed floodlights.

Across the table, Hendrix again spoke, his tone soft, persuasive.

'They buried it because they could. And when it was just

Masters and Jukes they could do that, but it's not just them any more is it?'

Hendrix nodded across the table at the still-silent Ros, but he didn't complete his thought process because he didn't need to. But Ros didn't answer, not because she didn't want to but because all that Hendrix was now saying to her was something she herself had been trying to resolve ever since Jukes had been found dead in his car, his throat cut in what had become, by now, a trademark slash across the windpipe.

Then a signal sounded on the table in front of them announcing the arrival of their starters.

Hendrix looked across at a still-distracted Ros as she looked down at her food, the final events in those files flashing again in front of her eyes, Ros trying again to imagine what had happened next but, and as previously with Joey, failing totally once more.

Even now, just reading the bare bones summary in the case notes Hendrix had accessed, Ros had felt her stomach somersault again.

It was every undercover cop's worst nightmare. The one intangible that no-one could do anything about, the chance encounter, the one in a million sighting in the wrong place at the wrong time.

And, in the case of Ryan and Jen, what a wrong place and what a wrong time.

After settling in the remote seaside refuge, Jen had taken to walking the beach at low tide. As she rounded a rocky outcrop she came onto another section of beach which was virtually private. A single house did front onto the sand but she'd never seen anyone moving around inside. The occasional dog walker aside, it was as if she had the whole world to herself. She'd walk on to the end of that section of beach until the waters of the estuary barred any further progress. Then, before the tide turned and mindful of warnings from locals that any incoming tide could speed back across the sands faster than a human being could run, Jen would turn and make for her temporary home again.

Which was when, one week into her retreat, Jen saw the family of four walking towards her. She didn't take any notice of them at first. She wasn't exactly in the frame of mind to make idle conversation with strangers, and the family seemed rather more concerned with taming a small puppy, a task which was clearly beyond the two young boys charged with executing it.

The small puppy bounded up to Jen and circled her evermore excitedly as the two boys, from a distance, urged it back. When that failed they dashed up to retrieve it, only managing to excite the small dog further. It was left to the mother and father to sort everything out a few moments later, which was when Jen looked up into the eyes of the man she'd fallen in love with three years before, the man she'd been seeking for the previous few months.

Ryan must have steeled himself for all sorts. An idle, sideways, glance in a crowded bar, a train door opening and an old contact or colleague stepping out. But how could he have anticipated this?

A deserted beach.

A day out with his family.

A woman to whom he'd professed undying love and commitment staring at him. A wife staring at the woman in turn, registering the look in her eyes, then catching the expression on her husband's face, fast becoming aware this was all a little bit more than an innocent encounter with a stranger courtesy of an over-exuberant dog.

Ryan handled it as well as he could as the case notes made

clear. He affected a pleased and casual-sounding greeting. He expressed surprise they should have run across each other again in this out-of-the-way place. He introduced Jen to his wife as a colleague he hadn't seen for some time. And then he rounded up his two boys and the small puppy and marched his family back along the sands towards their holiday cottage.

Ryan didn't look back once, but the eldest of his two boys did and he wanted to know why that strange woman was just standing there looking after them with tears running down her face? Ryan's wife wanted the same answer to precisely that same question, but Ryan didn't answer. What could he say? With the holiday now ruined anyway, Ryan packed the car that afternoon and handed back the keys to the holiday let.

If Ryan had left it at that he might possibly have rescued his marriage, but he didn't. Ryan dropped his increasingly-frantic wife, his sulky kids and their still over-exuberant puppy off at home, then turned straight round and drove back to the seaside village where he had little trouble locating Jen. She'd had to be rescued from the incoming tide as she'd remained on the beach, seemingly unaware of its approach and had become the talk of the locals, particularly as she refused to actually leave, even with the waters completely filling the inlet. She just remained on the sand, looking out at the distant horizon as if she expected some vision to suddenly materialise before her eyes.

But maybe she knew something the locals didn't. Because within a few short hours her faith was rewarded as, for the second time in one day, the man she'd never stopped loving appeared before her again.

And now Ryan came clean to her. Now he told her exactly who he really was and what he'd been doing. He laid bare the deception that had been at the heart of their relationship since the start. And he told her the truth because he couldn't live with it any more. He could no longer bear the casualties he'd created, meaning he now created a new one in their wake of course.

Previously, Jen believed she'd been abandoned by a volatile and unstable lover. Now she discovered she'd been duped from the very start. The fragile hold Jen retained on reality vanished almost in an instant. Ryan's act of charity in opening his former lover's eyes to his mendacity seemed to have become the ultimate coup de grâce.

Meanwhile, the officers alerted by Ryan's evermore hysterical wife arrived half an hour later and arrested Ryan before he could do any more damage and took Jen into protective custody too until the next move could be assessed. Ryan was released back into the care of his largely-bewildered family but it was a temporary respite. Ryan left the marital home three weeks later and never returned.

As Ryan's absence lengthened, the suspicion grew on the part of his employers that their former golden boy had committed suicide. That, as the case notes again made clear, was also their fervent hope.

In fact Ryan returned to Jen and the pair went into hiding. They stayed together for some time too. But then Ryan had suffered his breakdown. At the time it was believed that the double demands of his lifestyle and emotions had finally caught up with him. They now knew there was another reason of course.

But whatever the reason, it led to his current stay in that secure unit in Scotland and it also led to Jen being committed to the tender, if somewhat bewildered, care of Doctor Rahman.

'So it was Donna?'

A few hours previously, still parked outside that door set

into that large brick wall, Masters had hesitated, still reluctant – like Jukes before him and even now, after all this time – to put any of this into words.

But Ros just looked at him, her eyes demanding that he answer.

'Ryan had stayed out of sight all that time, putting some sort of life back together with Jen. But once all that happened to Donna, that's when he fell apart?'

Masters hesitated again, then nodded.

'Ryan and Donna were close. Very close. We didn't know that. He'd taken a special interest in her after everything that had happened to her mother. He saw her as another casualty of the whole thing I suppose, maybe the real casualty, who knows?'

Masters paused.

'So yes, what happened to Donna seemed to have been the final straw. Ryan flipped. He started this whole thing before he was finally caught, taken up to Scotland.'

Masters paused again.

'And then Jen flipped too.'

And how, reflected Ros.

Ros looked out through the car window again.

Of the two remaining loose ends, Kezia had been found safe and well as Ros always suspected. Having lost all faith in officialdom to keep a vulnerable soul safe, Jen had resolved to do that herself. And she might have succeeded too – Jen herself had remained out of sight for all that time with Ryan after all.

It would also have given Jen the chance to make some kind of amends. It had never been her intention that the young child find her father's body, despite Ros and Hendrix's previous suspicions to the contrary.

For his part, Leon was now in hospital being patched up. Physically he was OK, psychologically he'd need years for the mental scars to heal. They'd still no real idea what had happened to him after he'd been spirited away from that apartment in the centre of the Hayes and made to pay his price for all that had happened to Donna.

All they did know was that he was, now, yet another casualty, as Masters had put it.

But maybe not quite as innocent as some.

Back in that restaurant, with a mini iPad in place of a menu, and a distant view of the Senedd across the water, Hendrix hesitated, but – now – didn't speak.

Hendrix reached out and placed his hand on Ros's hand instead.

Ros looked away from the water and down at his fingers, resting now on hers.

Ros wasn't exactly unused to physical contact. It was what the club was all about after all.

The physical coupling of strangers.

No commitment.

No strings.

And no real emotion either which suited her just fine.

By comparison, all that was happening now was the very slightest of physical contact, but this promised the exact opposite. This promised commitment and it promised strings and it promised real emotion too.

The strange thing being that this felt as if it could suit her just fine too.

Ros looked up at Hendrix, ready now to answer the question she knew he was asking, the question she'd been asking herself ever since she journeyed as that empathetic, invisible ghost, first with Joey as he found out the truth about his marriage and the mother of his child, and then with Jen as she found out the truth about Jack Ryan.

Then Ros stopped as she looked beyond Hendrix.

And saw a nervous-looking Conor hovering in the doorway behind him.

Across the restaurant, Conor paused as he saw Ros.

Then Conor stilled as he now also saw Hendrix sitting opposite her, his hand still on hers.

But then Conor approached, and he approached because he had no choice and he knew it. He still didn't know exactly why, but Ros had made it clear that in the case of this particular client he absolutely had to contact her at any time, be that day or night, wherever she might be.

So Conor nodded at his immediate senior officer as he came up to her table, noticing that Hendrix's hand remained on hers all the time.

'That Category A again.'

Conor hesitated again as Ros stared back at him, Hendrix now instantly forgotten.

'There's a problem.'

It should have been one small note of hope. One small light illuminated in a world still enveloped in darkness as Jamie hunched down by the side of Kim's chair and told her all about the death of the woman who'd made them believe Aron was dead.

He told her that the evil that had visited their lives, the evil that had tried to destroy her mind and their family, had been destroyed in turn. That the devil had been dispatched and that part of the nightmare, at least, was over.

And Jamie rehearsed all the words he'd told himself would help, hoping against hope that some magic might prevail, that some comfort might, finally, be derived from it all.

And Kim listened to all he said. And she seemed to take it in too, her forehead creasing in apparent concentration now and again, a faint flicker visible from time to time in her eyes.

But then Jamie finished and fell silent and Kim remained silent too. And Jamie knew, without a shadow of a doubt, that all he'd just said had been a waste of breath. Whatever had happened to their persecutor in the present couldn't now alter the past, because that was all Kim could see.

In time there might be some sort of path to be found through all this, but for now there was none. What had visited them back in their flat had forfeited his partner's future, blasted apart their present, and made their past a horror she could never forget. Now they were in that no-man's-land common to all victims of evil, which was purgatory. Unable to move forward or back.

Which was when Jamie saw the blood.

At the same time, tears began to flow from Kim's eyes and the former, thin, trickle of blood fast became a flood.

A panicky Jamie immediately put Kim into the recovery position, distant memories of long-forgotten first aid courses swimming through his head, but the blood simply didn't stop. By now another of the protection officers from the unit had appeared and an ambulance was swiftly summoned.

At first the paramedic thought Kim had suffered some sort of haemorrhage, that some internal organ had ruptured for some reason and in quite a major way. Within seconds his suit was drenched with blood that continued to pump from the still-silent Kim's mouth, blood that showed absolutely no sign of abating and which would not abate either, not without the later intervention of a hospital surgeon and some careful needlework.

Because Kim had bitten off the end of her tongue. Later, that same surgeon told Jamie she must have been pressing down on it with her teeth for some time, grinding away, ripping through the skin and tissue until, finally, she'd amputated the very tip.

At which point she'd opened her mouth and the now-useless flap of skin she'd severed had fallen out onto her chin, before being washed away a second or so later by the first of the blood, issuing first in a trickle, then coming out in a torrent from a mouth that had been filling all the while.

And still Jamie could see it in her eyes. Kim should have been beyond everything now. Everything should now be blotted out aside from the lacerating agony in her mouth. But nothing had been blotted out. Despite all she'd done before to Francesca and now to herself, she still couldn't get beyond the one thing she was desperately trying to erase. She could still see what she quite clearly believed to be her dead infant in her eyes.

Jamie held his partner's hand while they waited for the ambulance and she, with the faintest of grips, held onto his, two souls clinging to the wreckage.

3 2 .

Ros scanned her electronic key onto the reader. A faint click sounded and she pushed against the gate. The concerned concierge, with whom she'd barely exchanged more than a few words in all the time she'd been there, came out of his hut in a vain attempt to find out what was going on, but Ros didn't enlighten him.

Ros moved on into the yard instead where an equally-bewildered-looking plain-clothes officer was sitting on a small bench by a flowerbed hosting different blooms, but all sharing the same desperate struggle to stay alive. An elderly man sitting next to him looked to be doing the same.

In any other circumstances, Macklyn would have been in a police cell. But given the alert on his file, the first port of call had been the Protection Unit instead. It didn't mean he'd evade justice for the crime he may or may not have committed, although there didn't seem to be too much doubt about that given the dead body that had been discovered in his small house. It just meant special measures needed to be put in place to deal with it all.

The plain-clothes officer hadn't exchanged a single word with the old man since he'd picked him up. But then there'd been a slight, but definite, shake of the head as they approached the communal front door that led to the first-floor apartment he'd been told to use to house the old man while assistance from other officers was summoned. For some reason the old man didn't seem to want to go inside. Short of putting him in a headlock and frogmarching him up the stairs, there wasn't a great deal his escort could do about that, so he'd seated him on the bench instead and settled down to wait.

Ros took the thin file from the plain-clothes officer, comprising the initial report from the scenes-of-crime officers, then nodded at him. She'd take over now. The officer stood and made his way across the courtyard, moving past the concierge who was still watching while trying to make it seem as if he wasn't.

Ros didn't look after the departing officer or at the curious concierge or at the file. She just looked at her silent father instead.

But Macklyn didn't even seem to see her. All he was looking at was a toy truck in his hand, a toy truck he was turning over again and again, painted in a distinctive-looking livery with paint that seemed to have been recently applied as faint traces of it were already beginning to stain his fingers.

Meanwhile, Conor returned to the unit offices to find the department had just enjoyed one piece of good fortune at least.

Ros and Conor had been liaising with contacts in Social Services for some weeks now and, finally it seemed, a foster family had been found for Kezia. The family in question had taken in several children with problem backgrounds in the past. A couple of such placements had been so successful that the children were now living with them permanently. Whether the same happy outcome would obtain for Kezia no-one knew, but at least the young girl was going to start living a halfway normal life again with other children for company, two adults to care for her, even a garden to play in and nearby woodland to explore.

Conor, trying not to think about Ros and Hendrix as he did so, watched as Kezia's new surrogate mother and father gently escorted the small girl to their car and packed her bag inside the boot. Then Conor kept watching as the boot was closed and the young girl was driven out of the gates.

Conor gave a small half-wave as the family saloon turned the corner and the young girl was, briefly, in half-profile, but Kezia didn't look back once.

Once Macklyn started he couldn't stop.

He'd begun, hesitantly, by telling Ros all about Aidan, about his unexpected approach and the way he'd been taken in by it all. But then everything began pouring out.

He told his daughter about the headaches and the feeling that not just his head but his whole being was being split into two. He told her about the relief he started to feel on those solo trips to places he was never supposed to revisit, the calm that had descended courtesy of the simple acquisition of a few toy trucks and vans, the feeling that maybe, finally, he could do it, that maybe this was the way he could cope.

The body that had been discovered by uniformed officers back in his small house hardly featured. Aidan simply didn't seem to matter. From the little Ros had been told about the small-scale wannabe blackmailer and all-too-active paedophile, that seemed fitting, although she had a suspicion things weren't going to be as simple as that. But for now she just let her father talk.

Which was something of a new experience because they'd never done this before. Perhaps Macklyn had talked at one time to one of Ros's elder sisters, but Ros herself had been five years old when their lives had been blasted apart. She could never recall one single proper conversation between herself and her father before the act of violence that had then shattered all normality for ever.

After that none ever took place because what lay between

them was simply too much, the weight of all that was unsaid simply too great for anything else to make itself heard. And so they didn't even try.

They asked questions and supplied answers instead. Who wanted what for tea? What clothes needed washing for school the next day? What was the weather like outside? But apart from that there'd been nothing.

But now Macklyn was talking. Now, and for the first time, he was talking to her about Braith, about the sister she never really knew and could not now recall, at least not the living, breathing, Braith. All Ros ever saw in her mind's eye was a blasted head, all but detached from a twitching body.

And Macklyn was telling her about Di as well, Ditzy Di as they always called her, the family scamp, the scatterbrained middle sister, always getting into some scrape or other, until she'd met the man who'd seemed to change all that, the man who'd turned the overgrown schoolgirl into a young woman at last, a young married woman indeed with a future to embrace; in actuality creating a time bomb that would destroy, within days, all they were and ever would be from that moment on.

And, despite everything, despite the circumstances that had provoked it, all this was actually heady. Intoxicating even. And as it continued, Ros felt a dim echo of all her father must be feeling on his forbidden visits, the sense that some dead weight was being sloughed from his shoulders, that light was beginning to break through at last.

Dimly, she was aware of someone approaching from the direction of the gates and she was about to tell her father to stop in case some other resident of the apartments caught something of their conversation.

But this was now the old Macklyn. Briefly, he'd returned to the character he'd previously been and Macklyn didn't allow his daughter to speak, he just turned towards the approaching

354

figure himself and took charge, much as he'd have taken charge all those years before in his transport yard or in the kitchen of their old house issuing a curt dismissal to the unwanted interloper.

'Do you mind?'

And suddenly, listening to the new tone in her father's voice, it was like going back twenty years. Now Ros could almost smell the grass in their old garden, bringing with it at the same time the distant aroma from an equally long-forgotten herb garden.

Macklyn nodded, equally curt, at the now-stalled figure in front of them.

'I'm talking to Cara.'

Jerked back to the present in an instant, a shocked Ros stared at him. Then her eyes focused on Hendrix a few metres away, puzzled by the elderly man's abrupt command but even more puzzled by something else.

Hendrix looked back at Ros. Hendrix had followed her home to finally get Ros's answer to the question he'd posed back in that strange restaurant with iPads in place of menus and the distant view of the Senedd over the water.

But now Ros could see a very different question in his eyes.

Who's Cara?

3 3 .

A FEW DAYS later, Ros was travelling. The ancient Andalusian settlements of Cádiz, Jerez, Seville and Huelva flashed before her eyes as her train passed each and every one. Other passengers embarked and disembarked along the route taking little notice of the small, slight, young woman travelling alone, presumably destined for some stop further down the line.

But Ros didn't alight at any stop further down the line, at least for now. She was just doing what she always did at times like these, allowing her mind and body to adjust to changed circumstances by keeping that mind and body on the move.

The deal had been done with Masters. The zealous Hendrix had wanted to pursue the investigation into the past activities of his disbanded and disgraced unit and had wanted Ros's help to do so. Together, with all they both now knew, they could have blasted that whole sorry exercise apart. And, briefly, Ros had been tempted, and not just for Kezia's sake but for Donna's as well. Some belated attempt to atone for all those past sins and omissions.

But she hadn't and the reason was simple. It wasn't the fact that Masters could and would try to intervene in the investigation into the death of the small-scale blackmailer and paedophile found in her father's house, although she doubted whether even Masters could do what he'd done in the past and make all that simply go away.

It wasn't even the fact that any investigation of the type the evangelical Hendrix was currently espousing would have opened floodgates that would have drowned more souls than the definitely-deserving Masters.

It was that one word. Or, more accurately, that one name. A name that should never have been spoken, but a name that, once spoken, would never be forgotten as Ros knew only too well.

There was something between them, they both knew that. Ros had known it from the moment she'd seen Hendrix in that quiet Amsterdam square, and she was fairly sure he'd come to the same realisation as well. There was a connection there.

And, if Ros allowed that connection to flourish, then at some point in the future he'd return to that conversation that day, to that elderly man and his fateful slip and he'd press her, gently at first but then more forcefully as the days went on and as their relationship developed, wanting to know what he'd meant when he called her by a name that wasn't her own?

And then, having failed to get any sort of coherent answer to a question that should very definitely never have been asked, he'd have felt impelled to try and find out in some other way.

Masters wouldn't then be the only casualty. Because Hendrix wouldn't rest until he'd got his answer because he was that kind of man, and if he wasn't that kind of man he wouldn't have made it his mission to find out what was really going on with Roman and Kim and Kezia, and Ros wouldn't have responded to him either.

And then, sooner or later, he'd get to know all about her past, a past that would then threaten his present and future as it had threatened hers and all closest to her for as long as she could remember.

Kezia was out in the garden taking pictures of plants.

From the window, Kezia's new foster mother watched fondly, and smiled. It had taken a few days. They'd tried all the usual things to try and engage her, games or walks, they'd even tried bonding her with one of the small pets they'd also recently adopted.

But the actual breakthrough, when it came, always took her and her husband by surprise and so it had proved in this case.

Kezia had seen a small, cheap, digital camera on a table in the hall. She'd asked how it worked. They'd shown her. Then she'd gone straight out into the garden and started to snap away.

Kezia's new foster mother smiled wider as she kept watching her new charge. Maybe this was it. That all-important first step. The moment some connection had been made.

Out in the garden Kezia kept holding the camera to her eye and felt peace settle inside. A peace she hadn't known now for weeks, but that was nothing to do with the pictures she was taking, all of which she'd later delete.

Because she wasn't seeing plants. And she wasn't seeing the other children as they charged around the garden or the two small dogs who followed them, yelping all the while.

All she could see were the two people who'd taken her in, the adults who would now, so she'd been told, become her new Mum and Dad and, in a way, that was nice because they were nice and she couldn't say for a moment that she'd felt threatened by them or uneasy in their company and they'd made her welcome, more than welcome in fact. So why all she could now think about was hurting them she didn't know.

So Kezia put the camera up to her face and tried to hide behind it, but it didn't seem to stop it happening.

In fact the more pictures she took, the more she imagined other pictures instead, not of the plants or small dogs or the other children she could see, but of human beings in the most extreme pain and suffering, the same sort of pain and suffering she'd seen in that bedroom that day when she'd walked in and seen the dead, bloodied, body of her father.

Later that same evening, Ros looked at the chess players, declining with a small smile the various silent invitations that wafted her way to sit down and play. As with most things in her life she was there to watch, not participate. To observe, not take part.

Ros had arrived in Madrid on the next stage of her wanderings. She'd taken a table at the Café Comercial on the southern end of Glorieta de Bilbao, sited near to a roundabout dominated by a floodlit fountain.

Ros moved inside the main body of the café, pausing to take in the marbled columns and smoked-glass mirrors. Then she made her way upstairs where the regular congregation of chess lovers from the city habitually congregated.

As she watched, Ros's mobile briefly pulsed with an incoming text alert. Despite being away, she'd asked to be kept updated on the various cases they were currently overseeing. Conor had promised to do so and her junior officer was being as good as his word. With no replacement for Jukes yet appointed, they were all taking up any additional strain.

Ros looked at the short reports on the screen before her, ending with Conor updating her on the good progress Kezia seemed to be making in her foster home. Then she closed down her phone, looked at the chess game unfolding before her, now moving into its endgame.

But all Ros could now see was Kezia and that was nothing to do with the report she'd just read. There'd been others, but Kezia had been at the forefront of all the faces she'd seen for days now, a small figure in the dusty landscapes glimpsed out of all those train windows.

Ros watched as one of the chess players picked up his king, the traditional gesture of surrender, smiled at his opponent and laid the chess piece on its side.

Ros still didn't know exactly why the young girl was dominating all her thoughts right now.

All Ros did know was that every time she thought of the young Kezia, she grew cold.

The next morning Ros woke early. And if she'd felt cold the previous night, now her room felt arctic. But it was still the height of summer and the temperature outside was already climbing towards thirty degrees, so that didn't explain it.

Which was when the other face that had been keeping her company during the whole of that trip swam before her eyes again.

Because Ros understood everything else, the fractured souls that Jukes, Masters and their former department had created, as well as the desire of at least one of those creations to turn, Frankenstein-style, back on them.

The one intangible, the one loose end that no-one had satisfactorily explained was Donna.

Ros could see it in Masters's eyes. He didn't believe that was simply random either. But, equally certainly, it couldn't be laid at Jen's door. Her vendetta was against the guilty, not the innocent. Too many blameless lives had been destroyed already, the last thing she would have done was to scar any more and especially not hers.

Ros herself had been through the files relating to all the clients cared for in that safe house and all Jukes had said was true. Not a single soul seemed to have been compromised after the attack on Donna. Not a single life seemed to have been placed under any kind of threat so far as anyone in their department could see.

Ros moved to the window, looked out on the roofs of the buildings below her, the sudden thought she'd woken with sending the temperature dipping ever lower.

But what if all that had been nothing to do with Leon or Kezia or Kim?

What if it had been about someone else?

A much colder case altogether?

EPILOGUE

T HE KNOCK ON the door came just before seven in the morning, which was roughly the time Ros opened her eyes all those hundreds of miles away in Spain.

Macklyn had actually expected it sooner in the day. Dim memories of cheap thrillers and forgettable films swam through his mind, images of cops bursting in before dawn to rouse their bleary-eyed suspects.

But in a sense and irrespective of when this inevitable call came, Macklyn actually welcomed it. Now he was going to be taken to a place where there would be no need to affect the trappings of any sort of normal life. He was about to become all he'd felt himself to be anyway, a man apart, literally an outlaw.

A line from an old song from decades before floated through his head as he reached out for the handle to open the front door, something about living outside the law making a man honest. Maybe, for the first time in more years than he could now remember, Macklyn was about to start living like an honest man once more. A man who didn't have to pretend to be anything he wasn't, because what would be the point? What, or who, would he be trying to protect any longer? Courtesy of one moment of madness in an encounter that should never have happened, Macklyn now had literally nothing left to lose.

Macklyn opened the door. A single male stood outside, which was another slight surprise. Trading on those same memories of cheap thrillers and forgettable films, Macklyn always had the impression arresting officers arrived in pairs. But this caller was definitely alone and for a moment he didn't speak. And there was no reading of his rights either.

Behind him there was another jarring note as Macklyn glimpsed an upmarket car and a decidedly upmarket one too; he didn't see too many gleaming black Range Rover Vogues parked on his home street.

And when Macklyn looked back at his caller who was still just staring at him, he found he couldn't tear himself away from his eyes which were the most unusual colour Macklyn had ever seen – almost ice blue.

Then his caller gave a slight nod.

And it was that slight nod that did it.

Macklyn hadn't been there at the time but, courtesy of the forensic reconstruction the patient officers had extracted from Ros, he knew that Braith's assassin had done that. He'd looked into the eyes of the woman before him, checking her features against an image he'd been previously supplied and had then nodded slightly to himself, convinced that both images matched.

In Braith's case he'd been wrong. He hadn't been told of the close physical similarity between his real target, Di, and her sister, but in Macklyn's case there could be no doubt. And his caller now drew a gun from inside his coat.

Previously, Braith had moved, instinctively, to protect the small child behind her. But Macklyn had no small child to protect and nothing else besides. So Macklyn just stood there, staring into the eyes of the man who was now staring into his and waited as he'd waited for the past twenty years, only now the waiting was over.

It had been Braith's time then. Now it was his.

Briefly, in the second or so that followed, Macklyn wondered whether that was really what it had all been about? All that travelling back to locations from the past, was it really about making acquaintance again with all that had been lost, or something else?

Had he actually been seeking this in some way? Making himself visible in order that some circle could then be completed? Tempting those he knew were still out there and still looking for him back out into the open, and maybe the peace he now felt settling on him in the small hallway of his rented house was his answer.

It hardly mattered of course. He could see it in the gunman's eyes. It was over anyway. Finally, it was finished.

Only it wasn't. There was one family member still left. And that realisation washed over Macklyn a millisecond later, only by then it was too late. The bullet had by that time smashed into the front of his forehead and propelled him back, arms flailing as Braith's must have done all those years before, down onto the floor, blood spurting onto the carpet that had only been laid a year previously but was already looking a little threadbare.

Then Macklyn lay still.

Macklyn's visitor put away his gun. He checked, quickly, to both sides but no alert had sounded, no-one had called out from any of the neighbouring houses, meaning no-one had seen or heard him. He replaced the gun, complete with silencer, inside his coat and closed the door.

Not that it was the end of his task. As Macklyn had realised just a moment before, there was one final name on the list he'd been supplied, but for reasons best known to themselves, his paymasters had insisted that this final item on the contract should not be completed yet.

The gunman had no idea why. The mark in question was a woman this time and young, in her twenties. She'd know they were on her trail from the moment her father's body was discovered, but maybe that was the whole point he reflected, as he now unlocked the door of his Range Rover.

Maybe they wanted the young woman in question to live

with the knowledge that one day soon she would also hear that same knock on the door. Maybe that was all part of the same retribution for a transgression about which he hadn't been fully enlightened and, idle moments of reflection aside, he didn't really care too much about either.

All he'd been told was that at some point in the future the final part of his task would be activated and then he'd do what he'd done today.

This time it had been an old man whose name he didn't even know.

Next time it would be a young woman whose name had been supplied although it wasn't, apparently, her actual name.

All he did know was that in exactly one year's time that young woman would be dead.

Also by the author:

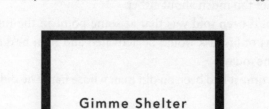

Gimme Shelter

ROB GITTINS

y Lolfa

£8.95 (pb)
£17.95 (hb)

Dylan Thomas's last days – and someone's watching...

THE POET & THE PRIVATE EYE

ROB GITTINS

y Lolfa

£8.95 (pb)
£14.95 (hb)

Secret Shelter is just one of a whole range
of publications from Y Lolfa. For a full
list of books currently in print, send now
for your free copy of our new full-colour
catalogue. Or simply surf into our website

www.ylolfa.com

for secure on-line ordering.

y Lolfa

TALYBONT CEREDIGION CYMRU SY24 5HE
e-mail ylolfa@ylolfa.com
website www.ylolfa.com
phone (01970) 832 304
fax 832 782